IS ANYONE LISTENING?

MYSTERIES UNCORKED - A PODCAST THRILLER SERIES #1

BARBARA FREETHY

Fog City Publishing

PRAISE FOR BARBARA FREETHY

"Barbara Freethy's suspense novels are explosively good!" — *New York Times bestselling author Toni Anderson.*

"A fabulous, page-turning combination of romance and intrigue. Fans of Nora Roberts and Elizabeth Lowell will love this book." — *NYT Bestselling Author Kristin Hannah on Golden Lies*

"Powerful and absorbing...sheer hold-your-breath suspense." — *NYT Bestselling Author Karen Robards on Don't Say A Word*

"Barbara Freethy delivers riveting, plot-twisting suspense and a deeply emotional story. Every book is a thrilling ride." *USA Today Bestselling Author Rachel Grant*

"Freethy is at the top of her form. Fans of Nora Roberts will find a similar tone here, framed in Freethy's own spare, elegant style." — *Contra Costa Times on Summer Secrets*

"Freethy hits the ground running as she kicks off another winning romantic suspense series...Freethy is at her prime with a superb combo of engaging characters and gripping plot." — *Publishers' Weekly on Silent Run*

"PERILOUS TRUST is a non-stop thriller that seamlessly melds jaw-dropping suspense with sizzling romance, and I was riveted from the first page to the last...Readers will be breathless in anticipation as this fast-paced and enthralling love story evolves and goes in unforeseeable directions." — *USA Today HEA Blog*

ALSO BY BARBARA FREETHY

Mysteries Uncorked - A Podcast Thriller Series

IS ANYONE LISTENING?

Mystery Thriller Standalones

ALL THE PRETTY PEOPLE

LAST ONE TO KNOW

THE OTHER EMILY

NOTHING BREAKS LIKE A HEART

Off the Grid: FBI Series

PERILOUS TRUST

RECKLESS WHISPER

DESPERATE PLAY

ELUSIVE PROMISE

DANGEROUS CHOICE

RUTHLESS CROSS

CRITICAL DOUBT

FEARLESS PURSUIT

DARING DECEPTION

RISKY BARGAIN

PERFECT TARGET

For a complete list of books, visit www.barbarafreethy.com

Is Anyone Listening?

———

For more information on Barbara Freethy's books, visit her website:
www.barbarafreethy.com

CHAPTER ONE

"You never know when you'll become a victim." Tessa Conway leaned forward and put her lips close to the microphone. "Or if anyone will ever know your story."

"Stop," I said with a laugh. "You're being overdramatic, Tessa."

"I'm selling our show, Cassidy," Tessa said.

"Cassidy is right. Too much." Morgan Kent set a bottle of wine on the folding table we used for our podcast and sat down next to Tessa.

"It's not too much," Tessa argued. "This is what our listeners are looking for. They want to be immersed in the story. Then they'll tell their friends about our podcast, and we'll be able to monetize. We won't have to keep looking for jobs or doing boring part-time work for no money."

As Tessa and Morgan bickered, I refilled my wine glass and looked around my tiny studio apartment on the twelfth floor of a high-rise in Manhattan. In addition to a full-sized bed, I'd managed to squeeze in a couch and this folding table, which served as my kitchen table when we weren't doing our podcast, *Mysteries Uncorked.* We'd started the show two months ago, after the company we worked for went out of business.

Bright Horizons, a midsize media agency, had been a great place to work for a while. But the owner had been more interested in his public persona than the bottom line and, eventually, reality had caught up. I'd done research and pitch decks, Tessa had worked in social, and Morgan in HR. Two devastating financial quarters for the company had resulted in massive company-wide layoffs that had put us all on unemployment.

While looking for new jobs, we'd decided to have some fun discussing our passion for true crime stories over bottles of wine. We'd never imagined that our informal podcast would have an audience of more than ten, but, to our shock, our numbers had grown as other true crime lovers joined us. Last week's podcast had gotten over ten thousand downloads across the various apps. That shocking fact had brought us our first sponsor, a wine distributor, who provided free wine for our podcasts.

Tessa thought it was just the beginning, and maybe she was right. Maybe we should start thinking bigger, because we all needed money. While we were three intelligent women with at least seven years of work experience behind us, none of us had been able to find another full-time job. Instead, I was picking up freelance writing gigs, Tessa was doing social media for a nonprofit and working as a caterer, and Morgan was editing employee manuals.

"You agree with me, don't you, Cassidy?" Tessa asked, drawing my attention back to her.

"Sorry, I wasn't listening."

"Well, that's great. I'm trying to save us, and you're daydreaming."

"What did you say?"

"What I said before. We need to think bigger."

"How?" I asked. "Specifically?"

"I was talking to a former client, who has been listening to our podcast. She's smart and well-connected, and she said if we really want to break out, we need to start doing more than talking about true crime cases."

"We do more than that," I argued. "I create timelines. I go through police files."

"So do I," Morgan added. "We dig in."

"But that's where it ends."

"Where else can it end?" I asked. "We're not detectives."

"Maybe we should be. My friend said if we take the podcast on the road, visit the scene of a crime, we'll triple our audience."

"What scene?" Morgan asked. "We mostly talk about cold cases. There's no scene anymore."

"We go to the town," Tessa said. "We talk to the neighbors, the friends. We shake things up. It doesn't matter if we find the truth; we just have to look for it and take our fans with us."

"You're crazy," Morgan said. "I need more wine."

Tessa raised her brows, a question in her gaze. "Am I crazy, Cassidy?"

"Maybe. We aren't investigators."

"Sure, we are. You're a researcher and writer, Cassidy. You always bring the scenes alive for our listeners. And Morgan is great with psychology, understanding people and motivations. And I can charm information out of just about everyone. What's the worst that could happen? No one talks? We don't solve the crime? Who will blame us for that failure?" She paused. "No one has solved any of these crimes. But we'll bring the story back to life. We'll put people right in the thick of it. I guarantee our numbers will grow, and so will our sponsors and advertisers. That means money, real money."

Tessa was a great salesperson, but not all of her ideas panned out. Still, where was the risk? "It is interesting," I conceded.

"Not you, too," Morgan groaned.

"I do need to make real money, or I'm going to be out of this apartment in a month, and I cannot stand the idea of asking my father for help."

"And I might have to sublet the other half of my bedroom to cover my rent," Tessa said. "I know you're not as financially desperate as we are, Morgan. You have Steven."

"He's not supporting me. We split expenses," Morgan said a little defensively. "We have to because Steven pays child support, and it's not a small amount."

"Then this money could help you, too," Tessa said.

Silence followed her words as we sipped our wine and considered her suggestion. Finally, I said, "I'm willing to entertain the possibility of taking the show on the road."

"Great! We need a good story, something that will resonate with our listeners," Tessa said, an excited light in her eyes now that I was on board. "You've been researching cases, Cassidy. Is there anything you've seen that would be worth digging into? How about a missing person?"

"A missing woman," Morgan interjected as her eyes lit up. "Someone around our age, our listeners' age."

"Exactly. Someone who disappeared, someone like us," Tessa added.

A shiver ran down my spine at her words, making me wonder if we were about to take a step we might regret. But we needed to take a risk to get to the next level. "I'll look through my files when we're done with tonight's podcast. We don't have to decide anything right now."

"But we do need to record tonight's show," Morgan interjected. "I have to be home by nine. So, let's get started, Tessa, and lower the temp this time."

Tessa made a face at Morgan. "Fine, I'll be less dramatic, but not too much, because our listeners love tension and mystery, and we have to give them what they want, or they won't come back."

We turned on our microphones, and I checked the camera on my laptop. The light in front of us cast a soft glow over our faces, and we looked pretty good. Tessa was the perfect one to be in the middle, her silky, straight blonde hair standing out between my wavy dark-brown hair and Morgan's sleek auburn shade. We were as different in personality as we were in looks, but the listeners seemed to think that made us more interesting, because we often didn't agree on potential villains when we speculated about the cases we covered.

"You want to count us down, Cassidy?" Tessa asked.

"Sure. Three, two, one..."

Tessa's smile broadened as she gazed into the camera. "Happy Wednesday. Welcome to *Mysteries Uncorked*, where we pop the cork on true crime's most fascinating cases. I'm here with my amazing friends, Cassidy and Morgan, and today's case is very intriguing. What would you think if I told you that a man found naked on the Santa Monica Pier ten years ago was not the Navy SEAL that everyone thought he was? In fact, he'd killed that Navy SEAL seven days earlier..."

"And that Navy SEAL was his best friend," I put in.

"It's amazing how friendship could turn to murder," Tessa said with a wicked smile. "I couldn't imagine killing either of these two."

"I can," I said sarcastically.

"Well, thanks," Morgan said dryly. "Although I'm sure that comment was directed to Tessa."

"Nice," Tessa quipped. "But we're not talking about us. Let's get back to the case."

"I don't think it's surprising at all that a friendship could lead to murder," Morgan said. "Most crimes have a personal element."

"That's true," I said. "It's just like they say—love and hate are two sides of the same coin."

As Tessa continued with the story, Morgan and I brought up other interesting twists that we'd discovered about the case, and the hour passed in a flash. Throughout the podcast, I could see the comments flowing in faster than usual. Every week, our audience grew and became more engaged.

"Before we say goodnight," Tessa said, pausing to give both me and Morgan a questioning glance, which I knew really wasn't a question. I could see the intent in her bright blue eyes. "Should I tell them about our upcoming project, ladies?"

"Nothing to say just yet," I replied.

"It's too early," Morgan agreed.

"Just a little tease then," Tessa said. "As you know, we love talking about cases in the news, but we think it might be time to take our show on the road. Stay tuned for more details." She paused. "Until next time."

We picked up our almost empty wineglasses and clicked them together. Then I turned off the camera and let out a breath. While I enjoyed making the podcast, I was always a little relieved when it was over. It was fun to talk about cases with my friends, but the growing audience increased the pressure to turn this fun project into a serious business.

"That was good," Tessa said. "Now we just need to find the right case to investigate in person. Let's start looking through the files."

Morgan stood up. "Sorry, I can't do it now. I promised Steven I'd be back by nine."

"No problem," I told her. "It might take us a while to find the right case."

"I'll see you tomorrow," Morgan said, grabbing her bag and heading out the door.

"I need wine and food before we start researching," Tessa said. "Do you want to order from that Thai place down the street?"

I picked up my phone. "On it." After ordering our favorites, I got up and grabbed a baggie of veggies from the fridge, poured ranch dressing into a small bowl and took it to the table.

"Thanks." Tessa immediately reached for a carrot. "I didn't have time to grab dinner before I came over."

"Me, either. Food will be here in ten minutes."

Tessa refilled our wine glasses, finishing off the bottle. "Morgan seemed stressed tonight. This is why I don't date men with children and ex-wives. It's far too complicated."

I nodded, popping a slice of cucumber into my mouth. "It wouldn't be my first choice, but I guess you love who you love."

"Or you choose to love someone else," Tessa said dryly.

"Speaking of choosing someone, did you hear from that guy you went out with on Saturday?"

"Nope. He gave me the usual, had a great time, let's do it again speech, and then nothing. I'm over dating, Cassidy."

"I hear you."

She gave me a more serious look. "I'm also over not having a real job and real money. That's why we need to make this podcast work."

"I get it." I paused, glancing down at my phone. "Our food is here. I'll go down and get it. Then we'll figure out our next case."

An hour later, we'd finished our late dinner and were deep into our computer files. But as I read through all the cases that I'd made notes on in the last few months, they all seemed wrong—too big or too scary or too far away. I was beginning to think our idea was only great in theory, not in practice.

Then the name of a town jumped out at me—*Stonecross, Maine*. I let out a breath of surprise.

"Did you find something?" Tessa asked, looking up from her computer.

"I—I'm not sure." My gaze ran down the news article about a woman who had gone missing a year ago in the small town of Stonecross. She'd last been seen at the Stonecross Inn. Now I remembered why I'd saved this story.

"Cassidy?" Tessa's questioning gaze brought my head up.

"It's...nothing."

"It doesn't sound like nothing. What's the case?"

"A year ago. Natalie Warren, thirty, from New York City, vanished after a three-day stay—checking out two days early from the Stonecross Inn in Stonecross, Maine."

"That sounds good," Tessa said with excitement. "Natalie is only a few years older than us. She's from New York. And Maine isn't that far away. Plus, the town name makes it sound kind of gothic."

"We can't go there," I said flatly.

Tessa's eyes widened in surprise. "Why on earth not?"

"Because...we can't. *I can't.*"

"I don't understand. What's the problem?"

"My father was born in Stonecross, Maine."

"Really? But why is that a problem?"

"My father left when he was eighteen and has never been back. There was some family drama that he refuses to speak about."

"Is that family still in Stonecross?"

"My grandmother runs the Stonecross Inn."

"Where the girl disappeared? Oh, come on, Cassidy. That's a crazy coincidence. This is our case. Every sign is pointing in that direction. You'll have the inside track with your grandmother. You'll be able to get information no one else can."

"I won't, Tessa. I've never met my grandmother. And my father would kill me if I went there. Whenever I asked about my grandmother, he refused to tell me anything except that his mother would never meet me unless it was over his dead body."

"Okay," Tessa said slowly. "I see what you're saying, but aren't you curious as to why you can never meet your own grandmother?"

"Of course, I'm curious. But my father is my only family, and he barely tolerates me. I can't cut the last connection I have to him."

"Does he have to know? You don't see him that often, do you?"

"A few times a year," I conceded. "But somehow he'll find out."

"How would he? Does he listen to our podcast?"

"God, no! I told him about it when we first started it, and he dismissed it like it was nothing."

"Then I don't see how he'll know. You're twenty-eight years old, Cassidy. Do you really need to factor your father into this? If you want to meet your grandmother, why shouldn't you? And she must be pretty old by now. Maybe it's time to connect before it's too late."

"He told me to forget about her a long time ago. If I go to Stonecross, he'll feel like I betrayed him."

"Now who's being dramatic, Cassidy? What on earth could your grandmother have done that was so horrible?"

"I don't know, but it was something."

"Don't you think it's time you found out what that was? And this isn't just about you, remember? This is about looking into the disappearance of a young New York woman, who disappeared from your grandmother's inn. What if we could find out what happened to her and bring her family closure?"

"Technically, she didn't disappear from the inn. She checked out, and no one saw her again."

"Either way, your grandmother is right in the middle of this case."

I frowned. "Even if I did agree to dig into this with you, I still don't see how we're going to find out what happened to this woman. Obviously, the police and her family looked for her."

"Maybe a year ago. Cold cases tend to crack as time passes. And when you put a bright light on a dark corner, sometimes the rats scurry out. You've always said your dream was to be a real journalist. Here's your chance."

I groaned. "Can't I be a real journalist somewhere else besides Stonecross?"

Tessa smiled. "Of course, but fate is leading you back to your past. I don't see how you can say no to that."

"Then I guess I'm going to say yes."

CHAPTER TWO

Two days later, early Saturday morning, Tessa and I packed up the white SUV she'd borrowed from one of her roommates. Before I could slide into the passenger seat, Tessa grabbed my arm and held up her camera. "Let's do a quick video, Cassidy."

"Here?" I protested. "You're double-parked and there are overloaded trash bins waiting for pickup right next to us."

"Exactly. It's the New York City vibe. Come on." She pulled me to her side. Using a selfie stick, she turned on the camera and said, "It's go time. Cassidy and I are headed for Stonecross, Maine, to try to find out what happened to Natalie Warren. If you don't know what we're doing, catch the latest episode of our podcast, *Mysteries Uncorked*, for all the details. We have an eight-hour drive ahead of us, and once we get to Stonecross, we'll post another video." She turned to me. "What do you think, Cassidy? Are we going to find out what happened to Natalie Warren?"

"I hope so," I said, looking into the camera. "Natalie deserves justice, and her family needs to know what happened to her. If you have any tips, feel free to drop them in the comments."

"See you soon," Tessa said, then clicked off the camera. "Let's go."

We got into the car, and I settled into my seat as Tessa navigated the Manhattan traffic with her usual impatience, leaning heavily on the horn when the car in front of her kept braking unnecessarily. I exhaled in relief when we finally left the city.

It had been months since I'd gotten out of Manhattan, and it felt good to see trees and grass and open roads. I had needed a change in perspective, and this trip was certainly going to give me that.

Tessa flipped through her playlist, finding just the right song to kick us off.

"This is going to be good," Tessa said, sending me a bright smile. "I just wish Morgan could have come with us."

I was sad that Morgan hadn't come for the road trip, but her complicated living situation had made it impossible for her to leave today. "We'll see her on Monday."

"So, let's talk about Natalie. I didn't have a chance to read the report you sent me last night, but it looked like you did a lot of research in the past two days."

"I did, and I will say that what I learned about her has made me more invested in her disappearance. Natalie lived in a studio apartment in Manhattan about three blocks from me. I probably passed her on the subway and didn't even know it."

"I didn't realize she lived that close."

"She moved there after she broke up with her boyfriend. She also changed jobs after the breakup because she worked with her ex. I contacted the company she was working for when she disappeared. HR wouldn't tell me anything, but I reached out to one of her coworkers, who said that Natalie was stressed before she went to Maine. That she said she desperately needed to get out of town. The coworker was the first one to worry when Natalie didn't come back. She tried to contact her, as did her supervisor, but their calls and texts went unanswered. Then Natalie's brother, Adam, showed up ten days later, asking if anyone had heard from her. That's when he got the police involved, but without evidence of foul play, the police couldn't or wouldn't do anything."

"Then the press got wind of the story."

"Yes. Adam also hired a private investigator, but he couldn't come up with anything, either. Natalie just disappeared off the face of the earth. I don't know how we're going to find anything, Tessa. It's been ten months since Natalie disappeared. The trail is very cold."

"It will be a challenge, but that will give us a good story to tell."

"I suppose. I also spoke to Natalie's brother. He said Natalie had been estranged from him and his parents since she'd moved to New York."

"You talked to her brother, too?" Tessa asked with surprise. "I feel like a slacker with you doing so much of the research."

"You were busy, and once I got going, I couldn't stop. Adam was reluctant to speak to me at first. He didn't want to open that old wound, but as we spoke, he loosened up and mentioned that there was some family drama, and he was a little bitter that Natalie had moved to New York with her boyfriend, leaving him to hold the family together. But after she disappeared, he felt guilty that he hadn't known she was gone for so long."

"What about Natalie's boyfriend? Was he ever a suspect?"

"Adam told me the police talked to the ex, but he claimed he hadn't talked to Natalie in six months, and there was no evidence to dispute his statement."

"So, there's not a lot to go on."

"That's what I've been saying."

"But we have a secret weapon—you and your relationship to the owner of the Stonecross Inn."

"We agreed not to tell my grandmother who I am," I reminded her. "That's why you booked the room under your name."

"Don't worry. I won't say anything. But eventually, you'll tell her the truth. Or she'll already know who you are because she's seen a picture of you, or because you look like your dad."

"I don't look like him, and I can't imagine she's seen a photo of me."

"You don't know that. Your father didn't want you to see her, but maybe she wanted to see you, if only from afar."

"I'm not sure that makes me feel better or worse."

Sympathy filled Tessa's eyes. "I know there's an emotional component for you, Cassidy, but until you want to deal with the family connection, we'll focus on Natalie's case and figure out the rest later."

"I just hope my grandmother isn't tied to Natalie's disappearance... I can't even contemplate what that would mean." I shivered as I watched the landscape slide by, wondering if we should turn around now, because it felt like the road we were on might take us somewhere we really shouldn't go.

———

Eight hours and several rest stops later, we took the exit for Stonecross. I sat up a little straighter, tired from the drive and stressed from my mixed emotions, but also excited to see the town where my father had spent the first eighteen years of his life.

It was a little after six p.m. when we drove along a winding and hilly road that led us past two schools. The first appeared to be a combined elementary and middle school, the second, a high school. Modest homes surrounded the schools, sitting on fairly large lots, but the homes got smaller and closer together as we reached the downtown area. Charming brick buildings boasting antiques, artisan jewelry, and unique gifts were mixed with cafés and bakeries, a bar and grill, and a restaurant that claimed to have the freshest fish on the coast.

"There's more here than I thought there would be," Tessa commented.

"I agree. But it's still strange to think my father grew up here. He's the picture of sophistication—tailored suits, the best whiskey and cigars, Michelin-starred restaurants, and expensive wine. He's about as far from rustic charm as you could get."

"Maybe that's why he left and never came back."

"Maybe." I glanced at the GPS. "Looks like the inn is a little up the coast."

As we left the downtown area, we drove along the harbor, with dozens of boats ranging from motorboats and sailboats to fishing vessels. Next to the harbor was a big boatyard that looked like it had seen better days, but the name on the building was mine. That made my chest tighten.

Tessa cast me a quick look. "Clarke and Sons Boatworks?"

"My grandfather's business."

"Who was the son? Your father?"

"No, my grandfather was the son. His father started the business. I don't know who took it over after my grandfather died." As the road wound upward, I could see an old lighthouse on a bluff, its lights going on as the fog began to roll in. A few miles past the lighthouse, the Stonecross Inn came into view.

The three-story Victorian was majestic but also weathered. It looked like the kind of house that might have been beautiful if it hadn't been pummeled by years of wind and the salty sea. As we turned into a long drive, I could see a wide porch circling the house, with Adirondack chairs placed at strategic viewing corners.

Tessa pulled into the parking lot and let out a sigh of relief. "We made it!"

I wasn't sure I was as relieved as she was, because now the reality of what we were here to do was going to begin. When I opened the door, the wind caught it, and I was surprised by the shocking burst of cold, damp air.

"It's freezing," I said, wrapping my arms around my body as I got out of the car.

Tessa came around to join me, camera and selfie stick in hand. "Let's do a quick video."

"Now? I don't look very good."

"You look...real. So do I. That's what we want."

Tessa's "real" was a lot better than mine, but she was already turning me toward the camera with the inn in the background.

"Hello, everyone," Tessa said. "Cassidy and I made it to the Stonecross Inn, the last place that Natalie Warren was seen alive. It's getting too dark to see much now, especially with the fog rolling in, which kind of gives this whole area an eerie feeling. Don't you think so, Cassidy?"

"It definitely feels like we're far away from New York City," I said as more chills ran through me.

"Wish us luck," Tessa added. "See you tomorrow." As she turned off the camera, she said, "Let's get our suitcases and check in before we freeze—"

As she abruptly ended her statement, I said, "Thanks for leaving out the *to death* part of that comment."

Tessa shrugged. "I wasn't going to say that."

I didn't believe her for a second, but I followed her to the back of the car so we could retrieve our suitcases and backpacks. Then we walked toward the iron gate with the brass plaque reading STONECROSS INN.

Opening the gate brought a squeaky squeal that heightened the anxiety running through me. I didn't know exactly what I was afraid of, but as we entered the front patio, I saw a curtain drop in one of the front windows, making me think that someone was watching, someone was waiting.

What if this was a horrible mistake? What if we checked in and were never seen again? What if we ended up like Natalie?

That was ridiculous, I told myself. My grandmother had been running this inn for fifty years, and as far as I knew, Natalie was the only one who had disappeared.

Still, I paused as Tessa brushed past me. "Wait," I said, the word escaping before I could stop it.

"Tessa looked back at me. "What's wrong?"

"Everything. I don't think we should do this."

"We just drove eight hours to get here. We're not leaving now. It's going to be fine, Cassidy."

"I don't know what it's going to be, but I'm pretty sure it won't be fine," I said.

Before Tessa could reply, the front door opened, and a woman stood in the entry, her features lost in the shadows.

Was this my grandmother?

Panic suddenly ran through me, and I had to fight the urge to run. But it was too late to turn back.

When we reached the front porch, the woman holding open the door beckoned us inside, and as the interior light reached her face, I sucked in a quick breath.

This woman was my grandmother, Ellen Clarke. I recognized her from the photo on the inn's website. But she appeared older and taller than I expected. In the photo her hair was brown. Now it was white and fairly short, the straight ends hitting at her collarbone.

She towered over me by at least five inches, making her probably five ten or eleven. In her gray slacks and navy sweater, she appeared thin, but she didn't feel frail or wispy, she felt strong and somewhat stern.

"Good evening," she said politely, but there wasn't any warmth in her brown eyes.

"Hello," Tessa said. "We're checking in. I'm Tessa Conway."

"Yes. I've been expecting you. I'm Ellen Clarke, the owner of this Inn." She stepped behind the front desk. "I was hoping you'd make it in before the fog got worse. Driving can be treacherous in weather like this. I'll need a credit card to cover incidentals," she added.

As Tessa went through the routine motions of checking in, I couldn't take my eyes off my grandmother. I wished I could say I would have recognized her anywhere, but that wouldn't have been the truth. She didn't look like my father, who had blondish hair and blue eyes. Maybe he'd taken after his dad, but I had no idea what my grandfather had looked like.

"And you are?" Ellen said, her voice cutting through my reverie.

I started at the question. I'd prepared for it, but I still wasn't ready. Finally, I bit out my answer. "I'm Cassidy Bennett," I said using my mother's maiden name. Although if Ellen knew anything about me, she'd probably recognize my first name.

Her expression remained guarded as she wrote down my name. Then, she said. "You're in luck. I have an extra room open. Instead of sharing, I'll be putting you in two rooms, just across the hall from each other on the third floor."

"We can't afford two rooms," I said. "We're happy to share."

"It's complimentary. And you'll be more comfortable with more space. Our rooms are not very big." She handed each of us a heavy metal key, in keeping with the rustic nature of their surroundings. "I'll have Ray bring up your bags shortly. There's no elevator, so I don't want you to have to take your luggage up two flights of stairs."

"That's great," Tessa said.

"Breakfast is served in the dining room from seven thirty to ten a.m.," Ellen added. "Our happy hour will be ending at seven, but you're more than welcome to grab a glass of wine and some snacks. We don't serve dinner, but I would hate to send you back into town with the weather changing, so if you'd like something more substantial, I can have our cook make you something simple to eat."

"We've been eating all day," I said. "Whatever snacks you have will be fine."

"The dining room is just beyond the living room." She waved her hand toward the archway behind us. "You'll also find a brochure in your room for our wellness offerings, but I did want to let you know that tomorrow morning there's a yoga class on the deck at ten. It's a beautiful way to start the day if you're inclined."

"That sounds nice," I said.

Ellen gave me a longer look that made me nervous. Did she recognize me?

"I did want to mention," she said, "that we prohibit camera use inside the inn, to respect the privacy of our guests."

"Understood," I said as Tessa nodded her head in agreement.

"Good. Welcome to the Stonecross Inn."

As Ellen finished speaking, a big, muscular man, who appeared to be in his forties, came into the reception area.

"This is Ray Connors," Ellen said. "He'll take your bags up. One room has a garden view, the other an ocean view. But they're both lovely, and the garden view room has a beautiful bathtub."

"That's the one I want," Tessa said. "I love a good bath. You take the ocean view, Cassidy."

"Are you sure?"

"Absolutely. This is my bag," Tessa told Ray, pointing to her blue roller bag. "The beige one is Cassidy's."

"I'll take them up," Ray said in a deep, gravelly voice.

As Ray grabbed each of our bags and moved quickly up the stairs, we made our way into the living room. An older woman sat by the fire knitting and chatting with another woman about her age. When we got to the dining room, we saw a young couple sitting close together, stealing a kiss between sips of wine.

Probably honeymooners, I thought, feeling reassured by the people I'd seen so far. I had been letting my imagination get the best of me. This was just a charming bed and breakfast that had been serving customers for a very long time. The fact that Natalie had disappeared after leaving here probably wasn't connected.

After a glass of wine and some delicious cheese and crackers, I started to feel more relaxed. "I needed this," I said.

"You do seem less tense. What did you think about your grandmother?"

"Don't call her that with people around," I said in a hushed voice, my tension returning.

"Sorry. What did you think of Ellen?"

"She was polite but not that friendly. She doesn't have the usual warm, outgoing inn owner personality."

"No, she doesn't. I was a little surprised." Tessa paused. "Maybe she recognized you, and that's why it felt awkward. She was waiting for you to say something."

"She could have said something if that was the case." I shook my head. "I don't think she recognized me. She didn't even flinch when I said my first name."

"Well, something seemed off."

"She might know something about our podcast. Maybe that's why she was guarded, why she warned us about taking photos inside. I guess we'll find out at some point."

Tessa nodded. "The guy who took our bags looked like a bouncer at a bar."

"And was also not that friendly. But we should try to talk to him tomorrow."

"Agreed." Tessa bit back a yawn at the end of her sentence. "I'm tired. I know it's early, but I want to take a bath and then get into bed. I'll have more energy tomorrow to get going on our investigation."

"Me, too. Let's go upstairs and check out our rooms."

Tessa poured herself another glass of wine, taking it with her, as we made our way back through the living room and up the stairs. When we reached the third-floor landing, I saw a woman entering a room at the far end of the hall. She was dressed in black jeans and a black sweater, and as she gave us a startled look, I caught a glimpse of her face. She was very pale, and she looked scared.

Before I could say anything, she opened her door and slipped inside.

I gave Tessa a questioning look.

She shrugged. "Maybe she just didn't feel like saying hello. Sometimes, I don't like talking to other people when I'm tired, which is one reason I don't usually stay at bed-and-breakfasts. Guests generally like to chat."

"True."

We paused in front of our respective doors. I felt reluctant to say goodnight. But Tessa, who was craving a night in a room without roommates, was eagerly unlocking her door, happy with our new arrangements, so I simply gave her a smile and said, "Sleep well."

"You, too. What time do you want to start?"

"Eight?"

She frowned. "I'm pretty beat. Let's do nine. We can get breakfast and figure out what to do first."

"Okay. See you in the morning." I slipped my key into the lock and turned the knob.

As I stepped into the room, the darkness unnerved me, and I quickly found the switch. As light warmed the room, I felt a little less uneasy. The room was charming, with a rustic wood-framed double bed and matching nightstands. A small desk and dresser were along the wall next to the entrance to the bathroom.

Letting out a breath that I felt like I'd been holding forever, I walked over to the window to pull the curtains. It was dark and foggy outside, and the window was so wet I couldn't see anything but condensation. Maybe that was good. I was too stressed out by everything; I didn't need a spooky landscape to add to my tension.

Closing the curtains, I sat down on the bed, thinking about my grandmother. It didn't appear that she'd recognized my name, which probably meant she'd never heard anything about me. Maybe she didn't even know she had a granddaughter. My father had left when he was eighteen, and he'd told me he hadn't had any contact with her since.

When I'd asked how he'd managed to survive without any parental support, he'd admitted that he'd had ten thousand dollars in a savings account that his father had started when he was born. He'd used that to pay for his first year of college, but he'd also worked while going to school. He was very proud of having made all his own money, and over the years, he'd created a great deal of wealth for himself.

I'd benefited as well. I'd grown up with privilege, and he'd paid for my college, but that's where it had ended. He'd always believed that I should make my own money, too. I just wasn't as good at that as he was.

But I'd get there. I wasn't going to ask him for help unless I was destitute, although that moment might not be too far away if I couldn't turn this podcast into a moneymaker.

Taking out the file I'd put together last night, I went over my notes and the list I'd begun making as to who we should talk to.

My grandmother was at the top of that list, but since we were staying at the inn, it seemed better to move her down for now. We didn't need her to kick us out before we got any information. It would be better to start with some of the employees, maybe even the yoga teacher. Someone not directly working for my grandmother might be more willing to talk to us.

As I flipped through pages of my notes on Natalie, I couldn't help wondering what room she'd stayed in. And as the window rattled from a gust of wind, a shiver ran down my spine. She could have been in this room for all I knew. She could have been sitting on this bed, just like I was, not knowing what was coming...

I drew in a shaky breath as I completely freaked myself out.

I was being ridiculous. Natalie could have been in any room in the inn.

Putting the file aside, I took out my phone to distract myself with social media, but I couldn't seem to relax no matter how hard I tried. Giving up, I opened my suitcase, changed into PJs, brushed my teeth, and then got into bed.

As I turned off the lamp next to the bed, I tried to think happy thoughts, but every muscle in my body was tense, and I began to wish I'd chosen the room with the bathtub. That might have helped me relax.

I also really wished there was a TV in the room. I could watch something on my laptop, but it needed a charge, and the only plug was by the desk.

I just needed to sleep.

Tomorrow, everything would look better. Closing my eyes, I tried to find a happy image to concentrate on. And then I heard a crash. I jolted up in bed, wondering if it had been the wind or something else. It was quiet now...or was it?

It sounded like someone was crying.

I got out of bed, moving closer to the wall vent where I could hear sobs and also a hushed voice, commanding someone to be quiet.

Getting down on my knees by the vent, I strained to hear more, but now there was nothing but silence. I sat there for several minutes, not knowing what to do.

Should I go downstairs? Try to find my grandmother? Tell her I heard a crash and then someone crying?

But I didn't even really know what I'd heard.

As my knees began to ache from the hard floor, I got up and returned to bed. But now I felt even more awake, and all I could think about was how much I wanted to go home.

I pulled out my phone and texted Tessa: *Are you awake?*

I waited for a long five minutes. No answer. Tessa was probably asleep. I couldn't just pound on her door and wake her up. Not just because I didn't want to interrupt her sleep, but because I was also too afraid to open the door and venture into the hall.

How on earth was I going to be an investigative journalist when my imagination was turning a quaint bed and breakfast into some sort of house of horrors? I should probably just be writing novels.

Telling myself over and over again that everything was fine, I closed my eyes and tried to focus on my breathing, but my mind kept drifting to Natalie Warren, to the woman who'd come here for wellness and then vanished.

I really hoped that wasn't going to happen to us. But alone in this room, I couldn't help wondering, if Tessa and I didn't come back, would anyone be able to figure out why?

CHAPTER THREE

I woke up a little after six on Sunday, and after a long, tense night, morning felt like relief. I needed to get out of bed and get my imagination under control. I didn't know what I had really heard last night. Another guest might have been in pain or had gotten bad news. Maybe someone had knocked a lamp off the side table, causing a crash.

Rolling out of bed, I checked my phone. Tessa hadn't responded to my late-night text, which meant she'd been asleep while I'd been wide awake and terrified. That was Tessa—she could sleep through anything, her conscience clear, her mind unburdened by the what-ifs that constantly plagued me.

It was too early for breakfast and yoga, but I needed to move, to burn off my lingering anxiety. Running had always been my escape, the one thing that cleared my head when everything else felt chaotic, so I pulled on a pair of warm leggings, a long-sleeve shirt, and a jacket. The temperature was in the low forties, so I also pulled out my running gloves and a beanie to cover my ears. Tucking my phone and room key into the zippered pocket of my jacket, I left the room.

The inn was very quiet as I made my way downstairs. No sign

of Ellen or Ray or anyone else. I slipped out the front door as quietly as I could, pulling it shut behind me with barely a click.

Outside, the fog was just beginning to lift. My breath puffed out in white clouds as I started down the driveway, my muscles protesting the cold before gradually warming up. The rhythm of my feet hitting the pavement was soothing and meditative. Left, right, left, right. Breathe in through the nose, out through the mouth. This I could control. This made sense.

I jogged down the path that ran along the road, past the lighthouse that stood sentinel on the bluff, its light still sweeping across the gray-blue water, past the large building with a sign that bore my last name, Clarke and Sons Boatworks.

I wondered if my father had worked there before he'd left town to start a new life far removed from here. But my father was the least of my concerns right now. Maybe at some point, I'd figure out why he'd left, but my primary focus had to be Natalie. We needed information for the podcast—something to keep listeners engaged so we could grow the audience and attract more sponsors.

Following the path into town, I ran past a quiet harbor with a few fishing boats heading out to sea. The shops were dark, the streets empty, and the eerie feeling crept back into my brain. I told myself it was just early. This wasn't a ghost town. It was a thriving small coastal town that I would come back to visit later in the day.

Turning around, I headed back up the hill. I was about a hundred yards away from the inn when I saw a sandy path leading down to the beach, and I decided to take a detour. The path was steep and rocky, winding between trees and scrubby vegetation. When I finally broke through onto the sand, I stopped, hands on my hips, catching my breath.

The tide was out, leaving a wide expanse of beach below the bluffs. The sand was wet and dark, scattered with seaweed and shells, and while the cove provided some protection from the wind, the ocean beyond was wild and rugged, and not at all inviting.

As I looked away from the sea, I saw a man by the rocks at the base of the bluff. He was tall and fit, wearing dark jeans and a black jacket. His gaze was turned upward, and he appeared to be studying the cliffs or the inn above us with an intensity that seemed a bit out of place, as if he wasn't just a curious tourist.

He turned suddenly, and our eyes met across thirty feet of beach.

I froze. For a heartbeat, neither of us moved.

Then, because standing there staring at him felt ridiculous, I gave a small wave.

He moved toward me.

"Good morning," I said. "I didn't expect to see anyone down here so early."

He studied me before responding, his gaze sharp and assessing. "You're lucky the tide is out. This beach isn't always accessible. This is the first day I've been able to get down here." Pausing, he added, "Are you staying at the inn?"

"Yes. I got in last night."

The words were out before I could think better of them. I didn't know this man. He didn't need to know my business. But something about the directness of his question had pulled a direct answer from me.

"What about you?" I asked.

"No. But I'm close by." He paused, then said, "Aren't you nervous about staying there?"

"What do you mean?"

"Women seem to go missing after staying at the inn."

My mouth went dry. "Women?" I repeated. "Are you talking about Natalie Warren? What do you know about her?"

"I know she disappeared."

"That was after she checked out," I said, repeating the official line I'd read in every article about the case.

"So I've heard." His tone suggested he didn't believe it for a second.

My investigative instincts kicked in, overriding my unease. "Do you think something else happened?"

"I do."

The certainty in his voice made my stomach clench. I stared at him, trying to read his face, understand what game he was playing. "If that's true, have you said anything? Have you spoken to the sheriff?"

"A lot of people have come here asking questions. No one is talking."

"Who are you? Why are you so interested in Natalie Warren's disappearance? Did you know her?"

"I didn't." His eyes narrowed slightly. "Did you? Because her name came right off your lips."

I'd been too eager, too quick to show my hand. "I didn't know her, but I heard about her disappearance."

"What's your name?"

I hesitated. Giving him my name felt like giving him power, but refusing would only make me look more suspicious. "Cassidy. And you?"

"Tyler."

"It doesn't sound like you live here."

"No, I don't."

A wave crashed closer than I'd expected, and I jumped back as cold water splashed across my feet. "Damn!" The icy shock penetrated my running shoes instantly, soaking my socks, chilling my feet.

"You should never turn your back on the sea, Cassidy." Tyler's voice carried a warning that felt like it extended beyond ocean waves. "At least not around here."

As I met his gaze, I became acutely aware of our isolation. If something were to happen to me right now, who would know? The calm I'd found during my run evaporated like the morning fog, replaced by creeping dread.

"I should go back," I said, but I didn't move because he was standing between me and the beach path.

"You should go back, pack your bag, and leave," he said, his tone grim.

"Are you trying to scare me?"

"I would hate to see anyone else go missing."

Anyone else. There it was again. That plural. "Wait a second. You said *women*. Did someone besides Natalie disappear?"

Before he could answer, his phone buzzed. He pulled it out of his pocket, glanced at the screen, and his jaw tightened. "I have to take this. Be careful, Cassidy. More careful than you think you need to be."

He turned away to answer his call, and I seized the opportunity to leave. I hurried past him and started up the steep path toward the inn, my pulse racing from our conversation.

Had he been warning me? Threatening me? Was he involved in Natalie's disappearance, or was he just another person who'd become obsessed with the case?

And what had he meant about other women going missing?

When I reached the inn, I felt breathless and unsettled. Ray Connors was outside the inn, high up on a ladder, nailing boards over a broken window on the third floor. My pulse jumped again. Was that my room?

As Ray climbed down the ladder, I approached, my wet shoes squishing with each step. He noticed me, his expression unchanging. Not friendly or unfriendly. Just... blank.

"What happened to the window?" I asked. "Is that my room?"

"No, not your room." His voice was curt, dismissive. "A guest had an accident. Knocked something into the window."

I wanted to ask, but Ray had already collapsed the ladder, slung it over his shoulder, and walked away. My mind raced with more questions. *Was the guest who'd broken the window the same one I'd heard crying through the vent?*

I pushed the questions aside and headed into the inn, telling myself I was overreacting. I needed to take a shower and get on with the day.

Back in my room, I stood under the hot water for a long time, trying to shake off not only the physical cold but also the unsettling conversation with Tyler. *Who was he, and why did he care so much about what was happening at the inn?* His words echoed through my head: *Women seem to go missing after staying at the inn.* Women. Not just Natalie. But who else? Why hadn't my research turned up other disappearances?

Unless they hadn't been reported. Or they'd been reported in other jurisdictions, no one connecting their disappearances to Stonecross.

Still thinking about that, I dried off and dressed in yoga pants and a tank top under a soft gray sweater. I needed to talk to Tessa. She'd either reassure me I was overthinking everything, or she'd be as alarmed as I was. Either way, I couldn't sit alone in this room, trying to make sense of everything by myself.

Tessa opened her door, a bright smile on her face. She looked pretty, her blonde hair shiny in the light, her blue eyes filled with energy. "There you are! I was just about to come find you. How did you sleep?"

I almost laughed at the question. "Not great."

Her smile faded. "That's too bad. Couldn't stop thinking? Or was the bed uncomfortable?"

"The bed was fine, but the night was not. Can I come in?"

"Of course." She stepped aside, and I entered the garden-view room, which was slightly larger than mine and did indeed have a spectacular bathtub visible through the bathroom door.

"That tub was heaven," Tessa said, following my gaze. "I stayed in there for an hour. Best bath of my life. Sorry I didn't answer your text. I crashed as soon as I got into bed.

"Lucky you."

She frowned. "Did something happen?"

I sat on the edge of her bed, and everything came tumbling out—the startling crash, the sound of crying, the voice telling someone to be quiet, my encounter with the man on the beach, ending with Ray and the broken window.

Tessa's expression shifted from curious to concerned to excited. When I finished, she was practically vibrating with energy.

"Holy shit, Cassidy. This is crazy. Multiple disappearances? How did we not know that?"

"Because it's not out there. Maybe someone covered something up, or maybe this guy was just blowing smoke."

"What if there are other women who left here and were never heard from again, but no one filed a missing persons report? Or what if they were filed in different jurisdictions, so no one connected them?"

"That's a lot of assumptions."

"But it's possible. And what about the broken window? It wasn't my room or yours. Do you think it was the room at the end of the hall where we saw that woman go inside?"

"I think that's exactly whose window it was. And maybe she was the one crying."

"How did she break the window?"

"No idea. Ray said it was an accident. It's hard to believe she threw something through the window. She looked so frail, like a gust of wind would knock her over."

"Maybe she was trying to escape," Tessa suggested.

"From the third floor?"

"Who knows what someone will do when they're trapped?"

"I don't think she was trapped. Why wouldn't she scream if she was? Why just cry? It sounded more like she was really sad, not terrified."

"We need to talk to her."

"She looked like she wanted to disappear into the walls, Tessa. I don't think she's going to talk to us."

"We have to try. We'll be friendly. Non-threatening." She stood up. "Maybe she's downstairs. Let's get breakfast and see who's around."

"Okay."

"By the way, did you tell that guy on the beach—Tyler—about our podcast?"

"No. I didn't tell him anything except my first name."

"Good. If he or anyone else asks, we stick to our cover story—we're researching historic inns for a book. We're writers doing background research. That's why we're so nosy."

I nodded, even though anxiety was pooling in my stomach. "Got it. But I think we need to be careful, Tessa."

"Of course, but we have to take some risks, too. Otherwise, we'll never find out anything."

Seeing the gleam in her eyes, I wondered if I was taking everything too seriously or if she wasn't taking it seriously enough.

I had a feeling we were going to find out.

———

The dining room was busy. The same young couple who had been kissing over wine and cheese was doing the same over bacon and eggs. Their oblivious happiness screamed honeymoon. The woman who'd been knitting in the living room had a table by the window, and her knitting needles clicked rhythmically as she worked on what looked like a scarf. A middle-aged couple occupied one of the other tables, consulting a guidebook as they ate. And in the far corner at a table by herself was the woman I'd seen entering the room next to mine.

She was hunched over a plate of food she wasn't eating, her fork moving listlessly through her scrambled eggs. In the morning light, she looked even paler than she had last night, almost translucent.

Ellen appeared from what I assumed was the kitchen, carrying a coffeepot. She wore the same neutral expression she'd had last night—polite but distant, the smile never quite reaching her eyes.

"Good morning," she said, gesturing to an empty table near the center of the room. "Please, sit anywhere you'd like. Coffee?"

"Yes, please," Tessa said with a warm smile as we sat down at the table. "This room is beautiful, and the buffet looks amazing."

"Thank you." Ellen poured coffee into our cups with practiced efficiency. "We have scrambled eggs, bacon, sausage, fresh fruit, yogurt, and pastries. Help yourselves."

"Wonderful," Tessa said. "Do you do all the cooking?"

"I have help," Ellen said, her tone making it clear she wasn't interested in elaborating. "Enjoy your breakfast."

As Ellen moved away, Tessa caught my eye and mouthed, "Warm."

I couldn't help but smile. In that regard, Ellen reminded me of my father. But that wasn't something I was going to think about now.

We got up and filled our plates at the buffet before taking our seats. The older woman gave me a smile as I pulled out my chair.

"Good morning," she said cheerfully. "I'm Dorothy Winters. Did you just arrive?"

"Last night," I said. "I'm Cassidy, and this is Tessa."

"Where are you from?"

"New York."

"What brings you to Stonecross? Or do I need to ask? More and more women are coming for Ellen's wellness classes."

"We're interested in that, too," I said. "But we're also researching old inns for a book we're writing."

"How lovely!" Dorothy's needles never stopped moving. "And you've picked the perfect inn. I've been coming here for years, and it's my favorite spot. My husband passed away two years ago, and since then, this inn has been my second home. I meet so many interesting people." She gestured at the honeymoon couple with her needles. "That young couple looks like they're in their own little world. Blissfully happy. They remind me of me and my husband a very long time ago. And then there's that poor girl." She lowered her voice, tipping her head toward my wispy neighbor. "She reminds me of how I felt after my husband died. Sad and lost. She's been here three days, barely eats, barely speaks. I tried to chat with her yesterday, but she practically ran away from me."

Before I could respond, the kitchen door swung open, and a young woman backed through it, carrying a tray laden with fresh pastries and a pitcher of juice. As she approached the buffet table, her foot caught on the edge of a rug and she stumbled. The tray tilted dangerously, and she overcorrected, sending a glass pitcher of orange juice sliding toward the edge of her tray.

"No, no, no!" she gasped, lunging for it, but she was too late.

The pitcher hit the floor with a spectacular crash, glass shattering everywhere, orange juice spraying across the hardwood in a sunburst pattern that somehow managed to reach our table, the honeymoon couple's table, and splattered across Dorothy's sensible shoes.

"Oh my God, I'm so sorry!" the young woman cried, her face flushing crimson. "I'm so, so sorry!"

Ellen appeared almost instantly, her expression thunderous. "Sophie."

The single word carried enough weight to make Sophie flinch.

"I'm sorry, Mrs. Clarke, I just—"

"Clean it up," Ellen said sharply. "Now."

As Sophie hurried back to the kitchen for cleaning supplies, Ellen turned to us with a tight smile. "I apologize for the disruption. Did the juice splash on you?"

"No, we're fine," Tessa said.

Ellen moved efficiently around the room, checking on the guests, refilling cups, and murmuring apologies, while Sophie came back with a mop and a bucket and cleaned up her mess with downcast eyes and a defeated posture.

When she got close to our table, Tessa leaned in. "Hey, don't worry about it," Tessa said. "Accidents happen. I once dropped an entire tray of champagne glasses at a party I was catering. Sounded like a bomb went off."

Sophie looked up, surprise and gratitude flooding her face. "Thank you. I'm normally not this clumsy. Actually, that's not true. I am clumsy, but I'm worse when I'm here. Mrs. Clarke makes me nervous."

Ellen's sharp voice cut through the room. "Sophie, when you're finished, please help Chef in the kitchen."

"Yes, ma'am." Sophie grabbed the bucket and mop and fled.

"Well," Tessa said quietly, "Sophie might be someone we could get to talk. She's clearly not a big fan of Ellen's."

"Maybe not a fan, but she is intimidated by her."

"It's still worth a try."

The kitchen door swung open again, and Sophie emerged, carrying a tray of fresh orange juice, and this time she moved with painstaking care, setting the new pitcher carefully on the table. Then she came back to us. "Can I bring you some juice?"

"I think we're fine," I said. "We're coffee addicts."

"Me, too," she said, appearing to relax as Ellen returned to the kitchen.

"Do you work here full-time?" Tessa asked.

"I split my time between here and Kelly's Pub. I'm saving up to get out of here." She glanced nervously toward the kitchen. "Don't tell Ellen I said that."

"Your secret is safe with us," I said. "Where are you planning to go?"

"New York City."

"That's where we live," Tessa said. "It's great there. You'll love it."

Sophie's face lit up. "Really? You're from New York. Maybe we could talk—"

"Sophie!" Ellen's voice rang from the kitchen doorway. "A word, please."

The light died in Sophie's eyes. "Coming." She hurried away, leaving Tessa and me exchanging another glance.

"We've got an in," Tessa said. "Maybe if we share info on the city with Sophie, she'll share info on the inn with us."

"That's a good idea," I said as I finished my food. Checking my watch, I added, "I was thinking of taking the yoga class at ten. It's almost that time now. What do you want to do?"

"Definitely not yoga. You know how inflexible I am."

"That's how you get flexible," I said with a smile, knowing that Tessa was not a fan of exercise.

Tessa took a sip of her coffee, then said, "I think I'll linger here, see if I can catch up with Sophie after breakfast ends."

"Okay. Just be careful."

"I don't think Sophie is dangerous. I'd be more likely to get hurt attempting to do yoga."

I gave her a faint smile. "I'll catch up with you after class. And, Tessa, I don't think we should assume anyone in this place is not dangerous."

CHAPTER FOUR

A lush garden path led from the side door of the inn to the yoga deck, which extended to the edge of the cliff. The platform was larger than I'd expected, maybe twenty feet by thirty feet, with a railing that looked sturdy but not particularly high. Beyond the railing was nothing but air and ocean—a sheer drop to the rocks and water below.

Five other women were already there, arranging their mats in a semicircle facing the ocean. I grabbed one of the rolled mats and found a spot next to the woman who was staying in the room next to me. I gave her a friendly smile. "Hi, I'm Cassidy."

She gave me a startled look as if she hadn't been expecting anyone to speak to her. "I'm Anna," she muttered.

"I think you're in the room next to mine. I saw you in the hallway last night."

Before Anna could answer, a woman stepped up to the front of the group, wearing a loose-fitting sweater over dark-green leggings and a crop top. She had kind green eyes and a warm smile.

"Hello, I'm Becca Thorne," she said. "Welcome to Sunday morning flow. For those who are new, this practice is about connecting with your breath, your body, and this beautiful natural setting. Let's start in a comfortable seated position."

I followed her lead and sank into the opening stretch. But as I did so, my gaze drifted to Anna. As she stretched forward, her T-shirt crept up, revealing purple bruises on her side that looked large and painful, making me wonder just how she'd gotten them. But I couldn't just come out and ask her, especially not now in the middle of class, so I refocused on the yoga moves, hoping I could talk to her more after class.

But we had barely settled into our final relaxation pose, when I saw Anna roll up her mat and walk quickly away. Clearly, she had no interest in speaking with me. It was apparent that someone had hurt her. I hoped whoever had put those bruises on her body wasn't still close to her. But I couldn't help but think about the crash I'd heard the night before, the broken window that had to be in her room, the hushed command to be quiet, and the sad sobs. *Who had been with Anna last night? And had they been there to help her or to hurt her?*

When Becca finally released us from the pose, I rolled up my mat and put it on the pile. Another woman was speaking to Becca, so I walked over to the rail to wait until they were done,

The view was spectacular—the ocean stretching endlessly before me, the white caps gleaming in the sunshine, seagulls flying overhead. When I looked down at the beach where I had stood earlier, my head spun. The drop was at least sixty feet, straight down to jagged rocks and now churning water. The tide was coming in, and the sand was almost entirely covered, just as Tyler had told me.

The railing came up to about my waist—high enough to be safe, but low enough that a stumble, a push, a moment of vertigo could possibly send me over. I gripped the wood, feeling the weathered grain under my palms, and tried not to imagine what it would feel like to fall.

"Beautiful, isn't it?"

I jumped, spinning around to see Becca's smile. "Sorry, I didn't mean to startle you."

"It's fine. I'm not great with heights." I backed away from the edge. "It's beautiful up here, but a little dizzying."

"When Ellen first asked me to teach out here, I wasn't sure about it," Becca said. "But she was right. There's something about practicing yoga with the ocean view offering a sense of space and possibility that's transformative."

"How long have you been teaching here?"

"About three years. That's when Ellen added a wellness program to the inn's offerings. The classes have become quite popular. Many of the guests who come here are looking for rest and a reset. Does that include you?"

"I could use a reset," I admitted. "I live on the twelfth floor of a high-rise in Manhattan where sirens and noise provide the soundtrack for my life."

"I went to New York once for a week, and I was so ready to come back to Maine for fresh air and peace and quiet."

"It is lovely here." I licked my lips, knowing I needed to talk about more than the view, but I wasn't quite sure how to get started. Finally, I said, "Do you know the woman who was next to me? Anna?"

"She came to a class on Friday," Becca said. "Why do you ask?"

"I saw a lot of bruises on her side, and she seemed...scared. I know it's not my business, but I couldn't help wondering if she was in some kind of trouble."

"She told me Friday that she was looking to start her life over," Becca said. "I hope whatever trouble she may have been in is behind her."

"That's good. I hope that's true."

"How long will you be staying? I have another class tomorrow and also on Wednesday."

"I'm not completely sure. My friend, Tessa, and I are writing a book on historic inns, and we want to include this one, so we're looking for historical information and maybe some old photographs, that kind of thing."

"So, this is a business trip, too."

"It is, but I'll try to fit in your classes as well."

"Great. I'm sure Ellen will love to have this inn included in your book."

I licked my lips, now realizing our lie might trigger others to ask Ellen about our book, and I wondered how long before the lie collapsed under its own weight "We haven't spoken to Ellen about the book yet. We're just starting our research, and we wanted to check out the inn without anyone trying to impress us," I said, searching quickly for a viable story. "But, of course, we'll talk to her once we decide if we're going to use the inn in the book."

"You should definitely do that. She's very protective about the inn's reputation."

Since Becca had opened the door, I decided to walk through it. "We heard there was an incident last year; a woman went missing after staying here. We wondered if that had any impact on the inn's reputation."

"I believe that all happened after she left the inn," Becca said quickly, her expression changing from friendly to guarded.

"Did you meet her? I think her name was Natalie Warren."

"She took one of my classes, but I only said hello and exchanged small talk. She seemed happy enough while she was here. If you want history on the inn and don't want to talk to Ellen yet, you should speak to Margaret at the Stonecross Library. She not only runs the library, but she's also the head of the historical society."

"Thanks for the tip."

"She's probably there today. She works most weekends since her husband died."

"I'm going into town later, so I'll definitely stop in. Thanks."

"Enjoy your stay. And I hope to see you in class again." Becca paused. "I'd give Anna her space. It's kind of you to be concerned about her, but sometimes people who have been hurt just need to be by themselves."

"I understand," I said.

"See you next time."

Becca stopped to talk to another lingering class participant, so I headed into the inn on my own. When I reached the third-floor landing, Tessa popped out of her open door. "There you are. I was about to come looking for you. How was yoga?"

"It was interesting," I replied, my gaze darting down the hall to Anna's closed door. "Let's go inside."

I opened my door and waved her into my room, shutting the door behind me. "The woman next door was there. Her name is Anna. I tried to talk to her. She didn't want to talk back. I also saw a lot of bruises on her side when she was doing a stretch."

"That doesn't sound good."

"I wanted to talk to her about it, offer my help if she needed anything, but she slipped out before class was over. I spoke to the teacher about her, and she said Anna arrived a few days ago and that she thought Anna had left whatever trouble she was in behind her."

"That's vague."

"Becca, the teacher, also suggested that I leave Anna alone, that she needed space. She said a lot of people come to the inn to reset. She was perfectly nice about it, but it also felt like a warning." I paused. "Oh, and I told her our cover story about writing a book on inns when she asked me what I was doing here. She commented that Ellen is very particular about the reputation of the inn. That led me to ask her if that reputation hadn't been hurt by the disappearance of Natalie Warren."

"You're getting bold, Cassidy. I like it."

I shrugged. "We have to start somewhere, right? Anyway, Becca said she met Natalie when she was here, that she took a yoga class, but it was her understanding that Natalie left, and her disappearance had nothing to do with the inn. So, I didn't really get anything new out of her. However, she did suggest that we go to the library and speak to Margaret, who apparently runs both the library and the historical society. She said Margaret would have information about the inn if we didn't want to talk to Ellen about our book yet."

"That's a good tip. Looks like we know who we're going to talk to next. By the way, I spoke to Sophie. She repeated what everyone else has said about Natalie's disappearance. She also told me she spoke to Natalie the day before she left, and she seemed fine, a little quiet, maybe even sad, but not upset or scared or anything. She also mentioned that a lot of single women act like Natalie when they come to the inn, which has become a haven for the lost and disheartened, most of whom seem to be women."

"That's interesting. Did she tell you anything about Ellen?"

"She's cold and judgmental with her employees, but much nicer to the guests."

"I'm not sure I agree with that."

"Well, we can talk to Sophie more later today. Her family owns Kelly's Pub, and she suggested we stop by tonight for their world-famous burgers. She's working but she'll take a break when we're there and talk to us about the inn and also Manhattan. She wants to pick our brains about where to live."

"That sounds like a good trade-off."

"I agree. In the meantime, I think we should go into town, check out the library, and see what we can learn about the history of the inn and the Clarke family. Then we poke around downtown and end up at Kelly's Pub for dinner, where we can talk to Sophie more freely. Hopefully, we'll get some information to share on our podcast tonight."

"Don't you think we should wait to do the podcast until Morgan gets in tomorrow? As soon as people in this town find out about our podcast, they'll stop talking. The longer we can work our cover story, the better, right?"

"I see your point. Let's decide later. If we come up with some good information, I don't think we should sit on it."

"Fine, but there's still a possibility we won't come up with anything."

"We already have stuff to talk about, the mysterious crash, the crying, the woman with bruises, the cryptic man on the beach..."

"We can't talk about any of that. We don't know what it means."

"We don't have to know what it means; we just have to let our listeners feel what we're feeling."

"Right now, I'm feeling a little sick to my stomach," I said dryly.

Tessa laughed. "Well, if we make our listeners a little queasy, they won't be able to walk away." She stood up and then said, "Oh, there's one more thing Sophie told me, and you're not going to like it, but it's going to be great for the podcast."

"What's that?"

"Natalie stayed here—in this room."

My stomach dropped. "You're right. I don't like that at all."

CHAPTER FIVE

The drive into Stonecross took less than ten minutes, winding down the coastal road past the lighthouse and the boatyard before reaching the main street. In daylight, with more tourists bustling about, the town looked even more charming than it had during my early morning run. It was still small, still quiet, but picturesque in a weathered New England way, with wind-battered wood, faded awnings, and storefronts that looked as though they'd been there forever.

Tessa parked in front of the library, and as I got out of the car, I smelled sea air and the scent of fresh-baked bread from a nearby bakery. "Something smells good. Maybe we should check out the bakery first."

"After the library."

I'd thought of Tessa as being the least focused of the three of us, but she was all business now.

The library smelled of old books and furniture polish that reminded me of weekends in college, when I'd spent hours studying while most of my friends were at parties or football games. My father had made his financial assistance contingent on my grades, and I couldn't afford to get anything less than an

A, so I had to hit the books even when there had been more appealing alternatives.

The woman at the circulation desk looked up from her computer as we entered. She was in her mid-fifties with chin-length dark hair going gray at the temples.

"Good morning," she said with a friendly smile. "Can I help you find something?"

"We're looking for Margaret."

"That's me." Her smile widened. "And you are?"

"I'm Cassidy, and this is Tessa. We're staying at the Stonecross Inn for a few days, and we're researching historic inns across New England for a book we're writing."

"How wonderful!" Margaret stood, clearly pleased. "I love talking about local history. The inn is certainly one of our most historic buildings. Are you researching anything specific?"

"Just general background," Tessa said smoothly. "The architecture, the families who've owned it, any interesting stories or legends. We're trying to capture the character of these old places. And sometimes the owners don't want to share all the good stuff."

"Well, you've come to the right place. I've lived in Stonecross my entire life, and my parents before me, and my grandparents before that. I have deep roots in the community. Follow me."

She led us into a back room that was packed with filing cabinets, old photographs on the walls, shelves of binders and books, as well as a long table with two computers.

"The Stonecross Inn was built in 1872 by Captain Josiah Hartwell, a whaling captain who made his fortune before the industry declined," Margaret said. "Captain Hartwell's descendants ran it as a boarding house and eventually a proper inn until the seventies, when it was sold to Richard and Ellen Clarke."

My pulse quickened at the mention of my grandparents' names, but I kept my expression neutral.

"Ellen has been running the inn for more than fifty years,"

Margaret continued. "And the past thirty-six on her own, since her husband died."

"What happened to him?" I asked, eager to learn more about my grandfather.

Margaret's expression shifted, became more somber. "Richard fell from the cliffs behind the inn. It was a stormy night with heavy fog, and he'd gone out to put some plywood on the windows. No one is really sure what happened. Ellen was already asleep and didn't know he'd gone out until the sheriff knocked on her door the next morning. A tourist had found Richard's body on the beach. It was such a tragedy. He was only forty-one years old."

"That's awful," I said.

"The whole town was devastated. Richard was very well-liked. He ran the boatyard—Clarke and Sons. It had been in his family for generations."

"We passed that building on the way into town," I said.

"Yes. It's still operating, but not by anyone in the Clarke family. Richard's son wasn't interested in taking it over. David left town shortly after his father's death and never came back."

"Why not?" I asked, wondering if I'd finally get an answer.

Margaret hesitated, and I could see her weighing how much to say. "It's a small town," she said finally. "People talk. There were... rumors. After Richard's death."

"What kind of rumors?" I asked, even though I wasn't sure I wanted to know the answer.

Margaret looked uncomfortable now. "I probably shouldn't gossip. It was a long time ago."

"We're just trying to understand the history of the place," Tessa said. "The full story, you know? The good and the bad. It makes for a more complete picture."

Margaret glanced toward the door, as if checking that we were still alone, then lowered her voice. "Some people thought David had something to do with his father's death. That they'd fought. That Richard fell during an argument." She shook her head firmly. "But the police investigated thoroughly, and it was ruled an accident. The cliffs are dangerous, especially in the fog."

My mouth had gone dry. People thought my father killed my grandfather? They'd suspected him of murder. No wonder he'd left. No wonder he'd never wanted to go back.

"Did his mother think that, too?" I asked.

"Ellen has never spoken to me or anyone about why David left. She made it clear the subject was off-limits. David was two years ahead of me in school, so I didn't know him well. Not many people did. He was polite but very private. All the Clarkes are kind of like that."

My father certainly fits that description now. He had excellent manners, but he was so guarded, so walled off from emotion, that no one could get close, especially me.

"I'm sure you're more interested in the inn itself and not the sad family history." She waved her hand to the nearby computers. "We've digitized all the local newspapers going back to 1920. Anything that's been written about the inn will be there. You can also access the bigger media sites in Maine and across the country." She paused, waving her hand toward the bookshelves behind her. "We also have some history books that were written about the town and the inn that you can check out. Let me know if you need any help."

"Thank you," Tessa said.

After Margaret returned to the circulation desk, I sat down in front of one of the computers, while Tessa took the seat next to me.

"You okay?" Tessa asked.

"Not really. I just found out people thought my father was a murderer."

Tessa frowned. "It was a rumor. We don't know that it was true."

"I can't imagine my father killing anyone. He's not violent. He's just...cold." Despite my words, I still felt unsettled by what

I'd heard. "But is this why my dad never talked about his past, never wanted me to meet my own grandmother?"

"Maybe your father was hurt by the accusations. Maybe your grandmother didn't defend him." She gave me a sympathetic smile. "You're probably not going to know the truth unless you ask one of them what happened."

"I'm not sure either one would tell me the truth. But I can't ask them right now anyway. We need to focus on Natalie. Maybe we can find something in the local papers that we haven't seen before."

"I can look for Natalie while you research your grandfather's death. I'm sure there was press about that, too. Maybe you'll find something reassuring in those reports. Right now, we just have Margaret's version of events, and we don't know if she has any idea what she's talking about."

"That's true." I turned my gaze to the monitor as I opened the search window and put in my grandfather's name. Several results appeared, the first one about his death. "Got something," I said.

"Already?" Tessa asked. "I barely finished typing in Natalie. Read it to me."

"Local Businessman Dies in Tragic Fall," I read. *"Richard Clarke, forty-one, owner of Clarke and Sons Boatworks, died Saturday after falling from the cliffs behind the Stonecross Inn. Clarke's body was discovered early Sunday morning on the beach below the inn. Sheriff Tom Holloway stated that the death appears to be accidental, though the investigation is ongoing. "The cliffs behind the inn are treacherous, especially in rain and fog," Sheriff Holloway said. "Clarke is survived by his wife Ellen and son David. Services will be held at Stonecross Community Church on Thursday."*

"That's pretty short," Tessa said. "There must be more than that."

"Here's an even shorter article from a week later. *The investigation into Richard Clarke's death has been closed, with officials ruling the death accidental. Sheriff Tom Holloway confirmed that there was no evidence of foul play."*

"Sheriff Holloway likes to close cases fast," Tessa commented.

"Like you said, I'm not going to find the answers about my family online. Maybe I'll see if I can find anything on other women who have gone missing from the inn. Tyler had to have gotten his information somewhere."

"Good idea."

I typed in *missing women Stonecross Inn* and hit search.

I was expecting to see Natalie's name pop up first, but instead, there was a short article from three months ago about a search being called off for a woman named Jessica Trent, who had rented a boat and failed to return to the harbor. The boat had been located several miles south, but there was no sign of the woman. Apparently, Jessica had been vacationing at the Stonecross Inn for several days before she'd rented the boat and never returned.

"Here's something interesting," I said to Tessa. "Three months ago, a woman named Jessica Trent rented a boat and failed to return. They found the boat, but there was no sign of her." I looked up from the computer to meet her gaze. "She was staying at the inn. Maybe that's who Tyler was talking about."

"I found someone else, too," Tessa said. "This article is from six years ago: *Woman Missing After Coastal Visit. Emma Rodriguez from Boston was reported missing after a visit to the Stonecross Inn for the summer solstice. Husband says she suffers from mental illness, and anyone with information should contact the sheriff's department."*

"If she was mentally ill, maybe that's why she disappeared."

"I found something else. But this goes way back," Tessa said. *"Lily Morrison, sixteen, of Stonecross, appears to have drowned during last night's storm. Her clothes were found on the beach below the Stonecross Inn, along with a suicide note. Lily worked part-time at the inn and was last seen leaving the property after her shift at three o'clock in the afternoon. Ellen Clarke expressed shock and sadness at the loss of such a beautiful, kind girl. A coworker remarked that Lily had seemed depressed the last few weeks, but she had no idea she was suicidal."*

"That's sad. But she wasn't staying at the inn; she was working there."

"Does that make a difference?" Tessa asked. "I think we've just found the tip of an iceberg. Natalie wasn't the only one to disappear. Tyler was right."

"But we don't know if any of these events are related. They sound more random."

"We could talk to Margaret about these other women."

"We could, but let's hold off for now. I don't want us to get too distracted by the other women when Natalie is our focus." I sat back in my chair. "I also don't want to get derailed by my family's story. Let's take a break. I need some air."

"That's fine with me. I want to shoot some video around town before we go to the pub. And, frankly, I don't think we're going to solve anything from this library. We need to get out and talk to people."

"I agree. I just hope they talk back."

CHAPTER SIX

After shooting video around town for the next hour and a half, we walked to Kelly's Pub, which occupied a weathered building near the harbor. Inside, exposed brick walls were covered with framed photographs showing the pub through different eras. The bar itself was dark wood, and behind it, shelves of bottles glowed in the soft light. Nautical touches were everywhere, with fishing nets draped in corners, a ship's wheel mounted on one wall, and old brass lanterns hanging from the ceiling.

It was only four-thirty, which was a little late for lunch and a little early for dinner, so only a dozen people were scattered about. An older man sat at the far end of the bar nursing what looked like whiskey. Two middle-aged women occupied a corner booth, laughing over glasses of wine. A group of younger guys played darts near the back, their competitive banter punctuating the low rumble of conversation and the classic rock playing from speakers I couldn't see.

A man stood behind the bar, wiping down glasses. He was tall and broad-shouldered, wearing jeans and a black T-shirt that showed muscular arms covered in tattoos. His dark hair was longish, curling slightly at his collar, and his eyes were a deep blue. He gave us a friendly smile as we sat down at the bar.

"Hello, ladies. What can I get you?"

"How about a name?" Tessa asked with a flirty smile. "You wouldn't be Sophie's brother, would you?"

"I am. Finn Kelly. And who might you be?"

"I'm Tessa, and this is Cassidy," she replied. "We met Sophie at the inn this morning. She told us this was the best pub in town."

"She's right. You must be the New York City writers she was telling me about. Have a seat. Sophie's in the kitchen, but she'll be out soon."

We settled onto barstools, and Finn immediately placed cocktail napkins in front of us. "Can I get you drinks? Food?"

"What do you recommend?" Tessa asked.

"Shipyard Ale if you like beer, and definitely my burgers. I know everyone says that about their local burger place, but I swear these are legitimately the best on the coast." He grinned. "Made with my own special sauce. Won't tell anyone the recipe, not even my sister."

"A man with secrets," Tessa teased. "I'm sold. Burger and a Shipyard for me."

"Same," I said, thinking how good Tessa was at being fun and flirty without really even trying.

Finn grabbed two glasses and started pouring our beers with practiced efficiency. "What do you two write?"

"We're working on a book about historic inns. That's why we're staying at the Stonecross Inn," Tessa said. "We wanted to see how it works from the inside."

"That inn definitely has history," he said, setting our beers in front of us. "It's over a hundred years old. My parents actually got married in the garden there."

"That's interesting," I said. "So, you grew up here in Stonecross?"

"I did, but I was gone for about twelve years while I was in the Army."

"When did you come back?"

"It's been about two years now. I hadn't really planned on going into the family business, but that's the way it worked out."

The kitchen door swung open, and Sophie emerged, her face lighting up when she saw us. "You came! I'm so glad. And I see you met Finn."

"I'm going to put their order in," Finn said as he moved away from the bar, heading into the kitchen.

"How was the library?" Sophie asked. "Did you learn anything interesting?"

"Margaret was helpful," Tessa said. "She told us about the death of Ellen's husband."

"That was a sad story from what I've heard. He died before I was born, so I never met him, but my parents knew him as well as Ellen's son, David. He left shortly after his father died and Ellen doesn't talk about him. There's some bad blood there." She paused. "Are you going to put that story in your book?"

"We're just gathering information," I said.

"We're looking for more atmosphere," Tessa added. "Ghost stories, local legends, that kind of thing. Facts are great, but we need the stories that make a place memorable."

Sophie smiled. "I've heard a few guests say they thought they heard voices in the night, but I'm pretty sure it was just the wind. The inn is old and creaky. It's always rattling."

"So, nothing?" Tessa asked with disappointment. "No resident ghost?"

"I don't think Mrs. Clarke would allow that. In fact, I would be careful what you write about the inn. If you say anything negative, she'd probably sue you. That inn is her whole life." Sophie straightened as the door opened, and a uniformed officer stepped up to the bar.

He had dark hair that was peppered with gray, a little too much weight in the middle and appeared to be in his fifties. He carried himself like someone used to being in charge and obeyed, and Sophie suddenly seemed a bit nervous.

"Sophie," he said with a curt nod. "Is Cole here?"

"I haven't seen him today, Sheriff," Sophie replied, and there was a carefulness in her tone that hadn't been there before.

The sheriff turned to us with a questioning gleam in his eyes. "Hello. I haven't seen you two in here before. I'm Sheriff Tom Holloway."

"I'm Tessa, and this is Cassidy," Tessa replied. "We're staying at the Stonecross Inn."

I was happy she hadn't used our last names, which seemed to be a deliberate choice on her part, probably because she didn't think I'd be able to say my fake last name without stumbling all over myself.

"How are you enjoying your stay?"

"It's been great so far," Tessa replied.

"How long are you in town?"

"Just a few days," she said.

"Sheriff," Finn said as he returned to the bar. "Can I get you something?"

"Just a coffee, thanks," Tom said, his tone clipped. "I'm looking for my son. Have you seen Cole?"

The door opened again, bringing with it a gust of cold air, and Finn said, "He's here now."

I turned to see two men approaching. The first was probably in his late forties, with an easy smile and tanned skin. The second appeared to be in his early twenties. Both looked happy and relaxed, until they saw the sheriff.

"There you are, Cole," Tom said, an edge to his voice. "I've been calling you for an hour. Where the hell were you?"

"Uncle Jeff needed me on a charter, and I left my phone in the truck," Cole said, not sounding that apologetic.

"You were supposed to be working at the boatyard this afternoon, remember? I asked Henry to give you some weekend hours so you could make extra money."

Cole's smile faded. "Oh, yeah. I forgot."

As Tom's gaze swung to Uncle Jeff, the man put up his hands in apology. "I didn't know anything about that, Tom. Cole didn't tell me."

"It's not a big deal," Cole said. "I'll apologize to Henry. I'm sure he didn't really need me anyway; he was just doing you a favor."

"And I was doing you a favor," Tom stated, anger reddening his face. "That's the last time."

"Got it," Cole said shortly. Turning to Sophie, he said, "Can I talk to you for a sec?"

She nodded and motioned toward the kitchen. Then she told Finn, "I'll be back in a second."

"I could use a beer," Jeff interjected. "Can I buy you one, Tom? Seems like you could use a drink."

"I'm on duty. And I have a coffee."

"Like you need more coffee. You need to calm down. You haven't been yourself since Diane—"

"I'm fine. I just need you to stop encouraging Cole to follow in your footsteps."

"You should be happy he wants to work with me. Otherwise, he probably would have left a long time ago. You have a history of driving people away."

The sheriff started to say something, then realized we were avidly listening to their conversation. "Sorry about this, ladies. I hope you enjoy your stay in Stonecross." He tipped his head, then took his coffee and walked out of the bar.

Jeff slid into the seat on the other side of Tessa.

"I don't think we've met. I'm Jeff Holloway, Tom's brother, Cole's uncle, in case you hadn't figured that out," he said with an easy smile.

"Tessa...Cassidy," Tessa said, tipping her head to me. "We're visiting."

"I figured. You're staying at the inn, right?"

"How did you know?" I asked.

"The inn gets a lot of visitors about your age these days. Ellen definitely found a way to drum up some new business, not that any of us are complaining. I run a boat charter service if you want to go out on the ocean."

"That sounds fun," Tessa said.

"Holloway Charters. I have an office on the pier, and if I'm not there, someone else will be. Or you can check our times and prices on the web. I'm always happy to give customers of the inn a special deal."

"We might take you up on that," Tessa said, pausing as Finn appeared with two plates loaded with burgers and fries.

"Why don't I show you to a booth?" Finn suggested. "You'll be more comfortable."

"Okay," Tessa said. "It was nice to meet you, Jeff."

"You, too."

Tessa and I followed Finn to a booth against the wall.

"Fair warning—these are messy," Finn said as he set down our plates. "Sophie is bringing you extra napkins. I know she wants to talk to you about New York, so I told her she can take a break, and she'll be right out."

"Great, thanks," I said.

"Was that a little weird?" Tessa asked. "Finn moving us to a booth?"

"It is more comfortable."

"Or maybe he didn't want us talking to Jeff Holloway."

"Why would he care? Jeff seemed friendly enough. Although he was in trouble with his brother."

" Family drama is everywhere."

"I wonder if we should talk to Jeff about the woman who took the boat out and then disappeared. If he runs a charter service, he might know something about that."

"Good idea, but I thought we were concentrating on Natalie."

"You're right, but still something to think about."

"Right now, all I'm thinking is about how good this burger is," she said, her mouth full of her first bite.

I laughed and joined in, completely agreeing with her assessment as the secret sauce overwhelmed my taste buds with its deliciousness.

"Napkins," Sophie announced as she came to the booth and slid in next to Tessa.

"Thank you," Tessa said, immediately grabbing one to wipe her mouth.

"So can I talk to you about New York?"

"Of course," I replied.

For the next half hour, Sophie asked us a million questions about which neighborhoods were the most fun for twenty-some-things, what the dating scene was like, how easy or hard it was to get a job, and whether the subway was safe to use.

I didn't want to discourage her with our unemployment, and Tessa didn't seem inclined to bring that up, either. Instead, we focused on how exciting it was to live in such a vibrant big city.

When Sophie finally ran out of questions, I decided it was our turn to get some information.

Clearing my throat, I said, "Sophie, when we were at the library looking for information on the inn, we couldn't help noticing that there were reports of other women disappearing after staying at the inn. One was only three months ago. Her name was Jessica Trent."

"Yeah. It's best not to talk about that here," she said, tipping her head toward the growing crowd around the bar. "It's a sensitive subject."

"Why?" I asked.

"Because the locals don't like the rumors and the bad press. We have enough trouble drawing tourists, and stories like that don't help."

"It is concerning, though," Tessa said. "Two women in the last year have vanished after staying at the inn. Do the employees talk about that?"

"Oh, no. Ellen wouldn't allow it. When the sheriff came to ask questions, she sat in on every meeting."

"That makes her seem like she's complicit," I said.

"Definitely not," Sophie said. "She's just protecting her business. Mrs. Clarke loves her guests. The only time I ever see her smile is when she's talking to a guest. I think it's just a terrible coincidence. And Jessica hadn't left the inn. She was staying there when she decided to get out on the water on her own. That had nothing to do with the inn."

Sophie spoke with a certainty that was hard to deny. Whether it was born of ignorance or protectiveness, I couldn't say. But she definitely seemed to believe what she was saying.

"I ran into a man on the beach below the inn earlier today," I said. "He said I should be careful, that more women check into the inn than check out. I have to admit he made me wonder if we should stay there."

"Is he a good-looking, brown-haired guy?"

"Yes."

"That's Tyler Pierce. He's an architect. He's looking to develop a piece of property down the road from the inn, but he's been asking questions around town the last week or so, and that's partially why everyone is getting skittish about the subject."

"Asking questions about Natalie?" Tessa asked.

"And the other one. I guess he's concerned about remodeling a house in the area if there's something going on less than a mile away." She let out a sigh. "Does any of this matter for your book? You wouldn't include these rumors, would you? If you did, no one would want to stay there, and the inn drives a lot of our tourism."

"We're not going to put it in the book," Tessa said quickly, reassuring Sophie.

"Oh, good. I was starting to worry. I better get back to work. Thanks for all the recommendations. I still need to save a bit more cash before I can make the move, but I'm hoping by June."

"That's a big move to make by yourself," I commented.

"Cole might come with me."

"Cole?" I echoed. "The sheriff's son, the one who was just here?"

"Yeah. He's dying to get out of this town, too." Sophie got up. "How long are you staying at the inn?"

"Another few days," I said. "We haven't decided yet."

"If you're concerned about the inn not being safe, maybe you should go somewhere else. There's a really nice inn on the beach in Cork Harbor. That's not too far from here."

"We're happy to stay at the inn," Tessa said. "We're not that concerned."

"Good, because there's nothing to be concerned about. Anyway, I'll probably see you tomorrow morning when I'll be trying not to drop any more pitchers of orange juice."

I smiled. "I'm sure that won't happen again."

"I'm not sure at all, but I can only hope."

As Sophie left, I turned to Tessa. "That wasn't particularly helpful."

"She definitely wasn't as open as I thought she'd be."

"She obviously has some loyalty to Ellen and doesn't want to lose her job because she's talking to two troublemakers."

Tessa smiled. "Women who make history are usually troublemakers."

"We're trying to make history now?" I said with a laugh.

"No, just a good podcast, but just saying..." Tessa's gaze moved around the bar. "This town likes to close ranks against outsiders. We need someone who isn't as entrenched in this town as Sophie."

"I can't imagine who that would be."

"Maybe Finn?"

I was surprised by her answer. "Why? He runs this bar, which seems to be the center of town drama. And he grew up here."

"But he was gone for a long time, and he's only been back a short while. Maybe he has a different perspective."

"I doubt it, but even if he was willing to talk, he's not going to do it here."

"Agreed. But I feel like we had a vibe. Maybe I could invite him to get a drink or a meal somewhere else. Maybe somewhere down the road, a little away from Stonecross."

"You want to ask him on a date?" I didn't know why I was surprised, because Tessa was very good at the charm offensive.

"Why not?"

"He could be...dangerous."

"I don't think he had anything to do with the missing women." Tessa gave me a determined smile. "We're going to get more information if we split up."

"Splitting up is not a good idea," I protested.

"It won't be for long. Why don't you go get the car? It's only about four blocks away, and I'll see if I can get a date with Finn for tomorrow night."

I liked her idea even less when I thought about walking to the car alone. But that was ridiculous. I walked all over Manhattan at two o'clock in the morning by myself. I could make it four blocks in a small town at seven o'clock in the evening.

"Okay. I'll get the car, and I'll wait for you in the parking lot. Just don't take forever."

"Getting a date rarely takes me long," she said with a confident smile.

I followed her out of the booth, then made my way to the door as she headed for the bar.

Once outside, I was surprised by the drop in the temperature, and I zipped up my jacket as I started walking down the block. The streets were quieter now, with most shops closed for the evening.

The farther I got from the pub, the more isolated I felt. The streetlights cast long shadows, and I found myself thinking about Natalie Warren walking these same blocks ten months ago, and about Jessica Trent, who'd disappeared three months ago.

Being alone on dark streets in a town where women kept vanishing felt reckless, and I couldn't believe I'd agreed to it. I picked up my pace, my keys already in my hand, when a figure rounded the corner ahead of me, and I gasped, stopping short before we barreled into each other.

I was more surprised when I realized it was the man from the beach, Tyler Pierce.

"Sorry," he said, holding up his hands in apology. "Didn't mean to scare you."

My heart was hammering. "It's fine. You just startled me."

"What are you doing out here by yourself? Where's your friend?"

"I'm just getting the car. She's at the pub."

"You two should stick together."

"How do you know about my friend?" I asked suddenly.

"I saw you two walking around town earlier."

Maybe he was telling the truth, or maybe he wasn't. "I heard you're an architect looking to build on a piece of property near the inn. Is that true?"

"I'm looking to rebuild a house near the inn," he corrected. "So, you've been talking about me?"

"Not exactly," I said quickly, not wanting to mention Sophie. "I'm just curious as to why what might have happened at the inn would be of concern to you."

"Because the value of the property will go down if it turns out something criminally bad is happening down the street."

It felt like he was telling part of the truth, but not all of it. "If you have any concern, why don't you just move on?"

"It's a good piece of property with an excellent price."

I gave him a long look. "I don't think you're telling me the truth, at least not all of it. Why are you really here?"

"Why are you?" he returned, meeting my gaze. "I heard

you've been asking a lot of questions, too, for some book you're writing."

"That's true. It's a book about historic inns. And the Stonecross Inn has a lot of history." I paused. "Who told you we were writing a book?"

"I heard it when I got a coffee this afternoon. The woman who works at the library was telling her friends all about you."

I wasn't surprised. Margaret had been eager to share gossip with us. No doubt, she did that all the time, all over town. I was happy now that we hadn't asked her too many pointed questions. She would have realized we were more interested in what happened to Natalie than the history of the inn.

His phone buzzed, and he pulled it out. "I have to go."

It was the second time in one day that our conversation had been interrupted by the phone.

That was fine. I didn't need to talk to him anymore. I hurried down the block, relieved to get into the car and lock the door. Then I started the engine and drove back to the pub.

As I stopped at a light, I caught sight of two people sitting at a window table in a café, and to my surprise, it was Tyler and a woman—Becca Thorne. She was smiling at him, and he was smiling at her, changing my impression of his dark, cold, dangerous exterior into something else entirely. And now I had more questions...

A car behind me hit the horn when I failed to immediately hit the gas on the green light, and I quickly turned my attention back to the road. A few moments later, I pulled into the parking lot next to the pub and texted Tessa. She came through the door and hopped into the car with a pleased smile.

"Well?" I asked.

"Finn and I have a date for lunch tomorrow. He's going to take me to a café in the next town over. I think getting him out of Stonecross will help me open him up."

"I guess lunch is a better idea than dinner. It will be safer in the daylight."

"I'll be fine with Finn," Tessa said, buckling her seat belt. "You're not that worried, are you?"

"I'm worried about everything. I ran into Tyler Pierce while I was getting the car. He said he'd seen us walking around town, and he heard Margaret tell her friends in the coffee shop that we were writing a book. I don't know if he's been watching us or it's just a small town and we're tripping over each other, but he makes me uncomfortable."

"Why? Did he say something else?"

"Not really. I said I heard he was an architect. He confirmed it was true, and that he was concerned about property values if the inn turned out to be a crime scene. But it just didn't seem like the whole story."

"Maybe he's also here looking for information on Natalie or Jessica and that's his cover story. He could be a private investigator."

"He could be. We should check him out."

"Maybe, but let's not waste time on him now. So far, he's just tried to warn you that the inn could be dangerous. Why would he do that if he was the danger?"

She made a good point. "I don't know. Maybe to make me trust him?"

"Well, don't trust him."

Tessa had a way of getting right to the point. I smiled. "Okay, I won't trust him. One other thing, after we parted ways, and I got the car, I saw him sitting in a café with Becca, the yoga teacher from the inn, and they looked very friendly."

"That's kind of interesting. I wonder if he's trying to get information out of her."

"No idea. It could have just been social, two attractive people. Did you get anything else out of Finn?"

"I got the date. That's all I was looking for. I didn't want to scare him off, so I just smiled and flirted and said you were going to be busy all day typing up our notes, and I would be bored."

I gave her a dry smile. "In other words, you told him the truth."

She grinned. "Sometimes, the truth works."

"And sometimes the truth is just a lie in disguise," I said.

A gleam entered her eyes. "That's good, Cassidy. We should use that on the podcast, a little tease for what's coming—the truth, or a lie in disguise."

"We don't know what's coming," I said darkly.

And I wasn't sure I was ready to find out.

CHAPTER SEVEN

We got back to the inn a little before eight. There were a few people sitting in the living room by the fire, and a young woman behind the reception desk, who greeted us with a smile and said her name was Moira if we needed anything. We made our way quickly up the stairs and headed into our rooms to freshen up before the podcast.

After turning on the light, I dropped my bag on the bed and turned toward the bathroom. But as my gaze swept across the desk, everything felt...wrong. My computer had been moved at least six inches, and my notebook was now on top of my Stonecross file.

Panic tightened my chest as I looked around and noticed other small details. The closet door was slightly open, and the pillows on the bed had been shoved to the side, as if someone had checked under them. Someone had searched my room. *Why? And had they found what they were looking for?*

I ran across the hall and pounded on Tessa's door.

The door flew open almost immediately. Tessa's face shifted from annoyed to alarmed in an instant. "What's wrong?"

"Someone was in my room." I pushed past her, my breath

still coming fast. "While we were at the pub, someone went through my things."

"What?" Tessa closed the door behind me. "Are you sure?"

"Yes, I'm sure."

As my words sank in, Tessa's gaze swept across her own room. She moved quickly to her desk, then her half-open suitcase on a luggage rack, and finally her closet. Tessa was messier than I was, so I had no idea if someone had gone through her things.

"I don't see anything missing," she said. "But it feels like things have been moved around." She met my gaze with a worried frown. "The door was locked. There was no break-in."

"Someone used a key," I agreed. "Which means they probably work here. They saw my Stonecross file, the information on Natalie, my personal notes... If someone wanted to know what we're doing here, then they do now." I sank down on the edge of her bed and Tessa did the same, as we both processed what we'd just learned.

"Was there anything in your room that had your real last name on it, Cassidy?"

"I don't think so. I had my wallet in my bag. Nothing else has my last name on it. You think Ellen suspects I'm her granddaughter?"

"Possibly. She could have recognized you."

"Wouldn't she just say something if she did?"

"You haven't said anything, either."

"So, what do we do now? Do we go downstairs and talk to her?"

Tessa didn't answer right away, her conflicted gaze matching the churning uneasiness inside me. "I'm not sure that would get us anywhere. Let's think about this. Nothing was taken. Your notes were clearly visible and easy to read through, but let's say they believe our cover story that we're writers putting together a book on historic inns. Maybe the papers back that up."

"Except that the focus is on Natalie. If they took time to

read everything, they would have seen that I spoke to Natalie's brother, that I compiled articles on her disappearance."

"Did anything in your notes mention our podcast?"

I stared back at her, then shook my head. "No. But you have the recording equipment in your closet."

"The backpack wasn't opened," Tessa said. "Even if it was, maybe they wouldn't necessarily put a microphone and a light together with a podcast about Natalie."

Tessa was trying to think logically while I was still caught up in emotional panic.

"Maybe we just sit on this and keep moving forward," Tessa suggested. "We need to get as much done as we possibly can before we get kicked out of here, which could happen as early as tomorrow."

"I suppose," I said. "But Ellen warned us about taking pictures inside the inn. Are we really going to break all the rules and film and record a podcast from here?"

"No one will know, and we have to do it. This is why we came here, Cassidy. We wanted to bring our listeners to the scene."

"I know. You're right. I'm just a little shaken."

"So am I. It's disturbing," she agreed. "But I don't think we're in immediate danger. Someone came in when we were out. It could have just been housekeeping. We don't know for sure if the rooms were searched." Pausing, Tessa added, "We were going to call Morgan before we did the podcast. Let's do that now." Tessa pulled out her phone and made the call. She put it on speaker as Morgan picked up.

"Hi, I'm glad you called," Morgan said. "I have some news."

"So do we," Tessa said. "Someone may have searched our rooms while we were out today."

"What?" Morgan asked in surprise. "Was anything taken?"

"No, but it's concerning."

"I'll say. You need to leave," Morgan said immediately. "Pack your bags right now and get out of there. I'm serious. This is getting weird. Just come home. We can investigate from here."

Tessa and I looked at each other. After a moment, I shook my head, then I said, "We're not quite ready to leave yet."

"We're just getting started," Tessa added. "And if we're going to investigate crime, we can't let a simple room search scare us off. Anyway, we can talk more about it when you get here tomorrow. With three of us, we'll have even more strength in numbers."

"I'm not coming," Morgan said.

"Because of this?" I asked in surprise.

"No. That was the news I mentioned earlier. I can't come. I have to take care of Aiden."

My heart sank. "Why?"

"Steven has to work overtime this week, and his ex-wife is out of town. I'm so sorry. I know you need me there, but I couldn't say no."

"It's okay," I said automatically. But it wasn't okay. Without Morgan, everything felt more precarious.

"I can still help," Morgan said. "I can do research, make calls, whatever you need. But I think you should both consider coming home. This feels like it's getting dangerous."

"We'll think about it," Tessa said. "In the meantime, we're going to record a podcast tonight with a recap of what we've learned so far. And we're going to do it from Cassidy's room, because we found out that's the room Natalie stayed in."

"That's creepy."

"It will make a good setting," Tessa said.

"You said record, not live?" Morgan questioned.

"We want to wait to post until tomorrow," Tessa replied. "Then we'll have another day in town before anyone realizes what we're up to. Do you want to be a part of it, Morgan? You can join us remotely."

"I can't. I'm sorry I'm letting you both down."

"You're not," I told her. "We'll talk tomorrow."

After we'd said goodbye, Tessa looked at me and said, "You don't want to leave yet, do you?"

"No."

"Good. Because I think if we're making people nervous, then we're doing something right."

"I hope so," I said as I stood up. "I'm going to get ready."

"I'll be over in a sec."

As I left her room, I realized my door was open. That was probably because I hadn't closed it when I ran out in shock. At least, I hoped that was the reason. I entered with trepidation, but nothing had changed in the past few minutes. I cleared off the desk and got us set up. Tessa came over a moment later with our lights and recording equipment. We put the camera on an easel so we could sit together on the edge of the bed and both be in the frame.

"Ready?" Tessa asked.

I nodded, then hit record.

"Hello everyone!" Tessa said. "Welcome to *Mysteries Uncorked*. As you know, Cassidy and I are in Stonecross, Maine, investigating the disappearance of Natalie Warren. We talked to a lot of people today, and one thing we learned is that Natalie is not the first or only woman to leave the inn and never be seen again."

As Tessa talked about what we'd discovered so far, my stomach tightened. We were crossing a line that we couldn't uncross. People in Stonecross and at this inn would hate what we were saying, but it had to be said, so I pushed my uncertainty aside.

I'd spent most of my life worrying about what someone else would think, whether I was pushing too hard, whether I was doing the right thing, and I had to stop. I couldn't live my life avoiding difficult conversations or confrontations. I'd always wanted to be a journalist, and I had the opportunity to do that now. I needed to push back against whoever was trying to intimidate us, and that started now.

As Tessa paused, I took over. "While we haven't gotten a lot of hard clues, as Tessa mentioned, we're clearly making someone nervous. When we returned to the inn tonight after dinner, we discovered that both of our rooms had been searched." I looked directly into the camera. "But we're not going to be scared away. Natalie Warren was thirty years old. She came to this inn looking for peace, for wellness, for a reset. And then she was gone. Her family deserves to know what happened to her. And if other women have disappeared from this place, their families deserve answers too."

"Before we sign off," Tessa added, "we're going to give you a look at the room where Natalie stayed during what might have been the last days of her life."

I maneuvered the camera to take a panoramic view of the room and then brought it back to us. Then I said, "As you can see, it's a charming room in a beautiful bed and breakfast on the Maine coast... But is it also the last place where Natalie was safe?" I paused, feeling unsettled by my own question. "We're going to try to find out."

"And you're going to come along with us," Tessa added. "Until next time..."

I turned off the camera. Done.

"That was good," Tessa said. "The best one we've done yet." She took the camera off the easel and then focused it on the bed. "I want to post a photo of the bed with a teasing caption: See where Natalie slept before she disappeared. Why don't you set the podcast to release at eight o'clock tomorrow night?"

"What if we find out more before then?"

"We can adjust. But at least we have something locked. I'm tired. And I need a bath. Are you going to be okay here by yourself, Cassidy? Do you want me to stay?"

"No, I'll be fine. Whoever was in here already knows what's here. I don't think they'll come back."

"I'm going to leave everything here, since this is where we'll want to record from," Tessa said, heading to the door with just her phone in hand. Then she stopped abruptly. "What's this?" She leaned down and picked up a piece of paper that looked like it had been slipped under the door. Her face went pale as she read it.

"What is that?" I asked impatiently.

She handed it to me without a word.

The message was written in block capitals, the letters harsh and angular:

LEAVE BEFORE IT'S TOO LATE

I sucked in a quick breath. This wasn't just someone poking through our things anymore. This was a threat.

"It must have been slipped under the door while we were filming," Tessa said. "Does this change your mind, Cassidy?"

"It probably should," I murmured. "But we're not leaving. Not yet anyway."

"I'll keep my phone close. You do the same. Text me if you need me."

"I will. You do the same."

After Tessa left, I stared at the note for another minute and then turned it face down on the desk. I picked up my phone, and before I could second-guess myself, I typed out a message to my father: *I need to know why you left Stonecross, what happened between you and your mother.*

I stared at the words for a long moment. And then I erased them.

My father wasn't going to tell me anything. I needed to find the answers for myself, and that's what I was going to do.

CHAPTER EIGHT

I jerked awake. There was a sound—too sharp to be the wind. Glancing at the clock, I saw it was a little past five a.m. And now I could hear the sound of hushed voices outside my room.

I rolled out of bed and moved quickly to the door, glancing through the peephole. There was movement just off to the side, and then Ellen came down the hallway. She paused outside my door, and I shrank back in alarm.

What was going on? Was she going to knock on my door?

And then I heard another voice. Anna?

I looked through the peephole again and saw Anna crossing in front of my door with a backpack on her shoulders.

What on earth was going on? Why would they be in the hall at this hour?

I turned the knob and cracked my door open, but the dimly lit corridor was empty now. I closed the door and locked it, then got back into bed. I stared up at the ceiling for several minutes, my mind racing with more questions and no answers.

I tossed and turned for the next hour, and then I must have fallen asleep, because sunlight was streaming through the curtains when I woke up again. I grabbed my phone, shocked that it was now half past nine.

My phone showed several missed texts from Tessa, starting about thirty minutes ago.

You up? Going down for breakfast. Want me to bring you something?

Cassidy???

Getting worried. Text me back.

I quickly typed: *Sorry! Didn't fall asleep until late. Just woke up.*

Her response came immediately: *I'm glad you're okay. I grabbed muffins and fruit. Coming up now.*

A minute later, there was a knock on my door. I let Tessa in, still in my pajamas, my hair a mess.

"Hope you're hungry. I grabbed a bunch of stuff." Tessa set a tray on the desk. It was filled with pastries, fruit, and coffee.

"Thanks. I must say you look better than I feel."

"I think it was the bath. The lavender knocked me out." She grabbed one of the coffees and took a sip. "Did you do any more research after I left last night?"

"I looked up Tyler Pierce. All I could find was a short paragraph about him on his company website. He is an architect for an NYC firm and got his degree at Yale. I couldn't find him on social media, but I was too tired to search further. I can do more today."

"Why don't you get Morgan on it? That's something she can do from New York and feel more a part of this. At least, we know Tyler is an architect. That part of his story holds up."

"It does. I'll text Morgan. I also want her to research Ray Connors. We've been focusing on Ellen, but Ray seems to be her right-hand man, and it's difficult to believe Ellen searched our rooms on her own." I paused. "There's something else I need to tell you, Tessa."

"What?" She sat down on the bed and sipped her coffee, giving me an expectant look.

"I woke up around five this morning to hear someone outside the room. It was Ellen and Anna. It looked like Anna was leaving."

"At five in the morning? That's odd. I guess she could have had to make an early flight somewhere."

"Sure. Or maybe..."

"She was checking out early, never to be seen again," Tessa finished.

"No one saw Natalie leave the inn, except for Ellen, who said Natalie checked out at eight. Maybe that was a lie. Perhaps she also left before dawn."

Tessa thought about that. "It's a possibility, but you're jumping to a lot of conclusions, Cassidy."

"You're right. I have no proof of anything, but my gut says I'm on to something."

"Okay. But I'm not sure there's anything we should do about it. I doubt asking Ellen will get us anywhere. We can ask Sophie if she knows whether or not Anna checked out. But I didn't see her at breakfast today, so I'm not sure if she's working."

"I can look for her later. What time are you meeting Finn?"

"He's picking me up at eleven."

"How are you planning to get info out of him?" I asked, turning my attention toward her upcoming lunch.

"I'm going to charm him into thinking he's just telling me about his life, his family, his friends, the quirky characters that make up the town, that kind of thing. I'm hoping that there's a bar where we're going, so I can loosen him up with a few drinks."

"Don't get too loose. You need to keep your wits about you. We don't know anything about Finn. And he was in the military for a long time, which means he knows how to fight, how to—"

"Don't say it," Tessa put up a hand. "Don't let your imagination get carried away."

"I just wish you were meeting him in town. I don't like the idea of him picking you up and taking you somewhere. It seems like a bad idea."

"Well, I can't bring you along on a date, which is how I pitched this thing. It's daytime. It's lunch. Nothing is going to happen. And if he expresses any concern about the missing women or Ellen, I'll confide in him, but I'm going to play that by ear."

"You need to let him do the talking, which is not always easy for you."

Tessa laughed. "You know me too well. But I hope you also know I can handle this."

"I do know that."

"What are you going to do while I'm gone?"

"First, I'm going to shower and get my head together. Then I'll go downstairs and talk to Ellen about the room search and the note."

"Really?" Tessa said. "What if she's the one who had our rooms searched?"

"Then I'll see how she reacts when I confront her." I grabbed the threatening note from my nightstand, where I'd left it. "If she isn't involved, then she needs to know what's going on. And if she is involved, I'm going to make it clear that we don't scare easily."

"That just might encourage her to do something worse."

Tessa had a point, but it was a risk I'd have to take.

———

Two hours later, Tessa was off on her date, and now I was headed downstairs. Moira was at the front desk. She told me that Ellen had gone into town. She offered her help, but I didn't want to talk to anyone but Ellen, so I said I'd catch up with Ellen when she got back.

Disappointed that I couldn't confront her about the note or the room search, I wandered into the living room. Dorothy Winters sat in a chair by the fireplace, her knitting needles clicking rhythmically, the scarf on her lap getting longer and wider.

"Good morning, dear," she said with a warm smile. "How are you today?"

"I'm fine. How about you?"

"Can't complain. Why don't you have a seat? It's nice here by the fire."

I settled into the chair across from her, watching her hands work the yarn. There was something hypnotic and soothing about the movement. But I couldn't sit here and do nothing. "Can I ask you something? About the inn?"

"Of course."

"You said you come here often." I paused, choosing my words carefully. "I've heard that there's been some trouble here in the past year, women who come to the inn but then disappear."

"You're talking about that woman who went missing last year," Dorothy said. "Natalie."

My heart skipped as Dorothy said her name with some familiarity. "You met Natalie Warren?"

"Yes. She was here the same week I was, last June. I actually gave her a knitting lesson. She seemed anxious, and I told her that knitting calms the mind. You seem a bit anxious, too. Would you like to learn a few stitches?"

The offer seemed so incongruous with what we'd been discussing that I almost laughed. But there was something gentle in Dorothy's expression, something that said this was more than just a random suggestion.

"Uh, I guess. But I don't know anything about knitting."

"Then let me teach you." She pulled extra yarn and needles from her large tote bag. "Come, sit next to me."

I moved to the ottoman beside her chair, and she showed me how to hold the needles, how to loop the yarn. Her hands were patient, guiding mine through the basic stitches.

"Natalie sat right where you're sitting," Dorothy said softly. "She was troubled, that one. Looking for a way to change her life."

"She said that?" I asked, trying to keep my voice casual even as my hands fumbled with the yarn. "Did she tell you why she was upset? Was she having trouble with someone, maybe an ex-boyfriend or a family member?"

"She didn't get into specifics. She just told me she needed to fix her life, and she wasn't quite sure how to do that. She didn't have any family support. She mentioned making some mistakes in her past that she wished she could take back. I told her we all have regrets at times in our lives, but the important thing is to look forward and not back. She had time to start over, to be whoever she wanted to be. She seemed to lighten with those words. And the knitting calmed her. She was less stressed after her lesson."

"Did she say anything about an ex-boyfriend or a man who might have been bothering her?"

"No. She said she was all alone."

"Did she say goodbye to you when she checked out?"

"I didn't see her. She left early in the morning, I believe. I didn't think anything of it until a few weeks later when I heard she was missing. I was very sad and shaken by that information. I hate to think anything happened to her. I prefer to believe she just did what she'd wanted to do—started her life over." Dorothy paused. "She had the prettiest locket. It was silver, and her initials were engraved on it. She couldn't stop playing with it. I asked her about it once, and she got a very pensive expression on her face. She said she didn't know why she still wore it, but she couldn't take it off. That maybe she would now."

Natalie's words in retrospect felt like a sign that she had been looking to change her life in a profound way. Had she just run away from her past? Was she completely fine living somewhere far, far away? I wanted to believe that. The alternative was very dark.

But if there was no mystery about Natalie, why had someone searched my room last night? Why had they left a threatening note? Why did they care what Tessa and I were doing here?

Unless the threat hadn't been about Natalie at all? Was it possible my grandmother just wanted to scare me into leaving before I found out something about my family?

"Natalie was a beautiful young woman, with her dark hair and deep-brown eyes," Dorothy continued. "You have similar eyes, Cassidy."

I didn't like that comparison, because there was already too much about Natalie's life I could relate to.

"Did you tell the police about your conversations with Natalie?" I asked.

"I mentioned to Tom that we'd spoken. He didn't think our conversation was important."

"Tom?" I echoed. "You know the sheriff?"

"Oh, sure. I've lived in Stonecross for more than fifty years. Moved here when I married my husband."

"I didn't realize. I thought you were visiting from somewhere."

Dorothy smiled. "No, I live in town. I find my home to be unbearably lonely at times, so I come here for a week every two to three months. I get to be around young people, which I enjoy very much. And I also get to spend time with Ellen, who has been very kind to me."

"Really? I have to say Mrs. Clarke is not the warmest person I've ever met."

"Ellen has a hard shell and high walls around her heart. But once she lets you in, you see a whole new side of her."

I wasn't quite sure I believed that, but Dorothy clearly knew my grandmother better than I did. "I heard Ellen is also a widow."

"Yes, but her husband passed a long time ago. I think she was maybe forty at the time."

"Does she have any kids?"

"She has a son, but I haven't seen him since he was a teenager. There was some sort of falling out."

"About what?"

"I'm not sure. You're very interested in people, aren't you?" Dorothy asked. "Is that because you're a writer?"

"Probably." I realized I'd probably pushed a little too hard for information. "I guess I love a good story."

"So do I. Especially a love story. I was married to the love of my life, and I am so happy when other people find their perfect match. That's why I like to talk to some of the young women who come here. They often seem to be at a crossroads, and I like to encourage them to see that good things are waiting for them. Being positive is the only way to live."

"It's definitely better than being negative," I murmured.

"You seem at a bit of a crossroads yourself, dear."

"I suppose I am. I lost my job a few months ago. And I've been trying to figure out my next path. I always wanted to be a journalist, a writer," I amended, quickly remembering my cover story. "And this feels like the right time to pursue it."

"It sounds perfect to me." She paused. "You slipped a stitch. Let me show you how to fix that."

"Thanks." For the next ten minutes, I concentrated on the knitting, as Dorothy chatted about random things in town or at the inn. I probably should be doing something more proactive, but it did feel good to focus on the needles and the yarn while my mind swirled with unanswered questions. But when I heard Ellen's voice at the desk, it was time to get back to business.

"I need to take care of a few other things," I said to Dorothy. "Thank you for the lesson."

"Anytime. Bring your friend if you want. I love to teach." Dorothy paused. "If you want to keep the needles and yarn to work on while you're here, you can do that. I won't be going home until Thursday."

I hesitated. "Maybe I'll just leave them with you, and if I have time to get back to it, I'll find you."

"I'm here most days."

I got up and moved into the reception area. Ellen was standing at the desk, looking at the computer. She lifted her gaze and gave me an inquiring look that was completely devoid of any emotion. "Cassidy, how can I help you?"

"Someone was in my room yesterday, while I was in town. And not just my room, but also Tessa's room."

"Was something taken?"

"No. But things were moved around."

"Sometimes my housekeepers tidy up when they change the towels. I'm sure that's all it was."

The casual dismissal made my blood boil. I pulled the threatening note from my pocket and placed it on the desk between us. "This was slipped under my door last night. Was that also one of your housekeepers?"

Ellen picked up the note and read it without any change in her expression, but when she set it down on the counter, she seemed to force an empathetic smile. "I'm sorry about this. We had some teenagers staying here last night, and I think they were playing a terrible joke on you. I don't know if you saw them, but they left with their family this morning. I don't think you'll have any more trouble."

It was a neat explanation. Too neat. I didn't believe it for a second.

We stared at each other for a long minute. I wondered if this was the whole point of the room search, the note. Ellen wanted us to leave, but she didn't want it to look like she was kicking us out.

But she wasn't going to get rid of me that easily. I not only wanted to find out what happened to Natalie, but I also wanted more information about my grandfather, my dad, and about why the family fell apart. I couldn't do any of that if I left.

"If you're concerned and would prefer to check out early, that's fine, too," Ellen said. "In fact, I'll be happy to comp you a night."

Ellen wanted us gone, and that made me want to stay. "I guess if you're not worried, then I'm not worried. Tessa and I will stay as we planned."

"Until Thursday, correct?"

That was the date we'd given on our reservation, so I just nodded and said, "Yes."

"Good. Let me know if you have any other...concerns."

I had a feeling I would have a lot of other concerns, but she wouldn't be the one I went to for help, because clearly that would not be forthcoming. "One more thing," I said. "The woman who was staying on our floor—Anna. Did she check out?"

"Why do you ask?"

"I saw her yesterday, and she seemed sad and upset. I just wondered if everything was all right."

"I can't discuss other guests. Is there anything else?"

A dozen questions ran through my mind, but a couple came through the front door with their suitcases, and I knew my questions would have to wait.

I headed back upstairs. My room was just as I'd left it, which was a relief. I sat down at the desk and looked through my notes, adding a new page of facts and theories that had come from yesterday's trip to the library, our talk with Sophie, and my most recent chat with Dorothy. It felt like we were making some progress, but not enough.

My phone buzzed with a text from Morgan: *Info on Ray Connors: Ex-con. Served eighteen months for assault and robbery. Got out three years ago. Working at the inn since his day of release. Previous to his arrest, he had worked at Clarke and Sons Boatworks for a number of years and lived in Stonecross.*

My pulse leapt at the new information: Ray was an ex-con. He had a violent past. And he'd been working at the inn during the time period when Natalie and Jessica had disappeared.

What was the assault charge for? I typed back.

Robbed a convenience store and put the manager in the hospital. Be careful around him. I have to run some errands, but I will dig into Tyler Pierce when I get back. Anything new there?

Nothing significant but still talking to people.

Sorry again for bailing on the trip. Let's talk later tonight.

I gave that message a thumbs-up and then sat back in my chair, processing what Morgan had told me. Ray had seemed intimidating from the start—big, muscular, taciturn. But lots of people looked intimidating without being dangerous. Clearly, Ellen trusted him.

A door suddenly slammed, making me jump to my feet. Tessa was still on her date as far as I knew. And if Anna had checked out...

I walked to the door and looked through the peephole just in time to see Ray carrying a rolled-up rug over his shoulder. He was coming from the direction of Anna's room. Anna, who had broken a window, who'd left before dawn, who'd looked like she was terrified every second of the day...

Without thinking it through, I opened my door and stepped into the hallway. Ray was already on the stairs, heading down, and didn't see me. I followed at a distance, my pulse pounding.

He went down to the main floor and then out a back door I hadn't noticed before. I slipped out that door a few seconds after him, watching as he carried the carpet toward the detached garage.

I should go back to my room, lock the door, and wait for Tessa to return. That would be the smart thing to do, but I really wanted to know what was so wrong with that rug that it had to be taken out of the room next to mine. While I was thinking, I moved into the shadows under a grove of trees next to the inn, not sure what I was waiting for.

A moment later, one of the three garage doors opened, and a truck backed out. There was no sign of the carpet in the bed of the truck, but Ray was definitely behind the wheel. He backed out, lowered the garage door, and then headed out to the road.

I debated what to do next. He was gone, and it appeared that he hadn't taken the rug with him. Maybe I'd just check out the garage. I moved across the property and found the garage door unlocked, so I slipped inside. There was a blue Mini Cooper parked at the far end, with two empty spaces next to it. Along one wall at the back of the garage, I saw a half-open door that invited me to look inside.

I quickly realized it was a storage room, filled with old furniture, filing cabinets, and...a rolled-up rug. I moved into the room and saw dark spots on the edge of the rug. It could be anything. But it looked like blood, and once that thought came into my mind, I couldn't get it out.

Kneeling beside the carpet, I carefully began to unroll it. More dark stains appeared. And my pulse began to race. *What the hell had happened in Anna's room?*

I heard a sound behind me. I dropped the carpet and jumped to my feet, spinning around in alarm. But it wasn't Ray who'd caught me snooping. It was Tyler Pierce.

I didn't know if that was better or worse.

CHAPTER NINE

I cried out in surprise, and Tyler immediately jumped forward, putting a hand over my mouth.

"Quiet," he said urgently. "I'm not here to hurt you. I'm looking for answers." He gave me a pleading look. "Are you going to be quiet?"

I nodded, and he slowly removed his hand from my mouth, his dark eyes searching my face. We stood there in the dim garage, both of us breathing hard, both of us where we shouldn't be.

"What kind of answers?" I asked in a hushed voice. "And don't lie to me that you being here has something to do with the property you want to develop."

Tyler's jaw tightened. He glanced toward the door, then back at me. "It doesn't."

"Did you know Natalie? Are you trying to get information on her?"

"No." He seemed to weigh how much to tell me. "I came here to find out what happened to another woman—Jessica Trent. She disappeared seven months after Natalie."

"I saw the articles about her at the library. I thought she took out a boat and never came back."

"That's the story."

"What does that have to do with the inn?"

"She was staying here at the time, and since another woman disappeared seven months before her, I think there may be a pattern. Your turn. What are you doing in here?"

"Looking for answers," I said, repeating his words.

"About Natalie or Jessica?"

"Actually, someone else. There was a woman staying in the room next to mine. She looked like she was terrified. I heard glass breaking in her room one night, then crying. I also saw bruises on her body. And that's not all. She left the inn this morning with Ellen before dawn. And Ray, the handyman, was cleaning out her room, and I saw him carry this carpet in here a few minutes ago. When he drove away, I felt the need to come in here and check out what was wrong with the rug."

Tyler moved past me, his gaze falling on the rug. He crouched beside it, examining the dark stains. "This looks like blood."

"It could be from when she broke the glass in her room."

"Or something else happened to her." He looked up at me. "This woman—Anna, you said? What's her story?"

"All I know is what I told you."

Before he could say anything, we both heard the sound of the garage door opening.

"Someone's coming," I said in panic.

He grabbed my arm and pulled me toward an old and very large armoire. There was just enough room for us to squeeze behind it. I held my breath as I heard a door open and close. My heart was hammering so hard I thought I might faint, but Tyler was pressed close beside me, his presence keeping me upright, preventing a full-blown anxiety attack.

The footsteps came closer. The door to the storage room opened. I couldn't see who it was, but I heard the sound of something being lifted, something heavy dragging across the floor.

The carpet. Someone was taking the carpet.

More footsteps. The sound of the main garage door opening again. An engine starting. Then the garage door closing.

We stayed frozen in our hiding spot for what felt like an eternity, but was probably only a minute.

"I think they're gone," Tyler whispered. "Let's get out of here."

We emerged from behind the furniture, and I immediately looked for the carpet. It wasn't there anymore. I met Tyler's gaze.

He grabbed my hand and guided me toward the side door, through the garage, and away from the building. I followed without thinking, my mind still reeling from what had just happened.

The bloody carpet—evidence of whatever had happened in Anna's room—was gone.

I was surprised when Tyler took me down a path behind the inn I'd never been on before. It was clearly a different way to get down to the beach and also a little longer, winding through tall trees and thick brush, the ground rocky and uneven beneath my feet.

When we finally emerged onto the beach, we were further down the beach than we'd been the first time we met, and the ocean stretched out before us, gray and restless under the cloudy sky. The wind whipped my hair around my face as he let go of my hand, and I had a chance to catch my breath.

"Why are we here?" I asked. "I could have just gone back into the inn."

"We need to talk. As I mentioned, I'm looking for Jessica Trent. And you seem to be looking for—what was her name?"

"Anna. And it's not just her I'm looking for; it's Natalie Warren. I think there might be something going on at the inn."

"So do I.

"How do you know Jessica?"

He hesitated, then said. "She's a friend. And she doesn't have anyone else to look for her. Her parents are dead, and she went through a bitter, ugly divorce a few months ago, where she lost most of her friends. When she first disappeared, I hired a private investigator, who discovered her last known sighting was at the Stonecross Inn. But when he came asking questions of the sheriff and Mrs. Clarke, he was shut down. He was told that she rented a boat for a morning sail and never returned. The next day, her boat was found crashed on the rocks about an hour north of here. There was no sign of her body. The consensus was that she couldn't handle the strong wind that came up that afternoon. She lost control of the boat and eventually ended up in the water, where she drowned."

"But they never found her body."

"No. Which is why I'm not convinced that's what happened. Since asking outright didn't get my investigator anywhere, I arrived last week with a cover story. Actually, it's not really a story. I am creating an architectural plan for the owner of the house I'm staying in. But that's not the only reason I'm here."

"I get it. This town doesn't like questions."

"They don't. Let's talk about you and your friend. You've been telling everyone you're writing a book about inns, but I looked you up online, and I couldn't find you anywhere. No website, no previous book reviews or listings. And you've been all around town asking questions about Natalie. What are you really doing here, Cassidy?

"We're not writing a book," I admitted. "Tessa and I have a podcast called *Mysteries Uncorked*. We investigate true crime cases. We picked Natalie because she's like us. She's about our age and lived in New York and just disappeared."

"A podcast?" he said, surprise running through his brown eyes. "That is not what I expected you to say. I thought you might have been a friend of Natalie's."

"I never met her, but I know a lot about her, and I've spoken to her brother. He's been devastated by her disappearance. I'd like to help him and her family get closure. And now that I know

Jessica and perhaps others have mysteriously vanished after staying here, I'm more determined to find out what's going on."

"How exactly are you going to do that? Do you have investigative experience?"

"No. But the police and investigators have come up empty, so it's not like we're stopping anyone else from doing the job. I wouldn't think an architect has much investigative experience, either."

"Fair point. But I'm determined to get the truth, and no one else is even looking for Jessica."

"Tessa and I feel the same way. Natalie had a family, but she was estranged from them. They didn't even know she was missing for a couple of weeks. By the time they started looking for her, the trail was cold."

"What if Natalie just walked away, changed her name, started over?" Tyler suggested. "That's the popular story around here."

"What if Jessica did the same? Maybe she used the boat to get somewhere else and disappear."

"I've considered that, but I spoke to her ex-husband before I came here, and he said she always got seasick when he tried to get her to go sailing. That doesn't sound like someone who's going to take a boat out by herself, does it?"

"No."

"I don't think so, either. By the way, where is your friend?" Tyler asked curiously.

"Tessa is having lunch with Finn Kelly."

"Why?"

"She's good at charming information out of men. She's hoping Finn is less committed to the party line since he lived away from Stonecross for many years."

"I don't know about that. Finn Kelly seems very close to the sheriff and his family. And his sister works at the inn."

"That's true, and nothing may come of their lunch, but it was worth a shot." I paused. "Speaking of getting information, I saw you with Becca last night. What was that about?"

He started. "I didn't realize you saw us."

"Well, you were sitting by the window. Did you get any information about Jessica?"

"Unfortunately, not. Like your friend with Finn, I was hoping to charm Becca into talking," he said with a small smile.

"And your charm didn't work? That's hard to believe," I said dryly.

"I was charming. She just didn't have anything to say."

"Or at least none she wanted to share. What about the sheriff? Have you talked to him?"

"Yes, but I didn't tell him why I was asking. He thinks I'm just concerned about buying property near an inn getting bad press. He reassured me there was no evidence of anyone being hurt at the inn. It was all just speculation."

"Maybe that's because they get rid of the evidence, like the bloody carpet that disappeared from the storage room." I paused. "Becca met Anna. She took Becca's yoga class. I wonder if she'd tell you more about Anna."

"I can bring it up next time we meet." He took out his phone and said, "What did Anna look like?"

"She had brown hair and eyes, average height, looked like she hadn't eaten a solid meal in days. Why?"

"I want to show you something." He scrolled through his photos and then held the phone out to me. "This is Natalie Warren."

I looked at the screen. "I've seen this picture." It was Natalie's professional headshot, from a social media site. She had been a pretty woman with dark brown hair, brown eyes, and a smile that didn't quite reach her eyes.

"Okay. What about this one?" Tyler scrolled to another photo, "This is Jessica Trent."

My breath caught. Jessica also had dark-brown hair, slightly different features, but the resemblance between her and Natalie was striking. Same age range, late twenties to early thirties, same coloring, same general build.

"They look alike," I said, surprise in my voice.

"Do they look like Anna?"

"A little."

Tyler's eyes met mine, and there was something intense and almost frightening in his gaze. "They also look a lot like you, Cassidy."

"I don't think so."

"Don't you? Isn't that why the blood just drained from your face? When I saw you on the beach yesterday morning, I thought you were Jessica, but then I realized you just looked like her."

I shivered at his words. I did have dark-brown hair and brown eyes. I was about the same age, the same height. "It's just a coincidence—"

"Or a pattern."

"A lot of women have dark-brown hair, and I'm sure many have stayed at the inn over the years and haven't vanished. I don't think two women, or even three, is that strong of a pattern when you think about how many women have stayed at inn in the last year." I didn't know if I was trying to convince him or myself. "And aside from looks, I'm not like the women who've disappeared. I'm not running away or searching for something more. From what I've read about Natalie, she was at a cross-roads. A long relationship had ended. Her family relationship was strained. She'd moved, changed jobs..." I licked my lips. "And didn't you say Jessica had gotten out of a bitter divorce?"

"She'd had a rough year," he admitted.

"And Anna showed signs of physical abuse. I'm not like them."

Silence followed my words as we stood there on the isolated beach, two people who'd come to Stonecross for different women but had found the same dark mystery at its center.

"You should still leave town, Cassidy."

His words reminded me of the note I'd received. "You didn't write that on a note and slip it under my door, did you?"

"No. Did someone leave you a note?"

"Yes, and it said I should leave. It also appeared that someone had searched my room earlier. Tessa's, too."

"Then why the hell are you still in town?"

"Mrs. Clarke said that there were teenagers pulling pranks last night, and she was sure it was one of them. She said they left this morning. And as for my room being searched, a housekeeper goes in every afternoon to refresh the towels and tidy up. She dismissed my concerns entirely."

"Well, you shouldn't dismiss your own concern. Trust your gut."

"That's what I'm doing. I'm not going to get scared away by a note."

He crossed his arms, giving me a speculative look. "All this for a podcast?" he mused. "Seems like you're not telling me everything."

"I could say the same thing about you. You're spending an awful lot of time looking for someone who is just a friend."

"I'm loyal to my friends. And Jessica doesn't have anyone else to look for her."

"I might not be Natalie's friend, but I'm still committed to finding out what happened to her. I'm not walking away now. I'm just going to be careful." I paused. "It might help if we work together, but not publicly. We don't want to tip anyone off that we're comparing notes."

"I'm willing to work with you, but my priority is finding Jessica, not Natalie."

"That's fine. I think there's a good chance there's a connection between them. Let's meet tomorrow. I can text you in the morning, and we can figure out a time and place."

"Sounds good. What's your number?" he asked as he pulled out his phone.

I rattled off my number, and he sent me a text in reply. Then he said, "I'm going to follow you back to the inn, but I'll stay a good distance behind you."

"Okay. Thanks."

His gaze followed me the entire way up the hill, and it was reassuring to know that he was watching my back.

It was almost four when I got back to my room. I knocked on Tessa's door, but there was no answer. I sent her a text, but she didn't immediately reply. As worry crept up my spine, I went into my room and checked for signs of anyone having been inside, but it looked the same as when I'd left it.

I sat down at the desk and felt immense relief when a text came back from Tessa. "*Sorry, we went out with one of Finn's friends on his boat, and I didn't have reception. Heading back to the harbor now. Should be back around six.*"

I couldn't believe Tessa had gone out on a boat with Finn after knowing that Jessica Trent had disappeared after a sail.

Of course, Tessa probably wouldn't have made that connection or would have decided it was worth the risk because she wasn't in Stonecross alone; I was with her, and Finn would know that I'd be able to tell the sheriff she'd gone out with him. Although maybe the sheriff wouldn't care. He and Finn were friends.

I decided to call Morgan and see if she was free to chat for a minute. Fortunately, she answered on the second ring.

"Hey, Cassidy. I've been thinking about you and Tessa all day. Have you learned anything new?"

I filled her in on the note from the night before, Anna, the bloody carpet, and my chat with Tyler Pierce. With each word, Morgan grew more concerned.

"This is bad, Cassidy."

"It's not all bad. Tyler Pierce seems like a possible ally."

"About Tyler. I did some research on him as you requested and found something interesting. Tyler has a brother named Marcus Pierce, who is currently awaiting trial for corporate fraud, embezzlement, and other criminal charges. He was in jail but is now restricted to his home with an ankle monitor. Did Tyler tell you anything about his brother?"

"No, but we didn't discuss his family or mine. I'm not sure his brother's issues are relevant."

"Maybe not. But isn't it a little odd that Tyler is in Maine looking for a friend when his brother is in a significant amount of trouble?"

"They might not be close."

"True. Frankly, I don't care about him. I'm more worried about you and Tessa. Where is she anyway?"

"Apparently on a boat with Finn Kelly. They were just supposed to go to lunch, so I don't know how that happened."

"A boat?" she shrieked. "After what happened to Jessica Trent?"

"You know Tessa; she's more confident and courageous than we are. If she thought she'd get something out of Finn by going out on a boat, she'd do just that."

"I'm afraid she's rubbing off on you, Cassidy. You're acting recklessly, too." Morgan paused, and I heard a commotion in the background. "I need to go. Aiden is home. We'll talk later."

"Okay. Bye." I set down my phone and thought about the information she'd given me on Tyler's family. I couldn't imagine how his brother figured into Tyler's search for Jessica. It was probably unrelated. We all had family drama. And I certainly couldn't object to Tyler holding back information on his brother when I had an even messier family relationship with Ellen Clarke, a woman who didn't even know I was her granddaughter.

Putting all that aside, I took out my notebook and wrote down my thoughts about Jessica, without mentioning I'd gotten the information from Tyler. If anyone searched my things again, I didn't want them to see the connection between us.

As the shadows lengthened, I turned on the lights and then decided to head downstairs around six. I was hungry, and I might as well go to happy hour. Maybe a glass of wine would settle my nerves.

The dining room had the usual setup—wine, cheese, crackers, and other snacks. Dorothy was chatting with an older couple while the honeymooners were lost in their own world. I smiled at everyone but took my plate and glass of wine to an empty table, not really in the mood to make small talk.

At seven, my phone buzzed. Tessa was finally checking in.

But when I looked at the text, my heart sank. It was barely readable, the letters jumbled, and autocorrect had clearly failed: *I'm back. U didnt answr ur door. Coming downstairs*

My stomach tightened. What the hell was wrong with Tessa? Was she drunk?

I texted back: *I'm in the dining room.*

No response.

I set down my wine glass and got to my feet. Before I could move, I heard a crash and a long, piercing scream that brought the dining room to silence. I ran through the living room and into the reception area.

And there at the bottom of the stairs was Tessa, crumpled in a heap, her leg bent at a horrible angle.

"Tessa!" I dropped to my knees beside her as Ellen came down a back hallway.

Tessa was conscious, but her face was twisted in pain. Blood trickled from a cut on her forehead. And her leg—oh God, her leg. I could see bone through the torn fabric of her jeans.

"Oh, my God," Ellen said, pulling out her phone. "I'm calling 911."

"Don't move," I said to Tessa, putting my hand on her shoulder. "Help will be here soon."

"What happened?" Ray asked as he came into the lobby along with the other guests, who were all now crowding around.

"I don't know," Ellen said, looking at me.

"I wasn't with her," I said. "I was in the dining room. I heard her scream. I guess she fell down the stairs."

Tessa was making agonizing, raw sounds of pain, her eyes squeezed shut, but the smell of alcohol on her breath was very strong.

Ellen crouched down but didn't touch her. "The ambulance will be here soon. Try to stay still, dear."

Tessa moaned in response.

Ellen's gaze turned to me. "Is she drunk?"

"I don't know."

Ellen got up to reassure the guests that the paramedics were on their way, while I tried to comfort Tessa, who seemed completely out of it. I wanted to ask her what had happened, but she was drifting in and out of consciousness.

Thankfully, the paramedics arrived within a few minutes. They stabilized Tessa's leg and carefully moved her onto a stretcher. She was barely coherent, and the words that did come out were slurred and confused.

I grabbed my bag from my room and followed the ambulance to the Seabrook Medical Center, which was about fifteen miles away. The drive felt endless, my mind racing with images of Tessa at the bottom of those stairs, her leg bent wrong, blood on her face.

She had to be all right. She just had to be.

CHAPTER TEN

At the hospital, I filled out forms for Tessa, who was being prepped for surgery. She had a compound fracture in her leg, and it appeared that she also had a concussion. The nurse asked me if she'd taken anything, as she couldn't speak clearly. I said I thought she might have been drinking, but I didn't know what she had consumed.

After being sent to the waiting room, I texted Morgan, who was as shocked and scared as I was, although all we really knew at this point was that Tessa had fallen down the stairs. I had never seen her get wasted to a point where she couldn't walk or talk, but it she'd apparently done a lot of drinking with Finn.

Thinking about Finn made me angry. *Why had he let her get out of his car in the condition she was in? And how had she gotten into that condition?*

After an hour of worrying and being told by the nurse that it would probably be another hour or longer before Tessa was out of surgery, I called the bar and asked for Finn. He came on the line a moment later.

"Finn Kelly."

"This is Cassidy, Tessa's friend."

"Sure. How can I help you?"

There was no trace of concern in his voice, and that annoyed me more. "You can tell me how Tessa got so drunk."

"What?" he asked, surprise and confusion in his voice. "Why don't you ask her?"

"Because she's in surgery. After you dropped her off, she fell down the stairs at the inn, her breath reeking of alcohol. She was completely incoherent. Did she take anything else? Or was she just drinking?"

"She's in surgery?" he echoed.

"Yes. She broke her leg. They said something about a compound fracture."

"Is she going to be all right?"

"I hope so. But I don't know. She hit her head, too. What did you do all day? I know Tessa. She drinks, but she doesn't get that drunk. And you were only supposed to go to lunch."

"We ran into a friend, and he offered to take us out on his boat. Tessa jumped at the invite, and I didn't have anything going on, so we went. It was a fun day. Look, I'm really sorry to hear Tessa is hurt, but I didn't think she was that drunk. She had drinks, but it was over a long period of time."

"You didn't notice she was slurring her words right before you dropped her off?"

"Actually, she slept for most of the ride back. She was a little sleepy when I woke her up, but she seemed okay. She said she'd talk to me soon and waved goodbye."

"She slept in the car? That doesn't sound like her. She's usually wired."

"I'm just telling you what happened. We had a lot of sun and some drinks, and I think she was tired. Where are you?"

"Seabrook Medical Center."

"That's a good facility." He paused. "She just fell down the stairs?"

"As far as I know. She couldn't tell me what happened as she was completely out of it. But I heard her scream, and found her at the bottom of the stairs."

"That's terrible. I'm sorry. I honestly didn't think she was incapable of making it up the stairs. If I had, I would have walked her up. But she said she was fine. She just needed some fresh air to wake up, that it had been a long day."

I didn't know if I believed him or not. He seemed sincere, but everything about their date felt off: the sudden boat trip, the delay in getting back. He could say *honestly* all he wanted, but until I spoke Tessa, I wasn't going to trust a word he was saying.

"Will you text me when she gets out of surgery?" Finn asked. "Let me know if she's okay. I'm about to head home. I'll give you my personal phone number."

"I guess I could do that," I said grudgingly, putting his number into my phone and then saying goodbye.

The next hour and a half seemed to take forever. I made a trip to the cafeteria to get a salad and some coffee. I didn't really feel like eating, but I had to pass the time.

It was almost eleven when the doctor finally made his way into the waiting room. He was an older man with gray hair and wise eyes, and I immediately felt more reassured.

"She's out of surgery," he said. "The fracture was severe, but we cleaned the wound thoroughly and stabilized the bone. Everything went the way we wanted it to."

"Thank God! When can I see her?"

"She's in recovery and will be asleep for several more hours. In addition to the leg, she has a mild concussion, which we are monitoring, but don't expect that to be a long-term problem. You're welcome to stay, but it might be better to come back in the morning, when she'll be awake and able to speak to you."

"I hate to have her wake up alone."

"We have a great care team here. They'll take excellent care of her."

"How long will she need to stay in the hospital?"

"At least two to three days. With this kind of fracture, we need to watch closely for swelling and infection. She'll be on IV antibiotics for the first couple of days, and we need to make sure her pain is controlled. It isn't anything unusual," he assured me, "just the safest way to make sure her leg is healing correctly. She has some rehab ahead of her, but her long-term prognosis is excellent."

I was relieved to hear that. "Thank you."

After he left, I debated whether I wanted to wait or not. But if she was just going to be asleep, it seemed wiser to go to the inn and then come back in the morning with some of her things. I sent Morgan a quick text to reassure her that Tessa would be okay. I sent an even shorter one to Finn, just because I'd promised, and then walked out to my car.

The drive back was dark, lonely, and a little eerie, with the fog and headlights occasionally blinding me. Pulling into the parking lot of the inn didn't feel any more welcoming. I didn't know if someone had pushed Tessa down the stairs, or if she'd simply slipped. I hoped it was the latter, but I couldn't be sure. Maybe someone had seen an opportunity to get rid of at least one of us. I couldn't let myself be the next casualty.

When I entered the inn around midnight, I was surprised to see Ellen sitting on a stool at the desk, looking at her computer. She took off her reading glasses and gave me a look of concern as she said, "How is Tessa?"

"She had surgery on her leg, and she has a mild concussion. The doctor said she'll have to stay at the medical center for a few days. I'm going back in the morning to see her."

"Did you have a chance to ask her what happened?"

Ellen's tone felt deliberately neutral, but I suspected this was why she'd stayed up to see me. "I didn't talk to her. She was in too much pain, and they took her away for tests and surgery."

"I'm so sorry she got hurt. I checked the stairs to see if there was anything there, any wet spot, or something she might have tripped on, but I didn't see anything." Ellen paused. "She did appear to be intoxicated. Was that confirmed at the hospital?"

"I don't know." I felt like Ellen was creating a defense for any potential lawsuit. "I'll talk to her tomorrow."

"Will you be staying here then? Or perhaps you'd prefer to stay closer to the hospital while she's recovering."

As much as I wanted to check out in the morning, I couldn't leave without talking to Tessa first. "I'm not sure of my plans. I'll let you know tomorrow."

"Of course. You must be exhausted. Can I get you anything? Tea or water, a snack?"

I was surprised she was being so nice all of a sudden. Cynically, I wondered if it wasn't because she was worried about getting sued. "I'm fine. I just want to go to bed."

"I'll see you in the morning."

I headed up the stairs, my gaze sweeping the landing where Tessa had started her tumble, but as Ellen had said, there was absolutely nothing there that could have tripped her up. On the third floor, all was quiet. Anna was gone. Tessa was gone. And I had no idea who was in the other room on this floor, but I felt very alone as I entered my room.

Everything was as I'd left it, but there were clean towels on my bed, so clearly someone had come inside while I'd been gone. I had put my notes away when I'd gone downstairs for happy hour, but if someone had gone through the drawers, they could have seen them.

At this point, I wasn't sure that mattered. Our reason for being in Stonecross would come out soon. That thought reminded me of the podcast that Tessa had scheduled to post tonight at eight o'clock. If I'd remembered earlier, I would have rescheduled it, but it was past that time now.

I pulled out my computer and opened the podcast, reading the comments below it. There were so many responses, three times what we'd seen previously. There were a ton of questions, showing that the listeners were really invested in what we were doing.

I didn't have the energy to answer any comments tonight. Checking my email next, I saw two emails from potential sponsors. They were very excited to see where the investigation was going to go.

How could I tell them it was probably going nowhere now that Tessa was incapacitated?

I couldn't. I had to do at least one more show on my own, so I could tell them what happened to Tessa, but that would have to wait until I knew what had happened. There was too much uncertainty to make decisions tonight. Tomorrow, hopefully, things would become clear.

———

I got to the hospital by nine o'clock on Tuesday morning. Tessa was awake with an untouched breakfast tray in front of her. Her face was pale, and there was a small bandage on her forehead. Her leg was propped up on pillows, wrapped from ankle to mid-thigh in thick white bandages. A hard, slightly curved shell hugged the back of her calf, held in place with elastic wraps. Only her toes showed at the end, swollen and a little bruised.

"Hey," I said, moving next to the bed with a smile. "You gave me a scare. How are you feeling?"

"Like I fell down the stairs, broke my leg and hit my head. That's what the nurse said happened."

"You don't remember?"

"It's fuzzy," Tessa admitted, tucking her tangled blonde hair behind her ears as she gave me a sheepish look. "I think I had too much to drink yesterday."

"Your last text to me was practically incoherent. That's not like you, Tessa. What happened on your date? Why did you stay out so long?"

"I'm not completely sure. I'm having trouble remembering. Maybe because of my concussion." She gave me an apologetic smile. "I'm sorry, Cassidy. I messed up." Regret filled her eyes. "I don't know how I'm going to help you now."

"I'm just sorry you got hurt. The most important thing is you're going to be okay. It just might take a while."

"That's what the doctor said. I can't go home for a few days. Something about wanting to make sure I don't get an infection."

"Which is good. And you'll get better pain meds in here."

"That is a positive," she said with a weary, pained smile.

"I don't want you to talk if it hurts. We can debrief later."

"I'm okay. They gave me some medication. It hasn't completely worn off yet."

I didn't want to press her, but I needed more information. "Can you tell me anything about where you went yesterday?"

"Finn took me to lunch at his favorite place in Cork Harbor. It's about forty-five minutes north of Stonecross. I didn't know we were going so far away, but it was a pretty drive, and he was fun to talk to. He told me about his military days, his family, and growing up in Stonecross."

As her voice trailed off, I tried to gently bring her back on track. "Did you ask him about Natalie or Jessica, the women who disappeared after staying at the inn?"

"Yes, I did," she said with a somewhat triumphant gleam in her eyes as she recaptured that fact. "Finn said he was bothered by those events, too. He didn't like the way the sheriff shut down the investigations so quickly. But he also understood why; the bad press could hurt the tourism, and the town needs tourists to survive."

"I get that, but two women have vanished in the past year. Those women had lives, families. Don't they deserve justice?"

"I think I said something like that, too. Finn said he didn't know what he could do about it. The sheriff and Ellen are tight. He doesn't really like Ellen, but she's Sophie's employer, and his sister is determined to work at the inn until she makes enough money to leave Stonecross. He said he even offered to loan her some money so she could leave now, but she wants to pay her own way, and he respects that."

"So, you didn't really get much information."

"I was trying. Oh, wait a second." A light came into her eyes. "That's why I went on the boat. When we were talking about Jessica, we ran into Finn's friend, Nathan, who was the one who found Jessica's abandoned boat. Nathan offered to take us out on the water and show us where he'd found the boat."

I frowned. "Weren't you at all concerned about going out on a boat with two men you didn't know?"

"Finn was nice. I didn't have a bad feeling about him. And Nathan seemed cool, too."

"It was a bad idea. And I don't understand how you got so drunk. What happened on the boat trip?"

"Nothing. It was beautiful out on the water." She paused. "That's where things get fuzzy." She paused, an unhappy expression on her face. "I don't really remember what happened or what we talked about. I guess it's the concussion. I'm sorry, Cassidy."

"It's okay. You'll probably remember more once you're feeling better."

"I hope so. What's going on at the inn?"

"Not much. Ellen smelled the alcohol on your breath last night. I'm sure she's preparing a defense in case you want to sue her for falling down the stairs."

"I don't really remember that, either."

"Maybe that's just as well," I said with a sympathetic smile. "You don't need to stress out about any of this."

"I can't help it. How am I going to help you from this hospital bed?"

"Maybe we just stop."

"We can't do that. Morgan texted me earlier and said last night's podcast quadrupled our audience, and it's still getting listens today."

"I probably should have canceled it, but I rushed down here with you, and I forgot all about it, until it was too late."

"I'm glad it's out. And I know it's a lot to ask, but I think you should keep going—if you're willing, of course."

I didn't know if I was willing or not.

"I think Nathan might have said more about Jessica, but I can't remember. I just feel like there was something he said that I wanted to tell you..." She sighed. "Dammit. I hate this foggy feeling."

"Don't fight it. You've been through a lot."

"You should talk to Finn. He was there. He'd remember what Nathan said."

"I don't know if we can trust Finn."

"Does he know what happened to me?"

"Yes. I contacted him to find out what happened. He said he didn't think you were that drunk, just tired. You apparently slept on the way back from your boat trip. He did express concern, and I texted him last night that you had made it through surgery."

"I think he's a good guy, Cassidy," Tessa said slowly.

"Well, I'm not convinced."

Tessa stared back at me. "You said I fell down the stairs. Do you think...is it possible that I was pushed?"

I sucked in a quick breath of air. "Do you think you were pushed?"

"I don't know. But I was thinking about the note we got. Someone wants us to leave, and now we're gone, or at least I am."

"I wondered about that, too, but it seems extreme, considering how little we actually know. We just have theories."

"Maybe our theories are a threat." Tessa let out a sigh. "Tell me what you did yesterday. Did you learn anything new?"

I told her about Ray, the bloody carpet, and my conversation with Tyler, and Tessa grew more amazed by the minute. "It sounds like Anna might be a victim, too."

"She might be," I said. "But I think I need to keep my focus on Natalie."

"Why? Anna just left. Her trail might be easier to follow."

"That's true. But I don't even know who Anna is. I have no

last name. And it's possible Anna isn't even her first name. Ellen isn't going to tell me anything about her; that's for sure."

"Have you thought more about telling her who you really are? That could open things up."

"I can't tell her until I know she isn't a... God, I don't even want to say the word."

"Killer?" Tessa put in. "It's possible she's something else."

"Like what?"

"A trafficker. Think about it, Cassidy. There are no bodies. Not Natalie, not Jessica, not Anna, and those are just the three women we know about in the past year. Maybe they weren't killed. They could have been trafficked, and your grandmother or Ray is part of the operation, picking women who are alone and vulnerable."

I nodded, just as depressed by that thought as any other. "If that's true, it's also horrible."

"The sheriff could be in on it," Tessa added. "Maybe he and Ellen are keeping each other's secrets."

"Or it's just Ray who's involved," I said, knowing that was a stretch, but I had this deep-rooted, misguided need to defend my grandmother for reasons I couldn't even verbalize.

"Maybe," Tessa said diplomatically, no conviction in her voice. "Either way, I don't think we can end our investigation here."

"No, we can't. We have too many questions. And there are real women's lives who might still be at stake. We have to keep going. *I* have to keep going."

"You're sure?"

"I am. I'm also hoping that your very public fall last night will keep me safe for a few days. If anything happens to me now, especially if it occurred at the inn, it would bring Ellen a ton of scrutiny. The podcast we just released would make her a prime suspect."

"I hope you're right."

"Anyway, there is a chance that Ellen might kick me out

before I decide to leave, but until she does, I'm going to keep digging. And I won't be completely alone in my effort. Tyler seems to be an ally. I'll tell him about Nathan and see if he got the same information you did."

"You should talk to Finn, too."

"I will."

"Do you want me to call Finn from here? He might feel sorry for me and tell me more."

Seeing the strain in her eyes, I shook my head. "You need to rest today, Tessa. Give your brain and your body a chance to heal. If I need you to make calls later, I'll let you know."

Tessa gave me a weak smile. "Okay. I'm proud of you, Cassidy, but I'm also a little scared. I don't want you to feel pressure to stay."

"If I need to bail, I will. I'll see you later. Get some rest."

As I walked out of her room, I felt both determined and terrified. This was on me now. And I couldn't help but wonder if that had been the plan all along.

CHAPTER ELEVEN

I got back to the inn around eleven in the morning and headed upstairs. Tessa had given me her key so that I could pack up her room and bring her some things when I went back in the evening.

As I entered her room, I saw the usual amount of messiness. Tessa had a tendency to try on a few outfits every day before she decided what to wear, and, clearly, she'd made a few changes before she'd gone out with Finn yesterday. I didn't see any clean towels neatly folded on her bed, as there had been on mine the night before, but maybe that was because housekeeping had been told she'd gone to the hospital.

With a sigh, I grabbed her suitcase and started repacking her clothes, then her toiletries, finishing off with her laptop computer and chargers, as well as the podcast equipment. I had just taken the suitcase into the hall when Sophie came down the corridor, pushing a cleaning cart filled with towels and other supplies.

She stopped abruptly. "Cassidy. I just heard about Tessa. How is she?"

"She has a broken leg and a concussion, but she's going to be okay."

"Thank goodness. I couldn't believe she fell down the stairs."

"Neither could I."

"I guess you're moving her things? Ellen sent me up to clean her room."

"I have everything packed up. I just need to move it all across the hall."

"I can help."

"Thanks." I pushed the suitcase into my room and then went back to Tessa's room to grab the case with our recording equipment while Sophie picked up Tessa's tote bag and followed me into my room.

"I'm really sorry for Tessa," Sophie said as she put the bag down on the bed. "Will you be staying here on your own?"

"For a few days. There weren't any hotel rooms near the hospital, so I'll just go back and forth until she's ready to leave."

"Will she come back here, or will you both be going to New York?"

"I don't know the plan yet." As she hesitated, I said, "Is there a reason you're asking?"

"Just wondering if there's something going on here I should know about. Finn has wanted me to quit for a while, but this morning he told me about Tessa, and he said I should quit immediately. But Tessa just had an accidental fall, right?"

"I don't know, Sophie. The other night, a note was slipped under my door telling Tessa and me to leave. And now she's gone."

Her eyebrows shot up at my comment. "Are you serious? Who would do that?"

"Ellen said it was just teenagers pulling a prank. She wasn't concerned at all."

"I suppose that makes sense. There were some teenagers staying here the other day," Sophie said.

Despite her words, there was uncertainty in her eyes. "Does it really make sense?" I challenged. "After two other women have disappeared in the past year, both with connections to this inn."

"I don't know. I want to quit, but I only need two more paychecks to have enough money to get out of here. It seems stupid to leave now." She paused. "And if you're that concerned, why are you staying?"

"It's just easier to stay here for another day," I said, realizing that sounded like a poor excuse after I'd just challenged her.

"It's easier for me to finish out the month than quit now," Sophie said. "Besides, Cole isn't ready to go yet, either, so it makes sense for me to just keep working here."

"Are you and Cole a couple?"

"Sort of. Not exactly." She gave a helpless shrug. "We've known each other since we were babies. We dated in high school, hooked up a few times in the last couple of years, but it's mostly because we're both bored. And we've each had a lot of family shit to deal with. My dad had a stroke two years ago, but he's finally better, and I want to go before something else happens to make me stay."

"I'm sorry about your dad. I'm glad he's doing better now." I paused. "What kind of family shit has Cole had to deal with?"

"His parents separated two years ago. His mom took off, leaving him with his dad, and Sheriff Holloway is not an easy man to deal with even on a good day. He hasn't had many good days since his wife decided she didn't want to be married anymore. I can't say I blame her. The sheriff is a hard person to live with."

"Why didn't Cole leave with his mother?"

"She didn't give him the option to go with her; she just left, and he's pretty bitter about that. He really needs a break. His dad rides him so hard. And he wants him to go into law enforcement, follow in his footsteps, like he did for his dad. There's always been a Sheriff Holloway in Stonecross for like the last hundred years, and he wants the next one to be Cole."

"And Cole isn't interested?"

"God, no. He hates rules, and he doesn't want to be anything like his father. Sometimes, I think he gets into trouble just to make his dad see he is never going to be sheriff material."

I could relate to Cole since my father had always wanted me to go into finance, and my decision not to had widened the gap between us.

"Anyway, Cole has decided he's never going to be able to change his father's mind, so he's going to leave. And it will be easier for both of us to go to New York together."

"That's probably true."

"I should get back to work before Ellen makes good on her never-ending promise to fire me if I don't shape up," she said dryly. "Then it won't be my decision to stay or go."

"Before you leave," I said quickly. "What do you know about Ray?"

"What do I know?" she echoed. "Uh, he's our handyman and also provides bell service and sometimes drives people into town. He does whatever Ellen wants."

"Has he worked here a long time?"

"A couple of years. He used to be at the Boatworks, but he had some trouble and went to jail for a while."

"That didn't bother Ellen when he came asking for a job?"

"I think she's known him a long time. I guess she trusts he's changed his ways. I've never had any problems with him. Why are you asking about him? Do you think he had something to do with the missing women?"

"Just wondered what his story was."

"I don't know much about him. Someone else in town probably knows more. I'll see you later."

As Sophie left, I got a text from Tyler.

Heard about Tessa. Is she all right? Can we meet?

I typed back: *She's going to be okay, but recovery will be long. I can meet you now. Where are you?*

The property I'm looking at developing. Half a mile north of the inn on Coastal Road. I'll send you the address.

A moment later, the address came through. I plugged it into my maps app. It was a ten-minute walk, maybe fifteen. I gave his text a thumbs-up, grabbed my bag and headed out the door.

I didn't see Ellen or Ray on my way out of the inn, which was a bit of relief since I didn't feel like talking to either one of them at the moment. The day was cloudy and cold, with wind coming off the ocean and the promise of rain by midnight.

Despite the blustery weather, it felt good to walk along the coastal road, with the wild and restless ocean on my left, the thick, towering trees on my right. A half mile beyond the inn, I saw a few smaller houses on large lots, and the last one matched the address that Tyler had given me. A gray sedan was parked in the overgrown driveway. I walked up to the front door and knocked.

Tyler opened it immediately, as if he'd been watching for me. He wore dark jeans and a gray sweater, his thick, wavy brown hair windblown. "Come in."

The house was dusty and filled with old furniture covered in sheets. But there was a sleeping bag on the couch, a laptop computer on the coffee table, and blueprints spread across the dining room table. I moved over to check out the building plans. "Are you actually creating plans for this house?" I asked in surprise. "I thought that was just a cover story."

"Since I'm here, I might as well work on the plans as well as the search for Jessica." He moved to stand beside me, pointing at one of the drawings. "If I were to buy this place, I'd leave some of the original structure, but I'd expand the floor plan and build a second story with ocean views."

His drawings were beautiful—detailed and thoughtful, showing a real understanding of how to honor old architecture while making it livable. "You're good at this."

"You sound surprised."

I shrugged. "I guess I am."

"How's Tessa?"

"She's hanging in there, but she won't be walking for weeks."

"What happened?"

"I'm not sure. Tessa had a lot to drink yesterday. She might have slipped or maybe someone pushed her. She doesn't know."

"That's disturbing. Didn't you tell me yesterday that she was out with Finn Kelly?"

"Yes. They went to lunch and then out on a boat owned by Finn's friend, Nathan, who apparently was the one who found Jessica's boat. At least, that's what Tessa remembers, but her memory is very fractured and hazy."

"Nathan Carmichael is the one who discovered Jessica's boat," Tyler confirmed. "He's a fisherman and charter boat operator out of Cork Harbor. That's in the police report. I went there to talk to him a few days ago, but he was on an overnight fishing trip, so I couldn't connect with him."

"Well, apparently, Nathan took Finn and Tessa to the spot where he found her boat."

"And..."

I shrugged. "That's all I know. I think it was by a cove, a small beach. You probably know more."

"That's the way it was described in the report," he confirmed. "Since there was no body found, there's speculation that she either drowned at sea or found her way up to the road from the cove. But if she did that, she would have walked to the closest place and asked for help. That didn't happen."

"Maybe she made it to the road, and someone picked her up."

"But she didn't resurface anywhere. She didn't take out any money from her bank account, didn't use her charge cards, nothing."

His flat voice didn't give me a lot of clues to his emotions. "What do you think happened?"

"I want to think she got off that boat, made it to land, and is safe somewhere."

"That seems overly optimistic based on what you just said."

"I have to hold on to hope as long as I can."

"Does that hope spring from the idea that maybe she wanted to disappear? Because that's what people suggest about Natalie, too, that she wanted to start over in her life. Maybe Jessica wanted to do the same thing. You said she'd had a bad breakup with her husband. Natalie also had an ex in her life."

"But people don't just disappear after bad breakups," he said.

"Only if they're desperate. Do you believe Jessica was desperate?"

"It's a possibility," he conceded.

"How long are you going to pursue this? She's been gone for three months. Don't you eventually have to go back to work?"

"Eventually, but I'm not ready to leave yet. I'm actually more hopeful now that you're here asking questions, shaking things up. Maybe that will get someone to talk who has previously been silent."

His phone buzzed, and he immediately pulled it out.

"Do you have to take that?" I asked.

"No." He put the phone away.

"Really? Every time we're together you get a call and you rush to answer it."

"It's fine. Just work."

"Do you still talk to the investigator you sent down here?"

"Sometimes. That wasn't him. That was...a family thing."

Maybe his brother, I thought.

"I've been thinking," he continued. "About the woman who left yesterday—Anna. Maybe we need to find out more about her. She's a fresh lead, a new angle."

"I thought about that, too, but I don't even know her last name."

"It would probably be on the computer at the inn."

I saw the look in his eyes. "Seriously? You think Ellen is going to let me on her computer?"

"It's not always attended, is it?"

"There are times when no one is at the desk, but Ellen is never far away. It would be risky."

"You're right. I'm going to meet Becca shortly. Maybe she can get me information on Anna."

"If you ask Becca about Anna after talking to her about Jessica, won't she start to think you're not just a nosy architect?"

"She already knows that Jessica was a...friend. She promised she wouldn't say anything. And I'll say my interest in Anna's quick departure is connected to Jessica."

I found it a little odd the way Tyler stumbled over the word *friend*, as if it wasn't the complete truth. *But why would he be looking for Jessica if she wasn't a friend? Why would he care?*

"I should get going," he continued, checking his watch. "Let's touch base later, compare notes."

"Okay." As I left the house, I couldn't help thinking that maybe one of the people I should be investigating further was him.

CHAPTER TWELVE

After leaving Tyler, I picked up my car at the inn and drove into town, arriving at Kelly's Pub around one. When Finn saw me, he said he wanted to talk to me, but he needed a few minutes to finish up the lunch rush. Seeing him moving rapidly between the bar and the kitchen, I grabbed a small table for two by the window and ordered clam chowder in a bread bowl from another server.

The soup came fairly quickly, and while I was eating, I watched everyone and everything going on around me. There was a mix of tourists and locals in the pub. Cole and his uncle, Jeff Holloway, came in and settled in at the bar to order lunch. There was no sign of Sophie, but she was probably still working at the inn.

Cole and Jeff seemed to get along well enough. I couldn't see any tension between them, lots of what looked like joking and laughter as they ate lunch. But their easy mood disappeared when the sheriff entered the pub.

He didn't say anything particularly dramatic that I could tell, but just his arrival changed the mood between the other two men. In fact, Cole got up and left, muttering something about meeting Sophie, despite the fact that there was a half-finished sandwich still on his plate.

Tom Holloway slid into Cole's empty chair. "What are you two doing here? I thought you had an all-day charter."

Jeff shrugged and said, "It got shortened. What do you want from me? I gave your kid a job. Sometimes, charters fall through. You need to loosen up, Tom, or you're going to lose Cole."

"What are you talking about?"

I couldn't help but eavesdrop as their voices rose high enough for me to hear them.

"Cole wants to leave with Sophie," Jeff replied. "He wants to go to New York."

"That's ridiculous. What's he going to do there?"

"I assume he'll figure it out."

"No, he won't. You need to talk him out of it."

"If you don't want him to go, you talk to him."

"He doesn't listen to me."

"Because all you do is order him around. And that's not fun. Trust me, I know," Jeff added dryly. "Cole wants to have a life, a bigger life than he can have here. Frankly, I think he's on the right track. I should have left a long time ago. But it's too late for me. Not for him. And he should go before he gets himself into more trouble than he can get out of."

"What does that mean?"

"It means he figured out the best way to get your attention, and I'm worried about how far he'll go to get it. Why don't you go see if you can find him now? He probably just went home because he told me he wasn't seeing Sophie until tonight."

"I can't chase him down now. I need to go to the inn. I have to speak to Ellen."

"About what?" Jeff asked.

"It doesn't concern you. Talk Cole out of New York. It's the least you can do for me after everything I've done for you."

As Tom got up, I looked down at my soup, not wanting to

call attention to myself, but I needn't have bothered; he was already out the door.

My phone vibrated on the table, and I saw an incoming text from Morgan, who wanted an update. I texted back that I was working on a few things, but nothing to report yet. We texted back and forth for a few more minutes, mostly chatting about Tessa's condition and Morgan's guilt about not being in Stonecross with me. When Finn slid into the chair across from me, I put down the phone.

"Thanks for waiting," he said. "How was your soup?"

"Excellent."

"Good. How's Tessa?"

"She's in pain. Her leg was badly broken. She'll be in the hospital for a few more days, and she won't be walking for a long while."

"Is she up for a visitor?"

"You want to visit her? Why?"

"Because I'm concerned about her. And I'm sorry she got hurt."

I used to think I was good at reading people, but since I'd gotten to Stonecross, that belief had definitely been tested. I didn't know what to make of Finn or of Tyler, or of anyone, really. They all seemed suspicious.

"Tell me what happened yesterday, Finn. Tessa said you went to lunch and then you ran into a friend, a guy named Nathan. He offered to take you both out on his boat, and you encouraged her to say yes."

"I didn't push it. She jumped at the idea after Nathan told her he was the one who'd found Jessica Trent's boat. I didn't realize you and Tessa were also interested in her disappearance."

"Both women stayed at the inn and disappeared within several months of each other."

"Under completely different circumstances."

"Maybe not so different, considering their last known days

were at the inn. But I want to know what happened when you were on the boat."

"Tessa started asking Nathan questions, and Nathan enjoyed her attention. He likes to boast about how he was the one who found the boat of the missing woman, as if that made him some kind of hero. And he took us out to the spot where he'd found the boat."

"I understand it was in a cove, with a beach nearby, that one theory is that Jessica got off the boat, climbed up the rocks, and disappeared from there."

Finn nodded. "Nathan mentioned that." He hesitated. "Look, Nathan talks a lot of shit. I'm not always sure how much of it is true."

"You don't think he found the boat?"

"No, I believe he found the boat, but I'm not as certain about what else he told Tessa."

"Which was what?"

After a momentary hesitation, Finn said, "Nathan told us that he found Jessica's diamond ring on the boat, but he didn't tell the police about it, because he wanted to sell it."

I looked at him in surprise. "I can't believe he would keep evidence like that. Did you see the ring?"

"He said he didn't have it on the boat. I'm also not sure he didn't make up the drama to add to his story." He paused. "But then he had second thoughts about what he'd said when Tessa mentioned the real reason you two were in town."

My stomach tightened. "What did she say?"

"That you have a podcast. That you're investigating Natalie Warren's disappearance, while pretending to be writing a book about inns."

His tone was flat, and I couldn't tell what he thought about our lie. So, I turned the focus back to Nathan. "You said Nathan regretted talking about the ring?"

"He was worried she'd talk about it on the podcast."

"So, what did he do?"

"He started backtracking, saying it wasn't really that expensive of a ring; he didn't even think it was a real diamond."

"Was he nervous because he'd stolen the ring, or because the fact that he had it might make him look like someone who might have had a hand in her disappearance? Maybe he didn't find the boat by accident. Maybe he knew exactly where it was. Or maybe he was responsible for Jessica's disappearance."

"That's a lot of maybes," Finn muttered. "I don't believe Nathan hurt Jessica. I think it's more likely he found a ring and kept it for himself."

"You should tell Sheriff Holloway about the ring. It could be an important clue to a woman's disappearance. I'm surprised you haven't done that already. Unless you're protecting your friend. Or maybe you're a part of it?"

"I'm not a part of anything. And I called Tom this morning."

His words took me by surprise. "What did he say?"

"That Nathan is a big talker, and he didn't believe a word of it."

"Because he doesn't want to believe anything that would make people look for Jessica."

"The sheriff does seem determined to downplay the circumstances surrounding both women," he admitted. "I told him to talk to Nathan, but I don't know if that will happen."

I leaned forward, fixing him with my most determined look. "What happened to Tessa on that boat, Finn? Why can't she remember the day?"

His lips tightened. "I've been wondering about that, too. I went downstairs for a few minutes. I had to make a call, but I didn't have reception on my cell, so I used the satellite phone. I was only gone about ten minutes, but when I got back it felt like Tessa was starting to slur her words. She laughed about it and said she must have had too much to drink. And then she curled up on a bench and napped as we sailed back to the harbor."

"She was dozing on the boat and then in your car, and you didn't think that was strange?"

"I did think it was off, but she woke up and we walked to my car, and she just seemed really relaxed."

"Do you think Nathan drugged her?"

"I really don't want to think that."

"Well, we're going to find out, because they took a toxicology screen at the hospital, and the results will probably be back later today. If you're trying to protect Nathan or yourself—"

"I already told you I spoke to Tom. Does that sound like I'm protecting myself?"

"I have no idea which side Tom is on. It certainly doesn't seem like he's trying to find anyone. And no one in this town wants to challenge him."

"It's complicated."

"Is it complicated?" I challenged. "I understand that tourism drives the local economy, but we're talking about the lives of several women."

He gave me a long look, then got to his feet. "I can't say you're wrong about the lack of investigation, Cassidy, but your podcast won't change that."

"Maybe it will. With enough public pressure, the sheriff will be forced to reopen these cases, and you should be part of that pressure. If Natalie and Jessica are safe, great. If they're not, then whoever hurt them needs to be brought to justice. The truth is not the enemy."

"Sometimes it is," he said heavily. "Sometimes it comes with a double-edged sword. The truth is never as simple as you want it to be."

CHAPTER THIRTEEN

The truth was never simple...

Finn's words rang through my head as I walked out of the pub and got in my car.

Maybe he was right about that. I had a personal truth that was very complicated and one I still didn't know what to do about. But that wasn't a problem I was going to solve today.

If Finn and the sheriff weren't going to follow up on the ring, I needed to do that. I picked up my phone and called Tyler. "I need to talk to you. Are you still with Becca?"

"No. I'm in line to get a coffee at the Daily Drip in Hanover."

"Hanover?"

"It's the town next to Stonecross, five miles south. Becca was teaching a class at the community center here. Want to come and meet me? Or I'll be back in about a half hour."

"I'll meet you. It's on the way to Seabrook, and I can visit Tessa after we talk. I'll see you soon."

Fifteen minutes later, I walked into *The Daily Drip*, a no-frills coffee house with a half- dozen tables, most of which were occupied by people sitting at computers. Tyler was at a table by the window, and I joined him with a smile.

He pushed one of two coffee cups in my direction. "It's Italian roast, with space for cream if you want it."

"Thanks. I'm good with this. How was your conversation with Becca?" I took a sip of the coffee, feeling immediately warmed and energized. "This is good."

"Better than anything I've had in Stonecross," he agreed. "Becca told me that Anna's last name is Franklin. She spent four days at the inn before she left. Two of those days, she took Becca's yoga class. I guess you were at one of those classes."

I nodded. "I was. Anna Franklin isn't an uncommon name. It might take some work to find her."

"I did a cursory search on my phone and found at least fifty," he said. "Becca also said that Anna mentioned she was from Chicago, that she'd heard about the inn from a friend. And that she'd really needed to get away from her life."

"Another woman who wanted to get away from her life," I murmured. "Seems to be a common theme."

"According to Becca, Anna arrived with bruises. Someone hurt her before she got to the inn. She said she felt like Anna was constantly looking over her shoulder."

"That's what I thought, too. Maybe she was hiding out at the inn until she felt safe to go somewhere else."

"I'm sure that's what Ellen and Ray would say."

I studied his face, his rather handsome face, I thought idly, shaking that out of my head as soon as I could. "Exactly what they would say," I agreed. "I should have knocked on Anna's door that first night when I heard her crying. I was just so rattled that first night. I was spooking myself out."

"Why were you rattled?"

"It was a long day of driving," I said vaguely.

"Or was it because you were going to the inn where a woman your age had stayed before never being seen again?"

I was grateful for the out he'd just given me, because I didn't need to tell him it had also felt strange to be in my grandmother's house, a woman I had never known and still didn't really know. "That's true," I said belatedly. "This is the first time I've ever tried to walk in the footsteps of a victim."

"It should probably be the last time. You're not an investigator, Cassidy. You don't have a personal stake in the victim. Why make yourself a target to increase your podcast ratings?"

"It's about finding answers for Natalie's family and for Jessica's, too."

"She doesn't have any family that I know of."

"But she has you, her friend."

He stared back at me."Right."

"Which is why I need to ask you something. You told me Jessica was divorced, that she had gotten out of an abusive relationship."

"That's correct."

"Would she have still been wearing her wedding ring?"

His gaze flickered. "What are you talking about?"

"According to the man who found Jessica's boat, he also found a diamond ring; that sounds like a wedding ring."

"That wasn't in the police report."

"Finn said his friend Nathan kept the ring to sell. He didn't tell anyone he'd found it."

"Except Finn."

"And Tessa, too. I guess Nathan likes to boast, especially to pretty girls, and it came out when he took Finn and Tessa to see where he'd found Jessica's boat. I wondered why she'd have her ring if she was divorced."

"I don't know," he muttered, a frown creasing his lips. "Did Nathan sell the ring?"

"I don't think so. Finn said he told the sheriff about it this morning, but he wasn't interested in pursuing it. He also thought Nathan was a liar."

"I need to talk to Nathan. If he lied about the ring, what else did he lie about?"

"I don't know. I'm hoping Tessa will be able to tell me more when her head is a little clearer. I think there's a chance Nathan drugged her."

"Why would you say that?"

"Because of the condition she was in. Finn told me Nathan started to panic when he realized how much he'd told Tessa, especially after Tessa told him about our podcast. Finn said he left them alone on deck when he went to make a call, and that Tessa was unusually sleepy when he got back. He thought it was just the sun and the alcohol."

"Do you think Nathan put something in her drink?"

"Yes, so she wouldn't remember their conversation. And it worked. She said the day is hazy."

"I'm going to drive to Cork Harbor and talk to Nathan," Tyler said decisively as he got to his feet.

"Wait. Let me see if Tessa is awake. If she's not, I'll come with you. I want to talk to Nathan, too."

"Okay."

He waited as I called Tessa. Her phone went to voicemail, so she must have turned it off while she slept. I left her a quick message and then followed Tyler out the door. "Should we take two cars?"

"Let's take one. I'll bring you back when we're done, since it will be on your way to see Tessa later."

"Okay." As I got into Tyler's car, I felt good about taking a proactive step forward. I wanted to hear from Nathan exactly what had happened yesterday, because I wasn't sure I trusted Finn's version. Not that I could necessarily count on Nathan to tell me the truth, but at least I could hear what he had to say and decide for myself.

———

Cork Harbor was about forty-five minutes north of Stonecross, and as Tyler merged onto the coastal highway, I settled back into my seat, watching the ocean appear and disappear through breaks in the trees. The silence between us felt comfortable, which surprised me. I barely knew this man, yet here I was, on my way to confront someone who might have drugged my best friend.

"How did you get into architecture?" I asked, partly because I was curious and partly because the quiet was making me tense.

"I always loved houses. Even as a kid, I'd draw floor plans, imagine what it would be like to design a home."

"That's sweet. Did your parents encourage your dreams?"

His jaw tightened slightly. "My parents died when I was twelve."

"I'm sorry. How did that happen?"

"House fire. My brother and I were at summer camp."

"Oh my God. I'm so sorry." The words felt inadequate, but what else could I say?

"Marcus was only eight when it happened. We went into foster care after that." He changed lanes to pass a slow-moving truck. "We managed to stay together most of the time, but there were a few years when we got separated. Those were the worst."

I thought about what that must have been like—losing your parents, losing the only family you had left, being completely alone. "When did you get back together?"

"When I turned eighteen, I became his legal guardian. We were on our own after that. I worked construction during the day, went to community college at night. Got a scholarship to Yale eventually. Marcus lived with me the whole time."

"That must have been hard on you."

"He's my brother. I couldn't let him live with anyone else."

"Do you see a lot of him now?"

He hesitated, then said, "Not that much."

"Tyler..."

"What?"

"I looked you up. I know your brother is awaiting trial for fraud and some other charges."

He shrugged. "I should have figured you'd do that."

"You could have told me."

"It's a difficult situation. Marcus is completely innocent. He was set up."

His words puzzled me. "If that's true, then why aren't you trying to help him? Why are you looking for Jessica?" I'd no sooner asked the question when I realized I already knew the answer. I knew why Tyler had stumbled over calling Jessica his friend. "Jessica is part of your brother's problem, isn't she?"

He didn't answer right away, then said, "Yes. She is. She ran away because she was scared. She knew Marcus was innocent, and she was afraid she'd get set up along with him. I need to find her because she's the only one who can prove my brother didn't do what they said he did."

It all made so much more sense now. As I processed what he'd told me, another idea occurred to me. "If she ran away from that situation, is it possible she's still running? Maybe she did get off that boat and disappear by choice."

"It's possible," he admitted. "Or someone else found her and made sure she couldn't come back and tell the truth. I have to know, either way, so I can help my brother. He's my only family, Cassidy. I have to save him. He would do the same thing for me."

"I understand. I wish you'd told me sooner."

"It doesn't change anything. I still need to find her and make sure she's safe. Then I'll have a chance to convince her that telling the truth will protect both her and my brother."

I was impressed with his loyalty to his brother. He'd put his whole life on hold to save him and also Jessica. "Then we better find her."

He gave me a smile. "It does feel good not to be doing this completely on my own."

"I feel the same way. I have to admit I'm a little jealous of your relationship with your brother. I always wished I had a sibling, especially after my mother died."

"How old were you?"

"Fourteen. She died of cancer. And then it was just me and my dad. But we had never been close, and without her loving presence, our house felt incredibly cold. My father had also been focused on work, but without her to come home to, he would stay later and later at the office. I don't think he wanted to be in that house any more than I did."

"Who took care of you?"

"I took care of myself. We had a housekeeper who would clean and cook meals we could heat up later, but that was it."

"That sounds lonely."

"It was. I tried everything to get his attention. Good grades, following his rules, going to the college he wanted, studying accounting and economics, even though I hated those subjects, but nothing really mattered. I finally decided to stop trying to be who he wanted me to be. I moved to New York and got into media, although my fact-checking job wasn't all that exciting, but it felt like the first step toward becoming a journalist, which is what I really want to do."

"And the podcast? How did that start?"

"The three of us got laid off from the same company a few months ago, and the podcast was just something fun to do while we looked for other jobs. Tessa, Morgan, and I are true crime fans. We'd drink wine and talk about crime, hence the name *Mysteries Uncorked*. To our surprise, we started to garner a following, and that's when we decided to dive deeper into Natalie's disappearance. You know the rest."

He didn't actually know all the rest, but he knew what mattered, and that was enough for now.

"I hope you won't regret the decision to dig deeper," he said.

"I hope not, too. But this is the first time in my life I feel like I'm actually doing something that might matter, might make a difference in someone's life. I have to keep going."

"So do I." He glanced at me and smiled as we shared a moment of truly being on the same page.

Then the GPS announced we were approaching Cork Harbor, breaking the moment.

I sat up straighter, looking out at the larger town emerging ahead of us. Cork Harbor was definitely bigger than Stonecross—more boats in the harbor, more restaurants lining the waterfront, more tourists walking the docks. The late afternoon sun glinted off the water, and I could see why people came here. It had that picture-perfect coastal town charm.

Tyler pulled into a parking lot near the marina. As we slowed, I caught sight of two men standing near a white pickup truck at the far end of the lot. One of them looked familiar—tall, lean build, dark hair.

"Is that Cole Holloway?" I asked, peering through the windshield.

Tyler followed my gaze. "Could be. Hard to tell from here."

The two men separated, the one who might have been Cole getting into the truck and driving off before I could get a better look.

"Why would he be here?" I wondered aloud.

"He works with his uncle, Jeff Holloway. Maybe they had a charter up here."

"That makes sense," I said. But something about seeing Cole here felt wrong. Or maybe I was just suspicious of everyone now.

We parked and got out of the car, walking through the marina that was busy with late afternoon activity—boats coming in from day trips and tourists browsing the waterfront shops. The smell of fried seafood permeated the air. It would have been more pleasant under different circumstances.

"There, Carmichael Charters," Tyler said, pointing to a small office on the dock.

We walked over, but the office was closed, a *Be Back Soon* sign hanging in the window.

"Damn it," Tyler muttered. "This happened to me the last time I came here."

"Excuse me," I said to an older man coiling rope on a nearby boat. "Do you know where we can find Nathan Carmichael?"

The man straightened, squinting at us. "Nathan? His boat's over there." He pointed down the dock. "*The Wanderer*. Third one on the left."

"Thank you."

We made our way down the dock, our footsteps echoing on the weathered wood. *The Wanderer* was a thirty-foot boat, white with blue trim, showing signs of wear but well maintained.

"Nathan?" Tyler called out as we boarded the boat. "Hello?"

A man in his late thirties came up the stairs, his long dark hair pulled back in a small ponytail. He wore jeans and a Red Sox T-shirt. "Can I help you?"

"Nathan Carmichael?" Tyler asked.

"That's me." His eyes were wary. "Do I know you?"

"I'm Tyler. This is Cassidy. We need to talk to you about Jessica Trent."

Nathan's expression immediately closed off. "I already talked to the police about that. Months ago. There's nothing more to say."

"Actually, there is," I said, stepping forward. "You took my friend Tessa out on your boat yesterday. Along with Finn Kelly. You showed her where you found Jessica's boat."

"So?" Nathan crossed his arms, giving me a challenging look. "Is there a law against that?"

"No," I said. "But there might be a law against withholding evidence. Like a diamond ring you found on that boat and never turned over to the police."

Nathan's face went pale, then flushed red. "I don't know what you're talking about."

"Tessa remembers," I said, which wasn't entirely true, but Nathan didn't need to know that. "She told us all about it. And she's at the hospital right now, being treated for injuries she sustained after spending the day with you. The hospital ran a tox screen. If you put something in her drink to make her forget what you told her, that's going to come out."

Nathan's face paled. "Finn told me she was in the hospital, but I didn't have anything to do with that. She fell down some stairs, right?"

"Because she was out of it," I said. "The doctor believes she had drugs in her system."

"Then she must have taken something after she got off the boat."

"The doctor will figure it out," Tyler interrupted. "They'll know exactly what time she ingested the drug."

I wasn't sure that was true, but Nathan looked trapped, and, finally, his shoulders sagged. "Look, I just gave her a little something to help her relax. She was getting all worked up, asking too many questions, saying she was going to put me on her podcast. I slipped a little something into her drink just to mellow her out."

"You drugged her?" I felt sick at the thought.

"It was just a sleeping pill. I didn't mean for her to get hurt!" Nathan insisted. "I just needed her to forget about the ring. If the police find out I kept it, I could go to jail. And it's not like anyone needs it—Jessica's gone, presumed dead."

"Is she?" Tyler asked. "Is she really dead, Nathan? Or is there something else the police don't know?"

Nathan looked at him, something shifting in his expression. "I told them everything that mattered."

"Everything that mattered to the police. What about Jessica's family? Her friends? She had a life. People who cared about her. Don't you think they deserve to know the truth?"

"We don't care about the ring," Tyler added. "We just want to find Jessica."

Nathan was quiet for a long moment, clearly wrestling with what I hoped was his conscience. "If I tell you what I know, you keep quiet about the ring. Deal?"

Tyler and I exchanged glances. "Deal," Tyler said.

I simply nodded, not wanting to mention that Finn had already talked to Sheriff Holloway about the ring. Nathan could find that out later.

"The day I found Jessica's boat, it was drifting near that cove, just like I told your friend," Nathan said. "But before I called it in, I went ashore. I wanted to see if maybe she'd made it to land, you know? And that's when I saw the ring in the sand. It was at least ten feet from the water's edge."

My pulse quickened. "You're saying that Jessica made it from the boat to the shore?"

"Could have happened that way. Or the ring just washed ashore when she drowned."

"You should have told the police this," Tyler put in, anger in his voice. "What the hell were you thinking?"

"I was thinking that selling that ring would keep me and my business going for another year," Nathan said, no remorse in his voice. "Plus, I still didn't know what happened to her, and that ring wasn't going to tell the story. Like I said, it could have been washed ashore."

"It's kind of amazing you could find a ring in the sand of a deserted beach," Tyler said, his voice harsh, his gaze pointed.

"I guess I got lucky," Nathan returned.

I could see that Tyler wasn't completely convinced that anything Nathan had told us was true, but I wondered if it was, and if Jessica had gotten off that boat. If she had, where had she gone, and why had she wanted everyone to think she was dead?

"That's all I have to say," Nathan continued. "Personally, I think Jessica got off that boat and had someone pick her up on the road above that beach. She's out there somewhere, living a new life. Maybe it's time to stop looking for her. It doesn't seem like she wants to be found." Nathan looked at Tyler, then me. "We have a deal, right? You don't say anything about the ring or the drugs?"

"For now," Tyler said. "But if we find out you're lying to us, all bets are off."

"I'm not lying." Nathan's voice was firm. "But even if I was, you can't prove anything. You haven't seen the ring. You can't prove I drugged Tessa. Finn was on the boat, too. He could have done it. You have nothing. Now, get off my boat."

Tyler hesitated and then turned. I followed him off the boat, and we didn't speak until we were back in the car.

"Should we go to the police?" I asked, breaking the silence between us as we fastened our seat belts. "Finn already talked to Sheriff Holloway, but maybe we could talk to someone in this town."

"And tell them what?" Tyler asked. "Nathan is right. We have no proof of anything. And whatever we say, he'll deny."

"I don't care about the ring, but how can I let him get away with drugging Tessa? He's the reason she's in the hospital."

"I understand how you feel. You can go to the police, but I don't think it will get you the result you want."

"I have to try. I can't let Nathan get away with this. He could be drugging other women, for all we know."

"Maybe you should talk to Tessa about it first, see if she has regained any of her memory, because I think there's a good chance Finn will renege on anything he told you to protect his friend. And then it will just be me and you, the outsiders, against Finn and Nathan, who are definitely on the inside. How do you think that will go?"

"I think it will get shut down like everything else," I admitted. "I'll talk to Tessa, and maybe I'll have more proof when the toxicology report comes back."

"I hope there is evidence because without it..."

"It's just our word against his."

"Exactly."

"What do you think of Nathan's suggestion that Jessica faked her death? It makes sense. You said she was on the run, scared that she was going to be set up, just like your brother. Maybe that's exactly what she did."

His lips tightened. "It's a possibility."

It suddenly occurred to me that Tyler could actually be the person Jessica was running from. Maybe she thought he would throw her to the wolves to protect his brother.

Which raised the question—should I be trying to help him find her?

CHAPTER FOURTEEN

Tyler was quiet as he drove away from the marina, and so was I. While I understood Tyler's motivation to find the person who could prove his brother's innocence and save him from jail, I wasn't sure whether we were both buying into the idea that Jessica had faked her death because it made sense—or because we needed her to be alive.

"Nathan's story about finding the ring on the beach is pushing us to believe that Jessica got off the boat and disappeared on her own," I said, breaking the silence between us. "But if Nathan was lying, and he didn't find the ring on the beach, then we really have nothing to prove Jessica got off that boat alive."

"Why would he lie about finding a diamond ring when the lie could get him into trouble?"

"Because he made it up to impress Tessa, and now he's caught up in it," I suggested. "Maybe it is true, but I don't want us to go down the wrong path because it's the path we desperately want to be on."

"I hear what you're saying, Cassidy, and you're right. Aside from Nathan's story, there is no evidence to suggest she survived the trip, but my gut says she did. That might be misguided, but that's how I feel. Maybe that's because I need to feel hopeful. My brother's life is on the line, too."

"I understand. And I want Jessica to be alive. I want the same thing for Natalie and also for Anna. But maybe Jessica's story is different from theirs. Did she register at the inn under her own name?" I asked.

"She registered under her maiden name, which is Trent. Her married name is Reese."

"Okay, but it seems like she would have used a completely different name if she were truly on the run."

"I'm not sure she was thinking that clearly. There was a lot going on. At any rate, I'm going to keep looking for Jessica. But you can go back to focusing on Natalie and Anna."

"We can focus on all three of them," I said. "I like working together. Two heads are better than one. We can challenge each other. Make sure we're not jumping to conclusions or falling for stories that are meant to take us in a different direction."

"It is nice to have someone to bounce ideas off of instead of going around in circles in my head."

"So, we keep working together."

"Yes. On that note, I did actually have an idea about Natalie," Tyler said.

"What's that?"

"I was thinking about how no one saw her leave the inn. There was no record of a cab picking her up. The inn is too far for her to have walked into town, especially with a suitcase. So, either a friend picked her up, as has been suggested in the police report—"

"A friend that has never been found," I interrupted.

"Or," he continued. "She left the inn another way. She didn't walk out the front door."

"What's the other way?" I asked with interest.

"Older houses built during prohibition sometimes had underground tunnels running to the beach for the purpose of smuggling."

"That's interesting. You think there's a tunnel under the inn?"

"I think we should find out. It probably wouldn't be on an official blueprint, but if I can get any of the plans from the city on the inn, I might be able to tell if there's a discrepancy of some sort, some indication that the cellar or basement has extra space, or what not... I'm definitely speculating here, but it's something I could check out for you."

"That would be great."

"You could also look around the inn, see if you can access the basement."

"That wouldn't be easy. Ellen is always roaming around, and she's already suspicious of me."

"Well, don't take any unnecessary risks. Let's see if I can find anything on the plans first."

"I don't want you to take any time away from looking for Jessica, though."

"Natalie is still important. Her family and friends need closure and justice. It was horrific when I lost my parents, but at least I knew what happened. I didn't have to spend every day wondering if by some miracle, they might come back to life. I feel for Natalie's family."

"So do I. And it's not just Natalie I'm thinking about. There's Anna, and also another woman who went missing about six years ago. Who knows how many more there are? The inn seems to be connected to a lot of mystery. Is that just a coincidence? Or is someone at the inn a part of something deadly?"

"Are you talking about Ellen?"

"Well, she's the one who's been there all along, but her handyman, Ray, is much creepier and has a record of assault."

"I looked him up, too," he admitted. "But he doesn't seem to have had any problems since he's been working at the inn."

"Is that because he never did anything, or because Ellen used her relationship with the sheriff to protect her handyman?"

"Impossible to tell. Small town law enforcement sometimes has a lot of layers."

"And Tom Holloway took over as sheriff after his father stepped down. The Holloways have been managing the law enforcement in this town for fifty-plus years, and Ellen has been here the whole time. Their loyalty bubble feels unbreakable."

"Nothing is unbreakable if you pound hard enough. That's what we keep doing," he said as he pulled up in front of the coffee shop.

"Do you want to visit Tessa with me?" I asked as I opened the car door.

"I'm going to let you do that on your own. I want to see if I can get any of the plans for the inn before the building department closes. Why don't you text me on your way back from the hospital and let me know how she's doing?"

"Okay. I'll talk to you later."

I'd no sooner gotten into my car when I got a call from Morgan, and I chatted with her on the way to the hospital. After updating her on what Nathan had told me, we discussed the podcast and the growing interest from sponsors. She was responding to comments and answering emails, and I was thrilled to have her take over dealing with all that. I needed to focus on unraveling the mysteries of Stonecross, which were multiplying faster than I could untangle them.

We hung up when I got to the medical center, and when I entered Tessa's room, I found her awake and looking marginally better than she had this morning. Her eyes seemed less foggy but there was still pain in her gaze.

"How are you doing?" I asked, glancing at the television that was on but muted. "Catching up on the *Real Housewives*?"

She shrugged. "I've mostly been sleeping. It's the best way to escape the pain."

"I'm so sorry." I sent her a sympathetic look. "I wish I could do something to make you feel better."

"I'll be okay...eventually. The nurse said today is probably the worst day. Fingers crossed."

Tessa was such a cheerful, confident, and outgoing person; it actually hurt to see her like this. "I should have talked you out of going to lunch with Finn."

"Oh, please, you couldn't have done that," she said with a spark of her usual fire. "And it wasn't Finn that hurt me."

"I know. It was Nathan. I went to see him today. He said you made him nervous when you talked about the podcast, and he realized you'd probably want to share the part about him finding Jessica's ring."

Confusion clouded her gaze. "There was a ring?"

"You don't remember?"

She shook her head. "It's all fuzzy. I thought my memory would be back by now."

"Nathan found Jessica's diamond ring in the sand near where he'd found her boat. But he didn't report it. He kept it so he could sell it. Finn seemed to think he was trying to impress you in some way by telling you a story that might or might not have been true. But when you mentioned the podcast, he panicked."

"I told them about the podcast. How could I do that? I don't remember that at all."

"Nathan put a sleeping pill into your drink to make you forget."

Her eyes widened. "He really did that? And he admitted it? I mean, I've been thinking that might have happened, but I also couldn't quite believe it. Where was Finn when that happened?"

"He said he went downstairs to make a call on the satellite phone, which also seems a little convenient."

"That's crazy."

"Nathan suggested that the ring on the beach proved that Jessica got off the boat and made it to safety and faked her own death."

"Or Nathan could have killed her and made up the whole story."

"There's that, too," I admitted. "Although, I hadn't considered that he'd killed her until just this second."

"If he didn't find the ring on the beach, maybe he took it off her hand."

"That's another scenario to consider."

"We need to put all of this on the podcast," Tessa said.

"I'm not sure I can say all that without proof."

"You can be a little vague and leave specific names out of it, but we have to keep feeding our listeners' hunger for more details." She paused. "I wish I could do it with you, but since I can't, why don't we film a super short teaser right here?"

"Here? You want to film from your hospital bed?"

"It's reality, and that sells. Let's do it now before I lose what little energy I have."

"Okay." I pulled out my phone. "How do you want to do it?"

"You start. Tell everyone you're visiting me in the hospital after I allegedly fell down the stairs, but that might not be what happened. I was sent to emergency surgery, and I'm now recovering. Then turn the camera to me. I'll give a wave, and then you put the camera back on yourself and say you'll be posting tonight with more details."

I nodded. "Are you ready?"

"Sure. I look awful, but that's the point. We want raw and real."

I patted my hair down, thinking I didn't have as good a reason as Tessa did for little makeup and windswept hair, but this was what I actually looked like. I started the camera and filmed the video as she'd instructed. We both reviewed it and then decided to post it immediately, as there was no point in waiting.

After I'd done that, I filled her in on what Morgan was doing about the sponsorships and then got to my feet as the nurse said they needed to draw some blood.

"You don't have to stay," Tessa said.

"Are you sure you don't want company? Or can I bring you food or something?"

"I don't feel like eating at all. And I'm probably going to sleep after this. I feel bad that I can't help you more."

"You just concentrate on healing. That's all that matters. We'll talk tomorrow."

"Okay. But...wait."

"What?"

"When you film tonight's podcast, you should say that you may have to move to another, safer location while we continue investigating. And tomorrow morning, you should do just that. I don't know if it's safe for you to stay at the inn."

"I don't know, either, but I'm not sure anywhere in town is safe. Like I said last night, Ellen can't afford to have another incident at the inn after what happened to you, so I think I still have a small window of time where that will protect me."

"I hope you're right."

"Me too."

Despite my resolve to keep going, just walking to the car made my nerves prickle, especially since it was six o'clock now and getting darker by the minute. But I didn't run into any problems, and I turned on some music to keep me company on the drive.

I was about ten minutes away from the Stonecross exit when I came across a detour. Several big branches were blocking the road, with a truck and two men working to clear the tree. I wasn't thrilled to leave the highway, but I had no choice.

The detour took me down a winding road that eventually led to the same coastal road that the inn was located on, but about six miles south. I hadn't driven this stretch before and became a little stressed out as I saw the jagged turns and steep drops along the ocean side of the road.

And then headlights came up behind me, blinding me even more. The car was right on my tail, getting closer by the minute. There was nowhere to pull over, and anxiety tightened my muscles as I pressed down on the gas. I told myself it was just a local, someone who knew this road well, who was just in a hurry to get home. *But was that really all it was?*

Fumbling for my phone, I called Tyler.

"Cassidy? Are you back?"

"I'm about six miles away on the coastal road south of the inn." I paused, hearing a crackle over the phone. "Where are you?"

"Driving home from town. Want to meet?"

"I think so." I glanced in the rearview mirror again. The car was getting closer. "There was a detour on the highway, Tyler. I'm now on a road that's clinging to the coastline, and someone is following me very closely. I don't have a good feeling—"

My words were cut off as the car behind me hit my bumper, and I bounced forward. Wrestling for control, the phone skidded out of my hand and landed on the passenger seat. I heard Tyler yelling, but I couldn't answer him because someone was trying to run me off the road.

CHAPTER FIFTEEN

I gripped the steering wheel with both hands, my knuckles white, my heart hammering my ribs. The headlights behind me were so bright I couldn't see anything in my rearview mirror except blinding white light.

The car hit me again, harder this time. My head snapped forward, and I felt the back end of the car fishtail on the narrow road. Ocean on one side, rocky hillside on the other, no shoulder, nowhere to go.

I pressed the gas pedal, trying to get distance, but the road curved sharply ahead, and I had to brake or I'd fly right off the cliff. The car behind me didn't slow down. It came at me again, relentless, purposeful.

The next impact sent me careening toward the flimsy wooden barrier, which was the only thing between the road and a steep, rocky drop. I yanked the wheel hard to the left, overcorrected, and felt the tires lose purchase on the asphalt.

Then I was airborne.

For one endless, suspended moment, there was nothing but the sound of Tyler's voice calling my name and the sick certainty that this was how I died—alone on a dark road, pursuing a story no one wanted told, investigating deaths that were supposed to stay buried.

The car slammed into the hillside with a crunch of metal and shattering glass. My head whipped forward into the airbag that exploded from the steering wheel, cushioning the impact but also suffocating me.

The car bounced, rolled, and tumbled down the rocky slope, every impact jarring my bones, rattling my teeth.

And then it stopped.

For a moment, or maybe it was longer, there was nothing but darkness and a ringing in my ears, the smell of something chemical, and a sharp, biting cold...

I blinked my eyes open, trying to understand where I was, what had happened. And that's when I realized I was pinned in my seat by an airbag, and the car was tilted at a steep angle, nose pointing down. Through the cracked windshield, I could see rocks and, beyond that, the dark churning mass of the ocean that didn't feel that far away.

I was close enough to hear the waves crashing, and that was a terrifying thought. When the car shifted slightly, my stomach lurched.

I was still on the hillside, but barely. I needed to get out. Now.

But my hands were shaking too badly to unbuckle the seat belt. My fingers kept slipping off the release button. And every movement I made caused the car to shift a little more, sliding incrementally toward the ocean.

"Hello?" A voice called from somewhere above me. Familiar, but I couldn't place it through the fog of shock. "Is someone down there?"

"Here," I yelled, but I wasn't sure he could hear me above the sound of the waves.

"I'm coming. Don't move," he shouted.

I was too frozen with fear to move, and as much as I wanted

help, I was also scared that if he got too close, the car would slide into the sea.

Before I could tell him to stay back, a light blazed through the broken window next to me, illuminating a face in the dark shadows.

Finn.

My breath caught in my chest. *What was Finn doing here? Had he been the one following me? Had he run me off the road and now had come to finish what he'd started?*

"Cassidy! Are you hurt? Can you move?"

I pressed back against the seat, unable to speak, my mind spinning with fear and confusion. "I—I..."

"Listen to me," he said. "We need to get you out now."

"I'm afraid to move."

As if to punctuate my words, the car shifted again, sliding another few inches down the rocky slope. Stones clattered down ahead of it, splashing into the ocean below.

I gasped. "Oh, God!"

"Can you unbuckle your seat belt?"

"I can't."

"Try," he ordered. "I'm going to get you out of here, but you have to help."

There was something about his firm, confident voice that calmed my nerves. I reached for the button again, finally getting it to release. As the belt snapped back, he reached inside the window to push the airbag out of the way.

"I'm going to open the door, and you're going to jump out as fast as you can. Got it?"

"I don't know if I can do it."

"You can do it," he said forcefully.

"Okay, one second."

"We don't have a second."

"I need my phone and my bag." I grabbed my phone, which was thankfully on the seat next to me and put it in my bag, then slipped the strap over my head. "I'm ready."

"One. Two. Three!"

He opened the door and I threw myself out of the car and into his arms. He caught me, bear-hugging me against his chest, and threw us both sideways against the hillside as the car gave one final lurch and tumbled away.

We lay there on the rocky ground, gasping, as the car crashed and bounced down the remaining slope, metal screaming, until it hit the water with a massive splash and disappeared beneath the dark waves.

I couldn't breathe. Couldn't think. I could only stare at the churning water where my car had vanished, my entire body shaking so hard my teeth chattered.

"It's okay," Finn said, his arm still around me. "You're okay. You're safe now."

"How did you get here so fast?" I asked in bemusement. "Were you following me?" As I looked into his dark eyes, I wondered again if he was the reason I'd gone over the side. But if he was, he wouldn't have rescued me, would he?

"I wasn't following you. But I saw your car go over the side."

"Because the car behind me hit me. They ran me off the road. You saw another car, didn't you?"

"Yes. I saw two cars, and then one crashed through the barrier and flew over the side of the road."

As he finished speaking, sirens wailed. "You called 911?"

"Actually, I didn't. I should have." He shook his head. "When I saw your car, I just scrambled down the hill to make sure whoever was inside was all right. Someone else must have called it in."

I lifted my head as the lights from the approaching fire engine lit up the area, and I heard another voice yelling my name from the top of the road.

"Tyler," I muttered. He must have heard the crash, then came to find me. He'd probably called 911, too.

A moment later, two firefighters rappelled down the hillside, secured by ropes, their headlamps cutting through the darkness.

Only then did I realize just how steep the slope was, how treacherous the loose rocks were, how easily Finn could have fallen trying to reach me.

He'd risked his life to save mine. *How could I have thought he'd tried to kill me?*

Finn helped me to my feet, keeping one arm around me so I wouldn't fall, which was a good thing, because my legs were shaky, threatening to give out. And I leaned into him more than I wanted to admit.

The firefighters reached us, immediately assessing my condition with practiced efficiency.

"Ma'am, are you injured? Can you tell me where it hurts?"

"I'm okay," I managed. "Just shaken up."

"We're going to get you up to the road," one of them said, already securing a harness around me. "Nice and slow."

The climb back up was painstaking as the firefighters guided me and Finn up over the loose rocks. When we reached the top, the paramedics immediately took me to the back of the ambulance to check me for injuries.

Tyler was right behind them, his gaze scanning my face. "Are you all right, Cassidy?"

"I think so," I said, although I was becoming aware of sharp, painful stinging sensations on my face and hands. I looked down to see some bloody scratches on my left hand, which must have come from the broken window.

"When I heard you scream..." He shook his head, his jaw tight. "I jumped into the car, but I didn't know what I was going to find when I got here. You were very lucky."

"I know. Finn wasn't too far behind me, I guess." My gaze moved beyond Tyler to Finn. He was talking to Sheriff Holloway, who had apparently just arrived.

"These cuts aren't deep," the paramedic said, drawing my attention back to her. "I've cleaned them, but you might want to go to the hospital and get checked out."

"I'm fine. I don't need to go to the hospital."

"Your call," she said.

As I stood up and surveyed the scene, I was reminded of just how lucky I was to be standing here on the side of the road, just a short distance from the end of my life.

"Are you really okay?" Tyler asked, his sharp gaze demanding the truth.

"I think so. Thank you for coming, for calling 911."

"It wouldn't have mattered if Finn hadn't gotten here first and pulled you from the car. I would have been too late."

"I know." As my gaze moved to Finn, I saw him turn, and then he and Sheriff Holloway made their way to me.

Sheriff Holloway gave me a nod, his expression serious. "It's Cassidy Bennett, right?"

"Yes."

"Can you tell me what happened?"

"Someone ran me off the road."

"Did you see who was driving?"

"I was blinded by the lights. I couldn't tell you what kind of car it was or who was behind the wheel."

"When did you notice the vehicle behind you?"

"Shortly after I took the detour." I paused. "It's weird about that detour. If those tree branches hadn't blocked the highway, I never would have been on this road."

"Unfortunate timing," the sheriff murmured.

Anger ran through me. "Unfortunate? I almost lost my life, and I can't help thinking it wasn't a coincidence. Maybe that detour was set up for the express purpose of getting me on this road, and it almost worked." My gaze turned to Finn, who was watching our exchange with a grim expression on his face. "If Finn hadn't been there to pull me out of the car, I'd probably be dead."

"I can't imagine that the detour was deliberate. The tree came down over an hour ago. Who would know you would be on this road at this time, and why would they want to hurt you?" the sheriff asked.

"I don't know. Are there cameras on this road?"

"No. This road is rarely used, because it's somewhat treacherous."

"What happens now then?"

"Well, it will take time to get your car out of the water, if that's even possible. Getting evidence off the car is unlikely." He paused. "Isn't it possible that driving on an unfamiliar road with sharp turns and a fast car behind you might have caused you to panic, take the turn too fast and then overcorrect, sending you over the side of the hill?"

"That isn't what happened," I said. "I can't believe you're trying to make this my fault."

"I'm just suggesting a more likely alternative," the sheriff said.

"It sounds more like you're trying to write this off as just an accident, when that's not what it was."

"We should do this somewhere else," Finn interrupted, his gaze sharpening on my face. "You're freezing and you've been through a lot. Can I take you back to the inn, Cassidy?"

"I can give her a ride," Tyler said. "I'm staying right by the inn."

"Do you two know each other?" the sheriff asked curiously, his gaze moving to Tyler. "You're the architect, right? The one staying at the Morrison house?"

"Yes," Tyler said.

"You've been asking a lot of questions about the inn," the sheriff continued.

"If I'm going to buy into the neighborhood, I need to know my neighbors," Tyler said.

"And how do you two know each other?" Sheriff Holloway asked, his narrowed gaze suspicious.

"We met a few days ago," I said.

"I think it would be best if I took you back to the inn, Ms. Bennett," the sheriff suggested. "I'd feel better knowing you were safe."

I didn't know if I was safe anywhere, especially at the inn, but all I said was, "It's fine. I'll go with Tyler."

"All right," the sheriff said, looking unhappy with my decision. "We'll talk again tomorrow when your head is clear."

I didn't really see the point of that, but I was happy to see him head back to his car.

"Are you sure?" Finn asked, shooting Tyler a speculative look. "Can you trust him, Cassidy?"

"She can probably trust me more than you," Tyler retorted. "Considering how her friend returned from a day out with you."

Finn's lips tightened, but he looked away from Tyler to me. "I just want you to be safe. You might not believe that, but it's the truth."

"I appreciate that, Finn. And thank you for risking your life to save me, but I think I'll get a ride with Tyler."

Finn seemed disappointed with my answer, but he walked back to his vehicle, and I followed Tyler to his car.

As I fastened my seat belt and Tyler pulled onto the road, I felt an unexpected sense of terror. I was on the side of the car nearest to the edge, and I found myself gripping my hands tightly together and focusing desperately on the road ahead. There was a fire engine in front of us and Finn was behind us, so I should have felt safer being sandwiched between those vehicles, but I didn't. It also didn't matter that I had Tyler at my side, that I wasn't alone, but I couldn't shake the anxiety that threatened to overwhelm me. Even breathing seemed difficult. Every gulp of air made me want to run. But there was nowhere to go. I just had to get through this.

Tyler suddenly reached out and put his hand on my leg. "You're safe, Cassidy. Just keep breathing."

"I need to get off this road."

"We're almost there. Two miles to go."

It only took five minutes to reach his house, but it felt like forever. When he pulled into the driveway, I practically jumped out of the car and immediately leaned over, fighting the urge to throw up. Tyler waited for me to pull myself together and then he let me into the house without comment. I felt another wave of relief when he turned on the lights.

I flopped down on the covered couch in the living room, happy to have the support beneath my shaky legs.

"I'll turn on the heat," Tyler said.

I nodded, rubbing my hands together as I tried to get warm.

He returned a moment later. "Can I get you something to drink? Something to eat?"

"Not yet. My stomach is still churning."

"Understandable." He sat down in the chair across from me. "I'm sorry about what happened, Cassidy."

"Me too." I paused. "The car is gone. It wasn't mine or Tessa's. She borrowed it from her roommate. We're going to have to buy her another car." I didn't know why I was focusing on that when I had so many other things to worry about.

"One step at a time. You're in shock. Don't try to fix anything right now."

"I couldn't fix it, even if I wanted to." I met his gaze. "Someone tried to kill me tonight. It wasn't an accident, even though Sheriff Holloway wanted to make it seem like I'd just gotten jumpy with someone coming up fast behind me. That wasn't what happened."

"I believe you."

His quiet reassurance helped more than he could know. "Thank you. But who would have taken the trouble to set me up like that, to create the obstacle in the road, the detour sign? How would they even know I'd be on that road? I know someone hit my car and forced me off the road, but I suppose it's possible they weren't responsible for the tree being down. Maybe they were following me from the hospital, and they took advantage of the opportunity. But I didn't tell anyone I was going to see Tessa, except you." For a split second, I wondered if I should have taken Finn or the sheriff up their offer to drive me back to the inn.

"I didn't tell anyone," Tyler said. "But I'm sure Ellen knew you were going to visit Tessa at some point today. Maybe Finn, too. He knows she's in the hospital. That means his family knows, and word gets around. He was also coming from that direction."

I let out a sigh. "You're just broadening the possible list of suspects," I said grumpily. "That's not helpful."

He gave me a brief smile. "Sorry. You've had a rough time. I don't have much in the way of food, but I have some fruit and cheese. Let me make you something to eat."

"Okay." I wasn't hungry, but I needed a moment alone to think about what happened.

As Tyler left the room to go into the kitchen, I pulled my bag over my head and set it on the couch next to me, trying to breathe slowly, to calm down. When I started to feel better, I pulled out my phone, seeing a bunch of missed messages from Morgan. I skimmed through them to see if there was anything urgent to attend to, but it was mostly just updates on the sponsorships and inquiries about what was going on here.

I would talk to her later when I had my wits about me. Right now, there was no point in worrying her or Tessa. Morgan couldn't do anything to help me, and Tessa needed to focus on getting well.

A few moments later, Tyler brought out two paper plates filled with peanut butter sandwiches, cheese, apple slices, carrots, and crackers. He set them on the coffee table and joined me on the couch. "You're not allergic to nuts, are you?"

"No. And I've eaten plenty of peanut butter in the last few months."

"Why is that?"

"I lost my job three months ago, and I live in a very expensive, very small studio apartment in Manhattan, so I've been watching my money."

"You've been living on peanut butter, but you still thought it was a good idea to come to Maine and spend a week at the inn and chase down an old mystery?"

"When you say it like that, I don't come off that smart."

He smiled. "Sorry."

"You're not wrong. But the podcast could be profitable, so Tessa and I thought of this as a work trip."

"What does she do for a living?"

"She has a lot of part-time jobs, same as me. We were working for the same media company when they decided to lay off half the workforce. We found ourselves unemployed with very little notice, along with the third person in our podcast trio." I paused, popping a piece of pepperjack cheese into my mouth. I swallowed, then said, "The podcast started out as a lark, an offshoot from a book club we were in. We loved true crime and no one else did, so we decided to have our own club, and then we turned it into a podcast. It started out slow, but eventually we got a following."

"And that's when you decided to become detectives, not just podcasters."

"Yes. And I'm starting to see the downside of that decision. I'm really out of my depth, Tyler. I always thought of myself as a good investigator, a great researcher, someone who could find small details and piece together clues to solve a mystery. I love to read. I love to write. I always wanted to be a journalist, and this seemed like a good way to test the waters. I never thought we'd end up targets."

"You didn't? You just said you're trying to solve a cold case. Don't you think that if someone killed Natalie and Jessica, and God knows who else, they'd want to protect that secret?"

"I guess I never thought we'd get close enough to the answer to make anyone nervous." I paused. "And I don't think we are that close. So why are they nervous? Why do they need to get rid of us?"

"Because you know more than you think," he said simply.

"I know very little." I took a bite of my sandwich, thinking about what I did know, and it didn't amount to much.

"Maybe it was Nathan who ran you off the road," Tyler suggested. "He drugged Tessa, so she'd forget what he'd told her. And after talking to you, maybe he thought you were a threat, too."

"But I wasn't alone when I saw Nathan; I was with you. Why wouldn't you be a target, too?"

As I finished my statement, we both stared at each other, and the house felt suddenly cold again and very isolated.

"I shouldn't have come here," I said. "You could be a target, too, and now we're together."

"Hang on," he said as I put my plate on the table, ready to get the hell out of there. "It might not have been Nathan at all."

"But he was the one who was nervous earlier."

"It could have been Finn," Tyler suggested. "He was with Nathan yesterday. He brought Tessa home in a bad condition. And he just happened to be very close behind you on that road."

I frowned at the reminder. "I thought that, too, when he first showed up. I had this terrible fear he hadn't come to save me but to finish me off. But that's not what happened. He risked his life to get me out of the car. He wouldn't have done that if he was the one who sent me down there in the first place. He would have just left me there. I probably couldn't have gotten out of the car or up that hill without him. And by the time you arrived, it would have been too late. I don't think it was Finn."

"Okay, but there's still Ellen and Ray. Maybe they never wanted you to make it back to the inn, and this was a way to get rid of you without tying your accident to the inn."

"That's true, but I need answers, not more theories," I said wearily. "I don't know what to do or who to trust."

"You can trust me, Cassidy. We're on the same side."

That seemed right, but my head was spinning, and I felt like I should be by myself, because the only person I could really trust was me. "I want to go back to the inn now."

"That's not a good idea. At least, wait until morning. You can sleep on the couch. You can get your bearings."

"Isn't this where you sleep? On that sleeping bag." I tipped my head to the bag next to the fireplace.

"I can sleep on the floor. It's not a big deal. I'd like to keep an eye on you."

"I appreciate that. I do. But I need to update my podcast. I need to clean up, and I need to sleep tonight so I can figure out what to do tomorrow. Will you take me back?"

His slight hesitation sent a moment of panic through me, but then he nodded and gave me a reassuring smile and said, "Of course. Why don't you finish eating first? Then we'll go."

I picked up my sandwich again and as I ate, I said, "Did you find out anything from the building department about the inn?"

"No, it was closed when I got there. I'll have to try tomorrow."

"Maybe I can look around the inn tomorrow morning, see if I can find any doors leading down to a basement."

"You should wait on that. I'd prefer you to stay above the basement level, preferably in the main area of the inn where there are lots of people around. You can't trust Ellen or Ray, and everyone who works there is loyal to Ellen."

"I think the sheriff is loyal to her, too. I bet he already told her about my accident."

"I wouldn't doubt it."

"I thought that Tessa's public fall down the stairs last night would create a protective bubble around me, that no one would want to take a chance on hurting me and bringing more scrutiny, but I was wrong. I wasn't safe."

"You also weren't at the inn, so no one can blame Ellen or Ray," he said. "Maybe it's time for you and Tessa to go home, or for you to leave Stonecross. Go to Seabrook, stay there."

"Without telling Jessica or Natalie's story? I can't quit now. And I'm not sure Seabrook would be any safer. It might be even easier to get to me there."

"If you don't quit, you might not survive. Is being a journalist, making money off a podcast, worth your life?"

I gave him a pained look as I said, "No, but I also want to live a life of courage and meaning, and sometimes that means taking a risk."

"You're not a quitter. That's an admirable trait."

I smiled at the irony of his words. "And a trait that has not been attributed to me in the past. My father would tell you that one of his biggest disappointments in me is how easily I give up, change my mind, and take the easy way out."

"Is that why you can't quit now, because you're trying to prove something to your father?" he asked curiously.

"It's more about proving something to myself." I got to my feet. "Will you take me back now?"

"I don't want to, but I will. And just for the record, if you change your mind, if you decide to quit on all this, I won't think any less of you. You'd be choosing the wisest possible course, and I don't really want to see you end up like Natalie or Jessica."

"I just wish we knew how they actually ended up," I murmured. "Because right now, we have no idea if they're dead or alive. I very much want them to be alive. I know that's not probable, but it is possible, and that makes me want to keep going."

CHAPTER SIXTEEN

Tyler pulled into the inn's parking lot just after seven. The building was lit up, and through the windows, I could see a lot of people milling about. Happy hour was just about to end, but the inn encouraged guests to enjoy the downstairs with its selection of books and games and the roaring fire in the fireplace.

"You're sure about this?" Tyler asked, as he kept the engine running.

"I am. I appreciate your concern. But there are some things I still need to do here. I'll lock myself in my room until morning, and then I'll figure out what's next." I could see frustration and doubt in his eyes, and it was nice that he cared about my well-being, but I needed to talk to Ellen before I made any other decisions. I certainly couldn't leave town before I did that. And I also needed to do the podcast that I'd promised to handle tonight. If I was on my way out of town soon, I might as well record what had happened to date. And then tomorrow, I'd speak to Ellen.

"Call me if you have any concerns whatsoever," Tyler said. "And I will come right over."

"Thanks—for everything." I unbuckled my seat belt and got out before I could second-guess my decision.

When I entered the inn, I was assailed by a reassuring warmth and the sound of conversation and laughter. There were a couple of people at the reception desk talking to Moira, and behind them, I saw Ellen and Sheriff Holloway walking into her office.

That was rather alarming. I was about to head upstairs when I heard my name called from the living room. When I turned my head, I saw Dorothy beckoning to me. She was sitting at her usual table, but she wasn't alone. She was with the sheriff's brother, Jeff Holloway. There was also an older couple playing backgammon at the table next to them, and in the dining room beyond I could see Sophie clearing tables while Cole hovered nearby.

It was definitely a full house tonight. I didn't really want to talk to Dorothy, but she was motioning me to come over, and I couldn't just ignore her, so I moved into the room, very aware of my disheveled appearance. There was dirt on my jeans and my sweater and probably in my hair, and I had cuts on my hands and on my face. But everyone would hear soon enough what had happened to me if they hadn't already.

"Cassidy!" Dorothy stood up, nearly dropping her knitting, her face filled with concern when I got closer. "Oh, my dear, we just heard what happened. Are you okay? You look terrible."

"I'm okay," I managed. "Just a little shaken up. I guess you all heard what happened."

"You had an accident on the Upper Coast Road," Jeff said. "My brother filled us in. Sorry to hear about that."

"Sit for a moment," Dorothy said, pulling over another chair.

"I was going to go upstairs."

"Oh, you don't want to be alone, do you? Sit."

I reluctantly sat because I didn't actually want to be alone, and I didn't want to draw more attention to myself.

"This is my godson, Jeff Holloway."

"We met at Kelly's Pub," Jeff said with a smile. "You were with your friend, a very pretty blonde."

"Yes, Tessa," I said.

"It's terrible what happened to her, and now you. It's like you're living under a dark cloud."

"It does seem that way."

"That road is treacherous in the dark, especially if you've never driven it before," Jeff said. "I've come close to running off the road myself."

"I didn't run off the road because of my driving. There was another car behind me. It bumped me from behind, and that's when I went through the barrier and down the hill."

"Oh, my goodness," Dorothy said, putting a hand to her chest. "That sounds terrifying. What happened to the other driver?"

"Nothing. They didn't stop. And it wasn't an accident. They deliberately ran me off the road."

Jeff's smile faded while shock filled Dorothy's eyes.

"Why on earth would someone do that?" Dorothy asked.

"I don't know. But that's what happened."

"My brother said you just lost control of the car," Jeff put in, giving me a speculative look.

"Well, that's not what I told him, but he seems to have his own unique narrative about anything bad that happens in Stonecross."

"Are you saying he's lying?" Jeff asked. "Why would he do that?"

"I have no idea. But I told him about the other car, and that's not the story he shared with you. If you don't believe my version, you can ask Finn. He witnessed the whole thing. Anyway, I should go. I'm exhausted, and I need to change my clothes."

"Is there anything I can do for you, Cassidy?" Dorothy asked with a kind and worried smile. "I feel like you haven't been having much fun lately, with Tessa getting hurt and now your accident... We need to change your vacation around."

"It definitely hasn't been much of a vacation," I muttered.

"You should take Cassidy out on your boat, Jeff," Dorothy

said. Turning to me, she added, "He has a beautiful boat. And he's a great sailor. You would be in good hands."

"I would be happy to take you out, show you a different side of Stonecross," Jeff said. "We could ask Sophie and Cole to come along. Cole told me you and your friend have been giving Sophie tips about living in New York. Those two can't wait to get out of this town."

"They don't appreciate how nice it is to live in a place where everyone knows you," Dorothy interjected. "My husband and I lived in Chicago for a couple of years, and I was so lonely in that big city. There was a lot to do, but it never felt like home."

"Anyway, the invitation is open," Jeff said, giving me a smile. "I don't have a lot of charters this week, so I have some free days. Just let me know. I'm usually in my office at the harbor during the day."

"I'll think about it. Thanks."

As I got to my feet, Ellen and the sheriff entered the living room, heading straight in my direction.

Ellen's eyes locked on me immediately, and I saw a myriad of emotions move through her expression—surprise, suspicion, anger...

"Good," Ellen said, her voice sharp. "You're back. Now it's time for you to pack your things and leave, Ms. Bennett."

The room went silent at her strident tone. Through the archway, I saw Sophie and Cole move toward the living room at Ellen's harsh words. Dorothy muttered concern behind me.

"Excuse me?" I asked, my tone as sharp as hers. "I was just almost killed—"

"Yes. I heard you nearly drove yourself into the ocean."

"That's not what happened," I said, unable to hide my frustration and anger.

"It doesn't matter," Ellen continued. "You haven't been honest with me. I told you and your friend when you first arrived that I don't allow the use of cameras inside the inn, that I protect the privacy of my guests, but you disregarded my wishes.

You recorded a podcast in your room, a podcast about this inn, about the nasty lies that have been circulating for the past year." Her face was tight with barely controlled fury. "You have been spreading vicious lies about this inn, and my staff, and this town, all the people here."

My stomach dropped. I'd known the podcast would eventually come out, but I hadn't expected it to be so public, so dramatic. My gaze moved around the room, seeing the mix of expressions around me. They couldn't look away from the crash happening right in front of them.

"Is that true, dear?" Dorothy asked softly. "You have a podcast about the inn?"

"It's true," the sheriff interrupted. "Cole gave me the link, and Ellen and I just listened to it."

My gaze flew to Cole, who now looked uncomfortable. And Sophie looked angry, sending an annoyed look in his direction.

"It wasn't just about the inn," Ellen added. "It was about the rumors we've had to deal with this past year."

"I haven't lied about anything." I tried to keep my voice steady, despite my racing heart. "Everything we said on the podcast is based on facts. Natalie Warren disappeared from this inn. Jessica Trent disappeared while staying here. Anna Franklin left before dawn a few days ago. Those are facts, not rumors. And no one seems to care about these missing women."

"Those facts have been twisted to make this inn look dangerous," Ellen said. "Facts presented to make me look negligent, to make this town look sinister. You came here under false pretenses, pretending to be an ordinary guest when really you were here to exploit a tragedy for entertainment."

"It's not entertainment; it's also an investigation. It's trying to find answers for families who deserve them."

"You abused my hospitality," Ellen continued. "You painted this inn as some sort of death trap when the truth is that one woman disappeared after she left here, likely because she chose to leave. And you've built a conspiracy theory around that."

"Jessica Trent disappeared while she was staying here."

"Because she took a boat out on her own."

"And then there's Anna."

"Anna Franklin left of her own free will," Ellen snapped. "A friend picked her up."

"Then why was there blood on the carpet in her room?" I challenged. "Why did Ray carry it out to the garage and then move it again in his truck?"

Ellen's face went pale, then flushed with anger. "You've been spying on my staff? You've been sneaking around—"

"I've been investigating," I interrupted. "Because women keep disappearing from this inn and no one is looking for them."

"That's enough," the sheriff said, taking a step toward me. "You need to leave. Ms. Clarke has every right to refuse you service."

"She might have the right, but I'm not going anywhere."

"Yes, you are," Ellen said, her voice edged with anger. "I've booked you a room at the hotel near the hospital where your friend is. I'll have Ray drive you there as soon as you get your things together."

"I'm not going anywhere with Ray, the man who moved a bloody carpet out of the inn."

"Why was there blood on the carpet?" Jeff asked from behind me.

I don't know which of the three of us was more surprised by the interruption.

"Stay out of this, Jeff," the sheriff ordered. "It doesn't concern you."

"Cassidy has a good question."

"Anna cut her hand on some broken glass in her room and bled on the carpet. Ray took it to the cleaners," Ellen said firmly. "You could find a mystery anywhere, couldn't you? And you don't need to answer that question, because as I said before, you're leaving. If you don't want a ride, you can call a taxi. Your investigation is over. Sheriff, would you mind escorting Ms. Bennett upstairs and waiting while she packs?"

"Hold on," I said, putting up a hand as Tom took a step in my direction. "I didn't come here just because of Natalie." My voice was shaking now, but I couldn't stop. This wasn't how I'd wanted to do this. I'd never planned to reveal my connection to Ellen in public, in front of all these people. But I had no choice. "Or the podcast. I came here to meet you."

Ellen stared at me in confusion. "No, you didn't. You're just trying to change your story now. This is another attempt to involve me personally in these disappearances, to make this about me—"

"No," I interrupted. "I'm not changing my story. I did come here to look for Natalie and to talk about our search for her on the podcast. But that's not the only reason I came. It wasn't just about Natalie or the others. It was also about your son, David. And why you two haven't spoken in more than thirty years."

The color drained from Ellen's face. She went rigid, her hands clenching at her sides. The room had gone so quiet I could hear the tick of the grandfather clock in the corner.

"That's enough," Ellen whispered, but now her voice was the one shaking. "You will not mention my son's name in this house."

"David isn't just your son," I said, forcing the words out. "He's also my father. I'm your granddaughter. I'm not Cassidy Bennett; I'm Cassidy Clarke. And I'm not leaving until we talk about why you and I have never met before now."

The silence that followed was absolute. Every person in the room stared at me, including Ellen, who stood frozen, her face ashen, her eyes wide with shock. For a long moment, she didn't speak. Didn't move. Just stared at me as if I couldn't possibly be real.

"You can't be my...granddaughter," she finally said.

"I am." I held her gaze. "I'm David's daughter. You really didn't know?"

She squared her shoulders. "How could I? David hasn't spoken to me since the day he left when he was eighteen years old." She paused. "Are you really his daughter? Or is this another lie?"

"I'm his daughter. And I think you know that, whether or not you want to admit it."

Ellen opened her mouth, closed it, opened it again. No words came out. She looked at the sheriff, at Dorothy, at the faces staring at her from the archway, and something in her seemed to crumble.

Without another word, she turned and walked out of the room. A moment later, I heard a door close.

The room remained silent. No one seemed to know what to do or say.

"Well," Dorothy said finally, breaking the tension. "I wasn't expecting to hear that. I don't think Ellen was either."

I turned to look at her. "I was going to tell her in private. I was waiting for the right moment."

"And you thought this was it?" Jeff asked dryly.

"I didn't know if I'd have another chance." My gaze moved to the sheriff, who didn't seem to know what to do now.

After a moment, he said, "I guess I'll let you and Ellen sort this out." He cleared his throat. "But the podcast needs to end. You're slandering the reputation of this town."

"Why are you so unwilling to admit that what's been happening here is real?" I challenged. "I didn't make up those women. They're gone. And no one knows where they are or what happened to them."

"Those cases were investigated thoroughly, and not just by me. There were private investigators involved, too. There is simply no proof that anything happened to them. That's why the cases were closed. Not because anyone wanted to hide anything. If you really want to tell the truth, you should put that on your podcast." On that note, he turned and walked out of the room.

I blew out a breath as he left. Then I turned to Dorothy.

"Did you know my father? Do you know why he left? Why Ellen won't speak about him?"

"I knew him as a child. But I don't know what happened between him and his mother. That's a question Ellen has to answer."

"I knew your dad," Jeff interjected. "He was Tom's age, which makes him five years older than me."

"What was he like?"

Jeff shrugged. "I don't know. He seemed like a good enough kid. He wasn't a troublemaker like Tom. But if he got pushed, he'd fight; he wouldn't back down."

"Your brother was a troublemaker?" I asked.

"Oh, yeah, big time. So was I." Jeff paused. "Tom thinks I still am. But he was way worse than me back in the day. Drove my father crazy."

"Your father was the sheriff, wasn't he?"

"Yeah, he was in charge of everyone and everything. It's ironic to me that somehow Tom turned out just like him."

I was less interested in the Holloway brothers and more interested in what Jeff knew about my father. "Do you know why my dad left? Why he never spoke to his mother again?"

"I think it had something to do with his dad dying. Some people even think David might have pushed his father off the cliff, but I never believed that."

"There's no way my father would ever kill anyone."

"Why don't you just ask him why he left?" Jeff asked. "He's alive, isn't he?"

"Yes, he is, but he won't talk about his family or the past."

"And Ellen won't speak of him," Dorothy interjected. "It's a sad situation. Maybe you can bring them back together, Cassidy."

"That seems pretty impossible right now. I don't know if Ellen is going to talk to me again."

"Well, she didn't make you leave," Dorothy said with a smile. "And she could have. That's a step in the right direction."

"I guess." I paused as Cole and Sophie came over to our table.

"Sorry I outed you," Cole said with a regretful smile. "I didn't mean to. I was telling Sophie, and my dad overheard."

I was glad Cole hadn't deliberately set out to expose the podcast, not that I could really blame him. It was public, and I had always known it would eventually come out. "It's fine. I knew someone would figure it out eventually."

"You look awful, Cassidy," Sophie said. "Do you need anything for your cuts? I can get you some first-aid supplies—antiseptic and bandages."

"I'll be fine. The paramedic cleaned the cuts. They'll heal."

"You must have been terrified," Sophie added. "I hate driving that road, especially at night."

"I was beyond scared. Luckily, your brother saved me."

"Really? I had no idea. Finn was there?" she asked in surprise.

I nodded. "Yes, and he's the reason I'm alive. He can also confirm that I didn't drive myself off the side of that road. He saw another vehicle behind me. I don't know why the sheriff won't acknowledge that."

"Why would someone want to hurt you?" Sophie asked. "It doesn't make sense."

"Sure, it does. She's stirring up trouble," Jeff said. "If someone did hurt those women, then maybe they're worried she's going to figure it out."

"I hate to think anything bad happened to Natalie," Dorothy said. "She was such a sweetheart. I really did think she just left and maybe wanted to start over."

"Tom says there's no evidence to prove she didn't do exactly that," Jeff said, sending a comforting look in Dorothy's direction. Then he pushed back his chair. "I should get going. Let me know if you want a boat ride, Cassidy, or if you want to chat more about your father."

"Thanks. I'll think about it. I need to talk to my grandmother again before I talk to anyone else. I'm going to head upstairs now."

"Take care," Sophie said. "And you have my number, Cassidy. Call me if you need anything."

"Thanks."

I felt a little less lonely as I climbed the stairs. Not everyone in this town hated me. I had some allies, or at least I thought I did. But maybe one of them was just pretending to be concerned. I really had no idea anymore. The only thing I knew for certain was that I wasn't leaving yet. Tomorrow would hopefully bring more answers, but first, I just needed to make it through the night.

CHAPTER SEVENTEEN

While I was exhausted and looked wrecked, I knew I had one more thing to do before I collapsed on the bed and went to sleep, and that was to film and record the podcast. It would be the first time I'd ever done it on my own. We'd gone from three women having fun, drinking wine and talking about true crime to Morgan being tied up with personal commitments, Tessa in the hospital with a great deal of pain, and me having survived an attack on my life.

Maybe this hadn't been the brilliant idea we'd thought it was.

I opened my laptop and set up the lights and microphone, but I didn't bother to brush my hair, change my clothes, or apply makeup to my somewhat ravaged face. Tessa had said being authentic and real would resonate better with the listeners, and I agreed. Plus, I just didn't have the energy to change.

Clearing my throat, I made a few notes on the pad of paper next to me, checked the audio and the video and then hit record.

"Hello everyone. As most of you know, I'm Cassidy, one-third of the *Mysteries Uncorked* podcast team. Tessa is in the hospital recovering from the surgery needed to repair her broken leg, which occurred when she fell down the stairs at the Stonecross Inn. At least, we hope it was an accident and not that someone gave her a push. Unfortunately, she doesn't remember much about that."

Pausing, I added, "I hope you saw the short video we posted on our page earlier with greetings from Tessa. She wishes she could be here, but she needs to focus on healing. Morgan is also absent, taking care of her family in New York, but I am proceeding with our investigation into the disappearance of Natalie Warren and several other women who have gone missing while staying at the inn or after their departure."

I took a breath and said, "You might wonder why I look so bad tonight. On my way home from the hospital, I came across a detour on the main highway. I took the road to the coast, the only one available. It was very twisty, with sharp turns, and perilously high drop-offs."

My voice shook as the memories flooded back. "And then I saw lights behind me, blinding lights. There was a car coming up fast, and I had nowhere to turn off. I hit the gas. I drove as fast as I could, but the car kept coming, and then it hit me. I barely maintained control with that first bump. But the second one was harder, and I yanked the wheel to the left to avoid the cliff, but the turn was too sharp. I lost control and went over the side. I can't even describe how it felt to fly through the air and tumble down a steep, rocky hillside. Luckily, my car didn't flip, and the rocks prevented me from crashing into the sea."

I let that sink in, then continued, "It was the most terrifying moment of my life, and I could feel the car precariously clinging to the hillside. Every breath I took, every slight move I made, the car seemed to slide just a little. Fortunately, someone had seen my car go over the side, and they came down the hill to rescue me."

Clearing my throat, I continued, "At first, I was afraid the person approaching my window was the same one who had sent me crashing, but I had to trust that they weren't. Because I didn't have a choice. The car wasn't stable. I had to get out. Fortunately, my rescuer was able to help me out of the car, and we hit the ground seconds before the rocks gave way, and my vehicle tumbled into the sea."

My voice shook as I relived that horrible moment. During my pause, I could see the comments flying in the chat window. I couldn't focus on them now.

"But I survived. And I know that it wasn't an accident. Someone tried to kill me tonight. Someone who thinks I'm getting too close to the truth. They wanted me dead, out of the way, no longer able to ask questions, to shed any kind of light on Natalie's disappearance. But I'm still here. I'm still filming from the Stonecross Inn. I might not be here much longer. The town wants me gone, but I'm going to try to stay, because I still have questions, and I still want to know what happened to Natalie."

I let that sink in, then added. "To catch you up, I want to fill you in on some other things I learned today. One involves a woman who was staying at the inn. She took a boat out and never returned. Her name was Jessica Trent, and no one knows what happened to her, either. A third woman who was staying at the inn when I arrived seemed to vanish in the early hours of dawn. There's a disturbing pattern going on here, and someone needs to find out why it's happening. I'm not sure that law enforcement is as interested as we are. I've been given a lot of explanations as to why all these women simply wanted to live their lives without scrutiny and just walked away, suggestions that they don't want to be found, and that I might actually be hurting them by looking for them. I don't think that's true. So, I'm going to keep looking, as long as I can."

Staring at myself in the monitor, I added, "I know that we're not investigators. That people have questioned how we can find answers when professionals have been unsuccessful. Maybe we can't. But we're still trying, and that counts for something. I wouldn't want to disappear and not have anyone look for me. These women deserve to have someone focusing on their cases, and maybe that will convince law enforcement to take another look at their cases. I hope to be back tomorrow with an update.

Let us know your thoughts. You're on this journey with us. Until next time."

I smiled and turned everything off, blowing out a breath as I did so.

A moment later, my phone rang. It was Tessa.

"Oh, my God," she said. "What happened, Cassidy? Why didn't you call me?"

"I assume you just heard the podcast."

"Yes. I watched it live. I can't believe you were run off the road. You should have texted me."

"I didn't want to worry you, and there was nothing you could do." I saw that Morgan was trying to call me, too. "Hang on, I'm going to make this a group chat with Morgan." I put us on the same call and said, "Before you ask, I'm fine."

"How can you be fine?" Morgan shrieked. "Someone tried to kill you."

"And who rescued you?" Tessa wanted to know.

"Finn," I said.

"Finn?" Tessa echoed. "I wasn't expecting that."

"Neither was I. I have to admit I wondered if he was the one who'd sent me over the side, but it was a steep hill, and he risked his life getting down to me, so I don't think it was him. He also backed me up with the sheriff by saying there was another car."

"You're talking about the bartender at the pub?" Morgan asked.

"Yes."

"Thank God he was there," she said.

"Tyler was there, too. He arrived a little later. I was actually on the phone with him when the crash happened. He rushed to find me and called 911. He was a good buffer between Finn and me and the sheriff when it was all over."

"The sheriff has to realize that something is happening, right?" Morgan asked. "He's going to investigate."

"No, he's not," I said. "He blew it off as me driving poorly on an unfamiliar road in the dark, and that it was just a local who knew the road and was driving fast behind me. He suggested that I got spooked and drove myself over the side. Not even Finn's account changed his mind, because Finn was too far away to give a description of the other car. Anyway, he's not going to investigate. He wants me gone. And so does Ellen. She tried to kick me out tonight when I got back to the inn."

"That's cold," Tessa said. "After everything you just went through."

"The sheriff was here when I got back. I made a short stop at Tyler's after the accident. I needed a breather before facing anyone. But in that short time span, the sheriff found out about the podcast and told Ellen. There were a lot of people around because it was happy hour, and I was in the living room talking to Dorothy when Sheriff Holloway and Ellen confronted me about the podcast."

"Damn," Tessa muttered.

"Wow," Morgan murmured. "What happened?"

"She tried to kick me out, said I was abusing her hospitality, trying to ruin the reputation of the inn. It was a brutal scene, and I knew I wasn't going to convince her to change her mind without playing my ace."

"You told her," Tessa breathed.

"I had to. It was the only way I could stop her from putting me in Ray's truck or some taxi to take me to another hotel."

"How did she take it?" Morgan asked.

"She looked genuinely shocked. I had thought maybe she suspected, but now I know she didn't have a clue. She knew we were up to something, but she didn't know what exactly until the podcast came out. She had no idea about the family connection."

"Are you sure?" Tessa questioned. "Maybe Ellen is just a good actress. Think about the note under your door a few nights ago, telling you to leave, and then me falling down the stairs or getting pushed...that would suggest someone at the inn wanted us gone."

"That's true. It could have been her or maybe Ray. My grand-mother might not know what's he's been up to."

"I believe Ellen knows absolutely everything happening at the inn," Tessa said dryly. "She's a sharp lady. So how did it end?"

"I told her I wasn't leaving until we talked about my father, and she just walked away. The sheriff left after that, and most of the others, too. And I decided to come upstairs and do the podcast. It might be the last one from Stonecross."

"It was a good one," Tessa said. "The way you described what happened to you was chilling."

"You're a great storyteller," Morgan said. "I could feel what you were feeling. It was so real." She paused. "The podcast comments are still going strong. We have thousands of people weighing in, and I already got an email from one of the sponsors who wants to send over a contract tomorrow. The podcast is definitely working. But, of course, there's been a huge cost to both of you. I feel guilty that I'm not with you."

"Don't feel guilty," I said. "You're where you need to be, and for the moment, we're all safe. At least, I hope so. I really don't know much, which is why it's weird that someone tried to kill me to shut me up. I wish I had more I could say."

"You need to leave tomorrow morning, right after you talk to your grandmother," Morgan said.

"I'm going to see what she has to say. I can't come back with nothing. I either have to find answers for Natalie's disappearance, or at the very least, I have to know why my father left, why my family shattered. I know it's a risk to stay. But I'm also hoping that maybe being outed as Ellen's granddaughter will put some kind of protective bubble around me."

"You thought that about my fall down the stairs and someone attacked you tonight."

"Yes, but that wasn't at the inn. It couldn't be tied to Ellen."

"What difference does that make? You still could have lost your life."

"You're right. But I need to speak to Ellen again before I decide anything."

"Ellen could be at the center of everything," Morgan put in. " I'm not sure she's going to let a long-lost granddaughter get in her way."

"Morgan is right," Tessa said. "From what I know of Ellen, she's cold and calculating. And if she's involved in trafficking these women, or, God forbid, getting rid of them, then what do you think she's going to do? She's not going to confess her sins to you."

"She's probably going to kick me out," I said realistically. "But I want to try to talk to her about my father, and I'm hoping that will unsettle her, so she won't be thinking clearly. Maybe I'll learn something, maybe I won't."

"What about Tyler? Can you stay with him?" Morgan asked. "Isn't he living nearby? I hate for you to be alone."

"He offered earlier, but it didn't make sense to me. I had the thought that maybe Nathan had come after me for what he told me about Jessica's missing ring. And if he came after me, he might go after Tyler, too. Anyway, after what happened with my grandmother tonight, the inn is probably the safest place I could be. I don't think she's going to let someone kill me on her property."

"She might find a way to have you disappear just like the others," Tessa said darkly.

"That would raise suspicions, and I think her standing in this community is as important to her as anything else." I let out a breath. "I appreciate the concern, but I'm beat. I need to take a hot shower and try to relax. I'll talk to you both tomorrow."

After a chorus of goodbyes, I set down my phone, rolled my tired head around on my shoulders and then grabbed my pajamas. A shower would feel good, but I was just too weary to attempt it. So, I changed into my comfortable PJs, turned out the lights and slid under the covers.

In the quiet, I could hear the wind blowing a branch against my window, and the waves crashing on the rocks below. At times there was a ringing sound, almost like a cry, that came through the vents, and the tension refused to leave my body. I felt like I was waiting for something to happen.

After several more minutes of anxiety-fueled thoughts, I got out of bed and pushed my dresser in front of the door. It was kind of a noisy process and, hopefully, whoever was below me didn't call down to the desk to ask what the hell was going on. But when it was done, I felt better. No one was getting in this room tonight. I was safe.

At least until tomorrow...

———

Wednesday morning, I woke up with aching muscles and a pounding headache, which got marginally better after a hot shower and a change of clothes. But when I saw the piece of paper slipped under my door, my tension immediately returned.

I unfolded the note with wary hands, expecting a threat, just like the last time. But this note was different. It was from Ellen, requesting that I come to her apartment on the first floor at my earliest convenience.

She was clearly ready to talk, or at least to tell me to leave again. I grabbed my phone and my bag and headed downstairs, feeling like I needed to be ready for anything.

Her apartment was at the back of the building in its own corridor, an area of the inn I had not been in before. I knocked on her door, and she answered a few seconds later.

She wore a pair of brown slacks and a caramel-colored cardigan over a white blouse, her stark white hair offsetting her pale face and brown eyes—eyes that were a lot like mine, but nothing like my father's brilliant green eyes. She waved me inside without a word, and as I stepped into her private apartment, it didn't feel much different from the inn. She had the same kind of décor, the same antique furniture, the same muted colors.

There was a living room, and what appeared to be a small kitchenette by a round dining table, with a door leading to a bedroom.

"Sit," she ordered.

I took a seat on a rather hard chair while she took the chair next to me, both of us avoiding the couch. Her gaze raked across mine.

"I don't see a resemblance," she said finally.

It wasn't what I'd expected her to say, but I was fine to put off the inevitable heavier conversation. "I look like my mother."

"Your mother," she echoed. "Who is your mother? What's her name? What does she do?"

"Her name was Pamela. She was a teacher."

"Was?"

"She passed away when I was a teenager. I don't have any other siblings, just an uncle on my mother's side, and a few cousins, but they live in Oregon. It's been my father and me for the past fourteen years." I paused. "You really didn't know about me?"

She shook her head but didn't explain.

"I don't understand," I said. "What happened between you and my father?"

"What did he say?"

"Nothing. He refuses to talk about you. He said he never wanted me to know you or for you to know me. And I guess you didn't want to know. Or you would have tried to contact me." I couldn't hide the bitter pain in my voice, and she flinched at my words.

"Your father made it clear he wanted nothing to do with me," she said finally. "I took him at his word."

"You still haven't told me what happened."

"It doesn't matter anymore."

"It matters to me."

"You need to talk to your father, not to me. It was his decision to leave."

"Was it?"

Her lips tightened, and I realized that if I pushed too hard, this conversation would end sooner than I wanted.

"Can you tell me about my grandfather?" I asked, changing the subject.

"He died a long time ago."

"What was he like?"

She appeared taken aback by my question. "Richard was...a lot of things."

"Give me a couple," I prodded.

"I don't know what you want me to say."

"I just want to know something about my grandfather."

"He was a hard worker. He took over the Boatworks after his father passed away, and he made it even bigger than it had been under his dad. He was selling boats all over the world, putting Stonecross on the map. He was determined to keep this town relevant and vital, a place where families could live and work and where their children would want to stay and raise their children. He was once the mayor of the town." Her gaze softened. "He could be very charming."

"It sounds like there's a but..."

"He could also be controlling, rigid in his views, a little too self-focused."

"Sounds like my father took after his dad."

She gave me a startled look. "Really? That's how you would describe your father?"

"Yes. I'd also say ruthlessly ambitious, very focused on money, and the kind of person you just don't get close to."

"He wasn't always that way. There was a time when he seemed like too much of a dreamer."

"Seriously? That doesn't sound like my father at all."

"He started changing even before he left. My son and my husband were often at odds. Sometimes I was at odds with both of them. They were strong personalities."

"Well, you don't seem like you have a weak personality."

"Circumstances forced me to be stronger."

"How did my grandfather die? I heard something about him falling from the cliffs."

"There are a lot of rumors about his death. This town loves to gossip."

"What happened?"

She hesitated, then said, "The year before Richard died, we were living in a house on Spring Lane. David was a senior in high school, and I was a stay-at-home mother and wife. But I'd always wanted to run a bed-and-breakfast like this inn. It was my dream to one day own this place. When the former owner decided to move away, she put it up for sale. It was in bad shape. It hadn't been operating as an inn for probably three or four years while she was ill. I knew I had to buy it. After many discussions, Richard agreed we would sell our house and use the money to buy this inn. Your father was almost an adult and thinking about going to college. Although Richard wanted David to work with him at the Boatworks. He wanted him to carry on the family legacy."

"I can't imagine my father working on boats."

"He was a very skilled carpenter. But he wanted a bigger life. Anyway, we moved here, and we started a long process of renovation. We weren't going to be able to open for guests for several months." She took a moment before continuing. "One night, there was a bad storm, and Richard went outside to check that the oceanfront windows were covered with wood so the glass wouldn't break. I was asleep when he left. I didn't know what had happened until the sheriff knocked on my door and told me a tourist had found Richard's body on the beach." Her lips tightened. "He must have gotten disoriented in the wind and the fog and slipped off the bluffs."

"I'm sorry," I said, seeing what appeared to be genuine pain in her eyes. "That must have been awful."

"It wasn't supposed to end like that for him, for me, for us..."

Silence followed her words. I wasn't sure exactly what to say.

Her story matched some of what I'd read in the old newspaper, but I didn't think she'd told me everything. And while it was a sensitive subject to broach, I had to do it. I had no idea if this would be the first and the last conversation we would have. "Why are there rumors that my father killed him?"

She gave me a startled look. "Is that what you heard from your dad?"

"No. I told you he didn't tell me anything. I read an old article about Richard's death. And then Margaret—"

"That damn woman is always spreading gossip," Ellen said sharply. "And she doesn't care who she hurts."

"So, you don't think my father killed his father?"

"Of course not."

"Then why would anyone else?"

"Because they argued a lot, especially when David was at the Boatworks. He didn't want to be there. He didn't want that to be his life, but Richard was determined that that's what he would do, and he told him he wouldn't pay for college. If he wanted out, he'd have to earn it." She paused. "Margaret's son worked at the Boatworks. I think he told her about a fight that got physical between them a few weeks before Richard died. That's where the gossip started."

"Did my father hear about the gossip?"

"Yes, but he wasn't that bothered by it, because he knew he didn't do it."

"Why did my dad leave a month later if he wasn't bothered by the gossip?"

She took a quick breath, then said, "Because he'd been wanting to leave for a long time, and now he could. That's really all I have to say."

"That isn't nearly enough. If my dad just left to go to college and have a different career, why did he stop talking to you? You were a widow. You had just lost your husband. And my father just turns his back and walks away? That doesn't make sense."

"He was angry with me, too. He didn't think I supported him

enough with his father. He told me he was done, and he left."
Her tone turned hard and cold. "I never heard from him again. I
never knew where he went or what he did. In the beginning, a
few of his friends tried to tell me, but I shut them down. I didn't
want to know until he wanted me to know. And he never did. He
could be stubborn, just like his father."

"And like you," I commented. "As the years passed, didn't
you ever want to look him up, to find out if he'd married or had
children?"

"He always knew where I was. If he wanted me in his life, he
would have told me."

I shook my head in bemusement. "I don't think I could have
let my child disappear like that and have absolutely no contact. I
feel like you're leaving something out."

"We've talked enough about the past. Let's discuss the
present and the future. You should go home, Cassidy. Your life
isn't here." She paused, tilting her head as she gave me a speculative look. "Does your father know you're here?"

"No. We're not that close."

"Does he know about your podcast?"

"I mentioned it when we first started it, but I don't think he
was listening. He just said it sounded like a foolish waste of time.
He was often disappointed in me. Ironic, since his father was
disappointed in him. Knowing what that felt like, he should have
acted differently."

"If David never wanted you to come here, to know me, to
learn about his past, then you should respect his wishes and go
home."

"I had more than one reason for coming here, and you know
that."

"There's nothing to find here, Cassidy. There is no crime."

"If there's nothing to find, then why did someone try to kill
me last night?"

"Tom said that you probably got spooked by the road and a
fast driver behind you."

"Finn saw the other car. It's not just my word being questioned. And I don't know why the sheriff is so determined to make up an alternative story for my accident. Just like he's so determined to force everyone to believe that the women who stayed here and were never seen again just chose to leave and disappear. I don't think that's what happened." I paused, unable to read her very guarded gaze.

"It is what happened," she said. "And Anna didn't disappear. I walked her to the door, and a friend picked her up."

"Before dawn? Why so early?"

"It was when her friend arrived."

"Anna had bruises on her body. She was scared, jumpy."

"She'd gotten away from an abusive situation," Ellen said. "And I was happy to put her safely in her friend's car."

"Who's the friend? Can I talk to her? Can I talk to Anna, confirm she's safe?"

"Anna didn't want anyone to know where she was going in case her past caught up to her. There are reasons people choose to disappear, Cassidy. Did you ever consider that you might be jeopardizing their safety by publicly talking about all this?"

"Did you ever consider that something bad happened to them either here at the inn or just after they left?" I countered.

"There's never been any evidence of that."

I was getting really tired of that line. "Everyone keeps saying that, but maybe there is no evidence because no one wanted to look for any. I understand that the sheriff wants to protect the reputation of the town, and I'm sure you feel the same way about this inn. But I would also think you would care enough about these women to want to find out what happened to them."

"I care about all my guests. But this is an inn. People come and go every single day. I don't know where they go. I can't go looking for everyone."

"How about just Natalie? How about we just focus on her? Or maybe on Natalie and Jessica."

"Jessica lost her life because she took a boat out without

having enough experience to deal with the changing ocean conditions, and Natalie simply left. If she disappeared after that, it's because she wanted to start over. No one at the inn had anything to do with either of those events. There's nothing bad going on here."

"Nothing bad? I almost died last night," I repeated. "And Tessa thinks someone pushed her down the stairs."

"That absolutely did not happen. I can vouch for every one of my employees."

"You know someone put a note under our door telling us to leave. What about that?"

"I explained about the teenagers."

"Yes. You have a lot of explanations, but I think you're wrong about the note, about the car, and maybe about Tessa."

"Your friend was drunk."

"Tessa was drinking, but it looks like she might have been drugged by Nathan Carmichael, who wanted her to forget he told her he found Jessica's diamond ring on the beach and kept it to sell."

Her gaze widened, and for the first time, it felt like I was actually telling her something she didn't already know.

"I don't know anything about that," she said. "He found a ring?"

"Apparently so, but he didn't tell anyone about it. Nathan also suggested that Jessica made it to shore alive and disappeared after that."

"Well, that actually supports what Tom believes, that Jessica had a reason to disappear, and that's how she chose to do it. I prefer that scenario than that she died at sea."

It was frustrating to have every theory I came up with rebuffed. Either my grandmother clearly believed that nothing had happened to anyone, or she was an excellent actress.

"I need to get to work," Ellen said, abruptly ending our conversation. "What are your plans?"

"I'd like to stay here for another day or two. Tessa won't be able to travel back to New York until the weekend, and I need to figure out what to do about a car, since the one we borrowed from Tessa's roommate is now in the ocean. Is there a car rental agency in town?"

"Not in Stonecross, but there's one in Cork Harbor."

"Okay."

"I'm not sure why you want to stay here. You clearly think I've done something to hurt these women."

"I don't think that, but I do believe you don't want to look at the situation too closely. Or consider the fact that someone else here might not be who you think they are."

"Are you talking about Ray?"

"He's an ex-con."

"You have done your research. Which means you know that he served his time and has had no problems since he was released. You don't have to be afraid of him. He looks rougher and tougher than he is."

"That's good to hear."

Ellen hesitated, then said, "You can stay until your friend is ready to leave, but you can't record or film in your room, and you can't interrogate my employees. Obviously, I can't stop you from talking to people in town or filming elsewhere, but this inn is meant to be a sanctuary for my guests, and I already had two check out this morning based on what they heard last night. Those are my terms. Take it or leave it."

"I'll take it. But I have a condition, too."

"I don't think you're in a position to be making conditions," Ellen said tartly.

I ignored that. "We talk again, at least once, maybe twice, and you tell me more about you, your family, about my father's childhood, and where I come from."

"David won't like that."

"But I will. And it's my decision, not his."

A small glint of admiration flitted through her eyes, but it was gone so fast I was sure I'd just imagined it. "All right. But now I have to get to work." As she stood up, she said, "I have a car you can use. It's in the garage. It's the blue Mini Cooper." She walked over to her desk and pulled out a key. Before she handed it over, she gave me a serious look. "If what you've told me is true, be careful."

"I'm going to try," I said as I took the key. "Thank you." As I left her apartment, I wasn't sure why either of us had agreed that I could stay at the inn or that we would talk again, because both seemed like perilous propositions.

CHAPTER EIGHTEEN

As I left Ellen's apartment, I paused in the corridor, my gaze drawn to a door at the far end. It was painted the same cream color as the walls, easy to miss if you weren't looking for it. A door that led somewhere—maybe to storage, maybe to a basement, or maybe to something else entirely.

I took a step toward it, then stopped. Ellen would be coming out any minute, and I couldn't risk getting caught snooping around her private quarters after she'd just agreed to let me stay. I'd come back later.

Turning, I headed back down the hallway, out the side entrance, and through the garden, ending up on the yoga deck, which was currently empty.

The morning air was crisp and a little salty. I walked to the edge of the property where the perfectly manicured lawn gave way to wild grass and then to nothing—just the sheer drop of the cliffs.

I stood there, looking down at the rocks and churning water far below, thinking about my grandfather. He'd allegedly come out here to nail some boards over the windows, to check on the property, and somehow ended up farther away from the house than he'd intended. He'd fallen to his death, and I felt almost dizzy as I looked down at the steep, treacherous drop.

In fog and wind, he could have taken a misstep. But it also felt like every other story I'd heard in Stonecross. Plausible but not entirely convincing. A neat explanation that raised more questions than it answered.

"Cassidy?"

I turned to find Becca approaching, her yoga mat bag slung over her shoulder. She looked concerned, her usual serene expression replaced with worry.

"I heard what happened to you last night," she said. "Are you okay?"

"I'm sore, but alive."

"Thank God for that. Tyler told me someone ran you off the road. That's terrifying." Becca shook her head. "I can't believe something like that would happen here." She adjusted the strap on her shoulder. "I've decided to take a break for a few weeks, until some of the rumors get sorted out. I just don't feel comfortable being here, which is kind of sad, because I always thought this beautiful deck overlooking the wild sea was the perfect place for people to get in touch with their inner spirit. But now there's nothing but a bad vibe around here. And when I told Ellen my decision to leave for a few weeks, even she seemed a little defeated."

"Did she say anything? Did she try to convince you there was nothing wrong?"

"She said she was disappointed and hoped I'd be back soon. That her guests love my classes, and she'll have a hard time replacing me. She was actually very nice about it." Becca paused. "I know Ellen comes across cold and hard at times, and after Tyler told me about his suspicions of her, I've started looking at her differently. But I still have a difficult time believing she could be involved with the disappearances of several of her female guests. She's very pro-female empowerment. That's why she has focused the inn's offerings on health and wellness."

I wondered whether that was the real reason, or if focusing on health and wellness programs had been the perfect draw for single, sometimes lonely, vulnerable women.

"Anyway," Becca said. "It was nice to meet you, Cassidy. I hope you get the answers you're looking for."

"Can I ask you one other question? Did you have much contact with Natalie Warren when she was here? Was she friendly, outgoing? Did she talk about her life with you or anyone else?"

"She took two of my classes and seemed to enjoy them. She wasn't jumpy like Anna or some of the others, but it felt like there was an air of sadness surrounding her." Becca paused. "She did mention she was having headaches, and we talked about stretches that might help. She was also going to see Dr. Garrett about it. Actually, I think the doctor was coming to the inn."

"A doctor who makes house calls?" I asked in surprise.

Becca smiled. "Ellen likes to provide the best service she can to every guest. She asked Dr. Garrett to stop by and talk to Natalie, but I don't know if they ever actually met. I just know what she told me." Becca gave me a speculative look. "Are you working with Tyler? It seems like you have similar interests. Only, he's looking for Jessica Trent."

"We've been comparing notes in case Natalie and Jessica are connected," I admitted.

"I spoke to Tyler a short while ago. I told him that a friend of mine who works at the harbor saw Jessica talking to Cole the day she rented the boat and thought they seemed pretty friendly."

"She just brought that up now?" I asked curiously.

"Well, your podcast has gotten a lot of people talking, and she mentioned it to me this morning, wondering if it was important. I told her she should talk to the sheriff and see what he thought. But she didn't seem to want to do that since Cole is the sheriff's son. Tyler said he was going to follow up with Cole."

"That's good."

"Cole is a nice kid. He's a flirt and drinks too much and likes to mix it up at the bar, but I don't think he's dangerous in any way. I'm sure he was chatting it up with Jessica. She was very pretty."

"I didn't realize he was a big flirt. I thought he and Sophie were together."

She shrugged. "I think they're more friends than anything, but I don't know. Anyway, I should go. Good luck."

"Thanks."

After Becca left, I walked back to the parking lot, thinking about Cole and Jessica. It was probably nothing. Cole worked at the docks with his uncle. She could have been asking him about renting a boat. But I wondered if there was any record of Cole saying he'd spoken to her; probably not, since his father was the sheriff and wouldn't want his son's name on anything that had to do with a missing woman.

As I moved into the garage, I noticed that Ray's truck was gone, and the storage door now had a padlock on it. I wondered if that had something to do with me mentioning that carpet to Ellen. They clearly didn't want me poking into anything else.

I got into Ellen's blue Mini Cooper. It felt surreal to be borrowing my grandmother's car. And I couldn't imagine what my father would say if he knew. At some point, I would tell him, but I had to find out more about my grandmother before I did that.

I was almost to town when my phone buzzed, and Tyler's number flashed across the screen.

"Hi," I said, putting the phone on speaker.

"How are you feeling today?"

"I've got some aches and pains but overall, I'm okay."

"That's good to hear." He cleared his throat. "I went to get coffee this morning, and the place was buzzing with gossip, all of it centered on you."

"Yes. The town found out about my podcast. Cole told his father, who told Ellen, and it spread from there."

"They weren't just talking about the podcast, Cassidy."

My stomach tightened at the suddenly hard note in his voice. "No, I guess they wouldn't be. Last night I had a confrontation with Ellen. She wanted to kick me out, and I couldn't let her do that, so I had to tell her something that she wasn't expecting."

"That you're her granddaughter."

"Yes."

"Was that a story to get her to let you stay or the truth?"

"It was the truth. My real name is Cassidy Clarke. Bennett is my mother's maiden name. I never knew anything about Ellen. My father refused to speak one word about his mother or his father or his past. And when I realized where Natalie had stayed right before she disappeared, I knew this was the story I had follow."

"I have to say I did not see that coming. You've had a hidden agenda all along."

"Not really. My main goal is to find out what's going on at the inn. But I do want to know more about my grandmother, too."

"You should have told me. I thought we'd built some trust between us."

"My personal story wasn't relevant."

"Not relevant?" he challenged. "Your grandmother could very well be trafficking or killing women. And you don't believe your relationship is relevant?"

"Think of it as a good thing. Maybe she'll open up to me now that she knows who I am."

"Well, she probably won't kill you, so I guess that's a positive," he said, a hard edge to his voice.

"I'm sorry, Tyler. I should have told you. I just didn't know what to say or whether I should bring it up. I wasn't even sure I was ever going to tell Ellen, because I don't particularly like her, and I definitely don't trust her. But I had to use the information so she wouldn't force me to leave."

"And is she talking to you?"

"We've had one brief conversation that didn't illuminate much of anything. But I'm hoping it's a start." I paused. "I ran into Becca. She said she talked to you about how Cole was seen chatting with Jessica the day she rented the boat."

"I just spoke to him. He said she just asked where she could rent a small boat. Since Holloway Charters doesn't rent small boats, he directed her to the Boat Deck, run by Stan Mitchell. He said he talked to Jessica for five minutes, and that was it."

"Did you believe him?"

"I don't know what to think about Cole. There's something about him that bothers me," Tyler said.

"Really? You think a twenty-three-year-old kid is responsible for what's happening?"

"Maybe not responsible, but a part of...possibly. I stopped by the building department, but the clerk told me I need to come back at three if I want to talk to someone about the plans for the inn. Apparently, only one guy can give me that information, and he's out until then."

"That's too bad. Where are you now? Should we meet up?"

"I'm driving to Cork Harbor. I want to see if I can find any buildings near that stretch of road that Jessica might have climbed up to, and see if they have any video footage."

"Did you want me to come with you?"

"I've got it. You could probably use a break today after everything you've been through. We'll talk later."

"Okay." As I put the phone down, I felt a little disappointed in Tyler's cool tone. But I couldn't blame him for feeling blindsided by the secret I'd held back. Now he seemed to believe I'd somehow joined Ellen's team, which wasn't the case, although I could see why he would think that.

As someone who was committed to family, Tyler probably believed that blood trumped everything. But while Ellen and I might be related, we didn't know each other. If Ellen was involved in Natalie's disappearance, I wasn't going to defend her or try to save her. In fact, it would just be corroboration for why my father had never wanted me to have anything to do with her.

A part of me wanted to pick up the phone and call my dad,

but I knew I wouldn't get what I wanted out of that conversation. He'd be furious that I'd come to Stonecross, and he wouldn't tell me a thing. I would have to figure this out on my own.

I pulled into the lot next to Kelly's Pub just before one. It was busy, but a bunch of people seemed to be finishing up and heading out.

I slipped onto a stool at the bar, and as Finn came out of the kitchen to drop off a burger to a customer a few stools down from me, he gave me a quick nod.

After taking care of that customer, he came over. "How are you feeling today, Cassidy?"

"Better. I wanted to thank you again for saving me."

"I'm happy I was there." He paused. "Have you eaten? Can I get you some lunch?"

"That would be great. I feel like a cheeseburger."

"You've got it." He paused. "I'd like to talk to you. Maybe after this rush dies down, and you've had a chance to eat?"

"That sounds good. I'd like to talk to you, too."

"I'll put a rush on that burger."

As Finn disappeared into the kitchen, a waitress set down a glass of water in front of me, and I took a refreshing drink as my gaze moved around the pub. The only familiar face belonged to Margaret, the librarian. She and another woman were just getting up after paying their bill.

As she neared me, she gave me a surprised smile. "Cassidy, right?"

"You remembered."

"Yes, and I've been hearing your name a lot today." She paused, turning her head to the woman next to her, an attractive blonde woman in her early fifties. "This is Cassidy, Ellen's granddaughter," Margaret said, then looked back at me. "And this is Joanne Garrett, our town doctor."

I straightened. "Dr. Garrett. I was just talking to Becca about you earlier today."

"Oh, why is that?" the doctor asked warily.

"Becca mentioned that you saw Natalie Warren when she was staying at the inn."

"Yes, I did. I already spoke to the sheriff about my very short conversation with her."

"Can I ask what it was about?"

"No," Dr. Garrett replied, her voice clipped and annoyed. "I believe very strongly in doctor-patient confidentiality."

"Of course. I'm just trying to find out what happened to her."

"Yes, I know. Margaret was just telling me about your podcast. I'll have to take a listen. I need to get back to work. It was lovely to meet you."

"You too," I murmured.

Margaret lingered behind. "Now I know why you were so interested in the history of the inn and Ellen and Richard's relationship."

"I would like to know more about my family," I said.

"I can't believe David had a daughter, although I don't know why that would surprise me. He left when he was eighteen years old. I'm sure he's had a complete and wonderful life since then."

"He's very successful. He runs an investment company."

"I always knew he was a smart kid. And he had big ambitions. Good to see they worked out for him. But sad that he doesn't ever come back to see his mother."

"When we spoke last, you said you thought he might have left because of the rumors about his father's death, but that doesn't explain why he stopped talking to my grandmother."

"I don't know, dear. Ellen is a closed book. It's very difficult to get her to open up about anything. But you might have the best chance of making that happen."

As the server dropped off my food, Margaret said goodbye, leaving me to wonder whether the doctor's visit to the inn could shed any light on Natalie's disappearance. But Dr. Garrett wasn't going to talk to me, and whatever she'd said to the sheriff had no doubt been erased or made to look like nothing.

The cheeseburger was so delicious that I stopped thinking and concentrated on eating. It was the first real meal I'd had since lunch yesterday, and I was suddenly starving.

Finn came over when I'd finished. By then, the pub had cleared out with only a few tables finishing their meals.

"How was it?" he asked.

"Great," I said. "Best meal I've had in a long time."

"Good." His blue-eyed gaze clung to mine for a long second, sending an odd tingle down my spine. "So, you're full of surprises, Cassidy. I thought the podcast was your only secret, but you were holding on to a much bigger one."

I nodded. "Yes, I'm Ellen's granddaughter. My father is David Clarke."

"And Ellen didn't know? She didn't recognize you?"

"She didn't even know I existed. She told me she has never had any contact with my father since he left, and that she never looked him up. He knew where she was. If he wanted to get in touch, he would have."

"That's cold but also sounds like Ellen."

"I don't really understand her, but there's a lot I don't know or understand. I didn't just come to Stonecross for the podcast; I came because I wanted to know who she was and why my father left. But she told me I need to ask my father if I want to know why, and I've already done that, so I'm not sure how I'm ever going to get any answers."

"I'm sure someone around here knows something."

"I doubt anyone will talk to me. I just asked Margaret, and she declined to answer. I'm an outsider, and, clearly, this town protects its own."

An odd light entered his eyes. "Well, I'm not an outsider, and I know some people who might be able to help."

"Really?" A tiny seed of hope took hold. "Who?"

"My father went to school with David Clarke. And I think my mom was a year or two younger but also in the same school."

"Would your father talk to me about him?"

"Well, he'd talk to me, and if you're there, too..."

"When can we go?" I asked impatiently.

He smiled. "Why don't we go now? I'm ready for a break. Just give me a minute."

"Of course. Thank you."

"Don't thank me yet. We haven't learned anything."

"I'm just appreciative that you're willing to help me. I'm sorry I accused you of running me off the road."

"I can see how you jumped to that conclusion."

"It wasn't just that you were there so fast; it was also what happened with Tessa," I said honestly.

He frowned. "I get it. How is she doing?"

"She's hanging in there. Improving every day."

"Good. I'll be back in a minute."

"Let me pay for this."

He held up a hand. "It's on me."

"You don't have to do that."

"I don't have to, but I want to. Don't worry about it."

As he went into the kitchen, I wondered if I should leave with him. While he hadn't run me off the road, I still didn't quite understand what had happened with Tessa and Nathan, who was his friend. Maybe I'd take my own car, or at least my grandmother's car, just to keep a little more control over my circumstances.

When Finn was ready to leave, we walked out to the parking lot. "I can drive," he said. "You obviously don't have your car."

"Ellen lent me her car."

"Okay, but I can still drive. It's not far."

"I'll follow you."

Something flickered in his expression—understanding, maybe, or disappointment. He knew I couldn't entirely trust him. Not after everything that had happened.

"That works," he said simply.

I got into my car and followed Finn through town and up a winding road. When he turned down Spring Lane, I realized this must be where my father had grown up. Ellen had said they'd lived in a house on Spring Lane before they'd bought the inn. Now, I wished I'd gone with Finn so I could have asked him which of the older, well-maintained, mostly two-story houses had been my father's childhood home.

Finn pulled over in front of a two-story colonial with blue shutters. I parked behind him and got out.

"That's your parents' house?" I asked, pointing to the blue colonial.

"Yeah. And there, the yellow Victorian—" He pointed three houses down. "That's where your father lived."

"So close."

"My parents moved into the house my father grew up in after his parents passed away. So aside from about eight years, my father has always lived on this street."

"It's pretty here. And this is where you grew up?"

He nodded. "Yes."

"You must have had a nice childhood."

"We did. But Sophie can't wait to get out of here." He gave me a smile. "I actually understand that feeling. I couldn't wait to leave, either. I enlisted when I was eighteen. Spent twelve years in the service. Probably would have stayed longer if my dad hadn't had a stroke."

"You came home for him?"

"I couldn't let the pub go under. He'd put his life into it."

"That's very admirable."

He shrugged. "Family is family. My mom still works, and she was busy juggling that job and taking care of him. Sophie helps out a lot, but she couldn't manage it by herself, so I'm here."

"Forever?" I queried.

"I don't think in terms of forever. Just for now."

"What does your mom do?"

"She's a seamstress. She works at the dry cleaners in town.

Aside from the usual tailoring, she makes everyone's special-occasion clothes. She's actually been sewing a wedding gown this week, so she's been working from home. You'll be able to meet both of them."

"Is your dad up for this? If he's sick, I don't want to upset him."

"He's much better now. Almost back to his old self. He keeps threatening to come back and take over the bar."

"Would that bother you?"

"No. But my mother would prefer he not get caught up in the stress of all that again."

As we crossed the street, my gaze moved back to the yellow house. "Do you know who lives in my dad's old house now?"

"A couple with two kids. They moved in about five years ago. Moved up here from Boston so they could live in a small town."

"Do you live with your parents?" I asked as we walked up to the front door.

"No, I have an apartment in town." He opened the door and stepped inside. "Mom, Dad, we have a visitor."

The house was warm and smelled like cookies. The woman who came out of the kitchen with curly brown hair and blue eyes, much like her son, wore an apron covered with flour.

"Finn, what are you doing here?" she asked with surprise.

"I brought someone for you to meet. This is Cassidy Clarke, Ellen's granddaughter. My mother, Katherine Kelly."

"Hello," I said.

"Oh, my goodness." Her gaze ran across my face with surprise. "I had no idea Ellen had a granddaughter. Or that David had a daughter, for that matter."

"What's going on here?" an older man said as he shuffled down the hall.

Finn's dad's hair was gray, but he also had warm blue eyes like his son.

"This is Ellen's granddaughter, Cassidy, John," Katherine told her husband. "David's daughter."

"Seriously? That's surprising. I've often wondered what happened to David. Is he with you?"

"No. He's in Connecticut. That's where he lives." I cleared my throat. "I actually don't know anything about Ellen or my dad's life here. He never wanted to talk about it, and Finn said you might be able to tell me about his childhood, that you knew him."

John nodded. "David and I were in the same grade, and he lived right down the street."

"And I was a year younger," Katherine put in. "But I knew him, too. Why don't we go into the living room and sit down? I just made some cookies. I'll bring them out. Would you like something to drink? I can make tea."

"You don't need to go to any trouble," I said.

"Oh, it's no trouble. Sit." She waved her hand toward the living room.

I followed Finn and his father into the room. His dad settled in the brown leather recliner while Finn and I sat on the couch. There was a ball game on the TV, but John instantly muted it.

"So, what do you want to know, Cassidy?" John asked.

"Well, my dad never wanted to talk about his past or his family. It feels like something terrible happened to cause that rift, but he won't say what it was, and when I asked my grandmother, she said it was his story to tell. But he's not going to talk, and neither is she, and I need to do something to end the standoff. If I could get some insight into what could have occurred, that would be helpful. Also, I would just love to know more about him as a kid."

"Well, I don't really know what happened between David and his mother. I have my theories, like everyone else. But it's their truth to tell or not tell." He paused as Katherine came into the room with a plate of cookies.

"The water is just heating up for our tea," she said, sitting in the chair across from the couch. "But you can start with a cookie. These are chocolate chip with coconut and oatmeal, my special mix."

I picked up a small napkin and a cookie, taking a bite to be polite, but the cookie might have been one of the most amazing cookies I'd ever tasted. "Wow," I said with genuine sincerity. "This is a great cookie."

Katherine smiled. "I am known for them."

"How do you have time to bake cookies?" Finn asked. "I thought you were swamped with sewing that wedding dress."

"I was, but the bride is postponing the wedding for a few weeks because her brother was in an accident. He's going to be all right, but they want to wait until he can be there."

"Sorry to hear that."

"Luckily, it's going to be easy enough for them to reschedule. Since I had some breathing room, I decided to bake." Katherine gave me a smile. "Now, you want to know about your father."

"She wants to know why David left," John interjected.

"We wish we knew," Katherine said.

"Margaret told me there were rumors that my father and grandfather got in a fight and during that fight, my grandfather fell to his death. She suggested that my grandmother sent him away, and that's why they never spoke again. But my grandmother said that my grandfather's death was an accident, and that it was ridiculous for anyone to think that David killed his father. But she didn't offer me a better explanation for why they're estranged."

"Richard and David were fighting in the months before his death," John said. "Richard wanted David to work in the family business. David wanted to leave town and go to college. Richard said he was deserting his family. David said he wanted to live his own life, that kind of thing."

"But there's no way David killed his father," Katherine said. "I agree with Ellen on that."

"At least not on purpose," John said. "It could have been an accident that occurred while they were fighting."

"I'd like to believe my father isn't a killer. But if he had done something to his dad, I don't understand why my father would be so angry at my grandmother. It seems like she should be the one who is furious and resentful for what he'd done."

"That's why I never bought into that story," Katherine said. "I thought there was something else going on with David. He had a lot of problems around that time."

"What kind of problems?" I asked curiously.

John and Katherine exchanged a brief look, then John said, "David was sweet on a girl named Lily. She was two years younger than us. Very pretty."

"But she had a hard family life," Katherine said. "Dad had a drinking problem. Mother had to work to make ends meet, and sometimes Lily and her mother looked like they'd taken a few punches, but they'd never told that to the sheriff, when he was called out a few times."

"Did my father go out with this girl?"

"David wanted to take her out," John said. "But Tom Holloway had staked his claim, and Lily seemed caught between them."

I was surprised by his words. "My father was in a love triangle with the sheriff?"

"Well, Tom wasn't the sheriff then; his dad was. And Tom was a troublemaker. Rumor has it that his dad used to knock him around, which is why he usually came out swinging when someone tried to cross him," John said.

"Tom told David to stay away from Lily," Katherine continued. "But David didn't want to listen. He was in love with Lily, and after his dad died, I think David was a little out of his mind. He was pressuring Lily to break up with Tom, and Tom was telling her that she couldn't leave him. I think Lily was scared of both of them. They were eighteen; she was sixteen. She was out of her depth."

I felt like they were describing someone passionate and

romantic, and that didn't sound at all like my father. "What happened? Who won?"

Katherine's smile turned sad. "Nobody. Lily ended up taking her own life."

I clapped a hand to my mouth. "Oh, my God, the girl who committed suicide, who drowned at the beach below the inn —her name was Lily? That's the girl my father was mad about?"

Katherine nodded. "Yes. She left a note by her clothes on the beach, saying she was sorry, but she couldn't go on anymore. She didn't mention David or Tom, and everyone knew her home life was bad, so she had a lot of reasons to be unhappy beyond them."

"And that's when my dad left?"

"Pretty much right after the funeral," Katherine said. "I think it was too much for him, losing his dad, all the rumors swirling around him, and Ellen was also in a bad place, which is understandable since she'd just lost her husband. The next thing we knew, David was gone, and Ellen said she didn't know when he'd come back."

"For years, we thought he was just at college somewhere," John said. "But we never knew where. Katherine and I moved to California to go to college and live a different life, so we lost touch."

I was less interested in John and Katherine's story than I was in my father's. "Did anyone stay connected to my dad? This is a small town. Didn't he have friends?"

"We all scattered after graduation, and David didn't seem interested in talking to anyone from here."

"And Ellen doesn't talk about him at all," Katherine said. "I once asked her about him. It was probably at least ten years ago now. She said she didn't know what he was up to, and she would prefer that I not speak his name to her. So, I didn't. She's a little on the intimidating side."

"I'll say," I muttered. "She just found out I'm her granddaughter last night, and I'm not sure she knows how to feel about that."

"She has to be happy," Katherine said. "I'm sure she misses David. And now she has a granddaughter."

"I didn't tell her who I was when I first got here. I actually also came because I have a podcast that investigates true crime stories, and my friend and I were looking into Natalie Warren's disappearance. The fact that it happened at my grandmother's inn made it a story I had to follow."

"I heard something about a podcast when I went to the market this morning. I didn't realize that was you."

"That was me."

"Well, I don't know what's going on at that inn, and I'm concerned about Sophie working there," Katherine said.

"I told Sophie to quit," Finn said. "I'll lend her the money she needs to go to New York."

Katherine looked rather pained at that statement. "I keep hoping she'll change her mind, but I know she won't, and I can't blame her. I had to live somewhere else, too." She paused. "I just got you back, Finn, and I hate to see her go, but I know everyone has to live their own life, and if there is something happening at the inn, then I don't want her there, either."

"Tom said that there's nothing to that disappearance, that the woman just wanted to start her life over, and she had a right to do that," John interjected.

"Tom needs to work a little harder," Finn said. "Because Cassidy has brought up some good points, and it's not just one woman with a mysterious disappearance; there are a couple."

"I didn't realize that," John said with concern.

"I don't have any proof," I said. "I just know that too many things have happened that don't make sense and can't be explained away with this plausible doubt I keep hearing."

"Well, that makes me more nervous," Katherine said. "How long are you going to stay at the inn? Are you concerned about your grandmother, about getting hurt?" Her gaze swept my face.

"I didn't want to ask, but were you in an accident? You have cuts on your face. That didn't happen at the inn, did it?"

"No. My car was run off the road last night. Finn actually rescued me."

"You did?" Katherine asked in surprise. "How did that happen?"

"There was a detour, and I ended up on the Upper Ocean Road, not too far behind Cassidy," Finn said.

"Someone ran you off the road?" John questioned, a sharp note in his voice now.

Before I could defend myself against another speculative question, Finn said, "Yes, someone did. I saw the other car. Unfortunately, I was too far away to see the make or the license plate."

"Why would someone want to hurt you?" Katherine asked, concern in her gaze.

"Because I'm asking questions. I'm shaking things up, and someone doesn't like that." I paused, then said, "My grandmother seems very sincere in her belief that Natalie checked out on her own, and her disappearance has nothing to do with the inn. You've known her a long time. Should I believe her?"

"That's a big question," Katherine said. "And we were David's generation. While I've had many short, casual conversations with Ellen over the years, I can't say we're close. I think the fact that we were David's friends has made her less interested in talking to us. We remind her of him."

"But Tom Holloway was David's age, and they seem very tight," Finn put in.

I thought about that. It did seem like an anomaly that Tom would be close to Ellen, since he'd been in David's class, and they'd had that alleged love triangle. But Tom hadn't liked David, and maybe that animosity had been easier for my grandmother to deal with once David had turned his back on her. "Perhaps she looks at Tom as the son she never had," I suggested. "Tom stayed and followed in his father's footsteps when David refused to do that."

"That's a good point," John murmured. "Personally, I never liked Tom that much, and I still don't. He's always had a short fuse, and it's worse now since his divorce. He rides his son hard, and Cole is unhappy and mixed up, too. I think he needs to get out of here more than Sophie does."

As the kettle began to sing, Katherine got up to get their tea.

After she left, John said, "I think you should be careful, Cassidy. If your father didn't want you to know his mother, your grandmother, then I think he had a pretty damn good reason."

"I just wish I knew what that reason could be."

"Well, I thought the rumors about David killing his father were completely unbelievable. But I always wondered if Ellen didn't have something to do with it."

I sat up straighter at John's unexpected words. "Why?"

"Because David left and never came back. Because he doesn't speak of his mother, and his mother doesn't speak of him. That sounds like a deep, painful trauma, and I can't imagine that trauma could be tied to something as simple as him not wanting to run the Boatworks. It had to be more than that."

"Maybe it was Lily's death," Finn said. "That's when he left."

"Perhaps, but why would he blame his mother for that?"

My heart began to race. "Was Lily's body ever recovered?"

"No, sadly, it was not," John replied.

"Oh, God," I murmured, looking over at Finn, who had the same awareness in his eyes.

"What?" John asked. "What are you thinking?"

"That Lily might have been the first girl to disappear from the inn, and maybe Ellen is responsible for that, too."

CHAPTER NINETEEN

Finn and I left his parents' house a half hour later. When we got to our cars, Finn said, "I think we should keep talking, Cassidy. About Lily being the first one to disappear."

"It was a long time ago, and it wasn't like the others. I could be wrong."

"Or you could be right. The way your father left and the fact that he has never wanted you to have contact with your grandmother, he either thought she had something to do with his father's death or with Lily's death—maybe both. I can't think of any other reason he would have cut off all ties with his mother. Have you thought about asking him?"

"Only like a million times, but every time I have tried in the past, his reaction is stone-cold anger. Our relationship is so tenuous, I feel like if I do one more thing wrong, it will snap, and that will be it, and I won't have family anymore."

"Why is it so tenuous?"

"It's a long story."

"I want to keep talking," he repeated. "About everything, and I want a chance to talk to you about what happened with Tessa and Nathan."

"I thought you told me everything you knew about that."

"I thought I did, too, but maybe I missed something. I think we should go over everything again. You need an ally, Cassidy."

His words reminded me of Tyler, but I wasn't sure he was my ally now that he'd realized I'd kept a big secret from him.

"And I want to help you figure out what's going on at that inn," Finn continued. "This is my hometown. This is where my parents and sister live, where I have a business. If someone is hurting female tourists, then I want to stop them."

"You're the first person in this town to say anything close to that."

"Why don't we go to my apartment? We can talk freely there, better than if we go to the inn."

I hesitated, and his gaze shifted.

"You're afraid to come to my apartment." he said flatly. "I guess I can't blame you."

"Is there somewhere we could talk that isn't your apartment? The beach, a garden, a park—maybe we could take a walk?"

"I know a spot. Follow me."

"Where are we going?" I asked as we walked to our cars.

He gave me a smile that made my heart skip a beat, and I had no idea what that was about.

"You'll find out," he said.

"Well, don't lose me," I told him.

"I won't," he said, his words seeming to have more meaning than they should have.

———

Finn led me through town and down a narrow road I hadn't noticed before. It wound along the coastline, away from the main tourist areas, until we reached a small parking lot near a weathered lighthouse. The white tower stood sentinel over rocky outcroppings that jutted into the sea, and a narrow path led down to a sheltered cove.

"This is beautiful," I said as we met up.

"It's one of my favorite places. Most tourists don't know about it. The main lighthouse is on the other side of town—bigger, more photogenic. This one's been decommissioned for years, but the town keeps it maintained." He gestured toward the path. "There's a bench down there where you can watch the water. It's peaceful."

We walked down the rocky path in silence. The wind carried the smell of salt and seaweed, and gulls squealed overhead, their cries echoing off the cliffs. When we reached the bottom, I saw what he meant—an old wooden bench sat on a flat outcropping, protected from the worst of the wind by the curve of the rocks.

We sat down, and for a moment neither of us spoke. The endless ocean stretched out before us, the waves rolling in with rhythmic persistence.

"I used to come here when I was a kid," Finn said finally. "When things got loud at home, and I needed to think."

"Things got loud?" I queried.

"Sophie is ten years younger than me. My parents tried for years to have a second kid, and when she came along, they were ecstatic. I was also thrilled to have a baby sister. But she was a loud baby and a loud toddler and a loud kid."

I smiled at his description. "So, you're saying she was loud..."

He smiled back at me. "I guess she was a typical kid, but by the time I was a teenager, I just felt like I needed to be out of the toy-filled chaos of our home so I could think about what I wanted to do with my life."

"That makes sense. And I can relate to needing quiet at times. I live in one of the noisiest cities in the world. Sirens blare all night long. Sometimes, I put the pillow over my head and ears so I can dull the sound, but then I tell myself I'm lucky to be living in New York, that it's where the opportunities are."

"To be a journalist or a podcaster? Or both?"

"That's not an easy question to answer. I always wanted to be a reporter, to write the story that everyone talks about, that changes lives forever, that speaks truth to power, but I'm finding that the reality of that kind of investigative work is pretty terrifying."

"And yet you haven't quit. You haven't run away. That says a lot about you."

"Some people might say that means I'm stupid," I said with a self-deprecating smile.

"Or some might call it brave. I personally lean toward brave. But maybe that's because I saw you last night, inches away from losing your life, and here you are today, back in the fight. And you're fighting for someone you don't even know. Natalie Warren wasn't a friend, was she?" he suddenly asked. "Is there more you haven't told me?"

"No. She wasn't a friend. We were looking for a cold case that we could relate to, that our audience could relate to. When I saw the Stonecross connection, it felt like all the signs were pointing to Natalie. I could relate to her. She lived in New York, about three blocks from my apartment. She'd broken up with her boyfriend, changed jobs, apartments, and she and her family were estranged. She was basically alone in the world, and I started thinking if I didn't show up somewhere, who would notice? Certainly not my dad, not for a few months anyway. Maybe around a holiday or Father's Day when I'd be expected to call in." I cleared my throat, realizing I was getting off track. "Anyway, that's how it all came together. Tessa and I headed up here, and our friend, Morgan, was supposed to meet us, but she couldn't come. So, it was just the two of us. Then Tessa got hurt, and it was on me."

"I'm really sorry Tessa got hurt."

"You've apologized several times. You don't have to do it again."

"Okay. Then tell me more about your father. About why your relationship is so tenuous."

I pulled my jacket closer as the wind picked up. "He's

just...disappointed in me. He always has been. I think when my mom died, all the softness in him died too. She was the buffer, you know? The one who made him laugh, who made him human. Without her, he just became this cold, focused machine. Work, money, success—that's all that mattered to him."

"And you don't fit that mold."

"Not even close." I let out a bitter laugh. "I went to the college he wanted. I studied accounting and economics like he insisted. I got good grades, but I hated every second of it. And when I finally told him I wanted to be a journalist, he looked at me like I'd just told him I wanted to be a street performer."

"Seriously?"

"Yes. He told me I was wasting my potential. That journalism was a dying field. That I'd never make any money or amount to anything. He was probably right about the money part. I lost my job three months ago. My studio apartment is barely bigger than a closet. I've been living on peanut butter and ramen, trying to make the podcast work, because my resume seems to fall into a big black hole wherever I send it."

"Well, the podcast is working. You've got thousands of people listening now."

"Yeah, but it took nearly dying to get that audience." I shook my head. "I don't know. Maybe my dad was right. I should have just become an accountant or an economist and made him proud for once in my life."

"Would that have made you happy?"

"No. But at least I'd have a family." The words came out before I could stop them, and I immediately regretted the vulnerability. "Sorry. That sounded pathetic."

"Everyone wants to belong somewhere. To feel like they matter to someone."

"I guess." We fell silent for a moment, and then I said, "What was it like being in the military?"

"It was great. I loved the structure, the purpose, the sense of being part of something bigger than myself. I had a team of men and women that I could count on, and I also got to travel. I was stationed in Germany and Japan and spent time in the Middle East. I saw horror and I also saw unexpected beauty, but what I really began to understand was how complex the world was..." His voice trailed off. Then he gathered his thoughts together and said, "But when my dad had the stroke, Sophie called me, crying. She was barely twenty-one and trying to manage the bar and take care of him while my mom was falling apart."

"So you came home."

"Just for a few months, I told myself. Just until he got better." Finn's smile was rueful. "That was two years ago. And now...I don't know. Part of me still wants to leave. See more of the world, have adventures. But part of me thinks maybe I'm supposed to be here. That this is where I belong."

"Your dad's better now. Couldn't you leave if you wanted to?"

"He's better, but he's not the same. And he's not sure he wants to run the bar full-time anymore. Sophie's leaving. My mom needs help with the house. And beyond all that..." He paused. "This is my home. Maybe it's time to accept that."

"As long as you're not living your life for someone else."

"Didn't you just say you wished you'd done that?" he asked dryly.

I smiled. "I didn't mean it. I can't live for my dad. Mostly, because it still wouldn't make him happy. And it certainly wouldn't make me happy. Maybe you should talk to your dad about what he wants. It's possible he doesn't want to take the bar away from you, that he sees it as yours now."

"He has made comments like that, but I don't know. Anyway, that's not something I'm going to figure out today. I'm here in my hometown, and the people who live here are my people, and if there is someone amongst us who is hurting innocent women, I want to stop them. You and Tessa have raised enough doubts in my mind to question the narrative I've been hearing the past year, and I don't completely trust the sheriff. Tom acts like he's a king and thinks he runs the town. Ellen also seems to feel that her inn is driving half the tourism in Stonecross, so it has to be protected no matter the cost."

"Does the inn bring in half the tourism?"

"Probably. But that doesn't matter if innocent women are getting hurt. We need to find out what's going on."

"We?" I echoed.

"If you're open to me helping you."

"Absolutely. But if we're going to be partners, I need to know if you're really willing to put yourself or someone you care about in the line of fire."

He stared back at me. "You're talking about Nathan."

"Yes. I know you went to the sheriff, who dismissed everything you said. Maybe you need to go back to Nathan and get him to admit what he did to Tessa."

Finn turned his gaze out to the sea, then after a moment, he returned it to me. "Nathan and I grew up together. He was a scrawny kid who had to wear a back brace for a long time. He was picked on, bullied, and I looked out for him. I guess I haven't let go of that habit. But he's not a kid anymore. He's a grown man, and I don't know him the way I used to. You're right. I need to talk to him again, and I'll do that today."

"You could do it now. You could call him."

He pulled out his phone. "Good idea. I'll put it on speaker."

"Thank you."

He punched a button and turned on the speaker. But the call went to voicemail. "I'll try his office," he said. "They might know where he is and when he'll be back." He put in another number. The phone rang once. Twice. Three times.

Then a woman's voice answered, high-pitched and panicked. "Hello? Who is this?"

Finn frowned. "This is Finn Kelly. I'm looking for Nathan. Who's this?"

"Melissa. I work with Nathan at the charter office. He isn't here. Something terrible happened." She was crying now, deep, racking sobs of shock and pain.

"What? What happened?" Finn asked.

"He overdosed. He might be dead."

My blood turned to ice. I grabbed Finn's arm, staring at the phone.

"Might be dead?" Finn repeated. "Tell me what happened."

"He went home for lunch around noon and when he didn't come back by three, Mike went over to check on him." Her voice broke. "He said Nathan was lying on the floor and there were pills everywhere. They think he might have tried to kill himself, but the paramedics got a pulse, so they took him to the hospital."

"When did this happen?" Finn asked, his voice tight.

"Sometime between noon and three, they think. The police are here now. They're questioning everyone. I have to go."

The line went dead.

Finn and I stared at each other in the sudden silence.

"Oh my God," I whispered. "He tried to kill himself?"

Finn's lips tightened. "And maybe succeeded, but I can't believe he would do that."

"Maybe it was an accident." I could see Finn processing that thought, but he clearly wasn't convinced. "What else could have happened?"

"I don't know, but I need to talk to the sheriff."

"I'm going with you," I said as we both jumped up.

We walked quickly back to our cars. I stayed close to Finn's tail, thinking about what had happened. Maybe Nathan had tried to kill himself. He'd drugged Tessa. He'd stolen Jessica's ring. Maybe there was even more to that story. What if he had killed Jessica, stolen her ring, and pretended to find her boat?

My phone suddenly buzzed, and Tyler's name flashed across the screen. "Tyler," I said. "I'm glad you called. I have news. Nathan tried to kill himself today."

"What? How did you hear that?"

"Finn called him, and they told him he was at the hospital. I guess he's still alive, but maybe barely."

"Damn. That's not good. He could still have information we need."

It was a bit callous to only think about the information and not the man, but Tyler wasn't wrong. "I'm hopeful he'll recover, and we'll be able to talk to him again."

"If he overdosed, maybe he was trying to kill himself."

"I had that same thought. I even wondered if he might have..."

"Killed Jessica?" Tyler asked grimly.

"He probably didn't, but—"

"We don't know."

"No. But Finn and I are on our way to talk to Sheriff Holloway."

"You're trusting Finn now?" he challenged. "Is that wise?"

"He's been getting me information about my father, and he seems like he genuinely wants to help me find out what happened to Natalie."

"Even though he's friends with Nathan, the man who drugged your friend? That's who you're going to trust?"

When he put it like that, it did seem like a risky move. Was I letting Finn's likeable charm blind me to who he might really be? I honestly didn't know.

"I'm not trusting him," I said. "I'm just going to see what he can find out from the sheriff, because I guarantee Tom Holloway will tell Finn more than he'll tell me."

"Will you keep me posted?"

"Sure. Did you find any security footage of Jessica?"

"No," he said wearily. "Not yet. But I'm waiting for a shop owner to come in. There's one place that looks promising, but the person in charge said he can't release the footage without the owner's permission."

"Good luck."

"Be careful, Cassidy."

"I'm going to try, but I'm not sure careful is even a possibility anymore."

"You can still get out. You can go home. Leave now. It's not too late."

"I think it might be," I murmured, knowing I was in too deep. That I couldn't walk away without knowing the truth. For better or worse, I was going to follow this to the end.

CHAPTER TWENTY

As I followed Finn into the parking lot of the Stonecross Sheriff's Department, I immediately noticed three men standing near a black pickup truck. When I got out of my car, their raised voices carried across the lot, and even from a distance, I could see the tension radiating from their bodies. It was Sheriff Tom Holloway, his son, Cole, and his brother, Jeff.

Finn slowed, holding up a hand as I moved toward him, and we watched from a distance as the scene escalated.

"I am done bailing you out of trouble!" Tom shouted, his face flushed red with anger. He stepped closer to Cole, invading his space. "You hear me? Done!"

"Good!" Cole shot back, not backing down despite his father looming over him. "I'm done with you and your lies!"

"I'm not the liar. You are!" Tom's voice was raw, furious. "Everything that comes out of your mouth is a lie!"

"Tom, come on—" Jeff tried to step between them, his hands raised placatingly. "This isn't helping anything. Cole is your son."

"Stay out of this, Jeff!" Tom snapped. "You don't know what the hell you're talking about."

"Don't yell at him," Cole shouted. "He's the only one who sees you for who you really are." Cole shoved past his father, heading for his own truck. Tom grabbed Cole's arm, yanking him back.

"We're not done—"

"Yes, we are!" Cole jerked free, almost knocking his father over with the violence of his movement.

He jumped into his truck and sped away as Tom stood there, his chest heaving, his fists clenched at his sides.

Jeff shook his head slowly, something cold settling into his expression. "You drive everyone away, don't you?"

Tom whirled on him. "This is not on me. I've done everything for that kid, bailed him out of every problem he's ever had. Same as I've done for you."

"That's the story you tell yourself, that you're the hero, and the rest of us are shit. But you're the reason everyone has to leave. It's always because of you." Jeff walked toward his gray Jeep, keys already in his hand. "You've been doing this your whole life, Tom. Pretending you're the hero, when you're anything but."

"Jeff—"

But Jeff wasn't listening to anything else his brother had to say. He got into his Jeep and pulled out with another squeal of tires.

Tom stood there for a moment, his shoulders rigid, before turning toward the building. That's when he saw Finn and me standing by our cars, clearly having witnessed the entire exchange.

His face, already red with anger, darkened further as we moved toward him. "What do you two want?"

"We need to talk to you about Nathan Carmichael," Finn said. "He apparently overdosed."

"Yeah, I'm aware. Cork Harbor PD is investigating. Looks like a suicide attempt."

"Or someone wanted to shut him up," Finn suggested.

"You getting him riled up now, too?" the sheriff asked me.

Before I could answer, Finn said, "Cassidy has nothing to do with this. I told you yesterday about what happened on Nathan's boat, the ring, Tessa, a possible drugging, and you said you were going to look into it."

"Didn't have a chance," the sheriff said. "But I'm planning to drive up there this afternoon and see what's going on. But it's either an accident or a suicide attempt. Nobody shoved pills down his throat."

"Well, glad to see you're keeping an open mind," Finn drawled.

Anger flared again in Tom's eyes. He definitely did not like his opinion being doubted in any way. "I always do," he snapped, then walked past us toward his cruiser without another word.

"Do you think he's going to tell the police in Cork Harbor what we told him about the ring and Tessa?" I asked.

"Hard to say. Our best bet is Nathan wakes up from all this and tells us what happened."

"I agree. What do you think about that scene with the Holloway men?"

"Not surprising. Tom can't stand it when people don't do exactly what he wants. And Jeff and Cole usually do the opposite."

"It was interesting that he told his son he was done bailing him out of trouble. What trouble is Cole in?"

Finn stared back at me through narrowed eyes. "Cole doesn't have anything to do with what's been happening at the inn."

"When Tyler and I went to see Nathan the other day, I could have sworn I saw Cole near the dock in Cork Harbor."

"Well, he works for Jeff, and they run charters to Cork Harbor."

"That's true."

"Look, Cole isn't a bad kid. I've known him his whole life."

"Seems like you just said the same thing about Nathan. Just because you've known someone a long time doesn't mean you actually know who they are now."

He frowned. "I must admit I've never seen Cole get physically angry before, and that bothered me. He's going to New York with my sister. I need to talk to Sophie about it."

"Maybe she can tell you what's going on with Cole and his father, because it feels like it's been brewing for a while. Every time I've seen them together, there's an underlying anger that's undeniable."

"I've seen it, too, but I guess I've just gotten so used to Tom's volatility, his temper, his arrogance that I don't question it, and I should be questioning it. I should be questioning everything. You're not the first person to come through town wanting to know what happened to Natalie Warren. Her brother was here, a private investigator, and in the beginning, there was press coverage, too, but Tom stuck to his story, and so did Ellen, and we all believed their version of events. Same thing happened with Jessica Trent. It was a sad story—a woman rents a boat and never comes back. But it just seemed like she made a bad decision, misjudged her abilities to sail that particular weather and current. It wasn't that difficult to believe."

"I've noticed how often Tom and my grandmother spout off plausible explanations, never questioning or changing their tune, and I can see why they seem believable."

"It took two outsiders to shake things up," he said with a small smile. "You and Tessa did that."

"I want to do more than shake things up; I want to get answers."

"So do I. And once we start talking to people together, it won't just be outsiders looking for the truth. I think I can get people to put pressure on the sheriff to reopen the investigation into Natalie's disappearance."

"That would be amazing, Finn." This was what I had needed: someone from Stonecross to join my side. "Tessa was right about you. She thought you could help us, and you're doing just that."

"Better late than never, right?"

I nodded, and as our gazes met an odd tingle ran down my spine. It felt like things were getting personal, but I couldn't mistake his help, his friendship, for something more. We were like ships passing in the night. I'd be gone in a few days.

"So," he began. "I should talk to my sister. What are you going to do?"

"I need to check in with Tessa and go back to the inn and speak to my grandmother. I'll tell her what happened with Nathan and see if that opens up a new conversation, but I'm not particularly confident that it will. She's a tough nut to crack."

"I can see that. You two share that trait. You're both very determined."

"Unfortunately, our determination is putting us on opposite sides. I don't know what role she plays in any of this. And that scares me. I want her to be innocent, because she's my grandmother, but it's hard to believe she is."

He nodded in understanding. "I get it. But if anyone can get her to crack even a little bit, it's probably you."

"I'm going to try. Will you text me if you get any more information?"

"Only if you promise to do the same."

"I will, and thank you, Finn. Thanks for joining my side."

"One other thing," he said as I was about to leave.

"What's that?"

"Your friend, Tyler."

"What about him?"

"Where is he? What's he doing? And how is he connected to Jessica?"

I thought about the secret Tyler had shared with me and wondered how to answer Finn's question without breaking that confidence. "He told me she's a friend, someone who doesn't have family to look for her, so he's the one doing it."

"Is that the whole story?" Finn challenged. "There's something about him that bothers me. He's been lurking around town for the past two weeks but never really asking questions, never really stating his concerns, just hovering, eavesdropping, always around but never right in the middle of things."

"He said he was afraid that announcing his intention would only close the channels of communication. The town closes down when outsiders have questions. It's the way I felt, too. That's why we started working together."

"He was there last night when you ran off the road."

"I was on the phone with him when I realized I was being followed. That's how he knew where I was, how he got there so fast."

"Interesting."

There was nothing but suspicion in that short word. "What? You don't trust him?"

"Do you?"

I thought about that. "I guess I don't really trust anyone. But he hasn't given me any reason to doubt him. And he wants what I want—to find out what happened to Natalie and Jessica."

"Where is he now?"

"He went to Cork Harbor to see if he could find any businesses with security cameras pointed toward the road that Jessica might have walked if she'd climbed away from that boat wreck."

He straightened, a new gleam in his eyes. "So he's in Cork Harbor? Has he been there all day?"

"Uh, I think he's been there a while." I could see by Finn's expression exactly where his mind was going. "You're wondering if he talked to Nathan again."

"You said the two of you went to see Nathan. Maybe he went back."

"He didn't mention it. I just spoke to him on our way over here. I told him about Nathan. He was as shocked as I was. If he'd spoken to Nathan, he would have told me. But I don't think he did because he thought Nathan was a dead end."

Finn nodded. "You're probably right. But be careful around that guy, Cassidy."

I couldn't help but smile. "I will, but you should know that he said the same thing about you."

He tipped his head in acknowledgement. "I guess I can't blame him for that. Until we know what happened, no one is above suspicion."

On that note, he turned and got into his SUV, and after a moment, I slid behind the wheel of my grandmother's car and followed him out of the parking lot. We parted ways at the first intersection, as I headed to the inn, and he went to find his sister.

It felt odd to see him disappear down another road. But it was for the best. I needed to think for myself. And I couldn't discount the possibility that both Finn and Tyler had hidden agendas. I'd kept my own secrets. I couldn't afford to think they didn't have secrets of their own. The only people I could really trust were Morgan and Tessa, and I owed them both a call.

I called Tessa first. Aside from everything else, I needed to know that she was healing and starting to feel better.

"Hey," Tessa said groggily. "I was just napping."

"That's good. How are you feeling? Are you still in pain?"

"It's not as bad as it was, but it's still there. The bad news is that I was spiking a fever last night, but the antibiotics seemed to have knocked that out."

"A fever? Is there an infection?" I asked with concern.

"Maybe, but the doctor was here a while ago and seemed to think the medication was taking care of that. But he wants to keep me here until Friday."

"That's only two days away."

"I know. And it's fine, because I need to feel a little stronger before I make the trek home. I guess we don't have a car anymore."

"No. We'll have to rent one. Or maybe we should fly. That might be easier on you."

"Probably."

"And we'll have to figure out how to get your roommate another car. I don't know if insurance will pay for anything. I guess I need to call someone."

"I already told my roommate what happened, and she will call her insurance company and find out what to do. I told her that there should be a police report because they responded to the scene."

"There should be, but whether there is or not, I can't say."

"So, is there anything new?"

"Actually, yes. Nathan Carmichael overdosed. He's in the hospital fighting for his life. The story so far is that it was a suicide attempt."

I could hear Tessa's exhale of surprise. "Wow, that's a shocker. When did this happen?"

"This afternoon sometime."

"How did you hear?"

"Finn called Nathan to ask him more questions about Jessica. When he didn't answer his phone, he tried his office, and they told us what happened."

"Why would Nathan want to kill himself?"

"With the timing, I can't help but think it has something to do with Jessica."

"Like what? He said he just found her boat and her ring. He didn't know her."

"Maybe he was lying. Maybe he was involved in something bigger, like her disappearance, maybe her...death."

"I guess that's possible. You mentioned you were with Finn... what were you doing?"

"He took me to his parents' house, and they told me about my father. They both went to school with my dad. It was interesting to talk to people who knew him when he was a kid. But they didn't know why he left. They did say my father didn't get along with the sheriff. That they were fighting over a girl named Lily."

"That name sounds familiar," Tessa said.

"Yes. It's the girl who allegedly killed herself, drowning off the beach, right below the inn."

"That's a crazy coincidence. Was your father still in Stonecross when that happened?"

"Yes. It was a couple of weeks after my grandfather died. And he left right after that."

"Maybe that's why."

"No idea. Anyway, that's what I was doing with Finn. And then we started talking about the missing women, and he said he believed we were on to something and that too many in the town, including him, had turned a blind eye to what was happening. He wants to help us now. He wants to shake things up, too. And since he's on the inside, he could be valuable."

"I'm glad he's been helpful. I thought he could be, if we could gain his trust."

"Your instincts were on the money."

"What about Tyler? Has he been helping, too?"

"He's definitely on the Jessica track." I paused. "Is it weird that Tyler went to Cork Harbor today to look for security camera footage on the road where Jessica appeared, which is the same town where Nathan overdosed?"

"That's a pointed question," Tessa replied. "You think Tyler had something to do with it? How? Why?"

"I don't know. Finn suggested it, but I can't imagine..." I rubbed my temples as the endless questions created a pounding in my head. "Finn doesn't trust Tyler, and Tyler doesn't trust Finn."

"And you?"

"I trust you and Morgan. Everyone else has a question mark."

"I'm glad you're not letting anyone get too close," she said. "Are you going to film another podcast tonight?"

"I should, shouldn't I?"

"I spoke to Morgan earlier. She talked to a lawyer friend who offered to draft contracts for our sponsors at a minimal cost. Two of the sponsors want to proceed, and I think we should jump on the opportunity now while the podcast listeners are engaged. Morgan said the comments are off the charts. I took a quick peek earlier, and she's right. But I know you have a lot going on, and I'm sorry the pressure is all on you."

"It's fine. I can do it. I'm at the inn now," I said as I parked in the lot. "I'm going to see if I can talk to Ellen. After that, I'll film something. I'll text you when I'm going live. Unless you want to join me on your phone?"

"I'm not feeling up to it. The pain makes my head fuzzy at times."

"You should just rest. Don't worry about anything. I'll handle it."

———

When I entered the inn, there were a couple of people who appeared to be checking in at the front desk with Moira. The living room was empty, and it looked like the servers were setting up the dining room for happy hour. I wanted to talk to Ellen before I did anything else, so I decided to see if she was in her apartment.

As I went down the back hallway, I noticed her door was slightly ajar, and I could hear two people speaking. It sounded like Ellen was talking to Ray. I crept a few steps closer to the open door, straining to hear what they were saying.

"Tom will handle it," Ellen said. "There's nothing for us to do. Just get back to work, Ray."

"There will be more questions about Jessica."

"That doesn't matter. We've been careful. As long as everyone keeps quiet, it'll be fine."

"Do you really think everyone is going to keep quiet when your own granddaughter is asking a million questions around town. And she's getting people like Finn to take up her quest."

"I'll handle Cassidy. Don't worry about her."

My heart jumped at the sound of my name, at the cold purpose in her voice. I whirled around and hurried away before they caught me eavesdropping in the hallway. I went through the side door and into the garden, taking deep breaths as I tried to calm down, to process what they'd said. They'd been talking about Jessica, probably about Nathan, and they knew Finn and I had talked to Tom, which meant Tom had called them. But why had he called them?

My stomach churned with a sudden nausea, a terrible fear that my grandmother was right in the middle of whatever was going on. She'd told Ray not to worry about Jessica, that they'd been careful. *What the hell did that mean?*

CHAPTER TWENTY-ONE

I pulled out my phone, feeling a desperate need to call someone, but who? Tyler? Finn? My father? The last one nagged at me.

Should I call my dad? Should I ask him if my grandmother was a...God! I couldn't even say it. Didn't even want to think it. But wasn't the evidence right in front of my eyes? How could I think anything differently after what I'd just heard?

Before I could change my mind, I punched in my father's number, holding my breath as I waited for him to answer, but he didn't pick up. And his cool voice on the message didn't make me want to leave one. I certainly couldn't ask this question in a voicemail. Nor did I want to text it.

As footsteps came up behind me, I whirled around in alarm, a fear that grew greater as I looked at Ray.

"Everything all right?" he asked.

"Yes," I said shortly.

"Good. Your grandmother is looking for you. She's in her apartment if you want to stop in."

"Of course. Thanks." As he didn't make a move to leave, I said, "Is there something else?"

He gave me a long look, then said, "No, that's it." And then he walked away.

I took a few more deep breaths, debating what I wanted to say to my grandmother, but I hadn't come up with anything by the time I walked into the inn and knocked on her apartment door.

She opened it a moment later, giving me a surprising smile. It didn't reach her eyes, but it did part her lips and surprised me with a warmth I hadn't seen before. But maybe this was part of her plan to handle me.

"Cassidy. Come in. I see Ray found you."

"Yes. I was in the garden. It's beautiful out there."

"I've always loved gardening. There's something about digging my hands in the dirt that's very satisfying."

It was the most personal thing she'd ever told me, and it put me off balance.

"Would you like some tea or perhaps a glass of wine?" she asked, as she motioned me inside.

"No, I'm fine."

"What have you been doing today?" Ellen asked as I sat down on her couch.

I thought about the best way to answer that question and decided that letting her control the conversation was a bad idea. She'd unsettled me. I needed to do the same thing. "Finn introduced me to his parents, John and Katherine."

Her lips tightened. "I see. And you spoke to them about me."

It wasn't a question, but I answered it anyway. "More about my father than you. I was curious to know what he was like as a child, and I didn't think you'd tell me."

"Because..."

"You don't seem to want to talk about him any more than he wanted to talk about you."

She shifted in her seat, and I knew my strategy was working; I just didn't know how long I could keep it up, because Ellen was a formidable woman, and I couldn't deny that I found her intimidating in the same way I found my father intimidating. Mother and Son certainly knew how to shut people down with just a look.

"I don't like to talk about David," she said finally. "It's painful. You don't have children, so you probably can't imagine what it feels like when the person you spent years protecting turns on you and never wants to see you again."

"There had to be a reason why he did that."

"As I said before, that's something you'll need to hear from him. What did John and Katherine have to say?"

"They told me that my father was in some kind of love triangle with Tom Holloway and a girl named Lily, the same girl who apparently walked into the sea, leaving a suicide note behind, never to be seen again." I watched for a shift in her expression, but she wasn't giving anything away. "A lot of people disappear from this town. And you and everyone else pretend that that's normal, but it's not."

Her gaze darkened. "That was a long time ago. Lily was a troubled girl who had a hard life. It was terribly sad that she made the choice to take her own life. I wish I could have helped her more. I tried. I gave her a job here, hoping the money she made would give her some freedom. But obviously, it wasn't money that could free her from her pain."

"My father left soon after that. Did he leave because she died?"

"I think that was a factor," Ellen admitted. "He suffered two losses in a very short period of time, his father and then Lily. I'm sure her death hurt him more than he was willing to share with me, although he never actually told me he was involved with her. I found that out after the fact."

"You don't seem like someone who is easy to share anything with. In fact, you seem like my father in that regard. He has huge walls up. I've never been able to scale them."

"But he was happy with your mother?"

"I think so. He was different with her," I admitted. "He was softer, happier; he smiled more. She could get through his walls, but she seemed to be the only one."

"How did she die?"

"She had cancer. It was pretty fast, less than a year. I was devastated."

"I'm sorry."

"The worst part of it was that I couldn't grieve with my dad. He shut me out. We were like two islands of pain. It was awful."

"He was never comfortable with his emotions. I assume you had family support on your mother's side?"

"Not really. She had family in Oregon, but we didn't see them much. They came out when she first got sick and then again for the funeral."

"Has your father dated anyone since then?"

"I'm sure he has, but he doesn't talk to me about it, and I haven't lived near him in a few years." I paused. "I thought coming here might help me understand him."

"I thought you came here because of your podcast."

"It was always about both. When I saw that Natalie had disappeared from your inn, it seemed like fate was telling me that this was the case I needed to look into. Because it gave me a reason to come here, to meet you."

"Why didn't you tell me who you were when you arrived?" she asked curiously.

"I was afraid you wouldn't let me stay. I didn't know if you knew about me. I also didn't know if you'd recognize me."

"You don't look like your father, but now that I know, maybe I do see some of him in you. I'm not sure. It's been so long since I've seen him."

"I still can't believe you never looked him up."

"As I said, he always knew where I was. He could have reached out if he wanted to. Obviously, he didn't want to."

"You both have a lot of pride. Probably too much."

"That's a possibility," she conceded. "And I think it may be time for you to leave. I can't tell you what happened with your dad and me. Even if I could, it wouldn't matter. What's done is done."

"The past isn't everything. There's the present. There's the future."

"Not a future we can share."

"Why not? I'm not my dad."

"Your father wouldn't allow that."

"I'm twenty-eight years old. I don't need his permission to know my grandmother."

"It would end your relationship. He would think you made a choice. And then he would make one." Ellen cocked her head to the side, her gaze sharp on my face. "Do you really want to choose me over him?"

I didn't answer right away because her question had cut through the polite bullshit we had going on. "I can't choose you, because I don't trust you."

Ellen stiffened. "Well, I appreciate your honesty."

"No, you don't. You don't want me to be honest. You want me to leave and never think about this place again. But I don't understand why, and maybe that's the reason I can't go yet."

"You have a life in New York. That's where you should be. You're young. You have years ahead of you to be whoever you want to be. I don't want to see your life defined by what has happened between your father and me, or what you think might be going on in this town. Go home, Cassidy. Find love, make a new family, and forget about this place."

There was a passion in my grandmother's voice that made me feel like she was speaking from her heart, like she wanted me to leave for my own sake, but was she really just protecting herself?

A knock came at her door. She hesitated, then got up to answer it. "Excuse me."

When she opened the door, I saw Moira. "I'm sorry to bother you," she said. "But Dr. Garrett is here, and she needs to speak to you."

"Have her wait in my office; I'll be right there." Ellen shut the door, then said, "I have to go."

"I heard," I said as I got to my feet.

"Think about what I said, Cassidy."

"I will. But I'm not leaving tonight."

"We'll talk again tomorrow." She ushered me out the door, then followed me.

When we got to the lobby, she went into her office, and I moved into the dining room where the servers had set out finger sandwiches along with other snacks. I made a plate, grabbed a glass of wine, and then headed upstairs to my room.

Once inside, I locked the door, then shoved the dresser back in front of it, feeling better with the added protection. Even though my grandmother had been relatively nice to me, I couldn't forget how she'd told Ray she would handle me.

That had probably meant convincing me to go home. At least, that's what I hoped it meant. Until I could figure that out, I was going to keep asking questions, taking steps forward, and hope that I could find the truth before someone found a way to stop me.

I set up my equipment and recorded a shorter podcast, ignoring my grandmother's request not to film from my room. I'd deal with her issues later. I related the new information about Nathan's overdose and how that might impact Jessica's case. I also said that the podcast was forcing people to listen to us, to ask questions on their own, to force the police to keep investigating, and we were going to keep at it as long as possible. I didn't mention overhearing Ellen's conversation with Ray. It was too personal. And it would put too much attention on Ellen and Ray, something I couldn't afford while I was staying at the inn. I was trying to be brave, but I was not that brave.

———

Thursday morning, I woke up with an ache in my neck and shoulders, probably from the tension that had grown in intensity every day I spent in Stonecross. Glancing at the clock, I was surprised to see it was after nine. I hadn't thought I'd sleep at all.

As I sat up in bed, I grabbed my laptop, which was next to me, and checked the podcast. I didn't think I'd done that great a job last night, jumping from one random fact to another, but the number of views had tripled from the previous podcast, and so had the comments.

I read through the first dozen or so, curious as to what the listeners were thinking. There was definitely shock and concern for my safety. Some people had questions about Nathan's overdose and how that might impact the investigation into not only Natalie but also Jessica.

And then there were the naysayers who thought I was just stirring up trouble, besmirching the reputation of the town, creating drama out of nothing, exploiting these women for ratings. One even went so far as to threaten me with retribution if I continued. That sent a chill of fear through me, but the threat wasn't completely unexpected.

It was certainly possible that some of the comments were from people in Stonecross, reminding me I was building a longer list of enemies every single day.

Shutting down the page, I checked my phone and saw several texts from Morgan. I decided to call her instead of texting back.

"Hi," I said when she answered. "I thought it was easier just to call."

"Did you see the views, the comments?" Morgan asked.

"I was just looking. Some of them are pretty negative."

"I was going to tell you not to read them."

"Too late. I didn't read them all, but I did see the threatening one."

"I know you want to see this through to the end, but there may be a point where you have to leave."

"I know. I'm taking a risk, but the podcast is taking off."

"It is, but I'm worried about the personal cost."

"If I leave now, it will be for nothing. We haven't found any answers."

"It won't be for nothing. You've put a spotlight on Natalie and Jessica. And with Nathan's overdose and Finn's help, there will be more pressure on the sheriff's office to investigate. One of the commenters suggested a write-in campaign to the mayors of both Stonecross and Cork Harbor to force further investigation."

"I didn't see that comment. Tom Holloway won't be happy about that."

"Maybe he'll start doing his job," Morgan said. "Seriously, what is the endgame here, Cassidy? Tessa said she's getting released tomorrow. She can't go back to the inn. Even if it was the safest place on earth, she said there's no elevator. And you don't have a car anymore. You're going to have to rent another one or fly, and Tessa can't do any of that on her own. You're at the end of the road."

"You're right. I probably just have one more day to get answers. I need to make the most of it."

"What are you going to do?"

"I don't know. But I'm hoping that Nathan is awake, and he can tell us whether that was an accident, deliberate, or something else entirely. Maybe he can clear up whether or not he actually saw Jessica on the beach when he found her ring."

"Do you think he did?"

"It's definitely a possibility. Why would her ring just fall off? Maybe he killed her and took her ring off her finger, and now he's guilty and wants to die before someone sends him to jail."

"That's dark but does make sense. Jessica's case seems to have more clues than Natalie's."

"Because of the way it happened. The boat trip created a trail. Natalie's exit from the inn did not." As I said that, I remembered Tyler's plan to check whether or not the inn had tunnels beneath it.

Tyler probably hadn't gotten back to the building department, or he would have said something to me. He'd never been as interested in Natalie's case as he was in Jessica's, and if he'd found video evidence in Cork Harbor, he would have followed up on that.

It was a little weird that I hadn't heard from him, though. I'd text him after I got off the phone.

"Cassidy?" Morgan said sharply. "Are you there?"

"Sorry, I got distracted. What did you say?"

"I asked if you've spoken to your grandmother again, if she's starting to open up to you?"

"We talked again last night. She didn't reveal much. She has a lot of pride and anger when it comes to my father. But I did unsettle her when I told her about the information I'd gotten from John and Katherine on Lily."

"What did she say about Lily?"

"The usual sad, tragic, 'wish I could have helped her' commentary. She did admit that Lily's death might have been a factor in my dad's departure, especially since it had come so soon after my grandfather's death."

"Could those two be connected?" Morgan asked.

"I don't see how."

"Do you think if you keep pushing her to talk, she'll eventually crack and spill the family tea?"

I smiled sadly at her words. "No, I don't think that. Something will have to happen to force her to change her mind, but it won't be me asking. As for my plan today, I'm going to go back into town and start talking to more people in the small shops and cafés. They all know who I am now. And maybe I can get Finn to go with me. If he joins forces with me, more doors will open, and more people will talk. He's my ticket to information."

"What about Tyler Pierce? What's he up to?"

"I haven't spoken to him since late yesterday afternoon. I'll check with him after we hang up. Maybe he got a lead on Jessica. That would be a good break."

"Okay, good luck. Let me know if I can help."

"Unfortunately, I think this is on me. But next time we decide to follow a cold case to its original setting, you can take the lead."

"Next time? I'm just hoping you survive this time."

"Me too."

Setting aside my phone and computer, I went into the bathroom to shower and then dress. Today was a new day, and I was going to go into it with confidence. I'd created some cracks in the wall surrounding these cases,and hopefully one of them would split right open.

CHAPTER TWENTY-TWO

I got downstairs at the tail end of breakfast and managed to grab some oatmeal and fruit before the servers started clearing. There was a new crew of guests in the dining room, no one I recognized, and maybe that was a good thing. I saw only polite smiles, no suspicious ones.

As I finished breakfast, Ellen came into the dining room and slid into the chair across from me. She had a folder in her hand.

"Good morning," I said tentatively.

"You want to learn more about our family, so I pulled together a few photos." She opened the folder and took out the first one. "This is your grandfather and me on our wedding day, fifty-eight years ago. I was eighteen when I married him. And I had your father nine months later."

"You were young," I said, staring at the picture for a long minute. My grandmother looked like a beautiful teenager with long brown hair and a hopeful, joyous smile that I'd never seen on her face. My grandfather was tall and lean with a warmth to his happy grin that made me want to instantly like him. Ellen had said he was rigid and demanding and set in his ways, but that's not what this man looked like.

"We were very young," Ellen said, a nostalgic note in her voice. "I met Richard the summer I came here to visit my aunt, uncle, and cousins. I grew up about two hours south of here. Richard was the cutest boy I'd ever seen. He was tall and tan with a sunburned nose that always freckled. He loved boats and being out on the ocean. He was full of life, and I was immediately taken with him. I was supposed to go home at the end of the summer. I was supposed to go to college, but I couldn't leave him. We got married that September. My parents were furious. But I was in love."

I lifted my gaze from the photo to look at her. "Was it a happy marriage?"

"For many, many years," she said, a nostalgic gleam in her eyes that turned a little sad. "But we had our share of challenges, arguments, differences of opinion. We grew up, and we weren't always on the same page. Richard wanted a stay-at-home wife who just wanted to take care of her son and husband. And I did those things for a long time, but I wanted more. I wanted to have something that was mine."

"He let you sell your house and buy this inn, so he must have come around."

"To be honest, I forced his hand. Your father was almost out of high school, and I told Richard that it was my turn to have something of my own." She paused. "He said I'd have plenty to do with my volunteer work. I helped out at the library. I was on the social committee for town events. It all sounded like more of the same, and I couldn't stomach the thought that that was all there was going to be."

I was shocked at how much she was revealing, and I didn't want to stop her by asking a question, so I waited for her to continue.

She cleared her throat. "After many discussions, some of which were very loud and very angry, I told Richard that wasn't going to work for me. The inn was up for sale, and I wanted to buy it. And if he didn't agree, then I was going to leave and find some other way to do what I wanted to do."

"That couldn't have gone over well."

"It was a difficult time," she said. "And there weren't just fights between me and Richard, but also between Richard and David. Our lives were changing, and we all wanted something different. But I believed in my heart that we would all be better off if we pursued our dreams. For me, that was this inn. For David, it was going to college and making something of his life."

"And for my grandfather?"

"He had his life. He had his business, his family. He had everything he'd ever wanted. It was our turn."

"So, you were on my father's side in terms of him leaving town?"

"Yes. He was too smart to just do carpentry at the Boatworks. I saw a bigger future for him, and I wanted to make sure he had it. But..."

"But?" I prodded.

"I had to walk a fine line. I needed Richard's support to buy the inn, so sometimes I didn't speak up the way David wanted me to. I thought it would all work out in the end. The inn deal was happening while David was still in high school. Once that was done, I could turn my attention to David's situation."

Her story cleared up a few things in my mind but also raised more questions. Before I could ask, she handed me the other photo in the folder. "This was taken at the church right after your father's first communion."

I looked at a slightly older version of my grandparents standing on either side of my father, who had a smile on his face that I had never seen. "He looks like a happy kid."

"He was happy when he was young. As he got older, not so much."

"Why? You have to tell me what happened. You can't take me this far and then stop."

"It's not my story, Cassidy." She gave a questioning look. "And would you even believe me if I did? You don't trust me. At times, I believe you think I'm a monster."

"Persuade me otherwise," I said, not denying that I had mixed feelings about her.

"I don't think I could," she said.

"I don't think you want to. Something is going on here."

"Sometimes it's safer not to know everything, Cassidy. Sometimes silence protects you."

"I don't believe that's true."

"Well, I do. The photos are yours to keep if you want to take them home with you."

"I would like to keep them. But I'm not leaving until tomorrow. That's when Tessa is being released from the hospital. I'd like to stay here one more night. Unless you don't think I'll be safe here?"

Ellen met my gaze head-on. "You'll be safe here, but I don't know about anywhere else. I watched your podcast this morning. I read the comments. Some were threatening. You're stirring up a hornet's nest. That's a mistake."

"I'm not going to let anonymous threats drive me away. That just means I'm getting closer to finding out what happened to Natalie and Jessica. You should want to help me so that you can clear up the inn's reputation, put the rumors away for good. If you have nothing to hide, why are you acting like you do?"

"If I could help you, I would, but I can't," she said with an unmistakable finality. Then she got up and walked away.

I watched her leave the dining room, her posture always straight, proud, confident, unbending. But I couldn't help thinking that *can't* wasn't a word my grandmother used often.

If she wanted something, she went out and got it, just like she'd gotten this inn. She could help me if she wanted to; she just didn't want to, and I still didn't know why. But I was going to keep asking questions until I found out.

Three hours later, my initial optimism had completely faded. No one in town would talk to me. Finn had gone to Cork Harbor to see Nathan. Tyler wasn't answering my texts. My allies were definitely not helping me, and neither was anyone else.

I grabbed a quick salad for lunch and took it down to the beach to eat, needing time away from the suspicious looks that seemed to follow me wherever I went. It was a Thursday afternoon, and the beach was fairly empty, but there were a couple of kids with their mother, making sandcastles and running back and forth to the ocean to fill their buckets with water. An older couple sat in chairs under a shaded tree, the woman reading, the man stretched out on a lounger.

It was a pretty, peaceful day, completely opposite to the turmoil in my head.

As I watched the young boy, I thought of my dad. He'd probably played on this very beach, Ellen watching over him. But maybe her gaze hadn't been on him. Maybe she'd looked up the coast to the impressive Victorian, the one she hoped to turn into a bed-and-breakfast.

She'd married so young. And while she'd spoken of instant love, she'd also mentioned troubles in her marriage. That was probably typical of all long-term relationships, but I couldn't tell just how happy she and my grandfather had actually been when they got farther away from the idyllic photo taken on their wedding day.

But I shouldn't be thinking about my grandparents and their wedding day when I had a limited amount of time to find out what happened to Natalie or Jessica before I had to leave town.

Picking up my phone, I tried Tyler again, relieved when he answered. "Hi," I said. "Where have you been? I texted you a few times."

"I know. I'm sorry. I've been trying to chase down a lead on Jessica."

"What kind of lead? The security footage?"

"Yes, I think I might have spotted the truck that picked her up."

"Really?" I asked with excitement. "That's great. Did you actually see her in the truck? Is she still alive?"

"I didn't get a good enough look at the passenger to know for sure, but if it was her, then she was alive the day Nathan found her boat."

"Do you think he saw her? Or who took her? Have you heard any more about his condition?"

"I heard that he survived the night, but I don't think anyone has spoken to him yet. Does that match what you know?"

"Finn went to see him, but I haven't heard back. So, how are you tracking this truck down?"

"I have a friend who's trying to clean up the video enough to see a license plate, but I'm not sure I need it."

"Why not?"

"Because there's a logo on the door of the truck, and it looks like the Stonecross Inn logo."

My heart leapt against my chest. "Are you serious? Are you saying it's Ray's truck?"

"I think so, but I don't have a clear enough view to take it to the police yet. And I'd really like to get facial recognition on the passenger, which my friend is also trying to do. You know this video will just get buried if it's not irrefutable."

I sighed as I saw the dead end he'd just run into. Even if it was Ray's truck, we couldn't prove it had picked up Jessica unless she was seen on the video. "This is so frustrating."

"Believe me, I hate finding bits and pieces as much as you do, but I'm excited to have a new lead. If I can confirm the license plate, my friend said we might be able to pick up the truck on the bigger highway cameras later that day, which would tell us where they went."

"Okay, that sounds promising."

"I think so," he said, a more hopeful note in his voice than

I'd heard in a while. "What's going on with you? Any more leads on Natalie? And, hey, I'm sorry about not getting those building plans."

"Don't worry about that. I can go by the building department, too, but even if there is a tunnel, it probably comes out at a point on the beach where there are no cameras."

"Probably," he agreed. "Are you still staying at the inn?"

"One more night. Tessa can't leave the hospital until tomorrow, and I'm still trying to figure something out before I have to leave."

"Are you talking to your grandmother about what happened?"

"She's talking but not about Natalie or Jessica."

"What's she talking about? Your family?"

"She's said a little about the family, but nothing that revealing. I think she's trying to tell me just enough to satisfy me and then send me on my way. But I'm not giving up yet."

"Well, I would steer clear of Ray. Don't be anywhere by yourself. Make sure you stay in public places with a lot of eyes on you."

"I will. Call me when you know more. If we can prove that Ray took Jessica somewhere, that could break everything open."

"I know how important this is," he said seriously.

"Have you told your brother you have a lead?"

"Not yet. I don't want to get his hopes up until I know more."

"Good luck."

"You, too." As I ended the call, I felt a little more optimistic, but I also couldn't help thinking that if that video pointed to Ray, then it might also point to my grandmother, and I might have to face the fact that she wasn't just a bad grandmother, she was also a horrible person.

That thought derailed my optimism, but I couldn't jump ahead. One step at a time.

I got up, threw out my empty salad container and returned

to the car. Wandering around town on my own hadn't gotten me very far, so I headed back to the inn. Maybe I could chat with Dorothy. She'd been friendly, and she knew everyone better than I did.

Unfortunately, when I got back to the inn, I found her usual chair empty, no sign of her or her knitting. I stopped at the desk to ask Moira if she knew where Dorothy was and discovered that she'd checked out that morning. That was disappointing.

With no one else to talk to, I went back upstairs and into my room. I sat on my bed, feeling frustrated and restless. I wasn't going to get anywhere by just sitting here, but I didn't know what to do next.

After a moment of debate, I took out my phone and called Sophie.

"Hello?" she said.

"Hi, it's Cassidy. I was wondering if I could talk to you. Are you at the pub?"

"No, I'm at home, waiting for Cole. With everything going on, we decided to leave today. We're heading for New York, Cassidy. I can hardly believe it, but Finn gave me the money I needed to go now, and Cole is fed up with his dad, so we're going to do it. We're actually going to get out of this town."

"I'm happy for you." I paused, then said, "Did you tell Finn you were leaving today? He and I witnessed a fight between Cole and his dad yesterday, and Finn was a little worried about you and Cole taking off together."

"We talked about that, but no one has to worry. I know Cole. He only goes crazy when he's talking to his dad. He would never hurt me. He's not like that."

Sophie sounded absolutely convinced by her words, and I didn't know Cole well enough to contradict her. "Well, that's good to hear. I hope it all works out."

"It will. I just need Cole to get here already. We were supposed to leave thirty minutes ago."

That seemed troubling. "Why do you think he's late?"

"I don't know, but I want to get on the road, so he better get here soon." Sophie paused. "When will you be back in Manhattan?"

"Probably Saturday."

"Great. I'll look you up. I wasn't sure you were going to leave without figuring out what happened to Natalie. What are your listeners going to think if there's no resolution?"

"I don't know. I'm still hoping to get a last-minute break. But in the meantime, I'm learning more about Stonecross and my family, so that's something."

"I still can't believe you're Ellen's granddaughter. You two are nothing alike."

"I would agree with that."

"Is she talking to you about your dad, their past?"

"Not really. I need to find more people in town who are willing to do that. Your parents were helpful, but I need more information. I was actually hoping to speak to Dorothy again, but I heard she checked out."

"You could go see her. She lives in town."

"Do you know where?"

"I don't know the exact address, but she lives in the white house with yellow shutters on the first block of Maple Drive. I dropped her off there once when she needed a ride home."

"Thanks. I'll check that out. Have a safe drive to New York, and, hopefully, we'll catch up there."

"I can't wait. Bye, Cassidy."

After hanging up the phone, I grabbed my bag and keys and headed back out to find Dorothy. On the way, I couldn't help wondering why Cole was late in meeting Sophie. Was his father trying to stop him from leaving? It seemed likely there was more family drama going on, and I hoped Sophie didn't get caught in the middle of it.

———

Dorothy's house was a modest white colonial with a garden that was beautifully maintained. I rang the bell and waited, hoping Dorothy might be able to tell me something I didn't already know. I wasn't actually that interested in finding out more about my father or family right now. I needed to find out what Dorothy knew about Ray, because he seemed to be a shadowy figure in everything that was going on. Maybe if I told her about the video footage, she'd tell me something in return.

A moment later, the door opened, and Dorothy's face lit up with surprise. "Cassidy! What a lovely surprise. Come in, dear."

"I hope I'm not intruding. I tried to find you at the inn, but they said you'd checked out."

"I came home this morning." She ushered me into a cozy living room filled with family photos and comfortable furniture. "Can I get you some tea?"

"No, thank you. I actually wanted to talk to you about something."

"Of course." She settled into a floral armchair and gestured for me to take the sofa.

I perched on the edge, trying to figure out how to phrase my concerns. "I've been hearing things about Ray. And I'm worried about what's really going on at the inn."

Dorothy's expression grew troubled. "I have to say all this talk has gotten me more concerned, too. But Cassidy, I've known Ellen for fifty years. She's a hard woman; I won't deny that. But she's not cruel. And Ray—he's had a rough life, but he's loyal to Ellen because she gave him a chance when no one else would."

"I understand your loyalty, but what about Natalie? What about Jessica and Anna?"

"I don't know what happened to them. But I don't believe Ellen or Ray hurt anyone," she said decisively. "They wouldn't do that. Sometimes people just leave, Cassidy. Sometimes they need to disappear and start over. All three of those women seemed lost when I met them. They were lovely women but sad, too.

They were running from things in their past. Maybe their pasts caught up with them."

"All three? Don't you think that's a bit coincidental?"

"I really don't," she said with a definitive shake of her head. "It's not like someone disappeared every day. It's been over the course of a year, and like I said, those women were searching for something. They weren't content. They were lonely. They wanted love, family, something to fill the void in their hearts."

"I didn't realize you'd talked to all of them."

"I talk to everyone. Anna didn't say much, though. She was like a scared little rabbit, darting away every time someone looked at her. But the others were a bit more open. And so pretty, too. It was sad. They had beauty and heart, but they were still unhappy."

"I just wish I had proof that my grandmother isn't sticking her head in the sand, that Ray or someone else isn't doing something that could come back to hurt her, too."

"Maybe you just need to trust your grandmother. Get to know her."

"How can I when she won't open up?"

"You keep trying. You seem like a woman with a lot of stubborn determination, much like your grandmother, in fact. Or maybe you need to press your father for information. Does he know you're here?"

"No. And he's as tight-lipped as she is. They have some secret. It might have to do with my grandfather, maybe Lily, or maybe both. But neither one of them wants to talk about it, and I don't know how to break this deadlock."

"Lily? I haven't heard that name in a long time."

"Apparently, my father had a crush on her. And then she killed herself."

"That was a very sad situation. I wish I could help." Dorothy stopped abruptly. "Maybe I can."

"How?"

"Pictures."

"I've seen a few photos of my grandmother and my dad when he was a little boy. I'm not sure more photos will help."

"What about when your father was in high school? When he was playing baseball? When your grandmother used to cheer him on at his games?" Her face grew more animated as she spoke. "Lily used to go to those games, too. I bet I have pictures of her as well. I didn't have children of my own, but I was always close to the Holloway family, and I used to go to all the games to cheer Tom on. He and David played on the same team."

"And they liked the same girl."

"I don't know about that, but I think it would be good for you to see your father and your grandparents in happier times so that you can get a better idea of who they really are."

"That could help, I suppose." Looking at family photos wouldn't get me closer to finding Natalie, but it might help me understand the two people who shared my blood but little else.

"Let's go downstairs," she said cheerily, leading me through the kitchen and down a stairway to the basement. It was quite a large room and very full, I thought, as she flipped on the lights. An assortment of random old furniture was along one wall, as well as a workbench with tools, and an area for gardening equipment. There were also quite a few boxes and a couple of old filing cabinets.

"Let me see," Dorothy muttered, moving toward a stack of boxes in the corner. "I think the yearbooks and photos are in these boxes. My husband, Harold, was always organizing things down here, but I haven't been through any of this since he passed. It was difficult enough to clear his things out of the house, the bedroom." She smiled sadly. "It's funny how the memories hit at the oddest times. Anyway, let's start opening boxes."

"Are you sure you want to do that? I don't want to create more clutter for you to clean up."

"It would be good for me to see what's here, and I won't have to do it by myself, so that's a bonus. I'll start here. You start over there."

"Okay," I said, my gaze moving to a stack of paint cans next to me. Tucked behind them was a large cardboard box. I was about to reach for it when the doorbell rang upstairs.

"Oh, who could that be?" Dorothy said, giving me an apologetic smile as she headed for the stairs. "I'll be right back. Keep looking."

I pulled the paint cans apart and grabbed the box, pulling it over to me. It wasn't taped like some of the others, and I squatted down to take a look inside. There was a colorful pink scarf on the top, but it had dark red spots on it, which reminded me of the carpet I'd seen taken out of Anna's room. I took it out and saw more odd items underneath, including a sparkly silver chain with a heart-shaped locket.

As I picked it up and turned it over, my hand began to shake. There were initials carved on the back: NAW. My breath caught in my throat. Oh, my God!

Was this Natalie's locket? The one Dorothy had described, the one I'd seen around Natalie's neck in some of the photos I'd found. It seemed impossible to believe that it was here. But those were her initials, standing for Natalie Anne Warren.

Holding the locket tight, I peered back into the box, seeing a silver bracelet, a turquoise ring, a woman's beanie, and then an envelope with strands of dark hair flowing out of it. *Why would there be hair in an envelope?*

I felt suddenly sick. I couldn't pick up that envelope. I couldn't look inside.

Getting to my feet, Natalie's locket still clutched in my fingers, my mind raced with questions. *Why were these things here in Dorothy's basement?*

She couldn't be a killer, could she?

No. That was impossible. She was a sweet old lady, and she'd brought me down here as if she had nothing to hide.

But I couldn't stay down here. I needed to get upstairs, to go to the sheriff, or maybe to Finn, to someone I could trust.

Before I could move, I heard someone come through the door, and then footsteps on the basement stairs that seemed too heavy to belong to Dorothy.

"Dorothy?" I called, turning toward the steps. I froze in shock.

It wasn't Dorothy coming down to the basement.

And any hope of escape had just vanished.

CHAPTER TWENTY-THREE

Jeff Holloway stood at the bottom of the stairs, his eyes moving from my face to the locket swinging from my fingers.

"You shouldn't have come down here, Cassidy," he said in a voice that was deadly quiet.

I took a step back, my mind racing. "Where's Dorothy?"

"When she told me you were down here, I sent her on an emergency errand to talk some sense into Cole before he leaves town. She won't be back...in time."

His last two words sent a wave of panic through my body, but I tried not to show it. "Then I'll just go back to the inn."

He moved closer, his big, broad body, blocking my exit. "You're not going back to the inn." He paused, his gaze turning very dark. "No one ever goes back."

I swallowed a knot in my throat, telling myself to stay calm, to think. I needed to keep him talking until I could figure a way out. Maybe Dorothy wouldn't find Cole. Maybe he'd already left with Sophie, and she'd come right back to the house.

"Nothing to say?" he challenged. "You? The woman who has so much to say to anyone who will listen? I've enjoyed your podcasts, listening to you scramble to find some reasonable explanation for what happened to Natalie. You wanted to tell a true crime story that would fascinate your listeners. But you know what's more fascinating than talking about murder?"

I really didn't want to answer that question. "Where's Natalie, Jeff?"

"She's not here. But you are. And you look like her with your brown hair and your dark eyes—eyes that are filled with fear right now. But you don't have to be afraid. You won't feel anything."

My heart was beating so fast, I thought it might jump out of my chest. "What did you do to Natalie?"

"You'll find out soon enough." An evil smile twisted his lips. "This will be fun. Not as good as planning, waiting, lying... But the spontaneity will be a nice change."

"Were there other women, too?"

"Of course. But no one came looking for them. I didn't think anyone would come looking for Natalie. She told Dorothy she was all alone. Her family hated her. Her ex had moved on. No one cared about her anymore. She was going to start over in a new place, create a new life. That's what they all think they're going to do, what they all want to do."

His voice took on a dangerous, nostalgic quality that made me shiver.

"Dorothy sent the women here? To you?"

"No. She wouldn't do that. She just told me about them, about the ones that made her sad, the ones who were all alone in the world, the ones who looked like you. She had no idea she was helping me choose."

"Choose?" I echoed, my voice barely above a whisper as the horror of it all settled in on me.

"Natalie wanted to be loved, to have someone obsessed with her, to feel that passion, and I provided that."

"She didn't choose you," I said, certain of that.

"She didn't know what she wanted. I did. I needed her. I needed all of them."

"Why?"

"You ask a lot of questions, Cassidy."

"If I'm never leaving this basement, then what's the harm in answering them?"

"You're right. It won't matter."

"Why did you pick women who looked like Natalie?"

"Because I couldn't have the one I wanted. But I could have them."

"Who did you want?" I asked.

He stared back at me for a long minute. "This is actually perfect that it's you."

"Why?"

"Because you're David's daughter. And David was one of the reasons I couldn't have her."

Realization dawned on me. "Are you talking about Lily?"

"They fought over her all the time—Tom and David. Lily went back and forth between them. She couldn't say no, even though they didn't treat her right. Tom hurt her physically, and David hurt her heart because he was going to leave her. I was right there, but she didn't see me; she only saw them."

"You killed Lily because she didn't want you?"

"No," he shouted, anger raging through his eyes, making me inch back toward the wall behind me. "She killed herself. Because of them, because of what they did to her."

"Then why didn't you kill your brother? It sounds like it was his fault that she committed suicide. Why hurt innocent women? Why are they paying for what Lily did?"

"Because they were just like her, running away from men who loved them, choosing the wrong person to make them happy. When the right person is there in front of them."

He was sick, delusional, definitely not in his right mind. I didn't know if that condition came and went, if he was normal sometimes and other times not, but it didn't matter. Right now, he was nothing but pure evil, and he was going to kill me. I couldn't let that happen. Not just because I really didn't want to die, but because I couldn't let him get away with another murder.

"Trying to think of a way out, aren't you?" he asked, his momentary rage turning back to confidence and a nauseating interest in me. "They all did. They all got the same look on their faces that you're wearing now."

"How many?"

He shrugged. "Not that many fit what I wanted, what I needed."

"And you've never felt any guilt about taking their lives?"

"Well, they didn't really want to live in the end, but, sure, sometimes I thought I was sick, that I took after my old man more than I wanted to. He used to beat us up, you know. And there's a good chance he killed my mother. I didn't want to be like him, but sometimes the dark takes over."

"You can choose something else," I said.

"That's what Natalie said, too."

"How did you get her to this house?" I asked, desperate to stall as long as I could. "Did you use Dorothy to lure her here?"

"No. I used my brother."

Surprise dropped my jaw, and he smiled. "You weren't expecting that answer, were you?"

"I wasn't."

"Tom and Ellen have their own operation going. You think they're better than me? They're not. They've been trafficking women for years. And it's always the same routine. The women are driven to the shopping center in Cork Harbor before dawn. Then they walk to the bus stop and get on the number twenty. At the first stop, they get picked up and taken away. Sometimes, I'm the one who takes them away. They think they're on some journey to freedom, but they're not."

I didn't really understand because fear was making it difficult for me to think. "What about Jessica? She got on a boat?"

"I don't know what happened to her. She didn't follow the

routine. Maybe they changed it up after all the people came asking questions about Natalie."

"And your brother doesn't know what you're doing?"

"That's the best part. Tom thinks he knows it all, but he knows nothing." Jeff's hands clenched into fists. "My brother destroys everything and everyone that he touches. And no one ever holds him accountable."

"So you kill innocent women to punish him?"

"To punish all of them!" His voice rose, echoing off the concrete floor. "Every woman who thinks she can walk away from me."

I glanced at the stairs. He was blocking them, but maybe if I could get past him—

"Don't even try. You'll just end up in more pain before this is over," Jeff said, reading my intention. "And there's nowhere to go, no one to help you. Do you think anyone in this town will be anything but happy if you disappear?"

"I'm not like the others. I'm Ellen's granddaughter. You don't think she'll look for me?"

"She has too many sins of her own to cover up."

"Someone will figure out what you're doing, and then you'll be the monster and your brother will be the hero when he puts you in jail. He'll win again, just like he always does."

"Shut up."

"But you could turn against him," I continued. "You said that Tom and Ellen are trafficking women. Why don't you tell people that? Why don't you take him down? Then you'll be the good one, and he'll be the bad one."

"I said shut up!" Jeff lunged forward, catching my arm and throwing me back against the hard wall behind me. My head bounced off the ragged wood, sending a shocking pain through my temple. But as he came toward me, I kicked him hard in the groin, the way I'd learned in the self-defense class I'd taken when I moved to Manhattan.

He let out a yelp of pain as he staggered backward. I tried to run around him, but he grabbed me again and dragged me toward him, a furious rage giving him what seemed like super-human strength.

I twisted and kicked, finally breaking free. I scrambled away from him, my eyes darting around the basement for something I could use as a weapon. Old gardening tools leaned against the far wall, but Jeff was between them and me.

He stood slowly, touching his lip, which I'd somehow made bloody with my fist. He looked at his fingers with something like surprise, then smiled. "Good. I was hoping you'd make this interesting." This wasn't the jovial man I'd met at the inn. The one who'd joked about Dorothy's stories being better than reality TV. That man was gone, replaced by something dark and twisted and utterly insane.

"Let me go. I won't tell anyone. I'll leave town."

"You had your chance to leave, but you didn't take it. You wanted your listeners to feel what Natalie felt. But they won't feel it; you will."

He rushed forward, shoving me backward, and I crashed into a stack of boxes. They tumbled down around me, old Christmas decorations and moth-eaten blankets spilling across the floor.

I grabbed a heavy box—filled with something solid—and swung it at him as hard as I could.

It connected with his shoulder. He stumbled, cursing, and slugged me in the face.

I made it to my knees before he caught me, throwing me down again, and as we hit the concrete floor together, the impact drove the air from my lungs.

His weight pressed down on me, crushing. I couldn't breathe. Couldn't think.

This is how I die, I thought distantly. *In a basement in Maine, and no one will ever know what happened.*

No!

Somewhere, I found the strength to push him off me and roll out from under him. I scrambled to my feet, gasping for air, my vision swimming. My face throbbed where he'd hit me. My palms were bleeding. Everything hurt.

But I was alive.

And the table behind me had tools, a screwdriver and a wrench. I grabbed the wrench and when Jeff came at me again, I swung the wrench at his head as hard as I could. He stumbled back in shock. "You bitch!"

I took advantage of his weakened state to hit him again, and this time he went down and stayed down. I stared at him in shock as I heard banging upstairs, then a crash, and someone running down the steps. I really hoped it wasn't Tom, because he would probably accuse me of trying to kill his brother.

I raised the wrench, tried to prepare myself for another fight, but my head was spinning, my vision blurring...

"Cassidy!"

Finn rushed down the stairs, his eyes taking in the scene—Jeff unconscious on the floor, me holding a bloody wrench in my hand with more blood dripping down my face.

"I—Jeff," I stuttered. "He was going to kill me. Like he killed Natalie."

"Oh, my God," he said as he came toward me and put his arms around my stiff body. "You're okay now. You're safe."

I was afraid to trust his words, but I was too weak to do anything but sink into his embrace. After a moment, he pulled slightly away to call 911. As he was doing that, I glanced back at Jeff, who was still unconscious, his forehead bloody from my last strike.

"I've never been in a fight before," I murmured. "Never hurt anyone. And definitely never tried to kill anyone." I glanced back at Finn's grim expression. "It was him or me. I couldn't disappear like the others. I couldn't let him win."

"You're saying Jeff killed Natalie?"

"Her locket is..." My voice trailed away as I realized I'd dropped the locket during our fight, then I saw it on the ground. "It's there. And in that other box are other pieces of jewelry and women's clothing. There's even some dark hair in an envelope. He said there were others... I don't know how many. But he killed them."

As I started to shake, Finn put his arms around me again. "You don't have to say everything now."

"If Tom comes here, he's going to try to spin this. He'll say I hurt Jeff. He'll hide the evidence. We have to do something." I felt panicked and desperate again. I'd escaped from Jeff, but Tom might be even more dangerous with the weight of the law behind him.

"I agree," Finn said. "I'm going to call the mayor. We need investigators here who aren't related to the suspect."

As Finn got on the phone with the mayor's office, I heard sirens, the second time this week they'd come for me. But I was still alive, still breathing, and that felt like a miracle.

Several minutes later, two officers came down the stairs who I didn't recognize, but Finn greeted them by name, telling them that Jeff had attacked me, and that he'd admitted to killing at least one of the women who'd disappeared from the inn.

That seemed to surprise both of them, and they exchanged a look of concern, as if they weren't sure what to do with the sheriff's brother being accused of murder. One dropped to his knees to check on Jeff, while the other turned to me.

"An ambulance is on the way. I'm Deputy Mendez," he said. "Can you tell me what happened?"

"Jeff Holloway tried to kill me because I found his stash of trophies that he'd taken from the women he killed, including Natalie Warren."

The deputy cleared his throat. "That's quite an accusation."

"It's not an accusation; it's the truth. Jeff told me everything because he didn't plan on my being able to tell anyone else. That locket on the ground over there belonged to Natalie Warren. Her initials are on it. In that open box you'll find items that belonged to other women, including a bloody scarf and some thick strands of brown hair."

The second deputy left Jeff's side to check on my claims. He looked in the box, then back at his partner. "It's just what she said—"

His words were interrupted by more sirens, followed by more voices, and then a trail of people came down the stairs, including the sheriff and two EMTs.

The first one to reach the bottom was Tom Holloway, his face red, his eyes burning with anger and what might have been fear.

"What the hell is going on—" He stopped mid-sentence when he saw Jeff on the floor. The color drained from his face. "My God! What did you do to my brother?" He turned to the EMTs. "Help him."

The two men rushed to Jeff's side.

"Jeff attacked Cassidy," Finn said, waving his hand toward my bloodied face. "As you can see, she had to defend herself."

Tom looked at me, then at his brother's unconscious form. "I don't understand," he said with a shake of his head.

"Jeff killed Natalie," I told him. "He admitted it to me. And other women, too, lonely women who had no one to look for them."

"There must be a mistake."

"There's not. There's evidence in that box, and probably on the locket on the floor, which belonged to Natalie."

"She's right," the deputy next to the box said. "There's a bloody scarf, human hair, and a bunch of other jewelry."

"It's not possible," Tom said. "No, this is wrong. She's trying to set Jeff up, tell a story to sell her podcast. She's a liar."

"Stop," Finn ordered, his commanding voice shutting down Tom's panicked ramble. "You need to step back, Tom. You can't investigate this. Jeff is your brother. It's a conflict of interest."

"I'm the sheriff. I decide who investigates."

"Not this time," another man said as he came down the stairs. "Deputy Mendez will be running this investigation, Tom. I want this scene secured. Every piece of evidence needs to be documented, and we'll need statements from everyone here." He paused, then turned to me. "I'm Mayor Brennan."

"Cassidy Clarke."

"You look like you need medical attention, Ms. Clarke."

"I'm okay. I just want to make sure that Jeff Holloway is arrested and that his brother can't let him go, that he can't bury evidence, can't try to pin this on me."

"I will make sure this investigation is run by the book," the mayor said. "Can you tell us what happened?"

"Yes, tell us what the hell happened," the sheriff said forcefully.

"Tom," the mayor warned. "Stay out of this."

"I came down here with Dorothy. She was going to give me photos of my family, but then the doorbell rang, and she went upstairs. While she was gone, I looked around for the photos. I opened that box, and I saw Natalie's locket. I had it in my hand when Jeff came down the stairs. Her initials are engraved on it, and she was wearing it in photos that I saw of her. I knew it was hers. And when Jeff saw me holding it, he knew I'd figured that out."

I waited for Tom to interrupt, but he was surprisingly silent. "There are other items in the box," I continued. "And Jeff told me that there were other women." I paused, feeling sick and in pain, but I had to get the words out. "He was preying on lonely women who had no family, who could disappear without anyone asking questions. I think Dorothy was giving him some information, but he said she didn't know what he was doing with that info."

My breath caught in my throat. "He was going to kill me. I was going to disappear like the others. But I couldn't let him get away with murder. We fought, and, somehow, I was able to grab a wrench and hit him over the head with it a couple of times. Then Finn showed up."

"This can't be," Tom muttered. "This is wrong—all wrong. There's been a mistake."

"No mistake," I said forcefully. "Your brother is a killer, and he said it's always been women who look like Natalie, like me, and most importantly, like Lily. He said he was in love with your high school girlfriend, and she rejected him, and she left him."

"She killed herself," Tom said. "This is crazy. Why are you talking about Lily?"

"Because Jeff was talking about her," I told him. "And you know I'm not lying. Jeff also said other things, too, that you and my grandmother have been trafficking women for years. He figured out where you moved them to be picked up, and he intercepted them, picking off the ones he wanted to fill the void in his life."

Tom opened his mouth, but no words came out. "None of that is true."

"It's all true." I leaned forward, putting my hands on my knees as the pain in my head sent a wave of nausea running through me.

"That's enough, Tom," the mayor interrupted as the paramedics came down the stairs. "We'll get a complete statement after someone takes a look at you, Ms. Clarke."

Jeff suddenly groaned as his eyes flickered open, and he took in the scene in confusion. One of the paramedics moved to him, while the other came to me.

"Why don't we go upstairs?" the EMT suggested to me.

I was afraid to leave, still terrified they'd cover up this crime like all the others.

"I'll make sure nothing is tampered with," Finn assured me.

"Okay," I said, allowing myself to be taken up the stairs as I heard Jeff telling them that I attacked him.

That almost sent me back down to the basement, but I told myself that Jeff couldn't lie his way out of this. It wasn't his word against mine. There was proof of his crimes, and he was going to have to answer for them, and there was no way his brother was going to be able to cover for him.

I sat down on the couch in Dorothy's living room as the EMT tended to my cuts.

"Looks like you have some older scratches, too," he commented.

"I was in a car accident two nights ago."

"Not your week, huh?"

"Definitely not," I said.

"How's the pain in your head?"

"Pounding. He slammed me into the wall and onto the floor."

"Did you lose consciousness?"

"No."

"That's good. I want to ask you a few questions," he said, then proceeded to ask me my name, birthdate, address, and where I was staying in Stonecross. After I answered those successfully, and he checked my vision, he said, "I think you're okay, but it wouldn't be a bad idea to get checked out at the hospital."

"I'll be okay. I don't want to go to the hospital. I feel better now that I'm sitting down."

"You're definitely going to want to take it easy tonight. And you'll want to put some ice on your eye. It's already starting to swell. You're going to have a shiner tomorrow."

I didn't care about my face right now. I was just happy to be alive. And to be able to tell everyone what Jeff had done.

"I'm going to help my partner with the other victim," the paramedic said as he got to his feet. "Will you be all right here?"

"Yes. And he's not a victim. He's a killer."

The EMT's lips tightened, but he didn't comment before moving down the hall toward the basement stairs. A moment later, Finn returned to my side while the others brought a noticeably wobbly Jeff up the stairs and into the living room, his hands cuffed behind his back.

When he saw me, he said, "She's a liar. You all know she's making up stories. She planted evidence down there. She's trying to come up with a killer for her podcast."

"Shut up," Tom said. "For the love of God, shut the hell up, Jeff."

Tom followed his brother, the EMTs and one of the deputies out the door. I assumed the other deputy and the mayor were still in the basement.

"I'm going to take you to the medical center," Finn told me.

"No. I have to go back to the inn. I have to confront my grandmother."

"Do you really think Ellen and Tom were trafficking women? That sounds like something Jeff made up."

I met Finn's gaze. "He didn't make it up. He told me how he intercepted the women. He knew where the pickup was supposed to be, where they would be expecting a ride from a stranger, and he became that stranger."

"Usually, in trafficking, the women don't go willingly."

"Maybe they didn't know they were being trafficked. But my grandmother will know, and maybe once she realizes what Jeff did and what information he has, she'll finally come clean."

"You should let the deputies talk to her first."

"No way. But you don't have to go with me. I'll go on my own."

I started to stand up and had to pause until a wave of dizziness passed.

"You're not going by yourself," Finn said. "I'll drive you."

"Thank you." As we moved through the front door, I suddenly realized Dorothy was still gone. "Dorothy," I said abruptly. "Jeff said he told her there was an emergency with Cole, and she needed to go talk to him. I don't think she should come back here and find the police here and that stuff in the basement."

"She was with Sophie at my parents' house when I left. She told me Jeff sent her there to talk to Cole, but he hadn't shown up. She mentioned that you were in her house looking for photos, and she hoped Jeff was taking care of you, and I thought that was odd, so I came straight over."

"I'm glad you did, because if that wrench hadn't worked—" Tears pooled in my eyes, but I didn't want them to fall, not yet, not when there was still stuff to do.

"It did work," he said quietly. "And I'll text Sophie to keep both Cole and Dorothy at my parents' house. She can stay there overnight if she needs to."

"I thought Sophie and Cole would be on their way to New York by now."

"Cole got delayed by his dad, who'd figured he was trying to leave. They got into another argument, which is why he was late. I'll text everyone now." Finn opened the car door for me and then sent his texts as I got into the car and fastened my seat belt, my body aching from head to toe. But I was safe, Jeff was going to jail, and I finally knew what had happened to Natalie. I just had one more person to talk to, one more person to confront.

Finn got in the car and started the engine, and I felt a wave of relief as we drove away from Dorothy's house. I know she hadn't meant to put me in danger, and it had been my idea to go and see her. But I thanked God that I'd been able to battle Jeff and come out on top.

As I looked down at my hands that were still shaking, I wasn't sure when I'd start to really feel safe, but it certainly wasn't happening yet.

Finn kept shooting me looks of concern, and I tried to give him a weak smile in return. "I'm okay," I said.

"I should have been with you. I shouldn't have left you alone today."

"I didn't think going to Dorothy's house was dangerous. I never imagined it was Jeff who had hurt Natalie, who had forced her to disappear. If anyone, I thought it was Tom or Ray, not Jeff."

"And yet in some ways, it makes sense," Finn muttered. "The Holloway family has a long history of violence."

"Jeff said his father used to knock him and Tom around, that

Tom did the same to Lily. He couldn't understand why Lily would want Tom, or even my father for that matter, because he didn't think David treated her well, either. But she only had eyes for them. She never saw him, and he was right there in front of her. It drove him crazy that women always chose the wrong guy when he was the right guy. I think that's what he said. It's all a jumble in my mind, and he wasn't always making sense."

"Because he's mentally ill," Finn said. "I wonder if Tom knew."

"He didn't. Jeff said the best part of it all was knowing that Tom had no idea what he was doing right under his nose."

"Then Tom is in the clear?"

"For killing Natalie, but according to Jeff, Tom and my grandmother were trafficking women, and he used their operation to find his victims. I hate the idea that she's been doing that."

"You should let the police talk to her."

"Who knows when they'll get to her? She might disappear before then. And I want to look her in the eye. I want to hear her try to excuse what she's been doing."

"She could be as dangerous as Jeff."

"Well, I'm going, and I'm hoping you'll come with me," I said.

"Oh, I am definitely not letting you talk to her on your own."

"Thanks." I paused. "I don't want my grandmother to be a trafficker or a murderer, but maybe my dad was right. Maybe it was a mistake to ever want to know her."

CHAPTER TWENTY-FOUR

When we pulled into the inn's parking lot and got out of the car, I saw Ellen standing on the porch, her arms crossed, her expression troubled.

She'd obviously heard what happened. Tom must have called her the second he'd left Dorothy's house. I was surprised she hadn't run. But then, this inn was her home, probably the only place she'd ever wanted to be. Unfortunately, her next place of residence might be a jail cell, and it might be because of me, her granddaughter.

I squared my shoulders, knowing I needed what little energy I had left. Ellen had intimidated me since the first moment I'd arrived, but not anymore. I'd just fought for my life against a madman. I could handle anything she was about to dish out.

"Cassidy, are you all right?" she asked.

"Jeff Holloway tried to kill me."

"Come in. Let's talk."

"You're not surprised."

"Tom called me. Let's not do this here. I'd like you to come into my apartment."

"Fine," I said, following her into the inn, past the reception desk, down the hall to her apartment.

She opened her door, then paused. "I'd like to talk to my granddaughter alone," she told Finn.

"Not a chance," he replied. "I'm not leaving Cassidy alone with you or anyone until we know everything."

She took a frustrated breath, then opened her door and motioned us inside.

"Can I get you some water or tea?" she asked. "Maybe some ice? Your face is swelling."

"The only thing I need right now are answers," I said as I took a seat on her couch, with Finn right beside me. I was glad to have his support because I was still feeling shaky, and I needed someone with a clear head to make sure my grandmother didn't get away with anything. "Jeff told me you and Tom have been trafficking women for years, that he simply took advantage of your operation to sneak a few for himself, and one of those was Natalie Warren. He apparently intercepted her up at some drop-off point."

Ellen shook her head, her face pale, her lips tight, her gaze hard and pinched. "We haven't been trafficking women."

"You can't keep making excuses," I said wearily.

"I'm not, Cassidy. Tom and I have been helping women escape from terrible, abusive situations. It started a long time ago, but it grew bigger in recent years as some women we helped sent others to us."

"What are you talking about?"

"An underground railroad," she said.

"A what?" I asked in shock.

"A system that allows us to help move women out of dangerous living situations. It's why I created the health and wellness programs here, so that it wouldn't seem unusual that so many troubled young women were making their way to Stonecross. They stay for a few days. We get them medical care from the doctor in town if they need it. We get them new identities, and we move them along to others, who set them up in their new lives."

"Are you serious? Tom is helping you do this?"

"Yes."

"Tom, the person who allegedly beat up his girlfriend, Lily, a very long time ago? A man who has anger issues and runs this town as if it's his personal kingdom?"

"Tom did hurt Lily," she said. "He was eighteen at the time. And he'd been beaten by his father and watched his dad hurt his mother. He was in all kinds of pain and all kinds of trouble. What he did to Lily was enough of a turning point for him to want to change his behavior, but it didn't happen right away. It took almost a decade before he finally cleaned up his act and tried to become a good husband and a good father."

"His wife left him, and his son hates him. It doesn't seem like he's good at either job."

"Well, maybe he's just gotten better at being a good person," she said. "He's been hard on Cole because Tom doesn't want Cole to turn out like himself. Tom didn't get himself together until his dad died and he became the sheriff. He believed the law saved him and that it could save Cole if he followed in his footsteps."

"They're not the same."

"I know, and I've told Tom that holding on too tightly never works. It only makes the person you're trying to keep close want to leave more."

I had a feeling she was talking about my father, but I couldn't let her derail me with a tantalizing glimpse of their relationship. I had to stay focused on what she'd been doing. "Tell me more about the railroad. When did it start?"

"Unofficially, a very long time ago. But in the past fifteen years, it has become a bigger operation." She paused. "I had no idea Jeff knew anything about what we were doing."

"He thought you were trafficking women."

"I don't know how he came to that conclusion. We've kept our circle incredibly tight. Only me, Tom, Ray, and Dr. Garrett.

Our other contacts are all outside of Stonecross. We have a social worker in New York and another in Boston. A woman who runs a shelter in Chicago is also in the loop. They send women here who need our help, who are often afraid for their lives." She paused, swallowing hard. "I honestly thought that Natalie had made it to her next location. But I don't have contact with the women after they leave here. It's too dangerous for us to know where they go."

"But someone had to know that Natalie didn't show up."

"They probably thought she changed her mind. That's happened a few times. Women want to leave, but once the immediate threat goes down, they get drawn back to their old lives."

"That's not what happened to Natalie. Jeff intercepted her and killed her in Dorothy's basement after doing God knows what to her. She didn't find the peace she was seeking; she found more violence. I don't know what he did with her body, and I don't know how many other women there were, but her locket was at Dorothy's house. And there were other items, belonging to other women there, too."

"I can't believe he used her house," she said with painful regret.

"He also used her. Dorothy would tell him about the women who were lonely and sad, who had no family, beautiful women who had brown hair and brown eyes, like Lily. It was about Lily, the girl he loved, but who didn't love him. Everyone who looked like her had to pay for her rejection."

"I had no idea," she breathed, new horror in her eyes. "Honestly, Cassidy, I didn't know Jeff was evil or sick. Tom didn't know, either. He wasn't protecting him."

It felt like she was being sincere, and I wanted to believe that this version of her was the truth. A grandmother who ran an underground railroad to save women was definitely better than a human trafficker.

"I have to interrupt for a moment," Finn said. "Because I

think we may still have a problem. And I don't want to wait on this any longer."

"Wait on what?" I asked, surprised by his words.

Finn gave me a worried look. "You told me that Jeff said he didn't kill Jessica."

"That's right. He said he didn't know what happened to her."

"That makes sense, because Nathan woke up, and he told me that Jessica escaped in a truck, driven by Ray."

Ellen sat up straighter, but instead of giving me a defensive explanation, she said, "That's true."

"That's true?" I echoed. "Why? Where did Ray take her?"

"After Natalie disappeared, there were a lot of eyes on this town, on this inn. I was going to take a break for at least a year, but then, Jessica needed my help. I was afraid to use our usual system. I didn't want it to look like there was a pattern. And as I said before, I believed Natalie was safe, like all the others. I wanted Jessica to be safe, too, so we set up the boat trip. She was to sail out to the cove, then push her boat out to sea so it would look like she drowned. But there was a problem."

"Nathan," I murmured.

"Yes. He saw her trying to shove the boat into the rocks. He came into the cove and asked her if she needed help. She said she didn't, and she'd make it worth his while to say he found the boat but never saw her."

"Oh, my God!"

"She gave Nathan the ring," Finn interjected. "To buy his silence."

"Yes. She told Ray what she'd done when he picked her up," Ellen said. "We hoped that Nathan would stay silent. The ring was worth a lot of money. But I knew Nathan when he was a kid, and he was always unpredictable. After some time passed, it seemed like we were in the clear."

"Where did Ray take Jessica?" Finn asked.

"To a bus station about thirty miles away, and then she made her way further up the coast to a safe house. She's fine. She's safe."

"I don't think she is," Finn said, his gaze troubled. "Nathan told me that Tyler came to see him yesterday. In fact, he thinks Tyler drugged him, intending to kill him after he told him about Jessica and Ray."

"Tyler?" I gasped. "That's crazy. He wouldn't kill Nathan."

Finn didn't look convinced, and neither did Ellen.

"Why would he?" I continued. "Tyler is just trying to find Jessica."

"Why?" Finn asked. "I know you said Jessica was his friend, but I'm not sure I buy that. Did he have another reason for wanting to find her?"

"Yes," I replied. "He did have another reason. Jessica is a witness to something that his brother is being charged for. He said she's the only one who can clear his brother's name, so he has to find her and bring her back, or his brother will go to prison."

"Jessica isn't safe," my grandmother said, jerking to her feet. "I have to warn her."

"Warn her?" I repeated. "You just said you don't have contact with the women after they leave here, that you don't know where they are."

"Jessica was...different."

"Different?" I questioned. "How?" At my grandmother's hesitation, I added, "Seriously? You cannot hold out on me now. I have to know everything. I almost died today because people refused to talk about what was going on. And maybe you don't give a damn about me, but—"

"Of course I give a damn about you," Ellen interrupted. "Jessica is different because she's the daughter of one of the first women I helped thirty-six years ago. When I helped that woman get away from a terrible situation, she was pregnant with Jessica. And she told Jessica if she was ever in trouble, she should come to me, that I was the only one she could trust."

Despite her explanation, there was something she wasn't telling me. I thought about what she had told me. "Thirty-six years ago," I said slowly. "That's about the time my dad left, isn't it? Are you talking about Lily?"

My grandmother nodded. "Yes."

"You helped Lily escape? She didn't kill herself?"

"We made it look like she did so no one would look for her."

As that sank in, I said, "Is Jessica Tom's daughter? Does he know?"

"Tom doesn't know anything about Jessica's past."

"You didn't answer my question."

Ellen twisted her hands, shifting from one foot to the other, as if she were battling some inner conflict. Then she lifted her head and met my gaze. "Tom isn't Jessica's father; David is."

"What?" I gasped. "Jessica is my...half sister? Does my dad know he has another daughter?"

"He doesn't. He thought Lily killed herself because of me, because I didn't want them to be together. He misunderstood an argument Lily and I had at the inn a few weeks before the night she allegedly killed herself."

"Why not tell him the truth? Set him straight? How could you let him believe that the girl he loved was dead? That is so cruel."

"It had to be done. Lily needed to be safe, and I didn't want him to look for her. She couldn't just disappear. It had to look like she was dead."

"I don't understand."

"I know you don't, but here's what happened. Tom abused Lily. Her father had done the same thing. But David was kind to her, and she said he found her one night crying, and he comforted her, and they ended up being together. He wanted them to be together forever. But her life was a mess. Tom was always drunk and always volatile. I was afraid he'd hurt David if he knew that David had slept with his girlfriend. And it wasn't just Tom; it was her father. She had to get away from him, but she was sixteen. She couldn't leave. She was a minor. If David tried to take her out of town, her dad would have come after him. And David could have been tried for kidnapping or statutory rape or any number of things. I had to protect him."

"So you helped Lily fake her death?" I asked.

"Yes. I told her that was the only way to be free, and that I would do it if she promised to never contact David again. I didn't want her to be an anchor around his neck. I didn't want being with her to make him her father's target. It had to be a clean and final break."

I shook my head. Her story made sense but still... "It was such a drastic thing to do. Couldn't you have gone to the police and had Lily removed from her father's home?"

"Other people had reported him, but neither Lily nor her mother would ever admit he was hurting her. And Lily didn't want her father to go to jail. She also didn't want Tom to go to jail. She just wanted to be free. And I helped her do that."

"What did my father think had happened?"

"He thought that I'd told Lily to stay away from him, that I'd fired Lily, and that she'd killed herself because she couldn't have him, and she'd lost her job, and she was afraid to go home and face her parents."

"You should have told him the truth."

Ellen gave me a direct look that held not even the tiniest bit of regret. "I couldn't do that. It was for her protection and for his. I may have lost my relationship with my son, but he went on to live the life he was supposed to live. And Lily did, too."

"Let's get back to Jessica," Finn interrupted.

"She came to me, terrified for her life. She said someone was trying to stop her from testifying in an upcoming trial. She needed help. Lily had died a few years earlier, and she'd told her if she ever needed someone, I was the one she should go to."

"Well, Tyler wants her to testify," I said. "He needs her to be alive. He's not trying to kill her."

"Let's hope you're right," Finn said shortly. "But just in case... you need to tell us where Jessica is."

"She's in Pinehaven, but that's three hours away from here, and Tyler has a big head start," Ellen said, pulling out her phone. She punched in a number, then gave me a fearful look. "Jessica isn't answering."

"We have to go find her," I said, jumping to my feet so quickly my head spun again, and put a hand on Finn's arm.

"You're in no condition to go anywhere except bed," he said.

"No. I'm going to find Jessica." I stopped abruptly, turning to Ellen again. "Does Jessica know you're her grandmother?"

"No. I didn't tell her. And, apparently, Lily didn't, either."

"I'll call the Pinehaven Police Department," Finn said. "They can send someone out to check her house and be on the lookout for Tyler."

"And then we'll drive there," I said.

"No."

"Finn. I'm not staying here, counting on some nameless, faceless police officer to save my sister."

"I agree. You're not staying here, and neither am I. My friend flies helicopter tours. I'm going to see if he can get us to Pinehaven in the next twenty minutes. If we're lucky, we might just beat Tyler there."

As Finn moved into the kitchen to make his call, my grandmother and I exchanged a long look.

"You wanted to know me," she said finally. "The truth isn't always what you want to hear, is it?"

"No. It isn't. I'm going to need some time to sort all this out. But right now, all I want to do is find Jessica." I shook my head in amazement. "I can't believe I have a sibling."

"She's strong, too, just like you, Cassidy. She's the one who blew the whistle at the company she worked for. She risked her life to stop a wrong." Ellen paused. "That's why I don't understand what you said about Tyler wanting her to help his brother.

I think the man awaiting jail is the one she's supposed to testify against."

My heart sank, because that made more sense than the story Tyler had told me. And hadn't I wondered at one point if Tyler was hiding something else? Hadn't I wondered if I was making a mistake helping him find Jessica? But I had been so desperate to have an ally, I'd pushed those misgivings aside.

On the other hand... "Tyler is an architect," I said. "I saw the blueprints he was working on at the house up the road. He's not a killer. Maybe he doesn't know that his brother is lying. Maybe his brother is using him to find Jessica."

"Maybe," Ellen said. "But we still don't know what his intentions are when he does find her."

"We've got a ride," Finn interrupted. "Are you sure you want to go, Cassidy? You're hurt. You might have a concussion."

"I can do this, and I want to do this," I said firmly. I might be running on nothing but adrenaline but I had to save my sister.

"Good luck," Ellen said as we left her apartment and headed to Finn's car.

I needed more than luck. I needed a fast helicopter and for Tyler to be stuck in traffic so he didn't get to Jessica before we did.

CHAPTER TWENTY-FIVE

I'd never been in a helicopter before, but I didn't have time to be nervous. On the way to Pinehaven, I texted Morgan and Tessa, giving them the highlights. Their replies came fast and furious, filled with concern and questions and worry that the danger still wasn't over. It might not be, but I wasn't alone now. Finn was a trained soldier. He was also carrying a firearm, which he seemed to have picked up from the pilot. At any other moment in my life, that would have made me nervous, but I was afraid we might need the gun, especially if I was wrong about Tyler.

As I chatted with my friends, Finn was on his phone, too, his fingers flying through his text messages as fast as mine were.

When the helicopter landed, we got off and ran to a parking lot near the airfield, where our pilot had arranged for us to get a car.

It wasn't until we had fastened our seat belts and started our drive to Jessica's house that I had a chance to ask Finn who he'd been talking to.

"One of my former team members does private security now," Finn said. "I had him look up Tyler Pierce."

"Are you going to tell me he's not an architect?" I said warily.

"Because Morgan looked into him, too, and she found the information on his brother, so that was true."

"He's an architect. But did you ever see a photo of him?"

"Why would I need a photo? I saw him in real life." At Finn's expression, my stomach twisted once more. "What?"

"I'm guessing when Morgan did her research, she didn't know what the man you were talking to looked like, did she?"

"I never sent her a photo."

He held out his phone. "This is the photo I just received."

I took his phone, shocked by the face of the man staring back at me. He had light brown hair that was thinning on the top, acne on his face, and thick-rimmed glasses. "This has to be a mistake."

"It's not, Cassidy. I think the man you met stole Tyler's identity and his life as a cover."

"If he's not the brother, who would he be?" I could see the answer in Finn's eyes. "You think he was hired to find Jessica and bring her back?"

"I don't think he's supposed to bring her back. I believe his mission is to make sure she never returns, never testifies."

I wanted to deny it, but I couldn't, because I knew deep down in my soul that Finn was absolutely right. "Can you go faster?"

Finn pressed down on the gas. "We're only a few miles away. The local police said they checked out the house, and Jessica wasn't home. They were going to stick around, but there's a multi-vehicle accident on the highway, so they'll be back as soon as they can. If Tyler, or whatever his name is, had to drive here from Cork Harbor, then we might still have a chance of getting to Jessica before he does."

"I hope so. Is it weird that there was a multi-vehicle accident nearby that took all the cops away? Or am I being paranoid?"

He gave me a shrug. "It's probably good to be paranoid. But Pinehaven is a small town with a small police force, so it could just be that."

"Maybe Jessica isn't even there. Ellen texted me a few minutes ago that she still hadn't reached Jessica."

"She might have moved on since Ellen sent her there," Finn suggested. "Maybe she just didn't feel safe and wanted to keep going just in case anyone tracked her the way Tyler just did."

"Ellen said she texted her like a week ago, so if she left, it was recently. And she didn't tell Ellen." I paused. "What if Tyler already has her? What if he kidnapped her and is taking her somewhere else to..." I really didn't want to finish that thought. "We have to save her, Finn. She's my sister. I can't let her die."

"We're going to do everything we can to prevent that."

I hoped our *everything* would be enough.

The address Ellen had given us led to a narrow gravel road that wound through a dense pine forest. The small, weathered cabin was set back from the main road, almost invisible unless you knew where to look.

"That's it," Finn said, pulling into a thick grove of trees about fifty yards away. "We should approach on foot. If Tyler's already there, we don't want to announce ourselves."

"I don't see a car."

"He might have hidden it somewhere, too."

We got out quietly, and Finn pulled his gun from his waistband, checking it with practiced efficiency. After everything that had happened, I was grateful he was armed.

We moved through the trees, staying off the road until we reached the cabin. It was surrounded by forest land. Perfect for hiding. Also perfect for trapping someone.

We approached the cabin carefully. The front door was closed, curtains drawn. Finn knocked softly. "Jessica? Jessica Trent?"

No answer.

He tried the door. It was locked.

"Let's check the back," Finn said.

We walked around the side of the cabin, our feet crunching on pine needles and fallen leaves. The back of the property opened up to more forest, and I could see a narrow trail leading into the trees.

The back door was closed but unlocked. Finn pushed it open slowly, gun raised. "Jessica?"

Still no answer.

We stepped into a small kitchen, tidy and sparse. Through a doorway, I could see a living room with a couch and a wood-stove. It looked lived-in but empty.

"She's not here," I said with disappointment.

"But someone's staying here." Finn gestured to a mug on the counter, still half full of coffee.

A sound from outside made us both freeze.

We moved back to the door and looked out. A dark-haired woman in jeans and a blue jacket was now visible about fifty yards away from the house. She was picking flowers and completely unaware of our presence.

"That has to be her," I said, moving in her direction. "Put the gun away so we don't spook her."

He tucked the gun into the back waistband of his jeans.

When we got closer, the woman suddenly whirled around in alarm, holding the flowers in front of her like some kind of shield. Then she dropped them and ran into the woods.

"Dammit," Finn swore as he broke into a run, and I quickly followed.

"Jessica," I shouted. "Ellen Clarke sent us. We're here to protect you. You're in danger. Please, stop."

At my words, she looked back, then stumbled over a branch and fell to the ground.

"I've got this," I told Finn. Then I slowly moved toward her. "Jessica," I repeated, bringing her gaze to mine. "You don't have to be scared. I'm Cassidy Clarke, Ellen's granddaughter. And that's Finn Kelly. He works at Kelly's Pub in Stonecross. We know why you had to disappear. We're here to help you. We think someone may be coming after you."

Jessica slowly got to her feet, her jeans covered in dirt and leaves, her face pale, her eyes wary. "Why did I disappear?" she challenged.

"Because you blew the whistle on fraud at your company, because a man named Marcus Pierce is awaiting trial, and your testimony could make sure he goes to jail."

"You could be here to make sure I don't testify."

"We're not the danger. That's a man calling himself Tyler Pierce, but he's not Marcus's real brother. He's been hired to find you. And he's on his way here. We need you to come with us."

"How do I know you're telling the truth? How do I know you're not the ones trying to kill me?"

I thought about that question, then gave her the truth. "If we wanted to hurt you, we would have already done that. Finn has a gun. He's an ex-soldier. He knows how to use it." I paused, looking back at Finn.

He took out his gun and pointed it down at the ground.

I turned back to Jessica. "We came to warn you, to get you out of here, to keep you safe. You have to trust me. I know about your mom, Lily, how Ellen helped her escape a long time ago."

Something in Jessica's gaze shifted. "You know about my mother?"

"Yes. I'm telling the truth."

"How did you find me? How does this other man know where I am? Did someone talk? Ellen assured me no one would know where I went. Was it that guy I gave my ring to? Did he rat me out?"

"He did," I said. "And Tyler tracked you from Cork Harbor."

"But I disappeared months ago. Why is this happening now?"

"Nathan didn't crack until today."

She let out a sigh. "I had a feeling he was going to be a problem."

A car engine suddenly sounded in the distance, growing closer. And there weren't many other homes in the area. I glanced back at Finn.

"I'm going to check it out," he said. "Go deeper into the woods. And don't come back until you hear me say it's safe."

"There's a trail that leads to a beach," Jessica said, already moving. "Follow me."

We ran through the tall pines, Jessica moving with the confidence of someone who'd walked this path many times. I couldn't hear the engine anymore. I also couldn't hear Finn or anyone else. But it felt like someone was coming, or maybe that was my imagination...

Jessica suddenly tripped again, sprawling onto her knees. She grabbed her ankle in pain. "Damn. I think I sprained it," she said, gritting her teeth together as she winced.

"Can you walk? We have to keep going."

"I don't think I can. You should go on without me. If we're together, you'll be a target."

"I'm not leaving you alone. If you can't walk, then we have to hide. Come on." I grabbed her hand and pulled her up, then wrapped my arm around her waist as she hobbled and hopped her way into the thickest brush we could find. We knelt down, staying close together, hoping we couldn't be seen from the path.

The forest was silent except for our ragged breathing and the distant call of birds.

Jessica gave me a questioning look. I shook my head, putting my finger to my lips, because I could hear someone coming. I really hoped it was Finn.

Then a branch snapped. Our hands were still linked, and we squeezed our fingers together. I wished I could see what was happening, who was coming. I desperately wanted to hear Finn say we were safe, but it wasn't his voice that broke the quiet.

"I know you're here, Jessica," Tyler said. "I want to help you.

There are people coming to look for you, people who will say they are here to save you, but they're lying."

Jessica bit down on her lip as she looked at me. I gazed back into her eyes, willing her to believe me. Thankfully, she seemed to understand that she had to trust me. She had to stay silent.

"Marcus confessed last week," Tyler continued. "You don't have to be afraid anymore. It's time to come back. The company wants to thank you for your honesty and your courage."

Tyler was good. He sounded believable, almost trustworthy. If I didn't know better, I might have thought he was telling the truth.

I heard more footsteps. Tyler was circling...hunting...

I could see him now through the underbrush—a shadow moving between the trees, gun in hand. He was sweeping the area methodically, professionally.

He was also getting closer to our hiding spot. Another few steps, and he'd see us. And once he saw me, he would know he couldn't keep lying.

Tyler stopped about ten feet away, scanning the forest. Then his eyes landed on our hiding spot, and a cold smile spread across his face.

"There you are. Ah, you have a new friend, Jessica. Isn't that interesting..."

He raised his gun, pointing it directly at us.

"Stand up. Both of you. Slowly." He paused. "Or I can shoot you now."

We had to buy time until Finn could find us. Jessica and I exchanged another look and then rose to our feet.

Tyler met my gaze. "Impressive, Cassidy. I thought I was way ahead of you. How did you find out?"

"Nathan woke up and told Finn about his conversation with you. You tried to kill Nathan, didn't you?"

"It was easy enough to spike his drink with all the drugs he had lying about. It's a pity he didn't die, but I didn't have time to waste making sure that happened." Tyler paused. "But Nathan didn't know where Jessica was. I had to track her here. How did you figure it out?"

"Ellen told me."

"Really? So, grandma knew all along, and she came through for you," he drawled.

"Yes. I also know you're not Marcus's brother, Tyler. You're also not an architect. Those drawings in the house—you didn't do them, did you?"

"The real Tyler did."

"Why go to such lengths to pretend you were an architect?"

"It was a good cover. And I kind of liked being an architect for a while. You should understand why I did it; you had your own cover story."

"It wasn't as far from the truth as yours. You lied to me. About everything. And the worst lie was that you wanted to bring Jessica back safely so she could help your brother when you never had any intention of doing that." I could hardly believe I'd once trusted this man, once thought about spending the night at his house. Thank God I hadn't done that. "Why did you pretend to work with me? Why warn me about the inn? Why get involved with me at all?"

"You were asking a lot of questions. I wanted to stay close in case you found a lead to Jessica before I did. "

"Did you run me off the road?"

"Why would I do that? You were helping me. That was Finn."

"No. Finn saved me. It must have been Jeff." I paused. "Jeff Holloway killed Natalie Warren. Did you know that?"

"No idea," he said casually. "But I never cared about her."

"Or about me. I thought we were friends."

"I cared enough not to kill you," he pointed out in a cold, pragmatic voice.

"Because I was useful."

"And because you weren't my target; Jessica was. But sadly,

you'll have to die now, too. I can't afford to leave any loose ends. You really are too nosy for your own good, Cassidy."

I couldn't believe someone was once again threatening my life, and now I had to save not only myself but Jessica, too.

I heard another snap of a branch, followed by Finn's voice as he came from the trees behind Tyler. "Drop it," he ordered, his gun fixed on Tyler.

Tyler didn't bother to turn around or lower his weapon. "You can't kill me before I kill them, and you've already lost the element of surprise."

"You might get a shot off, but I can kill you after," Finn said. "Either way, you're dead."

"So are they. You won't risk their lives. You have a conscience; I don't."

"You don't know anything about my conscience," Finn retorted.

I saw the gleam in Tyler's eyes. He wasn't going to listen. He was going to kill us.

Before he could squeeze the trigger, a shot shattered the air.

Tyler's body jerked, his gun falling from his hand as he crumpled to the ground.

I gasped in shock. Finn's gun was still raised, unfired.

And then I heard someone come through the trees to our left. Tom Holloway stepped into the clearing, weapon in hand, satisfaction on his face. He was followed closely by my grandmother.

I couldn't believe they were here, but I was thrilled they'd come.

As Tom walked forward to check on Tyler, Ellen moved toward Jessica and me, stopping a few feet away, her gaze raking my face, then Jessica's.

"Are either of you hurt?" she asked.

"We're okay," I said. "You all got here just in time." I still couldn't quite believe Tom Holloway had saved my life when his brother had tried to take it only a few hours ago.

Finn put his gun back in his waistband as he came forward. "Nice shot, Tom."

"Thanks for the assist," Tom said. "Your distraction allowed me to get into position."

"You two worked together?" I asked in surprise.

"I ran into Tom and Ellen in the woods," Finn said. "We wanted to make sure one of us had a good shot."

"Thankfully, I got the pleasure," Tom said.

"How did you get here so fast?" I asked my grandmother.

"Finn isn't the only one who knows how to find a helicopter ride," Ellen said. "As soon as you left, I knew I had to follow. I started all this, and I had to finish it."

"So did I," Tom said heavily, his gaze seeking mine. "I'm sorry about what my brother did to you, Cassidy."

"Then you believe me?"

"I wish I didn't," he said heavily. "But I do. I had no idea Jeff was capable of..." He shook his head, his jaw tight. "I had no idea," he repeated. Clearing his throat, he added, "The local police are on their way. I'm going to go back to the cabin and meet them, bring them down here."

As Tom left, Finn stood guard over Tyler's motionless body.

"Jessica sprained her ankle," I told my grandmother. "Can you support her for a moment?"

"Of course." My grandmother moved closer and put her arm around Jessica.

I let go of Jessica's hand and moved next to Finn, needing to take a closer look at the man on the ground. Tyler was on his stomach, a bullet hole in the back of his head, with blood pooling all around him. I couldn't see his face, which was buried in the dirt, and maybe that was a good thing.

"He was going to kill us," I murmured. "Jessica was his target, but he couldn't afford a witness. I can't believe I was friends with him. I am a terrible judge of character."

"Don't be so hard on yourself. You only knew him a few days. And I'm sure he played into what you needed to hear."

"He backed up all my suspicions about Natalie, and for a while, it seemed like he was the only one who believed there was something going on. But he didn't care about Natalie or Anna or any of the others. He was only interested because it gave him a reason to talk to me, to find out if I was getting closer to Jessica, if I could help him find her. And I was trying to do just that. I was bringing Jessica's killer right to her."

"You had no idea about any of this. And Jessica is alive because of you," Finn pointed out. "You got her away from the cabin. You helped her hide when she got hurt. And you stood next to her when she was facing a killer. You are one hell of a strong person, Cassidy. After everything you went through earlier, you faced death for a woman you don't even know."

"I don't know her, but she shares my blood. And that means a lot to me." I paused as I heard voices and saw the police following Tom down the path. As they got close, we backed away from Tyler to give them room to examine the body and secure the scene.

"Let's go back to the house," Ellen suggested. "They don't need us out here. Finn, Jessica could use your help."

"No problem," Finn said, putting his weapon away. "I'll carry you back."

"I'm kind of heavy," Jessica said.

"I don't think it will be a problem," he told her with a smile as he picked her up and carried her down the path.

I fell into step with my grandmother. "Thank you for coming," I said. "You and Tom saved our lives."

"I'm glad it worked out that way." She paused, looking me in the eye. "I didn't want to lose you, Cassidy, not like this, not because of anything I'd done."

"Why would you care if you lost me or not?"

"Because I do," she said with a shrug. "Believe it or not."

"I'd like to believe it." I gave her a long, thoughtful look, realizing what a complicated person she was, and someone I still didn't understand. But maybe over time, I could change that.

"Do you still have questions?" Ellen asked.

"Many," I said. "But one I would like answered now. Anna Franklin."

"She's fine," Ellen said. "I checked after I heard about Jeff. Anna made it to her next check-in, and she's safe. Jeff didn't hurt her."

"I'm very glad about that. And the blood on her carpet..."

"Just what I told you before. She was having a panic attack, and she knocked the desk lamp into the window, breaking not only the lamp, but also the window, and cutting herself in the process. Ray really did take the carpet to the cleaners."

I finally believed her. "Ray has been helping you with the network?"

"Yes. He's a good man. He made mistakes. He paid for them. And he changed his life. I believe in second chances."

"Then why didn't you give my dad one?"

She gave a helpless, sad shrug. "Why didn't he give me one?"

"Because he has too much pride, and so do you. One last thing... My grandfather's death was just an accident, right?"

"A tragic accident," Ellen said. "And it had nothing to do with your father leaving. That was about Lily, and to some extent, himself. David had ambitions. You might think that my actions forced him to take a path he didn't want to take, but he always wanted to go to college, to make something of himself."

"I believe that," I murmured.

We gave each other another long look and then started walking again. We didn't speak further until we got back to the cabin. Jessica was sitting on the couch in her living room while Finn put a bag of ice on her swelling ankle.

I sat down next to Jessica. "Is it bad?" I asked.

"Compared to what could have happened, it's nothing. Thank you all for coming. I wouldn't be alive if you hadn't." Jessica looked at Ellen. "My mother always told me the only person she ever trusted in her life was you. You came through for her, and you came through for me."

"There's something you need to know," Ellen said, then stopped abruptly, her gaze moving to me. "Do you want to tell her, Cassidy?"

"This is your story to tell," I said, remembering how many times she'd told me that my father would have to tell his own story, but this one belonged to her.

Ellen nodded and sat down on the edge of the armchair across from the couch. "When I saved your mother all those years ago, Jessica, she was pregnant with you."

"She told me," Jessica said.

"Did she tell you who your father was?" Ellen asked.

Jessica's expression shifted. "No. She just said he couldn't be part of our lives, and she didn't want to talk about him. Why? Do you know who my father is?"

"Yes. Your father is my son, David. You're my granddaughter." Ellen blew out a breath as if those words had taken a lot out of her. "And so is Cassidy."

"What?" Jessica asked in surprise, her gaze turning to me. "You're my half sister?"

"Yes," I replied. "And I just learned that today, too. Once I heard your story, and we knew where you were, I had to come and find you. I couldn't let anything happen to you, not when we hadn't had a chance to meet each other."

"Wow! I have a sister. That's crazy." Jessica shook her head in bemusement. "I always wanted a sister."

"So did I." I gave her a heartfelt smile. "And I'm very glad you're all right."

"Me too." Jessica's gaze returned to Ellen. "Is it really over?"

"I think so. But until we know for sure, we'll play it safe."

"My dad..." Moisture filled Jessica's eyes. "Does he know about me?"

"No," Ellen replied. "I made your mother promise she would never tell him if I helped her get away. I know that will sound as cruel to you as it did to Cassidy. At the time, I believed it wasn't going to be forever, just until David and Lily both had a chance to grow up. I wanted Lily to be safe from the people who were hurting her, and I wanted David to have the opportunity to be the man he wanted to be. But it didn't work out that way."

"I don't know what to think," Jessica said with a weary sigh. "It's been a long day and a longer year. I never really felt safe here. I kept waiting for something to happen, for someone to find me, and they finally did." She paused. "I'm going to have to go back and testify, aren't I?"

"I'm not sure," Ellen said.

"I don't understand why you didn't get more official help in the beginning, Jessica," I interrupted.

"I was put in a safe house for a day, but someone leaked my whereabouts, and I barely escaped," Jessica said. "That's when I ran to Ellen. My mother had trusted her completely, so I was willing to do the same. But now I don't know what will happen. I'm sure I can't just stay at Stonecross."

"Probably not," Ellen said.

I took Jessica's hand once more, feeling her tension. Gazing into her eyes, I said, "We'll figure it all out, Jessica."

Her lips trembled. "I haven't heard that word *we* in a long time. Not since my mom died."

"I'm sorry to hear that. My mother died, too. It was a long time ago, but I know what it feels like to lose a mother."

"But you had your father."

"Not really. He was too sad to be my father. But now I have a sister. And I think that's going to make everything better—hopefully, for both of us." I glanced back at Ellen and saw what appeared to be tears in her eyes. "You're crying?" I couldn't help asking.

"I'm sure you think I'm made of stone, but I'm actually not that tough." Ellen cleared her throat. "I'll let you girls talk. If you have more questions later, I'll answer them."

"I'll give you some space as well," Finn added. "But I'll be right outside. Call me if you need me."

As Finn left, Jessica turned to me. "Is he your boyfriend?"

"We just met like five days ago," I said, hardly believing how much had happened in less than a week.

"It seems like there's something there."

"Maybe," I murmured. "Maybe not. It's complicated."

"You look like you were in a fight, Cassidy. What happened to your face?"

"That's a long story. I'll tell you everything, but not right this second."

"That's fine. I need to catch my breath."

"So do I. Then we'll figure out what happens next."

CHAPTER TWENTY-SIX

A half hour later, Tom returned to the cabin, and he and Ellen sat down with Jessica to discuss her future. While they did that, I went into the bedroom to make a call that couldn't wait another minute. I needed to speak to Natalie's brother. I needed to let him know what had happened.

When Adam Warren answered, his voice was hopeful, and it hurt even more to crush that hope, to tell him that Natalie's murderer had confessed to killing her and that the police in Stonecross had her locket. I couldn't answer any of his other questions. I didn't know where Natalie's body was, or if it could be recovered, but I referred him to the Stonecross Sheriff's Department for more information. Not able to find any words to console him, I eventually just apologized for the bad news and hung up. It was the worst call I'd ever had to make, but I'm glad I could give the family some closure. I hoped that was better than nothing.

Maybe some point Ellen would share information with Adam about why Natalie was running away, why she'd needed to start over, but I wasn't sure if that would happen or not. My grandmother was still in many ways an enigma. But I would leave it to

Adam to press for more answers. In the end, nothing would bring his sister back.

Needing some air, I walked out to the porch to talk to Finn. He was on his phone but quickly got off when he saw me.

"Who were you talking to?" I asked.

"Sophie. Dorothy had to be taken to the hospital. She collapsed when she heard what Jeff had been doing at her house."

"Oh, no!" I said with alarm. "Is she going to be all right?"

"They think so. It was just an overwhelming shock. My mother and Sophie are with her now. She's resting comfortably, so they're going to head home soon."

"She's a sweet lady. She has to be devastated by what Jeff was doing. That kind of evil probably seems unimaginable to her. It was unimaginable to me until I saw the insanity in his eyes, the complete disconnect with reality. He had seemed so normal before that. Like Tom's easygoing, nowhere-near-as-intense younger brother."

"Jeff fooled everyone," Finn said. "I served him drinks and meals for the past two years and never had an inkling that anything was off."

"He hid his dark side very well." Pausing, I added, "I can still see his amused smile when I came back the night I was run off the road. That had to be him, don't you think?"

"Probably. Unless it was Tyler."

"Tyler said it wasn't him. He wasn't hired to kill me. And Jeff was at the inn when I got back that night. He was sitting with Dorothy when I told Ellen I was her granddaughter. He enjoyed that drama. He probably thought it was a great distraction from my search for Natalie, because now I was persona non grata with Ellen and everyone else in town."

Finn gave me a guilty look. "I shouldn't have left you alone earlier today. I should have taken you with me to see Nathan. That decision could have been a fatal mistake."

"What happened isn't on you, Finn. I brought everything on

myself. I stirred up trouble. I made Jeff nervous, my grandmother, too, because she feared I would expose her network. She was afraid that the women she'd saved wouldn't be safe anymore. I sure got her wrong. But that's one thing I am happy about."

"You have a lot to be happy about."

"I know. I'm grateful to be alive. And I'm glad we got some answers." I thought about that for a moment. "I asked my grandmother about Anna, the woman who was staying in the room next to mine who disappeared before dawn one morning. She wasn't one of Jeff's victims. She's safe."

"That's a relief."

"But there were other victims."

"We'll get their names. We'll get them justice," he assured me.

I nodded in return. "We will."

"How are you actually feeling physically after all this?"

"I feel numb, like I'm running on adrenaline, but I'm betting everything is going to hurt tomorrow."

"There's probably a crash in your future. I've ridden that adrenaline high before."

"I don't think that crash will compare to anything I've gone through today. I was almost killed twice. I really don't want to test my luck a third time."

"You won't have to do that. I'm not going to let anything else happen to you, Cassidy."

"I appreciate the sentiment, but I think it's over for me now. Jeff is in jail, and not even his brother seems interested in defending him. I'm guessing Tom will be more focused on protecting himself going forward. I'm not sure if this underground railroad is going to create problems for him and my grandmother, but I think they will have a lot of questions to answer, especially from the families who are missing loved ones."

"I agree, and I suspect their network will have to end. Or at least operate in a more overt way. I am glad to see that Tom does have a good side. I wasn't sure about that, especially recently, when you pointed out all the flaws in the investigation into Natalie's disappearance."

"I know now that Tom was covering up the railroad, that he and my grandmother genuinely thought everyone was safe. They just couldn't say why." Feeling suddenly exhausted, I said. "I need to sit."

Finn waved me toward the porch bench, and I took a grateful seat, happy when he sat down next to me. I was starting to really like his strong, powerful presence beside me. "Do you think Marcus Pierce will send other people after Jessica?"

"I've spoken to Tom about that. He didn't know much about the Jessica situation. Ellen wasn't as open when it came to Jessica, and now we know why. She didn't want to tell him that Jessica was Lily's child."

"That was a shocker," I murmured. "I never expected to get a sister out of all this. How crazy is it that I might have gone my whole life and never known about her? But, somehow, we ended up at the same place at the same time. I guess it was fate. I wasn't sure I really believed in fate before, but maybe I do now."

"It's hard to say it was anything else," Finn agreed. "Tom said he'll talk to the U.S. Marshals about getting Jessica back into witness protection until the trial."

"But she said that didn't work before."

"They'll try to make it work now. They'll also try to find links between the man who was pretending to be Tyler Pierce and Marcus Pierce. If they can establish that Marcus paid the man in the woods to kill Jessica, that should add more charges to what he's already facing."

"I wonder where the actual Tyler Pierce is?"

"They'll look for him, too."

"Do you think he's also dangerous?"

"No idea. But until the situation settles down, Jessica will need protection." Finn gave me a questioning look. "Are you going to tell your father he has a daughter he never knew about?"

"That's a good question. I have a lot to talk to him about.

But I need to get my head straight on all the details. That's going to involve a longer conversation with Ellen. And in the end, I really think she should be the one to tell him everything. But we'll see if I can make that happen. My grandmother and father are like two immovable objects. It might take a force of nature to bring them together."

Finn's smile warmed my heart. "I think you just described yourself, Cassidy."

I smiled back at him. "I didn't use to be a force of anything. Since I came here, I've become a different person. One who is willing to take risks, to push back, and to fight. I have never fought for anything the way I fought for my life today."

"You're stronger than you thought."

"I am. And while I might have misjudged my grandmother and Tyler, I wasn't wrong about you, Finn. My gut told me you were a good guy, and you are."

His smile faded. "I wasn't as good as I thought I was. I shouldn't have taken Tom at face value when he shut down the private investigators who showed up in town. I should have asked more questions. And that boat trip with Nathan and Tessa was a huge mistake. I was distracted by my friend's call. He has PTSD, and he needed to talk to me urgently, and dealing with him took my mind off what was happening with Tessa."

"That's why you disappeared for ten minutes."

"Yes."

"That makes sense. And I know you didn't think Nathan would do anything to Tessa."

"I really didn't." His blue eyes darkened as his gaze met mine. "It wasn't just your investigation that shook me up; it was also you, Cassidy. I've been a little stuck in my life. I got thrust back into a career I'd walked away from a long time ago. I told myself I couldn't say no, couldn't turn my back on my family, that it was only temporary, but then months turned into years, and I am still here."

"It seems like you enjoy running the bar."

"I actually don't mind it, but I never wanted to spend my whole life in Stonecross. And I don't know that I want to do that now."

"There is a big world out there. Maybe when Sophie moves to New York, you'll want to come visit."

He met my gaze. "I'm definitely going to do that, Cassidy."

My nerves tingled at the look in his eyes. *Was there something between us?* I didn't want to mistake the high emotion of the last few days for something more. But that cautious thought reminded me of how often I had chosen the safe path in the past. I couldn't keep doing that, and I didn't want to keep doing that. But so much had happened today, I couldn't deal with anything else at the moment.

"What are your plans in terms of leaving town?" Finn asked.

"Tessa gets released from the hospital tomorrow. I know she'll want to get back to New York. And I need to go with her. She can't travel alone."

"Well, I'm sure you're ready to get out of Stonecross. Unless you want to spend more time getting to know your grandmother."

"I think I need a little distance and perspective before I come back to talk to Ellen, and I do want to come back and sit down and discuss everything under the sun. But I also need to speak to my father, too. I'm hoping I can get him to come back with me."

"I'm not certain you'll get a happy family reunion. Your grandmother kept his daughter from him, kept his first love from him. How does he forgive that?"

Finn made a good point. "Maybe he can't. And maybe I can't blame him for that. My grandmother played God, and that wasn't up to her. She should have given Lily and my father a chance to figure things out. That was wrong."

"Even if he can't forgive his mother, that doesn't mean you can't have a relationship with Ellen, if you want one."

"I'm still deciding on that. But I do want to have a relationship with Jessica, and I hope my father will, too."

"I can't imagine he wouldn't want to know his daughter."

"He's a complex person and often unpredictable. But whatever he decides won't affect me. I finally have a sister. I'm excited about that, and I'm looking forward to a time when she is safe enough to live her life."

"Hopefully, that will be soon." He stood up. "But just so you know, sometimes sisters can be a pain in the ass."

I laughed. "You love Sophie."

"I do, but sometimes she can be a pain in the ass."

I got to my feet. "You have a great family, Finn. You're lucky."

"I don't think I realized how lucky I was until I got to know yours."

"Just don't hold them against me."

"I won't. I like you, Cassidy. You're an amazing woman. Unlike anyone I've met before."

Our gazes clung for a long minute, and I knew I had to speak what was in my heart. "I like you, too, Finn. I don't really want to say goodbye tomorrow."

"Then maybe we'll just say, 'See you later'".

"That sounds perfect."

———

Finn dropped Ellen, Jessica and me off at the inn just before eleven p.m. on Thursday night. Tom had stayed in Pinehaven to assist in the investigation.

While Jessica wasn't sure returning to Stonecross was the best idea, neither Ellen nor I wanted to let her out of our sight until we knew she would be in safer hands than ours. On that one point, we were definitely in agreement.

Ray was waiting for us when we got back. He was going to sit in the hallway outside Ellen's apartment to keep watch over

Ellen and Jessica. Tom had also assigned a deputy who would sit in front of the inn until morning.

Ellen invited me to stay in her apartment as well, saying she could make up the couch, but I decided to head upstairs. I was exhausted and I knew I would sleep better in a bed. But as I entered my room, I had to admit I still felt a little trepidation, and I didn't know why. So, I locked the door and pushed the dresser in front of it. Some habits were hard to break.

Then I went into the bathroom and winced at my reflection. I looked absolutely horrible. My left eye was swollen with a blue-black bruise that spread across my cheek to my nose. I had more bruises on my neck and other cuts that were raised and red, bright against my pale skin. My hair was tangled and there was even a small leaf stuck in the strands that apparently no one had noticed. I took it out and thought about brushing my hair but decided against it.

Returning to my room, I set up my computer, light, and camera and then sat down at the desk and hit record. It was a little late to go live, but it didn't matter. The audience would catch up with me the next time they got on.

"Hello," I said. "Welcome to *Mysteries Uncorked*. I'm Cassidy Clarke, and for those of you who have been following my investigation into the disappearance of Natalie Warren, I have a lot to report."

I almost added Jessica's name, but until I knew she was safe, I would leave her story for another day. In fact, I might just see if she wanted to film with me when everything was truly over for her. Our listeners would probably go nuts if they could hear her story firsthand. But that was for another day.

Clearing my throat, I realized I'd just created an inadvertently long dramatic pause. "Today I discovered that Natalie Warren is dead. I wish I had a better, happier ending to her story, but I don't. I'm sure the news will be hitting the papers tomorrow, but I wanted to share my version. Today, I came face-to-face with Natalie's killer, and after a terrifying battle, which you can tell by my face was not without injury, I managed to knock out her murderer with a couple of strikes from a heavy wrench. I know you're waiting for a name, and I'm going to give you one. Some might say that everyone is innocent until proven guilty, but this isn't a court of law, and I'm not a lawyer or a cop. I'm just the person who heard his confession."

I took another breath, then said, "Natalie's killer was Jeff Holloway, the brother of the sheriff, Tom Holloway. Before you ask, no, I don't believe the sheriff had any knowledge of his brother's crimes. I also believe those crimes extend back many years, and other women besides Natalie have lost their lives because of him. I'm very happy that tonight Jeff Holloway is behind bars, and I pray that he stays there for the rest of his life."

I could see the comments lighting up with shock, amazement, and concern for my physical injuries.

"I'm okay. I'm in a little pain. I'm shocked. Exhausted. Exhilarated. So many emotions are coursing through me. I spoke to Natalie's family today and gave them the news. There are a lot of details to come in the future, and I can't go into all those tonight, but in the coming days and weeks, we'll get into all the twists and turns that led to this day. I'll be back tomorrow with an additional recap. But for now, I'm signing off."

I shut everything down and leaned back in my chair, allowing myself to feel for the very first time a deep sense of satisfaction. I'd actually done it. I'd solved the mystery of Natalie's disappearance. I was a little shocked at that fact. Despite my optimism and determination, I had never been sure it would actually happen.

My phone buzzed. It was Morgan.

"Hi," I said. "I wasn't sure you were still up."

"We're both here," Morgan said as Tessa joined the group call. "We couldn't wait for you to do the podcast. It was great, by the way."

"I know it wasn't very long."

"It was perfect," Tessa said. "You gave them just enough detail to want more, and I'm sorry to say you looked like shit, but that made it so much more real."

"Happy to add to our authenticity," I said dryly.

"Are you really okay?" Morgan asked. "You downplayed your injuries when we were texting earlier."

"I'm starting to ache all over, but happy to be alive."

"You did it, Cassidy," Tessa said. "You found Natalie's killer, and you got him put away. It's unbelievable."

"I know. It feels surreal. But then I look in the mirror, and I know it was all too real."

"Where did Jessica end up?" Tessa asked.

"Downstairs with Ellen in her apartment. They invited me to sleep on the couch, but I think I need a bed tonight."

"Will she be safe there?" Morgan asked.

"Ray is standing guard. And Tom said that he'd have an officer in the parking lot tonight. They'll try to get some official protection for Jessica in the morning."

"And you have a sister," Tessa said. "Who would have thought?"

"Certainly not me."

"Have you spoken to your father?"

"Not yet. I'm going to need all my strength for that, and it's probably something I should do in person, so maybe in a few days."

"He might hear about you on the news."

"Maybe. If he does, I'll answer his call. But he doesn't pay much attention to anything but financial or sports news."

"The podcast is blowing up even at this late hour," Morgan commented. "What's your plan for the next one?"

"I think we should do it in New York with all three of us. Oh, by the way, Finn's friend, the one who flew us to Pinehaven in his helicopter, said he could take you and me to New York tomorrow, Tessa."

"Seriously? We don't have to drive?"

"Nope. Do you know when you're getting discharged?"

"The doctor said by ten a.m."

"I'll be at the hospital then, and we'll head back together. We should be home by dinnertime."

After we said our goodbyes, I couldn't drum up enough energy to change into pajamas. I just crawled under the covers and fell asleep, For the first time in almost a week, I wasn't worried about surviving the night or tomorrow...

EPILOGUE

Four weeks later...

I looked around my new one-bedroom apartment with enormous pleasure. I had so much more space than I'd had in the studio, and my windows now overlooked the river instead of an alley.

Since we'd returned from Stonecross, Tessa had also moved into a new apartment of her own and had no roommates for the first time in a decade. Morgan had actually broken up with Steven and had gotten her own place, too, so there had been a lot of changes in our lives.

The past four weeks had also seen *Mysteries Uncorked* climb to incredible heights, charting in the top five almost every week, and twice we had hit the number one spot in our genre. We'd done a series of podcasts on Stonecross, featuring different aspects of the case, including the underground railroad, which my grandmother had allowed us to talk about on the show, since it was no longer operational. She still had plans to help troubled women in the future, but she would have to find a different way to do that.

With our success, we'd signed up six sponsors, which had put enough money into our pockets to change our immediate living circumstances and given us a launchpad for the future.

My doorbell rang, interrupting my thoughts. Walking over to the intercom, I said, "Hello", expecting to hear Tessa's voice as she and Morgan were due any minute.

But it was Finn's voice that came across the intercom, and it sent a shiver down my spine that had nothing to do with fear but only with anticipation. We'd texted and chatted by phone in the past month, and he'd told me he hoped to visit soon, but he hadn't told me when. Now, he was here, and I was so shocked and excited, all I could do was stare at the intercom.

"Cassidy? Are you going to let me in?" he asked.

"Of course. Sorry. I'm on the eighth floor."

"I've got it."

I buzzed him in, then moved quickly to the mirror over the table in the entry to check my hair and makeup. It was lucky he'd decided to come now since I'd just gotten ready for our final podcast on Stonecross.

A knock came at my door, and I ran a hand through my hair as I went to open it.

Finn gave me a smile that took my breath away. For weeks, I'd told myself he wasn't that handsome, wasn't that great, but all those thoughts went out the window now.

"Hi," he said simply.

"Hi," I echoed. "Come in. It's great to see you."

"You too."

"Why didn't you tell me you were coming to New York?"

"I wanted to surprise you. Is it okay?"

"More than okay." As we gazed at each other a little too long, I cleared my throat and said, "Do you want something to drink?"

"No. I'm going to meet Sophie and Cole in a half hour. I just couldn't wait another minute to see you, Cassidy."

We'd been dancing around the subject of us being more than allies, maybe more than friends. It had been easier to leave everything undefined and up in the air while I was in New York and he was in Stonecross. But now we were face-to-face. And the air felt like it was sizzling between us.

"How long will you be in town?"

"I'll be here for about a week. And then I'll be back... permanently."

"What?" I asked, shocked again. "You're going to move to New York? What about Kelly's Pub? What about your parents?"

"My father and I have had some long talks. He's going to promote my assistant manager to manager, and he'll supervise. He's feeling good now, and he has been itching to get back into the bar more often; he just didn't want to get in my way."

"Which means what for you?"

"I'm going to open my own place, maybe in Manhattan, possibly Brooklyn, I'm not sure. I have some leads to check out this week."

"That's amazing, Finn. This is what you want?"

He nodded. "Yes. I finally stopped pretending I could be happy living my dad's life. There are parts of it I would like to live, like running my own bar and grill and finding the right person to settle down with."

My heart skipped a beat at the look in his eyes, and a wave of anxiety ran through me. *Was he moving for me? What if we didn't work out?* We barely knew each other, and the time we'd been together hadn't been real life. It had been high-stakes, drama-packed days, with life-and-death situations. *What would happen if we were just normal people living normal lives?*

"I didn't mean to scare you," Finn said with a knowing gleam in his eyes. "I'm not moving here for you, Cassidy. I'm happy you're here, but this is a career move I had planned to make a long time ago. I just got derailed by my father's stroke. Then I got stuck until you arrived band shook everything up. But there's no pressure. I'd like to get to know you better, see if whatever this is could be more. If you're not on the same page, that's fine. We can just be friends."

"I'm on the same page. I want to get to know you, too."

Relief flitted through his blue-eyed gaze. "Good."

"Good," I echoed.

He smiled. "I know you're doing the podcast tonight, so I'm not going to stay. I just had to see you as soon as I got here."

"I'm glad you came by. But you don't have to leave yet. Tell me what's happening in Stonecross."

"Well, Nathan is in rehab and is determined to get his life in order. He told me he sent an apology letter to Tessa."

"He did, and Tessa seems willing to accept that, although I think he should be in jail for drugging her, but I know it would be difficult to prove he put anything in her drink because her tox screen was not definitive. I guess rehab is the next best thing."

"Nathan also gave Jessica's ring to Ellen. I assume Ellen will get it to her. He's trying to make amends. I think almost losing his life woke him up, and he wants to do better."

"I'm glad to hear that."

"And the other piece of news is that your father showed up."

"Seriously?" I asked in shock. "He finally went to see Ellen? I've been asking him for weeks, and he told me to back off. If he decided to go, he'd go."

"I guess your experience didn't bring the two of you closer."

"That may never happen, but then I didn't think he would ever go to Stonecross, so I guess there's still hope."

"Well, he didn't just come to town; he went to the inn. He apparently stayed for a couple of hours. After he left the apartment, he walked out on the deck and looked at the ocean in a contemplative way. Then he got in his car and drove away."

"Did Ellen tell you that?"

"No, someone Sophie used to work with. You know gossip flies fast in Stonecross."

"Well, I'm happy they talked."

"Has your dad spoken to Jessica?"

"She told me yesterday he reached out and asked to meet

next week. She's nervous about it but also excited. I hope he doesn't let her down. But whatever happens, she and I will have a relationship."

"Jessica is safe now, right?"

"Yes. She gave her testimony and turned over all her evidence. She can no longer be silenced. The police also found a money trail between Marcus Pierce and the fake Tyler Pierce in his murder-for-hire scheme. Apparently, Marcus's real brother washed his hands of Marcus years ago." I paused. "Sometimes, I still can't believe I got taken in by a hit man. I was just lucky I wasn't the hit. He could have easily killed me."

"Let's not think about all the *what-ifs* anymore. Look at your beautiful apartment."

"It is nice," I said, giving him a proud smile. "You didn't see my other place, but it was about a tenth of this size and in a really noisy area. This feels so much better."

"I like the neighborhood. It has a good vibe."

"I can't believe you're moving here, Finn."

"I just wish it was today. But I have to find a place to live and a place to work until I can figure out how I might open my own restaurant."

"That's a lot to do."

"But it's exciting, and I can't wait."

"Me, either," I said. We stared at each other for another minute, and then I said, "Can I—"

He cut off my needy question with a hug, followed up by a kiss that was as hot and wonderful as I'd imagined it would be. One kiss turned into two as we sank into an embrace, we'd both been thinking about for a long time.

I could have stayed in his arms for a lot longer, but my doorbell rang, breaking us apart.

"We shouldn't have talked so long before we did that," I said breathlessly.

He laughed. "We'll make more time later."

"We better." I walked over to the intercom and buzzed Tessa and Morgan in. "Morgan is dying to meet you, by the way." I went over to the door and opened it.

A moment later, Tessa came in with her usual burst of energy, walking with the aid of a cane, but it was good to see her on her feet and looking like her usual self. She gave Finn a friendly hello, having forgiven him ages ago for not realizing she'd been drugged on Nathan's boat.

As Tessa stepped back, I introduced Morgan.

"I've heard a lot about you," Morgan said.

"Mostly good, I hope."

"How long are you in town, Finn?" Tessa asked.

"About a week, but I'm planning to move here."

Tessa's jaw dropped, and she flashed me a quick look. "Well, isn't that great?" She smiled as her gaze moved back and forth between us. "And if there's something going on here between you two, that's also great."

Finn smiled. "We'll see. I'll let you ladies get to your podcast."

I followed him to the door and stepped out into the hall with him.

"Give me a call when you're done with the podcast," he said, giving me another kiss before walking down the hall.

I let out a little sigh and then stepped back into my apartment to see two very curious faces.

"You and Finn?" Morgan asked. "Really?"

"Maybe. I didn't know he was moving here, so I didn't think anything could happen, but now...who knows? I guess we'll see where things go."

"I'm happy for you," Tessa said. "Where's Jessica? She's not here yet?"

"She's on her way." I had barely finished my statement when my doorbell rang again, and I buzzed Jessica in.

She arrived a moment later, looking happy and well-rested,

her eyes no longer filled with fear, her face no longer stressed with worry lines. I gave her a hug and then introduced her to Morgan and Tessa.

"I feel like I already know you. Cassidy has talked a lot about you," Jessica said.

"Is everything good for you now?" Morgan asked.

"Yes. I'm finally free, and I'm ready for a fresh start here in New York and a chance to get to know my sister, and, hopefully, my father."

I smiled as her gaze swung in my direction. "I'm excited about all that, too. So, are you ready to do this? I know our listeners are eager to hear directly from you."

"I'm ready. This podcast is probably the reason I'm still alive so, let's do it."

I motioned everyone to my round kitchen table where I'd set up the microphones and camera.

"Why don't you start, Cassidy?" Tessa said. "This story has really been yours from the beginning. And this is our last podcast on Natalie, Jessica, and Stonecross."

"Okay," I said, much more comfortable with being the lead now. "Welcome to *Mysteries Uncorked*. I'm Cassidy, and I'm joined by Morgan and Tessa, and a very special guest, one of the women we hoped desperately to find, Jessica Trent. Tonight, we'll be wrapping up our series on the Stonecross disappearances, and we'll hear directly from Jessica about what it felt like to run and hide, fake her own death, and face down a killer."

"Which she didn't do alone," Tessa interjected.

"She's right," Jessica said. "Cassidy was right there with me, and I wouldn't be here without her."

"Let's start at the beginning," Morgan interjected.

As Jessica launched into her story, I looked at the comments pouring in and then at the faces of my dear friends and my unexpected sister. The podcast had started as a lark, a way to kill time while we looked for other jobs. And now it had become not just a job but a career, with listeners and sponsors and the opportunity to change lives, to put a spotlight on people who had fallen into the shadows, and hopefully to do some good.

I had no idea where we would go next, but I couldn't wait. So many people needed their stories to be heard, and I was going to make sure that happened.

ABOUT THE AUTHOR

Barbara Freethy is a #1 New York Times Bestselling Author of 87 novels ranging from contemporary romance to romantic suspense and women's fiction. With over 13 million copies sold, thirty-three of Barbara's books have appeared on the New York Times and USA Today Bestseller Lists, including SUMMER SECRETS which hit #1 on the New York Times!

Known for her emotional and compelling stories of love, family, mystery and romance, Barbara enjoys writing about ordinary people caught up in extraordinary adventures. Library Journal says, "Freethy has a gift for creating unforgettable characters."

For additional information, please visit Barbara's website at www.barbarafreethy.com.

www.ingramcontent.com/pod-product-compliance
Lightning Source LLC
Chambersburg PA
CBHW061600190726
48288CB00007B/2105